Larry Plumb Is Still Here

P.A. Kane

First edition: 2024

ISBN:978-1-7359800-1-0

Also by P.A. Kane

Written In The Stars: The Book Of Molly
Leaving Jackson Wolf
The Last Playlist (A Sonic Epitaph)

Offical: PAKane.net

—To those who who lace 'em up everyday and find the strength to engage and evolve.

One

As his eyes popped open at 3:41 a.m. Larry Plumb was filled with a momentary sense of dread. Though he hadn't smoked a cigarette in decades, he sometimes found himself tangled in a dream hacking on a Marlboro Red just prior to waking—producing the first disappointing thought of the day: *Goddamnit, I started smoking again.*

He moved his vigorous fifty-six-year-old body to an upright position from the sofa bed where he slept by himself and quickly realized, as the fog of sleep lifted, that he'd been dreaming and hadn't started smoking again, which was a big relief.

Rooted back in reality, he began prepping for the first task of the day: feeding the chickens. Already dressed in sweatpants and a clingy T-shirt, he flicked on the light, grabbed his yard hoodie, pulled it over his torso, and secured his Bills cap over his closely cropped, graying hair. Reality came further into focus when he fixed his thick-rimmed black glasses into place. The woman at the optical store said they looked great as she placed them over his symmetrical ears, but he was sure they made him look like an older, dorkier Buddy Holly. "No, not Buddy Holly—Clark Kent," she said with a flirty smile, staring into his blue eyes.

Exiting the room where he spent most of his inside hours, he noticed someone had placed the small metal placard emboldened with thick, austere letters that read **MAN CAVE** on the frame above the door. He had received the placard as a Father's Day gift but resisted displaying it, joking to his daughters not to pigeonhole him that he might surprise them one day in a culotte and heels, which he could so rock.

However, Larry was reluctant to accept what the trendy placard stood for because it didn't fit. His flat screen, books, laptop, and desk, from which he managed his family's life, didn't quite comport with present-day accepted man cave standards of neon beer logos, sports memorabilia, and banners. But what really disqualified the room was the soft, worn copy of Anne Sexton's *The Complete Poems* on his desk and facing him near the doorframe the 1949 print of Ella Fitzgerald at Downbeat Club singing before an enthralled Duke Ellington and Benny Goodman. These, among other artifacts, made the man cave designation null and void in Larry's mind.

In the past, it might have annoyed Larry that his family and people, in general, had failed to consider this type of distinction. But his opinion about what a room was or wasn't, like most of his opinions, went unsaid. These days, with necks, craned toward hand-held devices, the whole world was absorbed in their own self-styled enclaves and had zero patience or need for his nuanced opinions, no matter how salient. The loudest and proudest carried the day.

Larry also understood that all these bent-headed people were so over patriarchal white men—even thoughtful, nuanced white men. Of course, there was strong pushback from the red-hatted, grab-em by the pussy crowd, but circumspect Larry was hardly a red hatter. Alienated from every partisan corner of society, he conducted the business of living with quiet resignation, keeping his mouth largely shut and his opinions mostly to himself.   He had set up the coffee the previous night. Though plagued by a burning semi-erection and a need to void his bladder, he sidestepped the bathroom, went into the kitchen, and hit the button on the coffee maker. With his mug anchored beneath the exit spout, he circled back to the bathroom. As he stood over the toilet watching the urine haltingly exit from his shrinking penis in dribs and drabs like an old leaky faucet, the day's second disappointing thought entered his mind—that perhaps he was past his prime.

He quickly brushed the thought aside, deeming it self-indulgent to linger on these natural bodily changes, and checked the floor. Sometimes, little urine droplets ended up on the bathroom tile, and his wife Maureen pestered him about sitting down to pee. But Larry had been steadfast in his refusal to take a seat. He had been upright his whole life and wasn't going to change over a few drops on the floor, no matter how much she nagged or flippantly hypothesized that he wouldn't comply because it would be emasculating for him to sit like a woman. He hated the cheap emasculation argument, but not as much as he hated that after being together for nearly thirty years, how little Maureen still knew about him or how his mind worked.

Back in the kitchen, as the coffee staggered through its paces, he smoothly removed his mug from beneath the exit spout and put the ten-cup pot back in place. The family cats, Betty and Friedan, met him in the kitchen and were wild with anticipation, rubbing up against him as he opened a can of turkey in gravy sauce to split between them. The Plumb dogs, Donald and Lydia, named after the characters in the John Prine song, came with Larry's soft whistle from the living room, where they slept on opposing ottomans. Larry got down on one knee and greeted each golden retriever with warmth and affection.

After sipping some coffee, he sprinkled a touch of whey into a water jug fitted with a stainless-steel nipple and then filled a feed bucket near the back door. As he stepped out into the dark, frosty November morning, the dogs fanned out like sentries, sniffing and peeing along the fenced perimeter of the double lot.

The Plumb house was a four-bed, two-and-a-half-bath bungalow built in 1920. It had good fundamentals that were enhanced by Larry's regular updates. In the decades Larry, Maureen, and the kids lived there, he renovated every room in the house. He also updated most of the electrical, windows, and water lines and generally had a project going with one on deck. It was a safe, comfortable first-rung suburban home outside Buffalo, New York.

This close to the city, it was odd to be raising egg hens. But animal-loving Maureen, after watching a million YouTube videos with the kids, was convinced they had enough space and tending to the chickens would require minimal work or commitment. Larry made a reasoned argument against the chickens, noting in a big-picture kind of way the relatively short duration hens produced eggs and the hassle of feeding them and cleaning the coop. The inconvenience of clearing the snow in the winter and the vigilance it would require to keep the dogs from killing them. After enlisting the kids to her side, Maureen prevailed. In short order, Maureen was also right about the work being minimal, since after the initial rush of obtaining the hens had faded, Larry did most of it.

Larry named the four egg-producing hens: Dumbfuck, Stupidshit, Lazyass and Littleballs. They had trendy proper names: Kendall, Odin, Elly, and Wynn, given to them by the girls, but Larry preferred to identify the chickens by their personalities. Dumbfuck and Stupidshit, left to their own devices would gladly walk into the jaws of the dogs and be torn to pieces. Lazyass was a classic underachiever, producing a single egg every three or four days. Littleballs was passive, always sitting back and waiting for her turn at the feeder instead of asserting herself like the other hens.

Their oldest daughter Samantha, was among those skeptical of Larry these days. Like many Millennials and Gen Z-ers, she was consumed with the "resistance" and "MeToo" movements and seemed to think of him and most white men his age as close-minded, racist, and suffering from toxic masculinity. While Larry was certainly plagued with old codes, he appreciated the struggle of women and marginalized people for equity and worked to be both self-aware and non-toxic. But with Sam, there was little room for error. She policed his language and called out his middle of the road views cruel and inhuman. At first, this kind of characterization hurt, but he recalled his own idealism at her age and wrote it off as that, thinking she would come around in time. But that time was still a way off.

In line with present-day conventions, she called Larry out for the offensive nicknames he gave the birds: "You can't call a female bird that."

"What?"

"Littleballs, it's anatomically incorrect."

"Sam," Larry said, hoping his daughter would catch the irony of her less-than-feminine name. "It's meant to describe her personality, not her sex parts. She's passive."

"Those names are obnoxious."

"Would you rather I call her Sissypants or Littlepussy? Remember telling me how slurs of weakness almost always refer to women's genitalia? See how well I learn?"

"How about you just call her by her real name—Wynn?" she said indignantly and turned away from him.

Piqued by the conversation, Larry was happy to be done with it, too.

Whether he was toxic, obnoxious, or whatever, the hens responded to him, especially Littleballs. Her underdog status quickly turned her into his favorite. Sometimes, he would enter the coop, lock the other chickens in the henhouse, and feed her from his hand. She not only tolerated him picking her up—she loved it, cooing and gurgling with contentment as he stroked her feathers.

As he changed out the water jug through a little door built into wire fencing, the birds rose with excitement. The top-loading feeders made it possible to avoid stepping into the coop, thus limiting the hens' exposure to the dogs. Another feature to keep the hens safe was a door atop the small house, making extracting the brown eggs easy. There was also a latched door on the side to clean out the pungent bedding and droppings that hit the senses like a well-placed sucker punch. Thankfully, with the colder weather, the bitter scent had dissipated.

As he completed these tasks, aided by a headlamp and the stored energy of the little solar lights fixed around the perimeter of the coop, Littleballs waited for a go at the feeder like a well-mannered lady. Larry encouraged her, "C'mon LB, get in there. Lazyass doesn't do a damn thing with that fuel. Get in there, beak that little malingerer."

Despite a harsh gust of wind that ripped through Larry's hoodie and up into his nostrils, a smile rose to his lips as he thought about the absurdity of having a conversation with a chicken and promoting hen-on-hen violence. He could hear the sound bite in his head. Coming up: Local man turns docile chicken into a KILLING machine.

With the day's first couple of disappointments behind him, he laughed and thought about how he loved those shadowy blue mornings when the world was sleeping and he was awake. But he was more than just awake—he was alive. He felt strong and vital as he inhaled giant gulps of the early morning stillness.

Out here in the blackness, he didn't have to endure the hassles of being ignored or argue his sensible points with challenged people. He was also thrilled to complete his morning tasks without hearing from all the whiners, complainers, and grievance-filled suburban white people he encountered all day long. Most of all, he loved that he was living while the rest of the world was sleeping.

These black and blue mornings had always been special to Larry. It never took much for him to go to that place in his mind when he was a kid delivering the morning paper. He could feel the snow crunch under his feet when he read the stunning headline: *Foreman Knocks Out Frazier In Second Round*. Then, months later, being equally stunned when Muhammad Ali regained the heavyweight title after somehow knocking out Foreman. Or waking up in his college days, taking a nip of marijuana, and reading a book like *Zen and the Art of Motorcycle Maintenance*. Or talking up his sleepy son in the minivan on the way to a 6 a.m. hockey practice. Or just sitting on the porch on a summer morning with a cup of coffee, listening to the nothingness as the moon slowly vacated the sky.

With these first tasks completed, he moved into the roomy two-car garage, which served as a workshop, workout area, and sanctuary for Larry. Followed by the dogs, he placed the feed bucket next to some empty egg cartons on an old kitchen countertop repurposed into a table. He slipped out of his yard boots, rolled out his mat on the interlocking rubber workout flooring, and with the dogs watching, went through a twenty-minute yoga-based core routine that included crunches, planks, and knee-kicks, among other exercises.

Larry sometimes flirted with six-pack abs, but to get over that last hump, the beer and whiskey he drank most nights would have to be removed from his diet, which to him, would have been like eliminating oxygen. Even in the most frigid parts of the Western New York winters, when the day's i's had been dotted and the t's crossed, Larry would realign himself by listening to highly curated podcasts and music while he sipped whiskey and drank beer in the insulated garage.

This life-affirming activity came about as the kids got older and needed less of his attention. Like everything in Larry's life, it was pursued with precision and discipline. He referred to his imbibing as an old football play, calling it a forty-two dive—four beers, two whiskeys. That's all it took to perfectly restore his equilibrium.

The prior night after completing a lower body workout while sitting in his padded Adirondack chair on a little carpeted ten-by-ten platform, Larry plugged in Dan Carlin's current event podcast, *Common Sense*. With the Trump nonsense sucking up all the oxygen, he listened to Carlin talk about possible opportunities and pitfalls, domestic and foreign, for the volatile President as he sipped his Rolling Rock/Jim Beam combo and replaced a power cord on the family's ancient Hoover vacuum. It was solid analysis, devoid of fluff and partisanship, unlike the corporate media or, heaven forbid, the guys at work whose in-depth inquiry led them to conclude Hillary was a cunt and Trump was some pissed-off god with a comb-over.

The podcast ended just as Larry had the vacuum cord locked in place. He poured his second Beam, opened his third Rock, and turned the lights down. He lit a few candles, opened the YouTube Music app on his phone, hit the shuffle button, and sat back and listened. First up was Frank Turner's angry rant, "Love Ire & Song."

He liked the energy of this Turner kid, who seemed to channel the spirit of Billy Bragg. Like Bragg, he didn't try to hide his British accent and had crisply phrased in-your-face lyrics. Absorbing the song, Larry wondered if he was one of the cowards Turner bitterly accused of despairing and selling out their ideals.

Like with most questions, if dealt with honestly, there were all these gray areas and no easy answers. Injustice was everywhere, from the degradation of the planet to innocent kids being gunned down in schools. Larry attended to his civic duties with pride, kept his property in good standing, and filled his recycling tote to capacity each week. Though he hadn't been to Catholic church since grade school, he learned the lessons of the Sermon on the Mount and the Beatitudes well. When people complained about taxes and programs to aid the most vulnerable among us, the Emma Lazarus quote, which he changed slightly and made his own, always popped into his head—*None of us are free until all of us are free.*

After a few reflective moments, he decided, in thought and deed, with his wallet and his vote, that he was on the right side of history on all these issues. The side of doing something—the side of throwing shit against the wall like FDR in the early days of his presidency—rather than doing nothing or protecting some moneyed interest bent on plundering the earth and exploiting the weak and vulnerable.

Further, he was cheered to think that, despite endless tragedies beyond his control, he cared for his own and still got after it every day. Though he didn't quite know where he fit in a rapidly changing world, he hadn't raised a white flag of surrender like some friends, coworkers and maybe even Maureen. As easy as it would be to get all sloppy and cynical, he still popped up in the middle of the night and attacked each day with vigor, knowing instinctively that despite all its trying moments, life was still worth living, still worth pursuing. Fuck you Frank Turner, he thought laughing to himself—I'm still here.

And a moment later, there was more evidence of Larry's continued engagement when the next tune-up was Bruce Springsteen's "Thunder Road," which he hadn't heard in some time. Overall, the song didn't quite work for Larry. After the beautifully grounded introduction, it bounded off into this cowboy, take-no-prisoners, American kind of hubris. The characters scream into the night free and unbridled, settling for nothing less than total victory. Larry knew everybody saw themselves in this scene, but it was fiction. People had to get up in the morning and go to work. It was nonsense to think you'd be feasting on the marrow of life with Mary at your side, screaming down some thunder road at four in the morning. Maybe there was a night or two in your youth when you felt free and alive like this, but those days were long gone, crushed by the monotonous pounding of the day shift, which provided food, shelter, and Netflix. Absent this relentless, monotonous pounding, you'd be even more screwed, living in a box on the side of that fictional thunder road.

And even if there were some transcendent wormhole of freedom, that's not what Larry wanted from life. What he wanted and needed was the infatuation and connection beautifully depicted in the song's intro.

With a yearning, Larry was sucked right into the imagery of the slamming screen door, of Mary in a breezy dress, and the sound of Roy Orbison on the radio over that pleading harmonica and those tinkling piano keys. It struck Larry at the core of his being, making him feel vulnerable and desperate. And rather than running from these emotions or just sucking it up as he had been programmed to do all his life, he embraced the emptiness and was filled with a strange kind of melancholy that felt so good. The emptiness made him sigh and take a deep breath as tears welled in the corners of his eyes.

But his reverie was soon interrupted when Maureen banged open the garage's man door, flicked on the lights, and began to yell above the music,

"Larry—the dishwasher—the dishwasher isn't draining—Larry—Are you crying, Larry?"

Two

When Larry came into the kitchen, the room that had really sold them on the house all those years ago, Maureen and their middle daughter Ashley were leaning against the pebble blue Corian countertop opposite the sink and dishwasher. He noted the broad grins on their faces and the light reflecting off the glass doors of the kitchen cabinets as he set down the portable sump pump and the tote containing his tools. He was initially annoyed at having his sanctuary time interrupted, but seeing them standing there with little twinkling halos, Larry's irritation was promptly replaced with an airy gratefulness amidst all the light and beauty.

Larry's know-it-all, get-shit-done pragmatism would have been how most people characterized him for much of his life. But in recent years, especially among the Plumb family, another more sensitive side had surfaced—a side that could be made to weep by a Bruce Springsteen song. And seeing the devilish cast on their faces, he knew they were going to push on that part of his personality.

"Okay," he said, "C'mon, hit me with your best shot."

"No sweetheart, 'Hit Me with Your Best Shot' is Pat Benatar, but I'm sure she could make you cry too," Maureen said, looking at Ashley.

Ashley was a fourth-year Elementary Education student at Buffalo State. Like her older sister Samantha, Ashley bought into the trendy notion of toxic white maleness and also looked sideways at Larry these days. Given her current outlook, she jumped at the opportunity to give Larry the business. She started strutting in a circle, slowly pumping her arms robotically and singing the Benatar song. Maureen quickly joined her.

Laughing, Larry asked, "How do you know Pat Benatar, Ash?"

"They played her like fifty times a day when I worked at Claire's in the mall— and I hear you bawling your eyes out to her all the time in your man cave."

Still laughing, Larry said, "How can it be a man cave if I'm in there crying at Pat Benatar songs. And, has any man ever cried to a Pat Benatar song?"

"We don't know, and we don't care. This is about messing with you," Maureen smiled, still following Ash's robotic movements.

"Yeah, Dad, we can't let you get away with this."

Then, almost in unison, Ashley and Maureen's phones buzzed, and Larry expected this charade to end. However, it was their daughter Samantha, a second-year Physician Assistant student at Cornell, and their son Bennett, who was on his way home from intramural hockey. Texts must have been sent while Larry was coming in from the garage.

With their phones on speaker, Ben made exaggerated sobbing noises while Sam started right in on her dad: "Mom, I hope you have the number to Crisis Services in case Dad loses it listening to those self-indulgent Joni Mitchell songs.

"Hey, don't talk like that about Joni. She's royalty," Larry said, fighting back.

Switching gears, Ben began singing "Big Yellow Taxi" in a loud, funny voice. Maureen and Ashley joined in bumped hips and did the Shoobopbop harmony with Sam. Despite being the punch line to this joke, Larry was delighted with this strange family interaction and loved the way Maureen's silvery hair vibrated around her shoulders as she bumped hips with Ashley.

After the first verse, Ben improvised some lyrics:
Dad played this song a million times in the car—Shoobopbop
Heard it so much my ears have begun to rot—Shoobopbop
Watching him boo hoo hoo left a massive scar—Shoobopbop
Wish I could bury this song in a parking lot—Shoolotlot

"Wow, Ben," Larry said in a loud voice, straining to be heard above their laughter, "Not bad for a C student."

And all at once, they shouted passive-aggressive invectives at Larry about being a bully and a bad sport until he finally said, "Okay—okay, uncle—uncle. You all got me."

As the banter dissipated, there was some small talk, and everybody assumed their rightful roles. Larry said he hoped Ben had pulled to the side of the road to use his phone. Sam inquired about putting a new coffee maker on the family Amazon account. Maureen informed her about an opportunity for a summer internship at Lakeshore Human Services, where her friend Rose was the office manager, which Sam graciously declined.

The call ended, and Ashley fell back into humming the Benatar song. Larry was getting the sump pump in place and was on one knee in front of the dishwasher. Unexpectedly, Ashley went over to Larry, kissed him on the head, and then went to do homework. Maureen dried and put away the dishes from the broken-down dishwasher. When that task was completed, she also kissed Larry on the head as he was about to power up the sump pump. Before she could get away, he stood up, pulled her close at the waist, and kissed her on the mouth. As the kiss dissolved, he looked her in the eye and said, "This shouldn't take long. Meet me upstairs."

"You smell like whiskey," she said, turning away from him.

"I can fix that."

"I'm really tired, and Ashley's home and Ben will be here in a minute."

"C'mon Moe, they'll be in their rooms. I'll whisper Benatar lyrics in your ear," Larry said in his most seductive voice.

A little color washed over her face, giving him momentary hope, but then she paused and said, "Not tonight, crying boy." and removed herself from his embrace. From there, she walked out of the kitchen into the living room and turned on some cop show.

***

After tending to the chickens and doing a quick workout the following morning Larry sat at his desk in the man cave and mused about the previous night's events. The playful interaction with his family, even if it was at his expense, delighted him. But within the interaction, a contradiction emerged that left him a bit rankled. To his daughters, and to some extent Maureen, he was viewed as a toxic knuckle-dragger. Yet, they wasted little time roasting him when his sensitivities surfaced. He wasn't surprised they didn't see the contradiction, but it burned in his craw a bit.

While Larry received zero credit for his efforts to evolve, the last thing he wanted was to whine or complain like some fragile snowflake. Still, his family failed to recognize what Larry and other men were up against. Society prescribed that he and his male cohorts not acknowledge their feelings and emotions. The quintessential male was stoic and remote, viewing interior sentiments with disdain. When these feelings occasionally appeared, the move was to hide and bury them.

Feelings equaled weakness, and rather than being seen as delicate or fragile, men overcompensated. Working-class guys grew beards, got tats, and bought F150s. The well-to-do professional class donned aviators, procured BMWs, and applied for club memberships. All of life's toil and struggle reduced to a skull tattoo or three-thousand-dollar golf clubs. How sad, Larry thought, it was to be a man.

For the most part, Larry was able to rise above the noise. He cultivated those feelings and emotions that society wanted him to bury. At least a couple of times a week, a book or some piece of music would move Larry to tears. Though most would consider this a deficiency, Larry knew it was a strength, even when his family made fun of his reaction to a Bruce Springsteen song.

As in tune as he was with his emotions, he had a problem with misplaced sentimentality and excess. All too often, Larry watched people around him cheapen emotion with excess. Whether it was Maureen tearing up at Christmas coffee commercials or an old high-school friend getting teary-eyed at the wake of a classmate they hadn't seen in thirty years—they were missing the point. These disproportionate reactions in Larry's mind diminished what Christmas was about and lessened the impact of someone gone before their time. Further, he was aware of how hard it was for men to react to life's calamitous events with proper perspective instead of some hollow, culturally approved construct.

Larry felt strongly about this, and when he had more currency with his family, he encouraged his kids to keep perspective, see the big picture, and not cheapen their emotions with excess—from boyfriends and girlfriends to work and school. Going through life at an even pace made truly special moments more impactful and powerful.

It was a hard point to sell because everybody accused him of being "a know-it-all" and of telling them what to feel, which was not the case. He was simply trying to impart the knowledge he had gained that was often overlooked—to analyze and manage feelings rather than being managed by them when some fateful event occurred. It was training yourself to respond in a measured, even way.

But, instead of trying to understand what he was saying, they made fun of him. When he tried to explain this, he saw the looks on their faces and the eye rolls—like the out-of-touch dad in a bad teen movie asleep on the couch. Though this hurt, he got over it and took solace in having planted seeds that might bear fruit someday.

He also wasn't upset that Maureen had turned down his amorous advances. Besides them not sleeping together because of Larry's odd hours, in recent years, her enthusiasm for sex had declined or, more to the point, her acceptance of his amorous advances had declined. If Larry could make the sale, she would be all fire. The problem was making the sale. And Larry did try—all the time. His libido was that of a slightly aging pubescent boy, and though he remained very attracted to Maureen, there wasn't much cooperation for all the effort. When they talked about it, Maureen casually said, "I guess I just don't want it the way I did when I was younger."

"So, what am I supposed to do?" Larry asked.

"Take care of it yourself." She smiled, cupping her hand and making the universal back-and-forth action of male self-gratification.

"Not funny, Moe."

"Soy," she said. "I hear a diet rich in soy lowers testosterone levels. Eat your Cheerios with soy milk."

Like everything over which he had little or no control, he accepted this with quiet, grudging resignation.

But getting teased or shot down by Maureen wasn't the only thing that annoyed Larry that morning—it was the goddamn cop show. Watching his gracefully aging wife from the kitchen doorway lean back on the couch's armrest, he was irked that she turned on an episode of *Law & Order.* Larry found these cop shows—all of them—*CSI, Blue Bloods, Bones* predictable and boring. Maybe Maureen didn't want him crawling all over her, but for chrissakes, read a goddamn book or put on PBS; something other than Law & Order.

But a visual popped into his head as he sat there, recalling his annoyance of the previous night. It was of a man having sex with a woman and working really hard at it while she watched Criminal Minds with a blank look on her face.

Larry was a great fan of the short story master Raymond Carver, whose fiction was flat, unadorned snippets of banality—it was extraordinary for its utter commonness. Carver's lean prose often left you hanging without resolution and judgment. Instead, these little stories just floated in the continuum of human drama, discharged only by the next bit of human drama. Carver's stories were so open-ended and unsatisfyingly satisfying that Larry was always filled with a sweet, hopeful kind of numbness after reading them. The point was not some predestined beginning or end but all the sad and beautiful living between the beginning and the end. If you missed this, you'd wonder how this Carver guy ever got published, but if you got it, it sang like Dylan's "Corrina Corrina" and glowed like Van Gogh's *Starry Night*.

His love for Carver was such that it had inspired him in recent years to get up in the middle of the night and spend a couple of hours before work pecking out Carveresque stories on his laptop after tending to the animals and doing his abbreviated workout. Though his efforts had been rewarded with a couple of one-offs in small literary magazines, Larry felt he had yet to fully achieve his voice—his stories still needed to flatten out and become more vacant and emotionless. It was slow going, but Larry loved being locked in the solitude of his own head, trying to strip away all the varnish of life, reducing it to its most essential elements with lean, fat-free words.

Although he was already working on other stories, he couldn't resist mapping out this new narrative in his head. It was of a guy named—Gus Ehrman, and he was with a disinterested woman named Rowena, who was watching Criminal Minds while they had sex. Gus was a welder in his mid-thirties at a failing family-owned steel plant where they mostly fabricated industrial valves and pipe fittings. Though he wasn't part of the family, he always seemed to find himself cleaning up messes made by the clumsy heir to the business, Tony Jr.

In addition to cleaning up Tony Jr.'s mistakes, he was having a lunchtime affair with the office admin, Eileen, who was bored at home and drawn to Gus's strong, drama-less disposition, which was a counterweight to her barely-kept-in-check volatility. Sometimes, they would carry on at a cheap motel, or sometimes, impulsive Eileen would have him between the yet-to-be-fabricated steel containers—getting a rush at the possibility of getting caught. Eileen contrasted nicely with Gus's uninterested *Criminal Minds*-watching girlfriend. Her daring and craziness were a welcome sidebar in his otherwise staid life.

From the shadows, Eileen appeared in the dark, cold warehouse where Gus was checking some inventory. With greedy eyes, she kissed him and started to undo the buttons on his coveralls. With a production deadline looming Gus thought for a moment he might turn her away—make her wait until lunchtime. But before the thought could even be processed, she had his coveralls below his waist and was working him with her hands.

Given his wealth of practical knowledge and willingness to dig into even the dirtiest jobs, Larry's affinity for the arts and letters might have surprised his coworkers at the West Seneca Highway Department, where he was a Senior Utility Specialist.

He had been an honors math and science student when he started out at Brockport State in 1980 with the idea of pursuing an engineering degree. But throughout high school and beyond, he never could shake the pull of Vonnegut, Roth, and, of course, Carver and the questions of human existence their literature raised. Further, engineering always had one correct answer, but the answers were endless in a novel or a poem. Literature was vast and open-ended, while engineering was stuffy and closed. Larry found it exciting to meditate on Prufrock's anguish or wonder what might have become of Holden Caulfield's little sister, Phoebe. However, due to circumstances beyond his control, the intellectual debate in his head hardly mattered because he would never quite make it through college.

On October 12th, 1981, the Buffalo Bills defeated the Miami Dolphins on Monday Night Football, 31-27. Besides being a big win for the Bills, Larry got lucky with an enthusiastic coed from Long Island named Angela that night. There was, however, an emergency looming for Larry's family back home, and it was several hours before his roommate found him in Angela's dorm room with a message to call his mom immediately.

Some random fifteen-year-old kid out joyriding in his family's Delta-Eighty-Eight had T-boned Larry's dad—the original Larry Plumb—as he was making his way home from watching the Bills game at Bar Bang Bang in South Buffalo. Besides going through the intersection at South Park and Tifft Street at ninety-five miles an hour, the kid wasn't wearing a seat belt and was ejected from the car—his young body splattered and dead on the pavement fifty feet from the collision. Larry's dad was hemorrhaging internally from the direct impact. After he made it to the hospital from Brockport in just over an hour, he lasted just long enough to tell Larry that he loved him and needed to take care of his mother, brother, and sister. And that's what Larry did.

The senior Larry Plumb was the town's chief electrician and a jack-of-all-trades. A giant, affable guy, the senior Plumb drank too much and was a terrible gambler. A point made very real when the funeral breakfast was ending, and a swarthy guy with slicked back hair and a pinky ring rolled up on Larry and spoke to him in hushed tones about settling his deceased father's account—Larry Sr. had a nickel on the Dolphins. Not surprised, Larry left the breakfast, his grief momentarily replaced by dread for the coming shitstorm that was going to be of his father's financial exposure. Larry withdrew the five hundred dollars from his own bank account and paid the first of his dad's many debts.

Vinny, the swarthy guy with the pinky ring, complimented Larry for being a stand-up guy at such a moment and returned a hundred to him. Not knowing whether he should thank Vinny or punch him in the fucking head, Larry took the hundred and got all sloppy that afternoon with his old high-school buddies Mac and Burbs, drinking whiskey at Bar Bang Bang, where his father had been a regular.

Larry did countless side jobs with his father growing up, and most of the money his dad made, in addition to his ample town salary, was pissed away on booze and sports bets. So much so that he let the payments on his term policy lapse, leaving his wife, a Highway Department secretary, and his younger brother and sister with nothing. There was a small auto insurance payout, but it was not nearly enough to cover his father's exposure, and Larry had little choice but to leave school and take a job with the town.

He loved his dad and was grateful for the countless hours they spent doing side jobs, from roofs to circuit breakers to hardwood floors. This off-the-books apprenticeship had essentially turned Larry into a jack-of-all-trades as well. However, given the financial mess thrust upon him, Larry was motivated to keep track of every dime he made and how it was spent.

In those years, he was a tireless worker, taking all the overtime he could get and any side job that became available. Bit by bit, he straightened out the family finances, allowing his brokenhearted mother to retire comfortably several years later. He was also able to scrape together a sizable amount of cash for his siblings' college education.

Despite how hard he was working Larry squeezed in some classes himself. In fits and starts, he pursued his degree until his late twenties, trying to figure out if he should go the pragmatic engineering route or with books and literature, where his head and heart were. In the end, though, because of his relentless schedule and responsibilities, he came up just short of that degree.

By then, he had met Maureen and settled in at the Highway Department, where he ran multiple crews. He completed jobs on time and under budget, much to the delight of fiscally conservative town residents and elected officials. At 27, Larry's star was rising, and he was asked to run for Highway Commissioner, which he did and won.

In the commissioner job, Larry was very competent at ministering to the town's needs—keeping the budget straight, getting the garbage picked up, and clearing the snow. But he was very uncomfortable with the back-slapping and ass-grabbing of town politics. After four four-year terms, he gave the job up. His high school buddy and right-hand man, Kevin McNamara, was elected with Larry's strong endorsement. Larry was kept on with the title of Senior Utility Specialist, which allowed him to run crews and do jobs at Highway and beyond. Mac tended to all the self-congratulatory political functions expected of a commissioner while Larry kept the ship up and running.

Brick by brick, Larry had built a nice life for himself. He had a solid family and a wife he adored, even if she didn't always cooperate with him to his liking. He garnered the respect and admiration of his neighbors, friends, and coworkers. Larry also had the pleasure of seeing the tangible results of his work—whether it was getting someone a job and mentoring them or making sure the town was open for business after a brutal Western New York storm. Additionally, he was thankful for his progress in his secondary occupation as a yet-to-be-discovered author.

In spite of all of this, there was a certain emptiness in Larry. A growing sense that the hard, careful work that had always characterized him was no longer necessary in a world of bent-headed people consumed by their devices, where the biggest and loudest voices—whether right, wrong, or crazy—sucked up all the oxygen.   These new forces left Larry weary and uncertain about how to move forward. In the past, there was little ambiguity in his life, from cleaning up the financial mess his father left him to building a home and life with Maureen. Now, he wasn't sure where he fit or what the world expected of him. Though he still got after it every day, more and more, he was having trouble seeing the benefit of his continued participation in this loud, obnoxious world that seemed to be rejecting him.

Three

On the Monday after Thanksgiving, Larry received a midafternoon text from his daughter Ashley asking for help with her car. She said it had been making "scary noises" between school and her internship at the old St. Ignatius School/Church on East Ferry in the city. Larry sent some return texts, hoping to diagnose the problem and pass it to roadside service. But Ashley's response was a terse, all caps text: "WORKING. CANT TALK. HERE TILL 6. PLS HELP."

With a shake of his head, he said, "Millennials," and added this new task onto what had already been a trying workday. It was the worst time of year at Highway—leaf removal season—and Larry, who was supervising a couple of different crews, had been getting shit all day from town residents about the shoddy job they were doing. In recent years, leaf removal had become a tightrope walk of waiting till all the leaves were off the trees and getting them picked up before the first snow. This year, they were aided by a lake-effect storm that accelerated the process, but only briefly. The problem was that with climate change, autumn (and spring) were slowly being eliminated from the weather landscape in Western New York. Summer now extended well into October, and the leaves remained on the trees longer and longer, which left a very short window to get them picked up before the crush of winter.

The crews would go out in a town truck with a giant vacuum-like arm that fed into a thirty-cubic-foot container. One of the guys would swing the arm back and forth, sucking up the leaves at the curbs of residents as the truck inched along, while two other guys would follow behind, raking up the excess debris. The leaves would then be deposited at the town's compost site.

As they worked along Dover Drive in Zone 3, a tiny, bejeweled woman in a black Chevy Suburban pulled to the side of the road looking for—"the *slackster* in charge." Without hesitation the guys in the crew directed her toward Larry. Like one of those trashy real housewives from TV, the compact woman donning oversized sunglasses immediately pointed her finger at Larry and began to yell at him for the long delay in picking up her leaves. Larry tried to explain the climate-change tight-window issue, but she was not having it. "These leaves are clashing with my Nativity scene and Christmas lights. How's my family supposed to enjoy the holidays with these filthy leaves everywhere?"

"It's a very challenging time for us. We're doing the best we can."

"Don't give me that—we're doing the best we can BS—do you know how much I pay in taxes?"

"Like I said, it's a challenging time of—

"Nonsense—What's your name?" she asked, looking for a name tag on Larry's reflective safety vest.

"Larry Plumb, Senior Utility Specialist."

"Well, Mr. *B*lumb, how about at the next board meeting I present a petition demanding that the town fire you and your crew and hire contract workers to do these menial jobs—for pennies on the dollar?"

"You're certainly welcome to voice your opinion at the board meetings," Larry said. He pulled out his wallet and shuffled through some business cards. When he found the card he was looking for, he took a pen from his shirt pocket, wrote something on it, and handed it to her. "This is Highway Commissioner McNamara's direct number. He answers his phone day and night and would be more than happy to address your concerns."

"Not likely," she said, returning to her SUV. Before slamming the door of the giant vehicle, she turned and said, "I'm not kidding about that petition."

Larry lingered for a moment while she pulled away and then walked toward the crew, which had been making progress with the leaves while he was being harangued. He half laughed to himself—Mr. Blumb—and he liked the idea of this woman calling his old pal Mac. It hardly mattered, though; Mac wouldn't be phased one bit. He was a world-class bullshitter and could talk circles around anyone. It's what made him a good commissioner. He didn't know squat about trucks, jobs, or the budget, but he could bullshit like no other.

Soon after that problem drove away, the manual arm that sucked up the leaves and fed them into the container went down. A bolt was loose on the hydraulic lift used to raise and lower the arm and was leaking fluid. Larry tightened up the bolt, but the gasket was trashed, and the replacement fluid on the truck wasn't enough to fill the system. The crew also needed to punch out at 3 p.m. The only call was to return the broken-down equipment to the town garages, or "the shop," as the workers at Highway referred to it and dispatch this crew to Zone 2, where the town's other leaf vacuum was still functioning. It wasn't the best use of manpower, but he had no other option. And he heard about it from Rocky, one of the guys in the crew.

Rocky was a stocky guy with wispy remnants of wavy blond hair and a long, scraggly beard that was the fashion among a particular set of working-class men. He had started at Highway about the same time as Larry but never went beyond his current position. Instead of putting his head down and working within the system, Rocky chose the well-traveled path of bitching and moaning about everything. Larry tried unsuccessfully for years to mentor him—to help him see the excellent work they were doing. Rocky didn't want to hear it.

In addition to not being open to Larry's apple-polishing bullshit, in recent years, Rocky had begun to challenge his authority. He voiced his displeasure about having to mop up in Zone 2, "With five of us raking, the vacuum's going to get overloaded and break down like this piece of shit," he said, pointing to failed vacuum arm.

With a shrug, Larry agreed to let him and the rest of the crew return to the shop, but they would have to punch out and lose ninety minutes of pay, which none of them wanted to do—even Rocky. All the way over to Zone 2, with Rocky in the lead, they grumbled about Larry and the shitty town equipment.

Back at the shop, Larry had a brief conversation with the mechanic about the gasket, then grabbed a pickup, went to Zone 2, and finished up the day with his aggrieved crew, who bitched the whole time.

At the end of his shift, Larry let out a giant, calming breath as he locked in the seatbelt of his Dodge Dakota. He was happy to leave the failed equipment and work crew problem behind for Ashley's broken-down car problem.

On the way, he listened to The Press Pool with Julie Mason on his SiriusXM radio. While the monsters in Washington continued to pursue outrageous policies, Larry was beyond outrage and listened with a placid detachment. But as he transitioned onto the freeway, he became distracted. He thought about that lady from Zone 3 and her gaudy jewels, earth-killing SUV, and stupid complaints. Quietly, he said to himself, *White people.*

The run-down old school/church where Ashley was doing her internship was far removed from suburban white people and their non-problem problems. Pulling up to St. Ignatius, Larry was taken aback at the condition of the building. Before the suburban exodus of the sixties and seventies, the east side of Buffalo was a Polish neighborhood, and St. Ignatius was a bustling Catholic church and school. Larry played high-school baseball just down the street at Schiller Park and remembered the area being much like South Buffalo, the working-class neighborhood next to West Seneca.

Larry texted Ashley that he was there, and she came out with her car keys. After moving the car ten feet and hearing a loud thumping noise, Larry got out, minimally jacked up the passenger side, and diagnosed the problem as a lower ball joint when there was some play in the tire.

They probably could have driven the car home, but Larry thought it best to get a tow. Ashley stood there, arms folded, looking annoyed and cold in a thin cardigan sweater. As Larry fingered through his wallet for his Triple A card, he said to her, "This place is pretty run down. Is it safe?"

"Yeah, I guess. I don't know. Is any place safe?"

"Right, but that's not what I mean. Is the building safe?"

"I don't know. Isn't there a building inspector or something that would have to approve it?"

"Yes, but—"

"Dad, can we talk about this later. I have to get back to work. Come inside when the tow gets here. I'll tell Darnell, the security guard, who you are."

Waiting on the tow Larry watched Ashley march with purpose back into the school and thought about what she had said about "any place being safe." He had been schooled by both his daughters and, to a lesser extent, Maureen, that for everyone except white men, safety was an illusion, and there was just as much danger for women in the suburbs as here, at a run-down school in the inner city. The danger and the perpetrators might look different and have different motivations, but the threat was the same, and caution was required in both places. Larry had spent a lifetime believing the opposite was true until his daughters had re-educated him.

Marked by old, ingrained codes, Larry had done well metabolizing these new facts and seeing the world through his daughters' eyes, but he fell back into his old belief system from time to time. When this happened, the women in his life were there with a quick and not-so-gentle rebuke.

After the tow came, Larry proceeded to the entranceway of the building. The security guard, Darnell, was standing at a desk with a woman, and they were going through a log or something. Darnell was dressed in street clothes and looked more like somebody's dad than a security guard. The woman wore a crisp blue suit, had mocha-brown skin, and had straight black hair parted just off-center, pulled back into a tight ponytail. A pair of glasses with a well-defined black frame sat on the bridge of her nose, giving her a professional air. After a moment, they both looked up, and Darnell asked, "May I help you?"

"I'm Larry Plumb. Ashley's father. Her car needs to be towed, and I'm going to drive her home."

"Sure, Ashley said you would be in. Have a seat," Darnell said, pointing in the direction of some steel folding chairs.

As Larry sat down, a small crash occurred in the hall. Darnell looked at the woman in the suit, and she gave him a slight nod, and he excused himself to check it out. Once he was gone, the woman removed her glasses, extended her hand, and said, "Mr. Plumb, I'm Dr. Johnson. Ashley's supervisor."

Larry stood up and shook her hand. "Pleased to meet you. It's Larry."

"Of course, and please call me Juanita. Ashley's been a real asset to our children and team. She has great instincts and is going to be a fine teacher."

"Really?"

A disarming smile came to her face, "You seem surprised?"

"Well, Ash has always been a top student, but I don't hear much about the day-to-day stuff anymore. I do know she's going to graduate on time. As the guy writing the tuition checks, that's a big relief. But as to what's going on minute to minute, I'm sort of clueless."

"Oh," she said as if she was sorry.

"Yeah, it's okay," Larry said, stammering a bit. "It's just they say less and less and want to hear less and less as they get older. It's a boundary thing, I'm told. Now, they just need me for my checkbook—and when their car breaks down."

"Yes, I guess that happens." After pausing for a moment, Dr. Johnson said, "That must be frustrating."

"Excuse me?"

"Frustrating. It must be frustrating when your kids only need you for money and when they have a problem," she said, nodding toward the door that led to the parking lot.

Her directness caught him a little off guard. Through the trials and tribulations of getting three kids through school, Larry became accustomed to educators being neutral and saying as little as possible. But her strong, no-nonsense face was devoid of pretense, and without really thinking, Larry said, "Frustrating is a good word. One day, they can't get out of bed without your help, and the next day, they think you're just off the turnip truck. And then there are all these boundary things. Do you have kids?"

"Just the students here at St. Ignatius and the teachers in training I supervise."

"So, you can probably relate."

"Oh yes. Most don't know what they don't know, but they come around."

"I hope so. It's tough sometimes," Larry said, feeling self-conscious.

"On our way to changing the world, the stars in our eyes can be so bright that we become blind to those who led the way."

"Is that Dumbledore or Shakespeare, maybe?"

"Haa," she smiled brightly. "No. I made that up on the spot for you, Mr. Plumb—Larry."

"Well, it's awesome. The first positive thing I've heard all day," he grinned.

"Thank you. Not much inspiration at West Seneca Highway today?"

"Never. And how did you know about Highway? Ashley?"

"No—I saw your profile."

"What profile?

"The one in the paper."

Larry could feel his cheeks redden, "From the News?"

This was a reference to Larry's 2000 profile in the Buffalo News, the year he won Erie County Civil Servant of the Year.

During a classic Buffalo storm that dumped nearly seven feet of snow on the city and the surrounding towns, Larry and his crews were responsible for liberating several group homes for developmentally disabled residents, some of which had no power or heat. He also was instrumental in getting medical personnel to countless town residents in crisis. And, maybe most importantly, when the worst of the storm had passed and people could get around on foot, he had town trucks plow out the lots at Consumer Beverage centers so residents could get beer while they dug themselves out from the storm. Over the five days of the storm, Larry slept just a handful of hours on a cot in his office.

The profile also documented his family history, including his father's death and his caring for his mom and siblings. Then, it highlighted his skillful management of the Highway Department after his meteoric rise to Commissioner.

"Yes, from the News. Before I take a prospective teacher into the program, part of the vetting I do includes looking into the background of the student and the family. Some might consider this unethical, but a quick Google search helps me to get a big-picture view.

"So, I helped Ashley get this internship?"

"I didn't say that. I said I do a Google search to help me get a big-picture view. I will say that after reading that profile, I was not surprised by her time management and organizational skills. They're real strengths for her."

"Really? You should see the clothes all over her bedroom floor."

"You'd be surprised. Do you want to see her in action?"

"Oh no, she'd flip if she thought I was—stalking—looking in on her."

"I showcase what we do here to people all the time. Trust me. She won't notice you at all."

And, though he had only just met Dr. Johnson—Juanita minutes earlier, Larry did trust her. She was charismatic yet disarming, and when Darnell returned, Larry followed her out of the entranceway into the facility.

Though the old school was run down and drafty, Larry could feel the buzz of positivity in the air. They took a leisurely stroll through the first-floor corridor, and Dr. Johnson pointed out what was happening in each classroom. Then they went into the basement where mass used to be held. The pews and pulpit had been ripped out, and the area was divided into large sections separated by cubicle walls. There was movement and activity everywhere.

They walked past Head Start kids learning about nutrition while some older kids were deep in thought, looking at algebra equations on a whiteboard. Ashley was teaching some middle schoolers what to do if an active shooter was in the building, which made Larry's heart sink. Also in the basement was an old kitchen where a group of ladies put together yogurt and fruit snacks. Adjacent to the kitchen was a play area with what looked like primarily preschoolers joyously riding tricycles, painting, and playing games. One of the old offices had been converted into a computer lab and a hodgepodge of different units sat on tables and desks.

As impressed as Larry was by everything he saw, he couldn't help but comment, "What's going on here is really great, but this building—how is it not condemned?"

Just then, Dr. Johnson, in a controlled yet stern voice, said, "Hakim," and stared down a middle school boy trying to elbow a girl out of her seat in front of an iMac. Under her watchful eye, Hakim got a small chair, pulled it up next to the girl, and sat in an orderly fashion. Dr. Johnson turned to Larry, saying, "We're a CAO—Community Action Organization and live on grants and donations. I'm sure you know how it works; you play up the good work you're doing to inspectors and ask for a little more time as you try to fund your capital improvements. We've made progress on the building, but obviously, we have a long way to go."

Looking around, Larry said, "Ah, funding—in the suburbs, that's called tax increases. How long do you have?"

"Maybe a year—tops. In that time, we have to show some real progress on the plumbing and possibly the boiler system, plus many other things, but those are the biggest priorities."

"Can you get it done?"

"I'm hoping. I've got calls out to politicians and community members trying to secure some pro bono contractors for us. These contractors are good people but need more education on what we do here. Not to stereotype or generalize, but many in the contracting community I talk to still have a certain "pull yourself up by your bootstraps" mentality and don't understand the positive long-term effects that programs like ours have on kids. We've had some success but no big commitments yet."

"Yeah, I remember. Contractors are not all that progressive."

"You know Larry, and I don't mean to impose, but that profile talked about your range of trade skills. Would you consider helping us on a project or two?"

For a second time, Larry was thrown off guard by her directness and stammered for an answer, "What would you need?"

"Anything and everything," she said with a measured smile, looking around.

"Boy, there's a lot to do. What about liability issues?"

"I can draw up waivers."

"Can I think about this some?" And then the real point came to him. "Of course, I would need buy-in from Ashley. I'm not sure she'd want me around."

"You guys really don't talk, do you? Remember how I said she was going to be a fine teacher? She loves these kids and the program and would do almost anything to get them more and better resources. Even if it means having her dad around. Also, she'll be moving on to student teaching at the end of the semester in a few weeks."

"All right. I'll talk to her and let you know."

"Great." Then, looking at her watch, she said, "It's almost story time at The Pit. Would you like to read a story to the children?"

"The Pit?"

"The Pit of Fun"—the preschoolers' area."

"Oh, I don't know."

"C'mon, it'll be fun." She smiled.

And, after pausing for another moment, feeling a weird connection with her, he said, "Sure, why not."

The kids receiving nutrition instruction earlier entered The Pit. Dr. Johnson directed Larry to the small library of books on shelves near the wall while she talked to Ms. Mohr, the teacher supervising the group.

Ms. Mohr instructed the children to sit on the carpeted floor in front of an empty chair while Larry found the perfect book: *Tthe Snowy Day* The by Ezra Jack Keats. Looking at the book's bright colors, Larry got a little choked up remembering how he had read this book a million times to his own kids and how not only did they love it, but he did as well.

Ms. Mohr announced: "Boys and girls, we have a special guest reader today, Mr. Plumb. Please welcome him." A smattering of "Hi Mr. Plumb ...Welcome Mr. Plumb" came back from the children. Larry chose to sit cross-legged on the floor in front of them instead of using a chair and introduced *The Snowy Day*. The book came right back to him, and a chill ran up his spine as he mostly recited the text from memory while showing the illustrations to the enthralled children. In some of the scenes, just like with his own kids all those years ago, he changed his voice for emphasis, and in others, he added cold, shivery sound effects.

There had been one brief lake-effect snowfall in Western New York in early November, which had since melted. When he finished the book, he asked the children what they did on that *snowy day*. Some said they looked at the snow out their windows, some helped shovel it, one little girl made a snowman with her brother, and a couple of the boys said they had a snowball fight.

One little girl named LaWanda, heard her grandma say, "It's too early for the goddamn snow." At that point, Ms. Mohr jumped in and talked about special words that adults sometimes use that they shouldn't repeat.

Larry was able to check his laughter at what LaWanda had said, but he felt an ear-to-ear grin on his face as he looked out at the innocent, beautiful kids in front of him. He was also delighted that when he gazed beyond the children to the back of the room, he saw Dr. Johnson and Ashley standing there, beaming.

Four

After climbing into the cab of the Dakota and placing her book bag between her feet, Ashley immediately changed the channel on the satellite radio to SiriusXMU—the college radio station. Teeming with good feelings from reading The Snowy Day and learning about Ashley's rising star, Larry resisted the urge to bring up what Dr. Johnson had said about her future teaching prospects. Given their current state of communication, almost any utterance from Larry would likely have been met with a shrug.

Looking at her as she scrolled on her phone, he also resisted the urge to tell her how much he liked the Spoon song on the radio. Unlike just about everyone he knew, aside from a few musician friends, Larry still sought out new music regularly. In fact, it was Larry who introduced Ashley and the rest of the family to Spoon, along with other classic indie bands like the Pixies and the Replacements.

As they traveled through the early evening Western New York darkness, he continued to look over at his daughter, whose face was illuminated by the light from her phone. Her glossy blue eyes, hidden by the sandy hair falling about her face, reminded him so much of Maureen when she was young. Suddenly, like waking from a dream, he realized Ashley was growing into a strong, beautiful woman right under his nose, and he was missing it. A wave of self-loathing washed over Larry, and he asked himself how this had happened.

Despite writing all those hefty tuition checks and watching her progress through school, Larry still saw her as a little girl. Why—he wondered. As they merged onto Main Street, he drifted back to one of his fondest memories of her. She was in the sixth grade, and one spring day, as Larry came in from work, she got up from the living room couch took out her earbuds, and with the weighty intention of Bertrand Russell, asked, *"Dad, have you ever heard of the band—Led Zeppelin?"*

Larry remembered the big grin on his face, telling her, "Yeah, I know Zeppelin. Not my thing."

"Not your thing?" But they kick so much ass."

"Ass—really, Ash?"

"Sorry, Dad, but they do."

"Yeah, well, they were and still are really overplayed. Besides that, every wannabe tough guy I knew growing up was into Zeppelin, which drove me crazy."

"So it's not the music—it's the people who liked the music? Lame Dad. Very lame."

"Let me finish. So, I was more of a Who guy back then, and Zep was okay, but all these Neanderthals driving around the suburbs in their dad's cars loved Zeppelin. That's all they ever wanted to listen to or talk about. It was so boring. And the radio played them all the time and still does—that's the real crime. So, I don't hate them as much as I'm just sick of them."

"Still, they kick a ..." she said, stopping herself.

In those days, Ashley was a cello player, and instead of riding the bus, she sometimes walked home from school and would stop at the music store on the way. The kid behind the counter let her jam on the display guitars along to Zeppelin. From there, she quickly hooked up with a few friends in a short-lived band called—the Slashers. They broke up due to artistic differences and because the lead singer had a Christian dad who wanted to sit in on practice sessions, which was stifling and a little creepy.

Even when it sometimes led to a bit of trouble—and not riding the bus home did get her in trouble—he loved her adventurousness. As he continued to look at her, a bittersweet feeling pulsed through his body: "Dad, have you ever heard of the band Led Zeppelin?"

Reminiscing this way made Larry long for the days when he was the arbiter of all things true and essential in his kids' lives. They used to come to him with everything from looking over homework to navigating tricky social situations to mapping out college and their futures. Now, he was a checkbook, a maintenance man, and often the butt of their jokes. As he'd told Dr. Johnson, he hoped it was a weird transition thing and that one day he would get his kids back and have conversations where everything he said didn't just produce an eye roll or an exaggerated sigh. Till then, he was resigned to quietly go about his business and try to be there for them when things like the ball joints went on their cars.

To that end, he needed to find a way to discuss Dr. Johnson's request that he help with some building issues at St. Ignatius. He wasn't thrilled to have to get Ashley's blessing, but it was necessary to keep their shaky peace. As they transitioned off the freeway onto Seneca Street, he turned down the radio and said, "In a weird way, I'm sort of glad you had car issues."

She looked at him momentarily, and by the light of her phone, he could see a hint of a smile.

"It was great to read *The Snowy Day* again and see you in action. And Dr. Johnson seems like an incredible person."

Half looking at him, Ashley said, "She's a *rock star*."

"Seems like it." And Larry couldn't resist, "She said a bunch of nice things about you."

"Dad."

"No, really. She said you had great instincts and organization skills."

"Dad."

"I was surprised, given the state of your bedroom floor, which I told her about in some detail."

"You did not."

"I sure did, but she still insisted that you would be an awesome teacher."

Larry could see her fighting back a smile and then he said, "I also told her it was hard to see you as a teacher, given your support of corporal punishment. But not the bad corporal punishment—just stuff like locking kids in closets and hitting them with rods till they bleed a little."

"You're a monster," she said with a smile.

"Monster? Add that to the list of names I've been called today."

"Who called you names?"

"Some of the guys on my crew when we had a breakdown. I wouldn't let them go home early with pay. That was mostly under their breath, but this lady was complaining that we weren't picking the leaves at her curb up quickly enough. She said they clashed with her Christmas decorations—called me a slackster and Mr. Blumb."

"Really?" Ash said incredulously, making direct eye contact with Larry.

"I kid you not. This lady threatened to organize a petition to get contractors to do menial jobs like the leaves."

"*White people,*" Ashley responded with a shake of her head.

"That's what I said. Goddamn white people."

They both laughed and as they turned the corner onto their street, Larry said, "There's one more thing. When Dr. Johnson was vetting you, she came across my old profile in the *Buffalo News.*"

"Yeah."

"Well, she asked me if I would help with some maintenance things around the school. I would like to do it, but I told her I had to run it by you first."

She smiled and said, "Oh my God. " Then she started laughing.

"What?"

"Sorry—sorry," she said, still smiling. "But she so played you." She began to laugh again.

"Played me? Whaddya talking about?"

Regaining her composure as they coasted into the parking spot in front of their house, Ashley said, "Dr. Johnson identifies people who can help the cause. She shows them around St. Ignatius, and like you, they're usually impressed. She then makes a pitch to them to donate some time, expertise or whatever they have to offer. She closes the deal with some interaction with the students—like reading *The Snowy Day*—rock star."

"Jesus Christ."

"Don't get mad, Dad. She's just looking out for the kids. And, yes, I'd be perfectly fine with you helping out. In fact, I'd love it for the few weeks I have left."

"Great," Larry said. He opened his door and removed his legs one at a time from beneath the dash. He stopped before getting out, struggling to suppress the urge to slam the door, pound the hood with his fist, or engage in some other semi-outrageous display of anger. Instead, he took a deep breath and just absorbed this blow.

Though upset, Larry would have been even more upset if he had given in to his anger, especially in front of Ashley, who had exited the truck and was making her way into the house. He also thought that given the never-ending battle to keep St. Ignatius open, he would have done the same thing. In a different way, he had done the same thing when he was Commissioner, schmoozing for reduced rates on labor and materials with contractors and suppliers on the golf course and at lunches.

After some calming breaths, he looked at Ashley's car, which the tow truck had deposited in the driveway. One at a time he placed his legs back into the Dakota, took out his phone, and called the local AutoZone. He would have liked to have gone right then to pick up the ball joint, thus giving him more time to process this Dr. Johnson information. But it was out of stock, so he would have to wait until the following day when one could be sent over from the warehouse.

When he went inside, Ashley was in the kitchen with Maureen and Ben. She was obviously telling them what transpired at St. Ignatius and how Dr. Johnson played him. As he passed them on his way to the bathroom to clean up, Ashley suddenly was mum with a barely hidden smile. After exiting the bathroom, Larry could hear them talking from the man cave while he changed into his sweats and yard hoodie. He came back into the kitchen; the three of them were having a hard time constraining themselves.

Larry opened the freezer door and pulled out a bag of frozen organic broccoli. He extracted a container of grilled chicken breasts from the fridge, a bottle of sriracha, and a hopper of Parmesan cheese. He put the broccoli in the microwave for five minutes and thirty seconds and chopped up his chicken breast with his favorite knife on a wooden cutting board. When he was done, he got a bowl from one of the cabinets embedded in the wall. As he deposited the little cubes of cut-up chicken into the bowl, it was obvious the three of them were ready to burst.

"Yes?"

Trying not to laugh, Maureen looked at both kids and said, "Ashley says you had a big day at her school."

"Big day? I was there for a little over an hour, but yes, the director or whatever her title is, Dr. Johnson, showed me around, and I read *The Snowy Day* to a group of kids. The place has a great positive vibe, and the work Ashley is doing is very impressive."

"I hear something else happened. Something about you being the new maintenance man," she said with a little snort as the kids turned away, trying not to laugh.

"Okay. I know it's hilarious to all of you that Dr. Johnson—what did you say, Ash—played me. But you know what, if I was in her shoes I'd do the same thing. In fact, I did do the same thing for years when I was Commissioner."

"You duped someone into doing work for free?" Ashley queried, laughing.

"You're kidding me, right?"

"Oh, don't be so sensitive, Dad. I'm just messing around."

"Let me get this straight. You call me for help. I come and help, and in the process, somebody else asks for my assistance. I agree to help them too. But, instead of thinking about how I stepped up for you and the school, you make me the butt of your fucking joke?"

"Larry!" Maureen said, surprised.

Ben jumped on it too, "C'mon Dad."

"Never mind," Ashley said as the microwave buzzed like an angry bell, indicating the start of a fight.

In the tense moments that followed, Larry removed the broccoli from the microwave, cut open the bag, and poured the contents into a colander to drain the excess water. As the steam from the broccoli rose to the ceiling, he asked, "So, what's the plan while your car's down?"

"Mom's going to drive me in the morning, and Sarah will take me to St. Ignatius in the afternoon. And I don't know about getting home."

"Really—you don't know? I'll be there at six."

Looking at the floor, Ashley quietly said, "Okay, thanks." She then picked up her book bag and headed out of the kitchen.

"Hey, wait. Where're you going? I'm going to need some help with the disassembly of that front end when I'm done eating."

"I can't. I have a ton of work to do."

"Guess you're going to have to stay up late."

"I already have to stay up late.

"Yeah, well, life is hard," Larry said with a certain dismissiveness while he dowsed his chicken and broccoli with sriracha and Parmesan cheese.

"So, what's this? You're trying to punish me because I made a little joke at your expense."

"Larry," Maureen pleaded.

"Right, I'm trying to punish you—please. And spare me with this—I have to stay up late stuff. I didn't sleep for eight years in my twenties."

"We know, Larry. You saved the world. Things are different now." Maureen said in an annoyed voice.

"I'm caught up with everything, I can help," Ben said, coming to the rescue.

"Thank you, Ben," Maureen snapped.

"Thanks, Ben," Ashley said in a voice trailing away.

"You sure?" Larry asked.

"Yep. I was headed to the gym, but I can do some sets in the garage," Ben said, nodding.

"Okay, I was going to do some sets too."

Rescued by her brother, Ashley stomped off with her book bag slung over her shoulder. Ben went out to the garage to get a head start on his workout while Larry ate his chicken and broccoli, and Maureen huffed around him in preparation for the argument that would come later. Her only words were an irate rebuke: "That doesn't go there," when Larry put his fork and bowl in the kitchen sink. Silently, he moved them to the dishwasher and then set up the coffee for the morning. They barely made eye contact on Larry's way out.

Though he might have been a little out of line dropping the "F-bomb" on Ashley, he wasn't sorry. He was resigned to his diminished role, but there was only so much of this nonsense he could take, and the "F-bomb" was a line in the sand that told them there were limits.

Going through the garage's man door, Larry found Ben doing a set of shoulder presses with dumbbells. He had also moved the car into the garage and removed the lug nuts on the driver's side wheel.

Setting the adjustable dumbbells back in the plastic carriage, Ben said, "I got the lugs off."

Larry extended his arms to the side and did some forward and reverse warm-up circles, telling Ben, "Thanks, but it's on the passenger side. Didn't you hear the noise?"

"Aw, I had my earbuds in."

Larry adjusted the weights from Ben's forty-five pounds and did a set of shoulder presses while Ben put the lugs back on. From there, they rotated sets and went through an upper-body workout. Ben set his earbuds on the repurposed countertop, and they listened to the latest Strokes record at a moderate level. Between sets, Larry jacked up the car and got the tire off. They scarcely said a word to each other while they worked out, which was fine with Larry and Ben, too, he guessed.

At six foot two, Larry was a couple of inches shorter than Ben and a few pounds lighter. Of the three kids, Larry found he still had a sliver of currency with Ben, mostly in what he thought were the deep, unspoken pools of their shared manhood. Though at opposite ends of the spectrum—Larry being phased out while Ben was phasing in—they both found themselves at an uncertain place in their lives, which rendered them more or less speechless. Ben, like Larry, was a big dude, clocking in at two hundred and twenty pounds, but on a six foot four frame. He had the same icy blue eyes and blond hair that was darkening as he got older. Ben had always been a decent, outgoing kid, but from about the tenth grade on, he had become a frustrating question mark.

"Ben, sausage or bacon?"

"I don't know."

"Ben, engineering or computer science?"

"I don't know."

"Ben, English or History?"

"I don't know."

"Ben, hockey or lacrosse?"

"I don't know."

"Ben, Arcade Fire, or Radiohead?"

"Radio—I don't know."

"Ben, Dungeons & Dragons, or Magic: The Gathering?"

"I don't know."

"Ben, boys or girls?"

"Girls," he said unconvincingly.

Ben held the utility light while Larry kneeled on a pad and tried to remove the bolts holding the ball joint in place. After struggling with little success, Larry said, "You want to give it a go?"

"Sure."

They changed positions, but Ben had no luck either, and Larry said, "Screw it, it's not happening. I'm going to have to drill those bastards out tomorrow."

Larry and Ben put away the tools as they finished with some sets of triceps extensions and then cleaned their hands. When they were done, Larry opened the freezer door on the garage fridge and removed his bourbon glass and a 1.75-liter bottle of Jim Beam. He free-poured the brown liquid into the short glass and grabbed a Rolling Rock from the fridge. Turning to Ben, he said, "You want one?"

"Sure."

A little surprised, Larry grabbed another beer while Ben moved a second chair onto the sitting platform—the sanctuary part of the garage, where Larry got right with the world via the forty-two dive and the ambiance of scented candles.

"Beam?"

"No way. That stuff smells like a research lab."

"Okay, but if you ever develop a taste, keep it in the freezer instead of icing it. The molecular structure of the bourbon will be compromised, but icing it down gets it all watery, and then you drink too fast and end up bombed. Keep it in the freezer and sip slooowly."

"Good to know, Dad."

From Ben's response, Larry got the hint that he was being an annoying know-it-all. With that, he sat down and resisted bringing up what made the Strokes sound, well—like the Strokes. There was something so unique about them that made you instantly know it was a Strokes song. But, instead of talking about it, they just sat there—listening—which was perfectly fine with Larry and again, judging by Ben's silence, him too.

When Ben had gone mute, Larry was alarmed, thinking he might be drinking and drugging or hanging with the wrong crowd. But there weren't any new faces, no new places he was going, no blurry eyes or funny smells. The evidence was nonexistent, and eventually, after Ben said, "I don't know," a million times, Larry took him at his word—*he really didn't know.*

At first, Maureen thought he was just being obstinate and lazy and tried yelling it out of him. This tactic only produced arguments and made Ben dig in deeper. While Maureen remained skeptical about why he had become so indecisive, she did back off when it became apparent yelling at him and pushing him wasn't working. And, despite SAT scores that were good enough to get into all the schools he wanted, it was decided by everyone, including Ben, that he should start out at community college where he could figure some things out. But even at the less demanding community college, he was struggling.

Recently though, Larry was seeing signs of life. He noted some curious digital purchases of books by Spinoza and Ta-Nehisi Coates on the Amazon account. And, as Larry looked at his phone for something to play when the Strokes record ended, sort of out of the blue, Ben said, "Have you ever read that Barbara Tuchman book that's been on the bookshelf in the front room forever?"

"*The March of Folly*?"

"Yeah."

"Sure. Great book."

"I liked it too, but the pundits think it's garbage."

"Garbage. Why?"

"They get stuck on the word folly—that her notion of what happened was destiny or something. But I like the folly angle. When I was a kid learning history in school, I didn't know the word folly, but I always thought King George was a complete asshole. He could've held on to everything if he had just given a little back to the States. And with the Medici popes, there would never have been a schism if they had just enacted some reforms. That's some major-ass folly, as she points out."

Hoping to draw Ben out some more, Larry tried to hold back the smile growing on his face and said, "I agree. Ultimately, they lost everything because of their greed and hubris."

"If Tuchman was still alive, I bet she would add the invasion of Iraq to the list and the Catholic sex abuse scandal."

"No doubt."

"Do you know Ta-Nehisi Coates?"

"Yes, I read that essay where he made the case for reparations a few years back."

"Do you agree with him?"

"About reparations—absolutely. The race issues in this country will never be solved till we own up to our sins. Reparations are a step in that direction."

"What's that thing you say? *None of us are free till all of us are free.*"

"Right," Larry said, unable to contain his smile. "Well, goddamn, you were listening."

"I listen," he said, pulling on his beer.

"Ben, what is all this?"

"All what?"

"This sudden interest in history and the world?"

"I don't know," he said, looking away.

Larry immediately recognized his mistake, but it was too late. He tried to bring it back by asking some questions about the Ta-Nehisi Coates book he had recently bought, but Ben just gave disinterested monosyllabic answers before finishing his beer and going into the house.

Though he ended the conversation prematurely by needing to know what Ben's sudden interest in history was all about, Larry was delighted they had a real conversation. As he sat sipping his Jim Beam, he was cheered that the coming fight with Maureen would end with him telling her about the conversation with Ben.

Five

I nside the house again, Larry sat down at his desk to prune his Gus Ehrman and Eileen story, which had a tentative title: Shadow Love. From the front room, he could hear the cop show Maureen was watching on TV. Donald, the male golden, tramped into the man cave and looked at Larry with his big, sad, wanting eyes. He turned in his chair, and the dog set his chin on Larry's thigh. The female Lydia was not far behind and did the same on the other leg. With a happy glow from the forty-two dive and the conversation with Ben, he smiled at the dogs and rubbed behind their ears as he re-read his story.

Gus sat with a beer at the kitchen table, watching Rowena listlessly mix meatballs into the pan of red sauce while the pasta came to a boil. Though her lack of energy annoyed Gus, he knew it made life easier, less complicated. She was so undemanding of him and their relationship that he wondered, as she lethargically fixed his plate, if she even noticed when he wasn't there...

Larry let out a muffled laugh when he predictably heard Maureen turn off the cop show, go to the kitchen, and loudly start putting dishes away. He knew she was mad at him for the way he had spoken to Ashley, and a moment later, she was in the doorway of his room with a stern look and said, "Larry, we need to talk."

Well aware of that tone, the dogs scurried away. Larry was still looking at his computer screen and said, "Okay."

Maureen sat behind him on the sofa bed, turned couch. She waited a moment and said, "Please look at me, Larry."

"One second, just let me finish reading this—"

"Larry!"

"And done. Yes, my love," he said, turning in his desk chair to face her.

"Larry, we need to talk about how you treated Ashley tonight."

"Yeah—I don't think we do. Unless you want to talk about what an entitled little shit she can be sometimes."

"Oh, stop it."

"Stop what? She was a jerk to me, and I called her on it. That's all."

"Stop it, Larry!"

"Again, stop what? Ash and I had a little dustup. People have dustups all the time. It's over."

"It's not over. She was very upset."

"Yeah, I don't think she was that upset. She was ready to escalate."

"You're being aggressive. Just like you were with Ashley."

"Aggressive? Do you even know what the word means? I'm not being aggressive. I'm frustrated with her and this nonsense conversation we're having."

"Don't talk to me that way, and having a conversation about how you upset our daughter isn't nonsense. She has a lot on her plate and doesn't need her father dropping F-bombs on her."

"So, she can say and do anything she likes to me, and I have to take it?"

"You're being unreasonable, Larry."

He recognized Maureen would never see his point of view, so rather than beat that dead horse, he did what he seemingly always did these days—resigned from the conversation. "Okay, okay. I'll back off."

The strange metamorphosis that saw Larry fall out of favor with his family corresponded with Maureen's rise. In the early years of their marriage, Maureen still possessed some lingering effects of her rigid Catholicism. She tended to see things in binary terms, often leading to inflexible judgments. Though she was a competent mother and elementary school teacher, she could be volatile. In those years, smooth and steady Larry was always there to temper her capricious impulses. To her credit, though, Maureen had worked hard to evolve, and by the time the kids graduated from high school, they were turning to her more and more, which was fine with Larry. What he didn't like was her tendency to appease them because it was easier, more convenient.

Larry did note the parallels between her exacting Catholicism and her tendency now to always agree with the children, especially when it came to him. In both cases, any complicated problem could be avoided if you relied on church dogma or just agreed with the kids regardless of the facts. Rather than take an unpopular stand, she went the path of least resistance, which sometimes made Larry not take her seriously.

But in a larger accounting of things, the good outweighed the bad with Maureen, and rather than fight this losing battle, Larry moved the conversation toward what had occurred with Ben.

"Hey, guess what happened with Ben out in the garage?"

"You crushed his soul for not holding the flashlight steady?"

"Will you stop, please?"

"What happened?"

"After we were done with the car and working out, he had a beer with me, and we talked."

"Talked?"

"Yeah, we talked."

"About what?"

"About some books he's been reading."

"When did he start reading?" she asked, smiling.

"Not sure. He asked me about *The March of Folly*, the history book that has been on the shelf in the front room forever. He's been ordering books on Amazon, too."

"That's great. What brought this on."

"Don't know. He shut me down when I asked."

"So, does this mean anything?"

"Maybe, but who knows. It might be a phase.

The smile on her face broadened, "Finally."

"It's hardly a done deal. It's probably best not to have any expectations."

"I know—I know. It's just I worry about him."

"He'll figure it out. He's a smart kid."

"You think so?"

"Absolutely."

She paused momentarily, and a troubled, faraway look came to her face.

"What is it?"

"I don't know. I'm feeling anxious. Is everything going to be all right, Larry?"

"What?"

"Is everything going to be all right with Ashley and Ben, you and me, Samantha—the family. Is everything going to be all right with us?"

"Yes. Everyone is doing great. We're fine. What's up with you?"

"I don't know. I hate it when you're angry with the kids. Sleep with me tonight. I miss you."

He was tempted to say he barely spoke to the kids but instead said, "You hate sleeping with me. My early hours wake you."

"I know. But I miss you. I want you close to me."

She moved to the edge of the couch, grabbed Larry's sweatpants at his knees, and pulled his desk chair forward. She picked up his right hand, brought it to the side of her face, and kissed his wrist. Leaning forward, he ran his fingers through her beautiful silvery hair and kissed her. Pulling away from the kiss and leaning her forehead against his, Maureen somberly said, "I'm sorry I'm not here for you as much as you want me. But I do love you. You're such a good man."

"I love you too," Larry whispered. "C'mon, let's straighten this out."

"Not that. I just need to be close."

"What?"

"I know. Please, just lie with me and hold me."

"You sure everything is okay?"

"I'm just anxious."

Though a little peeved, Larry did what she asked. They both had a restless night, and as Larry exited the bathroom at his usual waking time, Maureen went in.

She sat on the toilet, and Larry asked, "Are you feeling better?"

"Yes, but can you lie with me a little longer?"

"I got stuff to do and the chickens."

"I know, just till I fall asleep."

Laying wide-eyed on his back next to her, Larry's mind raced with the coming day. Maureen nestled close to him on her side and, after a few deep breaths, took him in her hand and started to stroke.

"Whaddya doin Moe?"

But she didn't respond. She just started kissing his neck and running her hands all over his body. Larry got the message and furiously removed his sweatpants and T-shirt and then attempted to dispense with her little nightie as he probed her body.

After he had not made much progress with her nightie, Maureen said, "Wait—" and climbed out of bed. She stood in the gauzy blue light, which threw wispy shadows across her face and around her body. With her hands at the bottom of her nightie, she started to sway gently and said, "You ready for this?"

Eagerly, he nodded and whispered, "Oh god—thank you."

Larry was always appreciative of any woman who would have sex with him and was pretty straightforward in his desires. The one thing that might have been considered a little messed up, which he told Maureen objectified but occasionally would play along.

For Larry, it was such a disappointment when they would roll by the intoxicating wiggling free of her garments in the heat of the moment. But when they went at a more deliberate pace, and she did disrobe for him, he could barely contain himself.

Though her body had softened with age, in the shadows of the night, his yearning was immense as she slipped off her nightie and moved her hips with careful, glorious precision from side to side before slowly dismissing her panties. "My god, you're beautiful," he whispered.

She sat at the edge of the bed and took him in her hand again. Larry grew greedy while she stroked, trying to Jedi mind trick her, thinking as hard as he could—SUCK ... SUCK ... SUCK.

But the mind meld fell short, and Maureen climbed atop him. He moved his hands all over her body. Eventually, they came to rest on her hips, and he gently guided her back and forth. Just as they both were reaching their breaking point, she climbed off of him, kissing him as she went, and said breathlessly, "Finish on top."

Larry did as he was told, and once he was inside again, Maureen closed her eyes and gasped softly. Feeling her breath and gazing at the purple hue of her eyelids, Larry's love for this beautiful woman was so complete at that moment.

When he was done, he rolled off her and reached for some tissues on the nightstand.

After he cleaned up, she nuzzled against him and said, "That was wonderful. You're wonderful. Why don't we do this more?"

"Are you kidding?"

"Oh yeah—I'll try to be better for you." She blanketed his neck with kisses and then said, "Not to be rude, but you can go now?"

Larry laughed, "Thank you."

"No, thank you. Now, let me get some sleep."

He kissed her once more and whispered, "I love you."

Once he had his sweatpants and T-shirt on and was headed for the door, Maureen said, "I love you too, Larry."

***

Larry had a little bounce in his step all day that Friday. The complaints he fielded from residents about the shitty job he and his crew were doing scarcely touched him. He recruited Hank Tomasi, the town plumber, for a reconnaissance mission the following day to St. Ignatius. Ben stepped up again that afternoon, offering to pick up Ashley from St. Ignatius while Larry finished the reassembly of her car's ball joint, which went off without a hitch.

But like a deflated ball, the bouncy lightness from his early morning intimacy with Maureen quickly dissipated, and life returned to normal. In a rare and careless misstep, Larry forgot to clean his dirty car hands in the garage and proceeded to wash them at the sink.

"I've asked you not to wash your hands in here after you've been working on the cars," Maureen scolded, exiting the basement with an armful of freshly folded linens.

"Sorry Moey," Larry said, smiling over his shoulder. "I'll clean the sink when I'm done."

"You say that, but you never do. And don't call me Moey."

Larry shook the excess water from his hands and grabbed a dish towel from the drawer next to the sink. He hoped her annoyance would be temporary, but she was exasperated when she returned to the kitchen after putting the linens in the closet outside the downstairs bathroom. "Jesus

Christ Larry, first you dirty up the sink, and now you're using my good dish towels."

Larry was wounded by her tone but resisted going back at her. Silently, he got the Comet cleanser out and scrubbed the sink as Maureen huffed about, placing junk mail in each family member's inbox sitting on top of an old writing desk in the dining room.

Larry used to go through the mail and weed out all the junk, but everyone got mad at him for throwing out their mail—even the junk—so the solution was these inboxes. Now, it just accumulated until Maureen got annoyed and threw the stuff out herself or got the kids to do it. Larry could see her inching toward the edge and was tempted to escalate with a bit of snark about how well the inbox solution was working, but instead, he kept his powder dry.

After he finished the sink, he took the dirty dish towel to the basement, came upstairs, grabbed a warm-up jacket from the man cave, and headed toward the front door. Maureen had moved on from sorting the mail to magazines, and walking past her, Larry announced, "I'm going bowling," which garnered zero response from her.

His irritation with Maureen promptly subsided once he was out in his truck. He hit the ignition, and the local classical station, which Ben had made a preset over the summer, popped on instead of SiriusXM. After dropping Ashley at home, Ben showed further usefulness by picking up a snowblower Larry was going to work on for one of his mom's neighbors. Ben was full of surprises these days, and thinking about him, Larry smiled.

He was instantly drawn in by the moody classical piece, which had this slow-building quality as if it were the prelude to some intense action in a movie. As he made his way through the dark pre-winter gloom to the bowling alley, Larry thought it might have been the kind of music playing just before Maureen came up the steps from the basement and scolded him. But the crescendo was a letdown. It was not the car crash he was anticipating. At any rate, pulling into a parking spot at the Centerview Plaza where the lanes were located, he waited a moment to hear who had written and performed the piece. Larry knew next to nothing about classical music, but since Ben made it a preset, he was learning and guessed this was the work of Debussy.

The composition went full circle and dropped back into its plaintive mood, and his mind wandered. The car crash that didn't happen in the music made him think of his old man—and the car crash that did happen. He got choked up for a moment and then saw a picture in his head of his busted-up dad trying to get himself out of his car as he motherfucked the kid who T-boned him.

Lost in these thoughts, he didn't realize for a moment that the music had transitioned to a march. Unless he waited, he wouldn't find out who the piece's composer was and who performed it. Not wanting to wait, he exited his truck, thinking about his larger-than-life old man, half-smiled, and muttered to himself, "Poor bastard."

Inside the alley, Larry bought two pitchers of beer and brought them over to a large common area at the head of the lanes where league play was taking place with the guys from the Highway Department. Because of his oversized responsibilities early on, Larry was only part of one team before he became Commissioner. That was for the best in Larry's mind. He liked the guys at work but only had so much bandwidth for their crude, ball-busting, and racist/misogynistic jokes. So, instead of being part of a team, he'd show up every couple of Fridays and have beers and shoot the shit with the guys and his buddies Mac and Burbs.

Mac and Burbs didn't bowl either, but they were there every Friday, unlike Larry. They were in their usual spot at the head of the ninth lane, sitting in a couple of high-back chairs with an empty pitcher. Coming from behind and looking at the pitcher, Larry said, "For ten bucks, you cheap bastards can get that thing refilled."

Both men smiled, and Burbs, the lean six foot five town carpenter, said, "Why would we buy when you're here?"

"Well, look who it is, Larry Plumb, out mingling with the little people," Mac said with a smile.

Larry climbed onto an empty high back and asked, "Can you get a new line? That one is so goddamn tired. And, for the record, the only little person I'm mingling with is you—the rest of us are just people."

"Are you making a comment about my physical attributes? Mac came back, gazing down at his pelvic area.

Laughing, Larry responded, "Wow, that's a leap."

Just then, a sturdy woman in a white apron with a bright smile came up and said, "Hey Larry."

"Lucy," Larry said with excitement. He got down from his chair and hugged her.

As the hug dissolved, Burbs said, "We were just talking about Mac's physical attributes or lack thereof."

"C'mon Burbs, easy. I have an image to uphold."

Lucy jumped at that. "Trust me, I never had any illusions about you or your physical attributes—the tiny hands, the overcompensating Mustang."

They all laughed as Mac raised his hands and looked at them quizzically. Given the reeducation he was receiving from his daughters and Maureen, Larry felt a tinge of discomfort with the coarse subject matter in front of Lucy. But she was a friend from the before times, and not only wasn't offended; she leaped at the opportunity to land a shot at Mac.

It was interesting to Larry that despite the hardened bubbles everyone lived in these days, there was still a certain elasticity depending on who you were talking to and what their predilections were. You had to be quick to keep up, even with old friends like Lucy.

Looking toward the far end of the alley, around lanes fifteen and sixteen, Lucy said, "Did you see who's here? —Ryan."

"Ha," Larry cracked, "they were talking about it on the truck today. I didn't think he was going to make it."

Ryan was Lucy's son. With Mac's help, Larry got him on a crew after he was a washout at college. On the truck today, one of the guys had been pushing Ryan to sub in tonight, but from what Larry heard, it hadn't sounded too promising. Ryan was a smart but sullen kid who maybe spent too much of his youth in front of screens. Like Larry's son Ben, he struggled to figure out where he fit.

"Yeah, he's not all that comfortable, but he's hanging in there," Lucy said with a half-frown.

"He'll be fine. He just needs some time," Mac offered.

"Here, let me get you guys another pitcher—on Gene," Lucy said, taking the empty pitcher.

"Plumb just brought two," Burbs gestured toward the beer.

"I can see that dipshit," she said with a smile. "It won't hurt anyone if Gene buys another one."

Gene was her boyfriend of some years and had a stake in the alley. During the day, Lucy managed a small dentist's office and took some shifts at the alley when they were short-staffed. She had never done well with men, and Gene was no exception. When she and Larry sometimes commiserated about their sons' lack of direction, the subject of Gene would come up too, and with a bitter shake of her head, Lucy would say, "How did I become such an asshole magnet?"

Lucy was back quickly, and setting down the pitcher, she said, "Thanks again—for Ryan."

"He's a good kid. It'll work out," Larry said.

As she was leaving, Burbs said in a loud voice, "Come and have a shot with us in the lounge later. "

"Gene's such a dick," Mac said to nobody in particular.

"Why don't you take her out?" Burbs asked.

"Isn't it enough that I got her kid a job? Plus, you heard her. My physical attributes might not meet her standards. It would be embarrassing."

"You—embarrassed?" Larry asked rhetorically.

"By the way Plumb, you're on my shit list. That lady on Dover Drive whose leaves are clashing with her Christmas lights called my phone fifty fucking times. Why didn't you pick her shit up?"

"Had a breakdown. We got them today. No worries"

"No worries for you. She's been calling me every twenty minutes. Listen."

Mac pulled out his phone and played her messages. They laughed as she complained about an endless array of problems, from the cost overrides on the new town library to the dirt from the freeway that was becoming embedded in her house's vinyl siding—stuff they had no control over. As guys walked by from the bar or restroom, they stopped, poured themselves a beer, and listened. Everybody had a good laugh, and they dubbed her *The Dragon Lady of Dover Drive.*

While they listened, a crowd started to gather down at the far end of the building where Ryan was bowling. Burbs asked a coworker headed to the restroom from that direction what was happening? Apparently, Ryan and

Ronny Wilkens were in a face-off on lane fifteen, each having thrown six straight strikes.

Ronny was a tall, gangly guy and former town worker. In the mid-nineties, he was a star left fielder and point guard at West Seneca North. He led North to the state basketball championship, but because of substance issues, he flopped at several colleges and had problems keeping a job, including one at Highway. Mac was forced to let him go after he called off thirteen times in a single month. These days, Ronny was the maintenance man at a couple of Off Track Betting joints, and despite his continuing substance issues, he was still a good athlete and a dominant bowler.

Larry, Mac, and Burbs went down to watch this duel with the rest of the guys. Ryan spared in the seventh, then had a strike in the eighth, then two more spares and a strike to finish out for a respectable score of 248. Ronny continued to strike into the tenth frame, but on his final roll, he was a fraction off, and the tenpin stood tall like the Queen's Guard at Buckingham Palace for a 299.

While Larry was pulling for Ryan, he was amused by Ronny's histrionics after each subsequent strike—the fist bumps, exaggerated high fives, flexing. Still, looking at Ronny in his moment of near triumph, he felt bad for him and men in general.

He thought about himself, Mac, Burbs, Ryan, Ronny, and the endless masses of boys who participated in youth sports. Every kid who bounced a ball, caught a pass, or scored a goal had dreams of making it big, and all but a few became casualties of those dreams. Life interceded with its temptations and excesses, and many ended up as some variation of a drunk maintenance man at a betting joint or a crew chief who got harangued by an entitled suburban shrew because leaves were clashing with her Christmas lights.

All this potential and unrealized glory gets reduced to obnoxious fist bumps and flexing on a Friday night at a fucking bowling alley. Somehow, it seemed to Larry, men everywhere deserved better, all of them, even guys like Ronny Wilkens, who could never get his shit together.

Larry's grim outlook continued when they entered the lounge for a bourbon. There, running his hand through his long beard Rocky was holding court with some of the younger guys talking about libtards and snowflakes. Standing at the bar with Mac and Burbs, Larry could hear Rocky's legendary dissatisfaction poisoning the newbies over his shoulder. He hoped they would be smart enough to see through the bullshit and take note that Rocky never went anywhere because of his constant grumbling. "Fuck him," Larry said to himself. He was his own misery.

After one bourbon, Larry left, and as he drove home, his thoughts drifted from Rocky's endless bitching to Lucy's never-ending quest to find a good man to Maureen's dissatisfaction with him earlier that night. Given how close they seemed to be after having sex that morning, he was extremely frustrated with her scolding words and cold behavior.

Though he was aware of attractive, bright women everywhere, he loved Maureen and never thought there would be anyone else for him. They had been through so much together, from the early lean years to caring for and burying her parents to patiently navigating their children into young adulthood. But he was growing tired of these little outbursts, her lack of curiosity, and how she and the kids summarily dismissed him.

Driving home on that cold November night, with a barely discernible measure of guilt, Larry asked himself if maybe there wasn't something more for him, something beyond Maureen.

Six

Maureen O'Donnell was the quintessential middle child. Born to Henry and Marion O'Donnell, she had two older siblings and two younger ones. Henry was a CPA, and Marion's older brother ran a successful State Farm agency in South Buffalo, where she worked after the children were relatively self-sufficient. Though Maureen was an adequate student and a happy kid for the most part, she was a bit of a wild card in the upright, God-fearing O'Donnell family. Her older siblings were earnest and obedient, and her younger siblings were whiny and spoiled. She found both older and younger to be exceedingly tedious and went her own way whenever possible.

She demonstrated her independence on several occasions in her early teens. In one particular instance, she and a few friends pulled the old trick of telling their parents they were sleeping at each other's houses and then stayed out all night in the park. Her older siblings would never be involved in such a ruse, and the younger ones would run home the second it got the least uncomfortable.

Maureen found deceiving her parents exciting, but staying out all night wasn't all that fun. It was colder than expected, the mosquitoes were unrelenting, and it was a little scary. Also, after they'd talk about why the Cars were better than Duran Duran and which boys were cute, trying to kill the hours became boring.

A couple of her friends' moms figured out the game while engaged in some small talk at the grocery store. This resulted in Maureen getting grounded for the last two weeks of the summer going into freshman year. She hated being stuck at home, but it was fun to deceive her parents, even if it didn't turn out to be that great of a time.

What was always fun too, during those years, was drinking a two-dollar bottle of Boone's Farm wine at the old Stone Bridge at Cazenovia Golf Course. The bridge sat between the eighth and ninth holes and became obsolete to golfers when construction workers building condos that butted against the course cut a path between the holes. The small bridge sat above a long- dried-out marsh with the fairways set on both sides and was surrounded by overgrown brush and some maple trees. It was an ideal spot for underage drinking since it was a fairway and an expanse of more maples away from the condos and houses that lined the course. And it was also challenging, but not impossible, for cops to get back there in their cruisers. As long as there were no big fights, and their empties were disposed of in the garbage cans the city provided at either end of the bridge, the police left them alone.

Unlike at home, where Maureen sometimes felt overlooked, she was quite popular with the Stone Bridge crowd, which was comprised of boys from the Catholic high school, St. Peter's, and her school, St. Bridget's, which had an all-female student body. Although she was pretty and intelligent, that's not what set her apart. Maureen had a certain kind of untamable confidence that saw her rise above all of her friends, many of whom were desperate for the attention of some St. Peters' boy. She saw herself as Joan Jett's sandy-blonde cousin, minus the leather. And as far as Maureen was concerned, she would decide who was worthy of her attention, not the other way around.

She made that clear during freshman year when she made out with Doyal Higgins for a few nights back at the bridge and then waved him off in front of everyone with a certain finality. Doyal was the Junior Class President at St. Peter's, and rather than hang out with him, Maureen chose to take home an eighth grader who was a friend of her younger brother and drank too much. This kid stumbled back to the bridge after making the rookie mistake of gulping down a pint of vodka and could barely stand. Everybody laughed and razed him, especially Doyal, which angered Maureen immensely. She walked the kid around till he was sober enough to go home.

Doyal Higgins was not only the Junior Class President but also the son of some wannabe hero legislator who was South Buffalo famous for always being on the six-o'clock news opposing Governor Cuomo. He took Maureen's public rebuke hard and went for the scarlet letter of Catholic retribution, starting the nasty rumor she had an abortion. Though the rumor lacked any credibility, it still managed to get around. Maureen was well aware of it and who started it but gave it zero oxygen and continued about her business of being pretty and confident.

All of this came to a head one day in the hallway after sixth-period study hall when Eileen Osgood, one of the girls always searching for a boy, asked her point-blank if it was true. "Yes," Maureen said. "It's actually my third abortion. I'm hoping to have another next week." She then put her hands on Eileen's shoulders and said, "Meet me behind the gym after school. I know some public-school boys who ain't shootin' blanks. It'll be fun."

The busy hallway seemed to come to a stop in a moment of shock. An uncomfortable silence hung in the air as if this were a slow-motion movie scene until Eileen protested in a shaky, worried voice, "You bitch. I'm not meeting you anywhere."

With a little self-assured smirk, Maureen casually turned around and moved down the hallway to her last class of the day.

Of course, the news reached her parents, and Maureen was asked to remain at the table after dinner.

Her father said casually, "We heard you were the center of a big scene at school today."

"It was nothing. It lasted about ten seconds."

"I wouldn't say it was nothing. Explanation, please."

"This stupid girl asked me about this rumor, and I wanted to shut her up."

"What rumor?"

"It's not important."

"What rumor?" her father insisted.

"Someone is saying I had an abortion."

"Oh Lord," her mother responded.

"It's not true. It's just stupid gossip."

"Why would someone start that kind of thing?" her father asked calmly.

"I don't know."

Then her older sister, Peggy, a senior at St. Bridget's and probably the person who told their parents about the incident, walked back into the kitchen and said, "Lots of people at school said they heard it from Doyal Higgins after Maureen dumped him."

"Why do you always have to be such an asshole, Peggy? I didn't dump him."

"Maureen Elizabeth, language," their mother said, slapping the kitchen table with the palm of her hand.

"Okay, okay," their father said. "Thank you, Peg. We can take it from here."

Henry lit a cigarette as she left, looked at his wife, and then turned to Maureen. "Look, sweetheart, next time something like this happens, talk to us. I don't want people saying untrue things about you, but if it happens again, try not to be so—expressive in your response. Reassure people that these are just unfounded rumors."

"What? I'm not doing that. Then those assholes win."

"Maureen Elizabeth—"

"I won't do it."

"Then think about this," her father said, setting his cigarette in an ashtray on the table. "Tomorrow, your mom is going to work, and your brothers and sisters are going to school. They will be asked about this rumor and maybe other things. At some point, someone will ask me as well. You don't want us to answer for this, do you? Can you see how this affects us?"

Reluctantly, Maureen did see and agreed to tone it down in the future, but being censored pissed her off. After thinking about it for some time, she came to the conclusion that she would just have to be more blunt in her responses. Instead of some clever hyperbolic comeback, she would just have to punch whoever was messing with her in the face, which was boring and inelegant.

Maureen's confidence and toughness could be traced back to her family. The O'Donnells presented an upstanding and devout image in their Irish-Catholic community and to the larger world. Public disrespect and misbehavior were not tolerated by her parents, but at home, Henry was partial to his Black Velvet, and Marion was prone to headaches.

This often resulted in their parents being unavailable, leaving the kids to sort out problems on their own. For Maureen, this meant kicking and scratching against her older siblings and intimidating and bullying the younger ones. She was not in the business of giving anyone a free pass, which made everybody think twice about crossing her.

Throughout high school and into her third year of college at the University of Buffalo, Maureen's confidence was marked as much by the sandy hair that curled beautifully about her shoulders as the stinging retorts that flowed effortlessly from her silky lips. Her classmates at St. Bridget's saw her as a badass and, like her siblings, thought twice about crossing her.

But then, in her third year at UB, she met a boy named Andrew Roth from New York. Andrew was different from the neighborhood Catholic boys who made up her world. He sat at the small table outside their classroom in Capen Hall, where Maureen was giving her astronomy paper, which was due that day, one last look.

"Mine's done. Want me to look yours over?" he asked.

"Excuse me?"

"Your paper. I can look it over for you."

"Thanks. I'm good."

"Do you mind if I sit here until class starts?"

"Suit yourself," she said without looking up from her paper.

After sitting quietly while Maureen checked her paper, he got up with her when everyone started to file into the lecture hall and again asked if he could sit next to her.

"What's up, dude?" Maureen asked severely.

"It's just that I see you have that Allan Bloom book, and I've been dying to talk to someone about it."

Roth was referring to *The Closing of the American Mind*, which Maureen had just picked up at the bookstore and was assigned reading in her Philosophy of Education class. Sitting down, she said, "I'm just starting it. What class are you reading it for?"

"It's not for a class. I read it on my own. It's a pretty hot book right now."

"Oh," Maureen said, perplexed. The idea that someone would read a book like this without it being assigned reading was foreign to her.

"My name is Andrew Roth," he whispered with a grin as class started.

Maureen didn't answer with her name, but she felt a warm half-smile come to her face as she perused his sturdy jaw and jet-black hair, offset by blue eyes that seemed to contain a hint of arrogance. He had little knowing crow's feet cropping from those eyes and wore a black Beastie Boys T-shirt.

At the end of class, when they passed their papers down the row to the teaching assistant, she noticed his was neatly encased in a plastic protector and perfect, unlike hers and others, which were beset with corrections and Wite-Out.

After class, as they walked, Andrew explained that he was an English/History major from Brooklyn and was headed to law school. When Maureen revealed she was a commuter, he had a million questions about her family, neighborhood, and high school. It was a pleasant, easy conversation, and she was surprised how hastily they made it to her car in the parking lot.

Although reading from the Bloom book wasn't due for a few weeks, Maureen started to plow through it over the weekend. Normally, she would've waited until the last minute, but something about this Andrew Roth kid was compelling. Embarrassed, like one of her dopey friends trying to win the affection of some guy—there she was, for better or worse.

She couldn't make much sense of the book since you needed all this secondary information about Plato, Rousseau, and Nietzsche for context. It was really annoying, and she wanted her goddamn $18.95 back because she didn't see how this was going to help her teach fifth and sixth graders. Despite the book's overall density, she understood but disagreed with how Bloom disparaged the American mind and the university system. On Monday, when she talked to Andrew over a coffee at the student union after their Astronomy class, much to her surprise, he argued Bloom's point.

She pulled out another book from her Philosophy of Education class, Since Socrates by Henry J. Perkinson, showed it to Andrew, and then said, "I don't get what Bloom's talking about. Nearly every education class I take has a discussion about these boring Greek philosophers."

"That's his point," Andrew began. "First, you're not really reading the Greeks. You're just getting Perkinson's interpretation of them. Second, in all likelihood, this guy is just giving you the accepted view of the Greeks prevalent in universities nationwide, which Bloom would argue is a kind of intellectual relativism. To get the Greeks, you had to read the original texts and critically think and debate them point by point. Hence, the closing of the American mind."

"That's another thing, the American mind," Maureen came back. "Until many more people went to college after World War II, I don't think America had this deep tradition where we sat around in our togas at the gymnasium debating Socrates and Plato. Maybe rich people had that luxury, but not the rest of us. It's bullshit to say there's this grand tradition in America that we lost."

Andrew smiled and responded that Bloom was talking about universities, not America in general. And the conversation went back and forth like this and fingered off into debates about music, TV shows, the '88 election. Their discussion only ended because Andrew had a night class. At her car, smooth as could be, he grabbed her by the hand, then leaned in and kissed her. Not only did Maureen not offer any resistance, but for the first time in her life, with the hairs at the back of her neck tingling, she felt the overpowering magnetic pull of a man.

Driving home, she was embarrassed by the silly rush of emotion scurrying through her body. It was almost as if she had raised a white flag of surrender against herself. She tried to fight it off, but thinking about Andrew's little stony blue eyes and jet-black hair, she giggled at her lightheadedness.

Soon, she was all in on Andrew, and Andrew was all in on her. A few nights after their first kiss, Maureen spent the night at the small off-campus apartment he shared with an old high-school friend from Brooklyn. After all this time, she finally found someone worthy of her attention, and she dove into this relationship with everything she had—caution and consequence be damned.

If anything marked their on-again, off-again relationship over the next three years, it was its combustibility. From the intense, physical, and loud sex to the knockdown, drag-out fights they had about everything from politics to music to books to the societal influence of *The Golden Girls*, theirs was a relationship defined by emotion and chaos.

Andrew, a future lawyer, had a well-reasoned opinion about everything. And Maureen, who was determined to never let anyone get over on her, met him head-on—often with explosive consequences. So ferocious was the competition between them that friends often felt uncomfortable in their presence. There were constant breakups and cheating on both sides, but eventually, they would find their way back to each other. Though there were tears, apologies, and promises to be kinder followed by weekends of sex, takeout, and watching old movies, they were always just an offhand remark or an opposing view from another eruption.

Early on, Andrew stumbled onto the ultimate trump card, which he used to great effect.

"It's incredible how much you're like your mom," Andrew casually observed after a dinner at the O'Donnell's.

"WHAT?"

"No, no—don't get mad. It's just you have certain mannerisms that are the same. And you look alike."

"What do you mean?"

"It's just how your mom sips from her glass and looks at someone when they're talking. You sip and engage like her, that's all."

"Oh," she hesitated. "But you said we look alike. She's a million years old."

"Yeah, but you can see, you know, in her day, she was a looker, like you."

"Really?" Maureen said, taken aback.

This exchange came early in their relationship, before Maureen understood that Andrew, noting her displeasure at the comparison, tucked it away and would reintroduce it at some opportune time to land a shot. Plus, it had some merit, no matter how much Maureen objected.

Andrew was also Catholic, and one weekend, they went to church with his observant parents in Brooklyn. Afterward, when they were alone, Andrew asked, "So, did you like our mass?"

"Well, it was weird with all those Black people there."

"What?"

Realizing her mistake, Maureen tried to walk it back, but it was too late, "No, I didn't mean it that way. It was just a different visual for me. That's all."

"Okay?" he said, smirking.

"Don't look at me like that," she said, raising her voice. "I'm not my mother. It wasn't racist. It was an observation."

Andrew would seize other opportunities to draw parallels to her mother. Shortly after getting back together after one of their breakups, where Maureen went on a few dates with a mutual friend, which angered Andrew, he landed a blow through one of these comparisons.

While washing the dishes at his apartment, Maureen lightheartedly said, "Maybe when I'm not around, you should think about using paper plates."

"Maybe you should just worry about your own dishes."

"Hey, c'mon, I'm doing something nice for you."

"Nice for me, or are you just trying to mother me—Marion?"

When Maureen wasn't up for sex, Andrew would accuse her of being a prude, like her mother.

"Prude? The woman bore five children and had two miscarriages. And we did it like two days ago."

"Please, I can see right through you. You have the same little parochial guilt as your mother. One day you're a porn star, and the next, you're the Virgin Mary."

"What are you talking about?"

"Quit playing dumb. It's obvious why Henry's in love with his Black Velvet."

As low as the lows were, the highs, like the enchanted week they spent in Manhattan after Andrew was accepted into UB law, were very high. But in the end, as much as she loved Andrew and as high as he could take her spiritually, intellectually, and sexually, it was just too exhausting to be with him.

While substitute teaching and working on her master's degree, she ended the relationship for good. It was the hardest thing she had ever done, but she knew this on-again, off-again cycle was incredibly toxic and not sustainable.

For six months after the breakup, she walked around like a zombie, but slowly, time worked its magic, and Andrew fell from her mind, and she started to date again. One of the first people she went out with was Mac. It was through him that she met Larry. This was when he was cleaning up his father's ledger and taking care of his mom and siblings.

When Larry was around, she could sense his attraction to her. She was impressed with his work ethic and determination, and when things fizzled with Mac—who was handsome, athletic and smooth, but far from serious about anything—she asked him to pass her number along to Larry.

Not only was she attracted to his sturdy six foot two frame, but she found his anti-intellectual—intellectualism and his unassuming, resolute demeanor incredibly sexy. Also, as Maureen was entering her mid-twenties, she had grown tired of the tough brawler facade she had erected and carried around since high school. Larry wasn't flashy or challenging like Andrew, and the highs with him would pale in comparison, but so would the lows. Ultimately, she knew she could build something solid and lasting with him even if it meant sacrificing some excitement and intensity—a trade-off she was willing to make at that point in her life.

Seven

J ust past 9 a.m., Hank Tomasi pulled up next to Larry in St. Ignatius'
parking lot. Hank and Larry had worked together for decades, and
stepping from their pickup trucks into the raw, dull Western New York
morning, they greeted each other with wordless nods. Hank carried a little
tool bag and walked with a certain deliberateness beside Larry from the
parking lot to the building.   They stood in the arched doorway, and Larry
pushed the entrance buzzer. Hank had been the town's master plumber
back to the days of Larry's dad. In Hank's face, Larry could almost see
his old gray friend calculating what he would extract from him for doing
this Saturday morning favor. Larry felt he was a little on the plus side of
the ledger with Hank after getting him some side work from one of his
neighbors recently. But the reconnaissance mission to this neighborhood
on Hank's day off would cost him a little more than he had in the bank.
Larry was taken aback when Dr. Johnson opened the heavy wooden door
a moment later, looking very fit and lean in a maroon tracksuit with three
rows of vertical gold piping that went from the top of her shoulders down
to her ankles. Larry was expecting the woman in the blue power suit he
had met a few days earlier.   Either way, she greeted them with a warm
smile, saying hello to Larry and introducing herself to Hank. Then she
said, "Fresh Timmy Ho's," and pointed toward the security desk inside the
vestibule where a carrying tray with three Tim Hortons cups sat next to an
open binder and papers.   She deftly removed the hot drinks from the tray
and handed them to Hank and Larry. Thin wisps of steam floated upward
as they dressed their coffees with cream and sugar. Looking at Hank stirring
his coffee, Larry said, "When I was here the other day waiting to drive my
daughter home, Dr. Johnson gave me a tour of the place. Great stuff going

on here. Lots of positive energy. She even talked me into reading a story to some of the kids."

Turning toward Dr. Johnson, Hank said, "You let Larry read a story? Was it nap time? Because if you've ever been in one of his meetings—they're real snoozers."

"It was a short story," Dr. Johnson responded with a smile.

They laughed, and Hank said, "I know we just met, but I can tell you're a good judge of character, Dr. Johnson."

"It's Juanita. Of course, I'm kidding. Larry did a great job with the children."

When their coffees were all put together, they passed the kitchen and the lavatories, whose plumbing Larry would potentially be upgrading, before heading to the basement to check the supply lines. Dr. Johnson asked Hank about his family and work history as they walked. Larry was impressed how she got Hank to talk so freely about himself and his wife, kids, and grandkids. At one point, she turned to Larry and gave him what he interpreted as an inside smile, letting him know the magic she had used on him the other day was now being applied to Hank to the same effect. It was a bit unsettling to Larry, but Ashley was right—Dr. Johnson was a *rock star*.

Once in the basement, Hank set down his coffee and his little tool bag. A moment later, he pulled out a couple of flashlights and, with Larry's help, inspected the lines coming in and out of the building. Hank removed a small notepad from his shirt pocket and wrote down measurements as they checked the lines. He also asked a series of questions: How many hours a day are people in the building? How many people drew on the water supply, and what's the ratio of children to adults? Is there any expansion of programs expected that would change water usage? How heavy is the food prep in the kitchen? And finally, the most pertinent question—how long do you intend to stay in this building?

Aside from a couple of crumbling return stacks that could be repaired cheaply with PVC, Hank declared the building to have good bones overall, even though it was old. The damage was minimal in the kitchen and lavatories on the first floor besides some faucets and shaky lines that provided minimal water pressure and needed replacement. The fixes, which involved opening up some walls, were relatively simple and inexpensive, provided PEX was used instead of copper. "It'll be a breeze for an old pro like Plumb. Take him a couple of Saturday mornings at best, Hank said with a laugh."

Hank moved on to the girls' lavatory after taking measurements and putting together a materials list in the boys' lavatory. There was a moment for Larry and Dr. Johnson to talk in the empty hallway. Very directly, she asked, "Could you do this in just a few Saturdays?"

"Hank overestimates my skills."

"You're so modest, Larry."

While Larry wasn't the kind of guy to necessarily talk himself up, he certainly didn't think of himself as modest. He quickly determined he was being played again and said, "That's great, the way you turn it on."

"Excuse me?"

"The charm—the way you work people."

"I'm sorry. I'm not following."

"The way you talk to Hank—to me. The charm you use."

"Oh look, you don't have to do this if you don't want to."

"No. I'm happy to do the work. I'm happy to contribute."

"So what's the problem then, Larry?"

"I don't like being played. This angle, you work to get people to help you," he said, unable to hide his frustration.

"Excuse me," Dr. Johnson said in a low, blunt voice as her dark eyes narrowed. I've been very upfront with you and Mr. Tomasi. Again, if contributing to our cause creates a problem, please step away. But do not accuse me of playing games with you. It's true that to do this job, to advocate for these children, I've learned how to persuade and flatter to get people on board with our mission, but always—always for the children.

Just then, Hank approached them, tore off several sheets of paper, and handed them to Larry. "I wrote the town's account number for Shaffer Supply at the top of the paper—you'll have to pay cash, but that account number will get you our price. I figure you can pick stuff up on your way over here."

Shifting gears, Larry looked at the little notepad papers and asked Hank, "If I need to run out and get an odd thing, who would be closest?"

"Leerb's."

"You should probably give me our number with them too."

While Hank pulled out his phone to check the town's account number with Leerb's, Larry and Dr. Johnson made eye contact again. The narrowness had receded, but there certainly was no warmth in her face.

After getting the account number, they all started walking out, and Dr. Johnson, as if putting on a show for Larry, thanked Hank profusely and talked with a passion that bordered on the sensational to him about the mission of St. Ignatius. She was smooth and inspiring without a hint of condescension.

At the exit, Larry made arrangements with Dr. Johnson to start work on the girl's first-floor lavatory next week and said she should be thinking about alternatives because it would be out of commission for some time.

As they walked to their trucks, Hank carried on about Dr. Johnson being a Halle Berry-like babe. Hank's words barely registered with Larry, who was preoccupied by his argument with her. Before getting into their trucks, Hank reminded Larry that he owed him a favor and, with a big smile, said he should expect an invoice first thing Monday morning. Larry responded with a less-than-heartfelt laugh.

Once inside his truck, Larry hit the ignition, shifted it into gear, and gave Hank a nod to go first. After he backed out and pulled away, Larry remained frozen with his foot on the break—full of agitation at the idea he was being played. He again thought over the argument with Dr. Johnson in his head before he quietly said, "Fuck it," and threw the truck back into park, turned off the engine, and marched back toward the school entranceway.

Larry stood in the arched door frame and pressed the entrance buzzer with a certain ferocity. A moment later, Dr. Johnson pulled open the heavy door. Looking a little surprised, she said, "Yes, Larry?"

"Do you have a minute to talk, Dr. Joh ... Juanita?"

She stepped back and waved him into the vestibule and then made her way toward the security desk. She sat on the edge of the desk facing him, folded her arms, and asked, "What can I do for you, Larry?"

"I'm not feeling so good about our arrangement, and I want to make sure we understand each other."

Her brow furrowed, and she asked, "What is it you don't understand?"

"I'm not sure. It just seems our conversation from earlier wasn't finished."

"Oh, you mean the conversation about how I advocate for the children. Is that it?"

"Yes."

"Tell me again what you don't understand because I thought we cleared that up."

"I feel like I was misled into helping you, and quite frankly, I'm not feeling all that good about it."

"The word you used Larry, was *played*," she said forcefully. "You think I'm playing you like you're a mark or something."

"Well, not like that."

"Then, what is it?"

The steam he had when he cut the engine and marched back to the building was fading. With slumped shoulders, he said, "I kind of feel like you're not appreciating what I'm doing for you—what Hank just did for you. It feels like I'm some kind of dupe you're manipulating."

"I'm sorry you feel that way. But I am, and the children are grateful for your help."

Regaining a bit of his mettle, Larry said, "It sure doesn't feel that way."

Dr. Johnson's eyes narrowed, and she drew him in for a long moment before a smile came to her face. That smile gradually grew into a muffled laugh, and she pointed her long, slender finger at Larry. She was about to say something but paused to giggle some more. When she stopped giggling, she raised her finger at him again and gleefully stomped her feet.

Frustrated and confused, Larry said, "I'm glad you find this amusing."

With a wide grin, Dr. Johnson said, "I know what this is. Oh, Larry, Larry, Larry. Your little white ego got hurt by the uppity black lady. And now, that little white ego needs to be massaged—right?"

"No. Whaddya talking about?"

"C'mon Larry, fess up. You'll help the black lady and her kids so long as they know *you* *in* charge," she said, moderating her voice.

"That's not true. In fact, as you were talking to Hank, I was amazed at how smooth you were."

"Amazed? You mean amazed at how I *played* him?" she said with the smile receding from her face. "And why would you think that? When you were Commissioner and some white business owner was trying to get a contract or sell you a piece of equipment, did you think these things? Or when some town council person was sucking up to you for a patronage job? Or do you think they're different than me? They occupy a different position and deserve respect, unlike the uppity black lady. Why don't you afford me that same respect? Don't answer—I know why."

She paused and locked her burning dark eyes on Larry. "Listen," she said quietly but forcefully, "For the last time, I am, and the children are grateful that you would offer your time and expertise to help St. Ignatius. It means the world to us." She then took a calming breath and continued in a softer tone, "I know you have a good heart, Larry. I saw it in that *Buffalo News* profile, in your wonderful daughter, and how you read to the kids. But you know how you could really help us and yourself? —Turn off that little white man privilege thing you got going on and see us. Not our building, not our neighborhood, and not the color of our skin, but see us."

Larry was stunned. After a few long moments, he stepped toward her, turned around, and leaned against the desk next to her. Staring straight ahead, he paused, took a deep breath and said, "I'm sorry. Holy shit. You're absolutely right. I'm such an asshole." He turned toward her and felt a smile come to his face, "Thank you, Juanita. You're right. I can't believe I'm that asshole."

"It's okay. I know you're a good guy. Those old codes are hard to keep in check," she said generously.

"It's nice of you to say that, but I don't need to be congratulated for meeting some minimum level of decency. I mean, two minutes ago I was a racist asshole to you."

"But now, you're owning it."

"Ah—" He hesitated for a moment and then looked toward the big heavy entrance door, "I guess, and I don't mean for this to sound like a rationalazation, but I guess since I read and listen, I'd like to think I'm beyond all this racist bullshit. But clearly, that's not the case. I should get out of the suburbs more."

"That's not a bad idea. Don't be so hard on yourself. We all have things we've been taught buried in us.

"You too?"

"Certainly. Being black doesn't make me immune. I'll tell you something, and I'm not proud of this, but after 9/11, every time I saw a Muslim woman in a headscarf, I expected her to speak in that broken militant language. Then, when they opened their mouths and spoke perfect English, I was shocked. These prejudices are in all of us."

"Me too about the headscarf thing. Sometimes, I still expect these ladies to talk that way." Larry said in a placid tone.

"It's very embarrassing."

"Why would you be embarrassed? The country was going through this huge trauma. Isn't it normal to make some assumptions?"

She smiled, "Yes, I suppose it is, but it's still embarrassing."

"Why?"

"Well, we saw it play out with you a minute ago."

"Oh, right."

"And it's different for white people, especially men. For me though, it's embarrassing because every single day of my life, the world lets me know I'm a black woman. It's the first thing people see about me, and I have to push back against it all the time, and it's exhausting. And then to use the same bias I fight against all the time? —I expect better from myself. I expect that I should extend the same goodwill to those Muslim women that I want for myself and for my kids. That's all."

"Ah, yeah, I get that."

"That doesn't mean I'm *not* going to call out that white privilege mess you brought today, Larry Plumb," she grinned.

"Please."

She measured him up for another moment, and before continuing, a mischievous expression came to her face, "Now that we understand each other, it seems like a good time to add another layer to this."

"What? You know I'm in the union. We don't add layers without a negotiation," he said playfully.

"I got this. Here's my offer: pay remains the same—at zero, but I'll provide you with extra manpower."

"Extra manpower? Interesting."

"Hear me out. Hear me out," she said, raising her index finger for Larry to listen. "I have a few workers that could benefit your endeavors here at St. Ignatius. They have zero skills and maybe a bit of attitude. But with some persuasion, they could be real assets."

"Really, just what every job needs—no skills and a bit of attitude. Can they at least make coffee?"

"I'll bring the coffee, and the workers, with some of my steely-eyed persuasion, will do whatever you ask, or I'll kick their butts. They can carry things, get tools, and do the job I hated most—hold a flashlight."

"Ah, the dreaded holding of the flashlight. Everybody hates that."

"Yeah, but not like me. My daddy was an academic and wasn't really good at any of this handyman stuff. He could delight you with Shakespeare's Sonnets, but a tape measure and screwdriver were his kryptonite. He did try though, and I had to help him, which meant standing around while he thought things through. Of course, the flashlight was the worst. He cussed me something fierce when I got bored and didn't hold it still."

"Yeah, I know what you mean. Until I was sixteen, I thought my real name was Dumb Ass. My old man was skilled at many things, but he had a special talent for yelling at me, "Light, over here, Dumb Ass—""

"Did it upset you?"

"No. Never. As you know from the profile, my dad died young, and that screwed me in a lot of ways, but before that, he took me on a ton of jobs and taught me all this stuff—like plumbing. Another thing was how to endure "ball busting," excuse my language, from those higher on the food chain."

"So, he taught you how to work with the Hank Tomasis of the world?"

"Very good. Yes, he taught me how to work with the Hank Tomasis of the world?"

"Okay, so back to our negotiation. You understand I asked you to let a few St. Ignatius students assist you, right?"

"Yes, I got that."

"And you're good with that?"

"Sure."

"Great. A few kids might really take to this kind of work. Myself or someone else will be in the building in case they need help keeping focused so you can get things done."

"Does this include teaching them how to work with the Hank Tomasis of the world?"

Dr. Johnson moved from leaning against the edge of the desk next to Larry to standing in front of him and smiling, "Please, no. They can get that someplace else."

Apparently, their conversation had ended, and Larry stood up too. Dr. Johnson extended her hand to him and said, "I'm glad you came back, and we talked this through."

"Yes," Larry said, shaking her hand. "Again, I'm sorry for being such a—such a—a Dumb Ass."

"She looked at him warmly and said, "No worries. We all have our moments."

As they started to walk to the door Larry nodded at Dr. Johnson in her maroon tracksuit and casually asked, "Headed to the gym?"

"The gym? Been there, done that. I have things to do and can't be wasting my Saturday morning at the gym. Lu Kim is waiting to turn my nails into a work of art," she said playfully, extending her long, slim fingers in front of her face.

They were at the heavy arched door, and Larry laughed, "Okay, sorry I asked." He opened the door, met her eye one last time, and said, "Thanks, Juanita. See you next week."

"Thank you, Larry. See you next week."

Not sure what just happened Larry walked to his truck feeling really good. He wasn't sure, but he thought he might have just been flirting with Dr. Johnson. Getting in his truck, he had a pang of guilt but fought it off, rationalizing that nothing had happened or was going to happen, and decided to just enjoy how playful she was with him after they got past his racist shit.

And that was it—that's why he felt so good. He was wrong about something, which he stepped up and owned, and rather than making fun of him or torturing him with it, like Maureen and the kids might have, they just moved on. She accepted his failure and just moved on, which was nice.

Truth be told, it was also nice to have a bright, pretty lady talk in a breezy tone and smile at him rather than being summarily dismissed.

Eight

Basking in the good Dr. Johnson vibes, Larry drove home blasting NRBQ at old-school party level. The cheerful melodies about cars and girls made him think of a simpler time—when he could hang with Mac and Burbs and drink beer all night, when pretty girls smiled and flirted with him like Dr. Johnson had today, a time when the world opened up to him with endless options and possibilities.

But a few blocks down from his house, after he'd strained his vocal cords belting out "I Want You Bad," these carefree thoughts of drinking beer and pretty girls invariably dissipated.

Not only did they dissipate, they floated back to his dying father, telling him he needed to take care of his mom and siblings. As his head churned, Larry could feel the weight of his life, both past and present, drag him down, which was so discouraging. Also, the nagging question remained of where he fit in this new world that seemed to be rejecting him.

Not wanting to give in to this pessimism, Larry took a deep breath and decided not to be a victim in his own story. He wouldn't hang an anvil around his own neck. For once, he wouldn't let his responsibilities and commitments dominate him. He was going to fight off feelings of rejection and irrelevance. Like other people, he would just roll with it. He would be free and untethered from his customary earnestness and uprightness. For once, he would be selfish and just think about himself.

It was easier to consider these selfish thoughts given the negative interactions he had with Maureen after they had sex two nights ago. Since then, she had yelled at him about a dirty sink and dish towels and scarcely made eye contact before he left for St. Ignatius earlier that morning. If she was still mad when he walked in the door, he wouldn't try to smooth over whatever was causing her foul mood as he would under normal circumstances. Today, he was going to take care of himself.

When Maureen still gave him the stink eye, but Donald and Lydia greeted him affectionately, Larry decided to take the dogs for a walk. Because of their big yard, these walks were less frequent than Larry and the dogs would have liked, but today, given the circumstances, this was a grand idea.

So, Larry put on his warm barn jacket and Bills skullcap, leashed up the dogs, and went out the door without saying a word. Before getting too far, he ran back into the house and grabbed some earth-friendly poop bags and a couple of tennis balls.

Once he got going again, he felt a real sense of purpose and had a bounce in his step, moving down busy Potters Road. He turned onto Tampa Drive, a residential street much like his own with vinyl-sided cape cods and bungalows. He noted the mostly barren trees and the piles of yellow-and-brown leaves at the curb, which in this context, were like soft little play spaces for rabbits and squirrels and not the bullshit that suburban assholes complained about to him endlessly.

He loved the dogs' bounce and optimism. They appreciated the new smells, places to leave their scent, and the possibility of devouring the occasional squirrel or rabbit that crossed their paths.

At the end of Tampa, he turned right onto Dorrance, where there was a park with a softball diamond and a couple of basketball courts. Larry walked over to the diamond along the third baseline, testing the firmness of the ground as he went. Once in the outfield, he decided it was good enough and set the dogs free.

Had the turf been softer, he would have kept them leashed and continued on. Donald and Lydia had a real knack for finding mud, and the last thing he wanted, given Maureen's current mood, was to bring home filthy, wet dogs in need of a bath. But given the ground's half-frozen state, Larry pulled out the tennis balls and began to chuck them high into the gray sky.

Donald was much more fun to play a game of catch with than Lydia. After chasing down the ball Donald would drop it at his feet and wait for it to be thrown again. Lydia, on the other hand, was much more work. She wanted Larry to chase her down and extract the ball from her jaws.

Eventually, she would give it up, but not before at least some half-hearted effort to get it from her.

Larry smiled to himself, noting the irony that all the women in his life, even his dog Lydia, required nurturing before they would cooperate with him. But after a few tosses, maybe sensing she was missing out on some fun, Lydia started to compete with Donald for the ball.

Just as his arm began to loosen up, the winded dogs refused to chase anymore. Donald gave up first and lay on his stomach with his front paws extended. Lydia held out a bit longer, trying to coax Larry into getting the ball from her, but eventually she stretched out on the cold ground too, when he wouldn't. Some retrievers, Larry thought.

Leaving the slimy balls behind, Larry leashed them up again and continued down Dorrance into South Buffalo. He went north at Abbott Road, walking past ever-changing storefronts and street corners where he used to hang out during high school. Though he was a West Seneca kid, some of his grade school friends ended up at the Catholic high schools in South Buffalo. Larry would sometimes follow them down there, especially when there was a girl he liked.

He cut up Cushing Place searching for the house of one of these girls he accompanied to the Mount Mercy junior prom. She was a sweet, quiet kid with a lot of sisters. He didn't quite remember why they stopped dating, but he did remember the total indifference of her father when Larry met him on prom night. He was an older guy who sat in a recliner reading a newspaper. After being introduced, he turned toward Larry for the briefest moment as if to say—you're the fifth schmuck in a powder-blue tux with a pink ruffled shirt that's come through here this spring—whatever.

Bopping down the street, Larry couldn't quite place the house but laughed, thinking about the girl's father's indifference and wondering what happened to her.

He turned left on Onondaga at the end of Cushing and was back on Potters again. This stretch of Potters ran parallel to Caz Golf Course, and he was tempted to cross the street and let the dogs run free on the empty course, but he kept going, thinking he might continue his Saturday rebellion by taking a nap when he got home. Again, he laughed to himself, trying to remember the last time he took a nap. But a few blocks up, he came upon his coworker/apprentice, JD—Joey Dionne, standing out-side the Golf Club Inn smoking a cigarette.

JD was the head maintenance guy at West Seneca North, one of the town's two high schools, and was well on his way to being Superinten-dent of Buildings & Grounds.

Larry found JD when he was just a kid sweeping out classrooms at Winchester Middle School, where Maureen also worked. Larry saw his untapped potential and pushed him to get maintenance certifications to run the boiler systems in the schools. JD was a natural bullshitter like Mac, but with an aptitude for managing people, budgets—most anything you threw at him. He was handsome too, with a chiseled jaw, thick black hair, and a long, lean body. His natural good looks drew too many people to him—mostly women.

Rumors about JD and women abounded throughout the gossipy lit-tle town. It didn't help that after he divorced his wife, a middle-school math teacher and the mother of his two daughters, he was linked to scandalous affairs with the Receiver of Taxes and the Town Supervisor, both of whom were married and ten years his senior. And though the talk continued, JD learned to keep his business on the down-low, never admitting or denying anything when it came to the ladies.

Seeing Larry, JD reached out his hand to shake as cars whizzed by on Potters, "Larry Fucking Plumb and his dogs out for a stroll. Son of a bitch, this is my lucky day."

"I forgot this was your weekend—you piece of shit," Larry said with an affectionate smile.

JD worked the day shift at the Golf Club Inn every other weekend.

"C'mon in and have a drink, you asshole."

"I got the dogs."

"So?"

"Isn't there some health code bullshit?"

"Yeah, the health code says you need to have a drink with me. And, besides, the health inspector suffers from sudden onset blindness the second I buy him a couple of shots. C'mon, have a drink," he said as he flicked his half-burned smoke away and pulled open the barroom door.

With some hesitation, Larry followed JD, who made his way around and behind the mostly empty rectangular-shaped bar. Natural light filtered into the smallish room outfitted with about a dozen tables and plenty of Bills, Sabres, Yankees, and Budweiser paraphernalia. Though the place had a buoyant, fresh scent, it still made Larry feel a little sad to be in a drinking establishment in the middle of the day.

This point was reinforced as he climbed up on a stool by three guys about his age, sitting like statues to his right and watching college football with draft beers in front of them. Larry didn't stop at the Golf Club Inn often, but these same three guys were always there whenever he did. On the other side of the bar to his left was a pretty girl scrolling on her phone with a couple of Michelob Ultras in front of her. She was probably one of JD's many admirers, wearing a tight turtleneck with streaky blonde hair flowing from beneath the same Bills skullcap Larry was sporting. Larry thought that if they had one of those "who wore it better" contests, she would win by a mile.

"What'll it be, Plumb?"   "You got a bar rag or something? My hands are gross from throwing balls to the dogs," Larry asked.

Sure," JD replied. After Larry cleaned his hands, he asked again, "What'll it be Plumb?"

"Blue Light," he said as he stared down and reassured Donald and Lydia everything was all right.

"Whiskey?

"No whiskey. Too early."

JD eyed him incredulously as he pulled two shot glasses and a bottle of Crown Royal from beneath the bar.

"You keep that pretty handy, huh?" Larry laughed.

"It's a best practice. I probably learned it from you."

After he poured two shots, they tapped glasses, and JD said, "To Larry Plumster—the plumest of all plums," and he tossed it back.

On the other hand, Larry took a small, controlled pull on his whiskey and said, "You should use some best practices on that."

As if backing up Larry's point, Donald let out a loud bark, which stunned them for a moment and made them laugh.

The woman with two Ultras in front of her looked up from her phone and said, "Where's the dog?"

"Not dog—dogs," JD said, turning toward Larry.

A big smile came to her face, and she nimbly got down from her stool and walked around the bar. When she saw Donald and Lydia, she said, "Aww, they're gorgeous." She met Larry's eye and asked, "Can I pet them?"

"Sure."

She bent over and started working both dogs around their yellow/reddish ears and necks. Soon, she was on one knee saying things like, "Pretty babies—Who's a coupla good puppies?"

Another woman in a tight turtleneck moseyed out from the restroom behind the guys watching football. She had dark hair, and when she made the right turn at the end of the bar and saw the dogs, her face lit up.

"Lynn, look at these puppies," the first woman said.

"You mind?' she said to Larry as she already had her hand on Lydia's head.

"Knock yourself out—Lynn."

Larry turned his gaze to JD as the pretty ladies continued to pet and baby-talk to the dogs. He shrugged as if he didn't know what was going on.

"Names?" the blonde lady in the skullcap asked.

"That's Donald, and that's Lydia."

"Those are fairly random names," Lynn said, meeting Larry's eye.

"From the John Prine song," Larry remarked as if it were all too obvious.

Upright again, the blonde woman introduced herself. She held out her hand to shake and said, "I'm Carrie, and this is Lynn. Who's John Prine?"

"He's like a country rock singer."

"Like Blake Shelton?" Lynn asked, still petting the very happy dogs.

Now, it was Larry's turn to be puzzled. "Blake Shelton?"

JD responded that Blake Shelton was a nu-country guy who hosted a TV show and was married to Gwen Stefani.

That struck a chord with Larry. "Right, I know who she is. I don't know any Blake Shelton songs, but I can't imagine he's like Prine. Prine is a seventies throwback. His songs make you laugh, cry, and dream of pork chops all at the same time."

Climbing up on a barstool next to Larry, Lynn asked JD to grab their beers and inquired about the song, "Is "Donald & Lydia" one of those happy, sad, pork chop songs?"

Sitting between Carrie and Lynn, Larry realized he was hanging out with two exceptionally attractive, great-smelling women who were not his wife. In this awkward situation, he felt his face flush. Stumbling a little, he said, "No, Donald & Lydia is a straight-up sad song about two lonely people."

"I don't get it," Carrie said. "These two puppies are so adorable and happy."

Just then, Lynn got off her stool, went to the digital jukebox on the wall, and dialed up "Donald & Lydia" and some other Prine songs.

"They were the runts of the litter that no one wanted, and I don't know; Donald and Lydia just came to me, and it stuck."

When the song started, Carrie appeared miffed. "Did he just call her fat?"

"Yeah," Larry responded.

Lynn shook her head, "That ain't cool."

"Yeah, but it's from 1970. Different standards and if you listen, he's empathizing with her."

After "Donald & Lydia" came "Sam Stone."

"So when is this Prine guy going to be funny?" Carrie asked.

"Or talk about his pickup truck?" Lynn followed up, reaching down and working the dogs around their ears.

Just when Larry started to feel defensive, "Linda Goes to Mars" popped up, followed by the hilarious duet with Iris DeMent, "In Spite of Ourselves." Both ladies laughed and maybe were won over a bit. Carrie even touched Larry's arm at one of the funny lines, making him uncomfortable. But he had a second beer and shot and told a funny story about when JD first started running the boilers at the middle school and ran up the heating bill an extra ten grand one winter.

"So the middle school principal, Joe Dokes—great guy," Larry explained to Carrie and Lynn, "tells JD he needs help with something at Town Hall one night. Being an ambitious little kiss-ass, JD is only too willing to help."

JD interrupted Larry, "Plumb, you evil son of a bitch, I can't believe you're telling this story."

Larry waved him off and continued, "So, being the ambitious little kiss ass he is, he shows up, and Dokes brings him into a meeting room where a lot of people are milling about. I'm there too and start talking to JD, and he asks me what's going on and if I know what Dokes needs. I was Highway Commissioner at the time and had no idea why he would need JD at the town board meeting.

So when the meeting starts, Dokes has JD sit beside him at the representative table. There are usually ten or fifteen concerned citizens at these board meetings. But there's always a small contingent that knows the budget inside and out, and maybe the second or third item on the agenda they want answers about the heating overruns at the middle school. Since it's his building, Dokes has to face the music for this. He gets up, lays out some bullshit, and then says, 'Our maintenance supervisor Joey Dionne, can provide more information,' totally throwing JD under the bus. And these budget psychos proceed to rip JD a new asshole."

At this point, Larry had to pause because he was laughing so hard.

"Plumb, you motherfucker," JD responded, smiling.

Lynn had an amused expression on her face while Carrie struck a note of concern, "Aww, poor JD."

"Screw that, poor JD stuff," Larry said, still laughing. "It was the best thing ever. He's twenty-five or twenty-six, and he's up there hemming and hawing still in his work clothes while this tight-ass resident from Reserve Road who has a million-dollar house is asking him why he's so stupid. It was the greatest thing ever. I thought he was going to cry."

"That's really mean. Why didn't you help him?" Carrie asked, frowning.

"Dokes eventually jumped in."

"Did that ever happen to you?" Lynn asked Larry.

"Yeah, about two seconds later, I got my ass handed to me by the same guy."

"It was kind of an initiation that I wasn't ready for," JD explained.

"Ready for?" Larry laughed and imitated JD from that night, trying to answer questions. 'Well sir'... 'You see sir'...'I wasn't aware of that, sir.'

The girls seemed amused. They took a couple more sips of their beers and then got their coats from a rack on the wall. They were headed to the mall to do some Christmas shopping. After one more round of petting and baby-talking to Donald and Lydia, they told Larry it was nice meeting him. Then, they both made Larry uncomfortable by giving him a little hug goodbye. Carrie looked at JD and said she'd text him later. Lynn said, "Bye."

After he watched them walk out, Larry turned to JD and said, "Who the hell are they?"

"Just a couple of neighborhood girls," JD smiled.

"Right, girls like that—in this neighborhood?"

"Oh, they're around. Trust me, they're around."

After finishing his second shot, Larry looked at JD and asked, "I wasn't too hard on you, was I?"

"Nah, you son of a bitch. It's great seeing you."

"Yeah, same. I have to remember when you're here."

Larry climbed down from the barstool, fist-bumped JD, and then walked out into the cold, gray afternoon with the dogs in tow. He felt good—not just from the beers and whiskey but from the day itself, first with Dr. Johnson and now with Carrie and Lynn. For once there were no thoughts of the rejection he often felt from his family and the larger world these days. Instead, he laughed and thought, I still got it as he rolled down Potters Road.

Nine

The house was empty when he arrived home from walking the dogs. Ben was probably working part-time as a hockey referee, and Larry couldn't quite remember where Maureen and Ashley might be, though he felt he should know. Given the happy little buzz spinning around in his head, he considered whether it was a good idea to check in with Maureen or just grab another beer and make a day of it. While thinking it over, his phone buzzed—it was Maureen. Actually, it buzzed three times before he decided to take the call. He also decided if she continued with her nonsense, he would end the call, and it would be full steam ahead on the day drinking.

At first, she was frustrated with him because she had told him several times that she was going to an education job fair with Ashley that afternoon. After her complaints about him not listening ran its course, Larry noted a change of tone in her voice. It was a simple maternal tone, which he knew well, and meant an end to the thirty-six hours of hostility toward him.

This was as close as Maureen came to an apology, and through the years, Larry had more or less learned to accept it. If he pushed on what had happened over the last couple of days, she would get her back up and stubbornly defend her anger. She'd point out what he had done to instigate her, and in the end, it would just create more hostility. It was another situation where it was easier to resign from the conversation and move on.

A feature of Maureen's non-apology apologies was usually some kind of peace offering. Today, after the job fair, she and Ashley were going to stop at Mitchell's, a little dive bar they all liked, for a late lunch, and she called to tell him she was bringing a roast beef special home for Ben and wanted to know if he wanted one too.

"Is that good, or maybe the chicken?" she asked.

"No, the roast beef is fine. Thanks."

"I know Ben will want the gravy. Do you want gravy?

"No gravy or bread. And could you get me a side salad instead of fries?"

"Sure. Is that it?"

"Yeah. Tell Ash everything went well at St. Ignatius this morning."

"Okay. Love you Larry."

"I love you too. See you in a while."

Larry hit the end-call button on his phone and shook his head. He again went over the events of the last thirty-six hours with Maureen, which included sex, dirty towels, anger over where he washed his hands, lack of eye contact, and now the roast beef special and an "I love you." Rather than dwell on the deeper meanings of all this bullshit, he decided to continue the theme of the day and just roll with it.

He gave a second thought to a nap but instead grabbed another beer, sat down, and worked on his Gus Ehrman story, *Shadow Love*. Thinking of Mitchell's, Larry spun a scenario in which Gus's lunchtime mistress, Eileen, happened upon Gus and Rowena, who were having a fish fry at one of Buffalo's great dive bars, like Mitchell's.

Gus saw her coming toward their table like a small, tornado while Rowena methodically cut her fish into neat sections. When she was on top of them she said, "GUS!" as if it were some coincidence. Without asking, Eileen sat at the table and introduced herself in the same exaggerated voice. Then, she went on about Gus at work—Gus this, Gus that. And while talking, she playfully kept reaching over and touching his arm. When this tactic failed to get a rise out of Gus or Rowena, she became frustrated. The wedge Eileen attempted to drive between them was met with modest, disinterested smiles as they methodically ate their meal. Having failed, she got up and stomped away.

Gus looked at Rowena and smiled. After a moment he said, "Coleslaw is good—sweet," to which Rowena did not respond...

The day rounded out nicely. As they consumed their roast beef specials at the kitchen table, Ben recounted a fight that had broken out between some parents at the rink for Larry.

Laughing, Ben said, "You really start to question this whole youth sports thing when two moms are throwing haymakers."

"What started it?" Larry asked as he turned over his salad.

"I have no idea. It wasn't anything on the ice."

Larry asked if Ben remembered jumping his mite teammate Justin Povlak after he told him Santa wasn't real just before a game. "Best fight ever," Larry laughed.

"Oh yeah, I remember. I still hate that kid," Ben grinned while sopping up gravy with a half-slice of bread.

After finishing his roast beef special, Larry sat on the couch with Maureen and the dogs and watched an artsy movie that Ashley recommended called Paterson. It was about a bus driver/poet and starred an actor Larry didn't know named Adam Driver, who was some sex symbol and a big shot in the *Star Wars* franchise.

Larry thought the movie was a little unbelievable, but even more unbelievable was that this Adam Driver guy was a sex symbol. But again, like everything else, maybe he was unaware of what made someone a heartthrob these days.

At any rate, whatever shortcomings there were in *Paterson*, Larry still thought it was a pretty good film. He liked the calm, understated tone and could relate to Driver's blue-collar literary aspirations. He also liked the poetry in the film, which he could process in real-time. Maureen thought it was unrealistic as well. She liked the poetry too, but without sexy Adam Driver, it would have been very dull.

When the movie ended, Larry and the dogs got up from the couch. He grabbed Maureen's hand and said, "Come out to the garage and have a drink with me."

"Wow Larry, you really know how to woo a girl. A cold, stinky garage—will you write me a poem?"

"No. But I'll recite some lines from the poet they talked about in the movie, William Carlos Williams, with giant provocative flourishes—and I'll dance with you."

Still holding her hand, he stood up and gracefully shuffled his feet, making her laugh.

As her laughter fizzled out, she studied his face for a moment and then pulled him in for a kiss. When she didn't release him, Larry got on his knees, and she embraced him as if he were a life preserver, clinging to him with all her might.

After disengaging from the hug, she looked at him as if she wanted to say something. But as the moment passed, her face became blank, as if she were a writer staring at an empty page, not knowing where to begin. A weird awkwardness followed, and she began searching for the TV clicker in the couch cushions. Larry examined her face and bumbling movements for clues about what was happening with her. Unable to discern anything, he asked, "Is everything okay Moe?"

Still looking for the clicker, she said, "Yes, everything's fine."

"What's with the hug?"

She paused and was about to say something but then joked, "I don't know. I love you and tried to express that with a hug. Maybe I'll write a poem. "Loving Larry Plumb One Hug at a Time.""

A little confused, Larry picked up the clicker that had fallen on the floor next to him, "Really, he said, smiling as he handed it to her, "you're going to write me a poem—I can't wait." He stood up and lingered for a moment, still staring down at her.

"Larry, everything's fine," she said, gesturing with her chin toward the back of the house for him to take his leave. "Go listen to one of those brainy podcasts or cry to some Joni Mitchell and Rickie Lee Jones."

Out in the garage, Larry decided not to think about all the drama with Maureen. He swept off the rug on his little platform where his chairs sat, lit some candles, and fixed his Jim Beam/Rolling Rock combo. Instead of Joni or Rickie Lee, he dialed up one of the indie bands he had been hearing on Sirius XMU—Big Thief. There was a dreamy truth in vocalist Adrianne Lanker's voice that went beyond authentic. It was a desperation that touched up against the divine, maybe like Joni on "Hejira." Watching a couple of live Big Thief videos on his phone made Larry think the Lenker's divinity wasn't limited to her voice, but it pulsed in her whole being from the way she moved in front of the mic to how she handled her guitar.

As much as he was enjoying the artistry of Big Thief, his mind drifted back to earlier in the day to the Golf Club Inn and, more specifically, to Carrie and Lynn. He logged into his secret Facebook account and, though a little embarrassed, stalked JD's page for links and pics of them. As creepy as this kind of reconnaissance was, Larry was fascinated by how people portrayed themselves on social media.

He liked Carrie and Lynn and was conflicted about what he wanted to find. On the one hand, he hoped they were "hot chick" posters who littered their feeds with provocative selfies. But as much as he would have enjoyed a bunch of images of these pretty ladies, he was hoping there was more to them than just being hot. And there was.

As it turned out, they were "party" posters with pictures almost entirely devoted to them engaged in bacchanalian pursuits on various holidays—St. Patrick's Day, Fourth of July, happy hours, benefits, and vacations. All the drinking pics with groups of people made sense, given their connection to JD. Larry was glad they weren't just "hot chick" posters, but still, the old, entitled codes buried within left him feeling a little cheated.

After looking for a minute at Carrie's and Lynn's party pages, Larry thought back to his first appointment of the day with Dr. Johnson. He paused, wondering if browsing her page would be some kind of ethical breach. He considered it for a moment and made a shaky rationalization—because of the free labor he was providing, it warranted a quick look. Plus, she was a little sneaky, delving into his past while vetting Ashley.

Given her position, he expected little more than a bunch of boring St. Ignatius stuff, but when the page loaded, Larry was shocked. It had all the St. Ignatius information, but it was also a "hot chick" page with a bounty of Dr. Johnson selfies dressed in outfits that accentuated her fit body.

From what he'd seen of her in the professional business attire and the maroon tracksuit, it was obvious she took care of herself. But he wasn't expecting this. Posed images in dresses that adhered to her body like the skin of some exquisite fruit. A range of facial expressions that were sometimes steamy and mysterious, sometimes tenacious and tough, and sometimes fun and playful.

This was buttressed with an "About" section that listed her extensive academic achievements—the MBA from the University of Buffalo and the Ph.D. from Northwestern. There was also a detailed list of her professional accomplishments. The juxtaposition of those provocative pictures next to that resume was weird and sexy—a party girl and a professor.

As shocked as Larry was, he lost any pretense of moral conflict and scrolled greedily until he came to a section of pics of Dr. Johnson on vacation in the Virgin Islands with three other women. He slowed down and looked at the women in a plush hotel suite getting ready for a night on the town. There was also a cache of pictures of Dr. Johnson and her friends prancing around in brightly colored bikinis on the beach with drinks in their hands. "Good lord," Larry said under his breath.

But most provocative was a group of photos with Dr. Johnson and her friends sitting atop four-wheelers near the edge of a shaded trail in their bikinis. They looked like a band of revolutionaries on their way to execute a raid—unsmiling and serious in dark glasses sitting on these redneck ATV machines. Dr. Johnson was so fierce in her aviators, her muscled brown shoulders and torso glistening in the sun.

Sitting there, enthralled by the pictures, Larry felt his mouth hanging open a bit. Embarrassed, he quickly clicked off her page and closed Facebook, but later in the house, he haltingly opened the page again on his laptop. And, like before, he was awestruck at how badass and sexy Dr. Johnson was sitting on that four-wheeler. It was such that Larry felt he had no choice but to take an unplanned shower. These showers carried on through the week as well.

The week itself was a good one for Larry. His crews buttoned up the last of the leaf removal, but because this job went so late into the season, he had fallen behind in his other duties and was scrambling to get the snowplows attached to the town's fifteen pickup trucks. He was also late doing an inventory of needs at town facilities and schools, shuffling in some freshly tuned snowblowers and removing others.

Additionally, he spent some time with JD, replacing hardware on North's Bobcat bucket. Larry jokingly pressed him to give up some information on Carrie and Lynn, but with a sly look, JD stuck to his line about them just being a couple of neighborhood girls.

At home, things continued to be a bit awkward with Maureen. Something was weighing on her, but she remained mum. She noticed and commented on the upward trend in the number of showers Larry was taking, which had been one per day before work. Trying not to sound defensive, he said, "I'm trying something new."

But of course, the truth was he was seriously crushing on Dr. Johnson, and the only way to get rid of the distraction, to cleanse himself of her sitting on that four-wheeler looking so fierce, was to take care of it in the privacy of the shower. He felt silly and undisciplined at his inability to keep this in check, and like a high school sophomore, he started to get nervous about seeing her on Saturday. He worried she would see through him and somehow know how he had used her social media to defile himself.

But it was fine. She was waiting for him again in a tracksuit, but this one was powder blue with white piping, and she had three sturdy preteen kids with her. After she introduced Makayla, Trevon, and Jaylen, they all went out to Larry's truck and started to bring in tools and materials. Though he felt sophomoric, he couldn't quite tamp down the swirling giddiness he felt in the presence of Dr. Johnson. He handed out gloves and safety glasses to the kids and told them these were theirs to keep and they were to be worn at all times.

Makayla, who Larry immediately identified as the most enthusiastic, said she hoped to get a hard hat. Larry accommodated her with an old, not often used one buried in the cab of his truck and told the boys if they wanted hard hats, he would bring them next week, to which Trevon responded after looking at Jaylen: "We cool."

Once they were past this initial phase, Dr. Johnson went to her office, saying she had some things to do but would be around and Larry could text her if anybody lost focus. Since he was finding it hard not to be totally consumed by her for the sake of the job, he was grateful to be freed from her presence.

Walking down to the basement with the kids to shut off the water leads he decided that though he felt embarrassed to be crushing so hard on Dr. Johnson, he wouldn't judge himself or try to blot these feelings out. He didn't know where they were leading, if anywhere, but he would make an effort to enjoy "liking her," as silly as that sounded in his old pragmatic head. All of this aligned with his belief in consciously embracing your feelings, good, bad, or giddy, rather than running from them.

With that straight in his mind, down in the drafty, dark part of the basement where the guts of the plumbing entered the school, Larry talked to the kids about the job at hand. He wanted to let them know what they would get from being here for the next few Saturday mornings. He began with a story about his father, telling them he was an electrician but also very accomplished in building and rehabbing and how he had done tons of jobs with his dad, just like this one they were doing.

"Did you like it?" Makayla asked brightly.

"Not really," Larry responded.

"Why?"

"Because he never told me anything about what we were doing. We'd be sitting at breakfast on a Saturday, and he would just say, 'We got a teardown today,' or 'Got a buddy who needs an install,' and I would have to go and work with him without any idea for how long or what the job was, and why I was there. All I did was carry things, hold flashlights, and get yelled at when things went wrong. If I dared ask a question or offered a suggestion, he would tell me, 'You're here to do what I tell you, not to think.'

"Eventually, I figured out what he was doing by having me help him. He was teaching me how to install, fix, and build things in his crude way. But it was hard because he never told me what we were doing or why I had to give up my Saturdays and quite a few Sundays, too.

"I don't want that for you, so here's the deal: We work till noon, you're going to get dirty, and you're here to learn something—how to take things apart like walls and pipes and then put those things back together and make them work and look pretty. While we're doing this, I want you to consider whether you like this work and feel you're good at it. You can make a very nice living as a plumber—a person who is an expert at installing and repairing water pipes. And if not, at the very least, you can pick up some skills to help you one day when you have your own home.

"Finally, feel free to ask a question or offer a suggestion. I promise not to yell at you like my dad did to me."

When he was done talking, he turned around and Dr. Johnson was standing at the top of the basement stairs with four bottles of water, smiling. It wasn't one of those tenacious or tough smiles he had seen on her Facebook page. It was a simple smile of delight.

Larry felt his face flush like a middle schooler as they walked up the stairs exiting the basement. He took the bottle of water and did his best to get past the lightheadedness he felt in her presence, saying, "Thank you."

From there, they walked to the first-floor girls' lavatory. Along the way, Larry didn't dare subject himself to further exposure to Dr. Johnson or that glorious smile for fear of some kind of juvenile response.

Once she was headed back to her office, Larry let out a sigh of relief, and he and the kids got to work. Larry didn't know what to expect, but all three kids were quick learners and took directions well. The only problem they had was a minor one. After scoring up the old wall tile that needed to be removed so they could get at the steel piping behind it, he couldn't get the kids to break it down gently enough to keep the dust at bay. After trying to correct them a couple of times, he let them have their way.   When tasked with this job as a kid, he always wanted to bash the walls down, but his dad insisted on the gentle method. So he stepped into the hall, took off his N95 mask, and with a certain amount of defiance toward his dead father, cheerfully watched them destroy the wall with abandon from the doorway. At the end of the morning, as Larry watched them shake the dust out of their hair and clothes, he casually told them that's why you use the gentle method.   Aside from this, the demolition of the first-floor girls' lavatory was a complete success. Walking back into the building to get his remaining tools after the children were gone, he was both hoping and not hoping to see Dr. Johnson, but there she was at the main entrance, looking at him playfully, "Looks like you accomplished a lot this morning."   "Yes—a good morning's work."   "You did an excellent job setting expectations and explaining what a plumber does. Very impressive."   "Thank you. I missed telling them what an electrician did when I was talking about my dad."   "Did you ever do any teaching?"   "Nah, you know, Nothing formal. I've mentored a bunch of guys and led some in-service training. Things like that. Of course, Ashley and her brother and sister for as long as they could put up with me."   "Well, you seem to be a natural," she said, laying that delightful smile on him again.   Dr. Johnson helped Larry carry his remaining tools to his truck. They talked about his impressions of Makayla, Trevon, and Jaylen along the way and made plans for the following Saturday. Thankfully, talking about the children brought out the serious educator again, and she put that smile on ice until they said a somewhat drawn-out goodbye at his truck. She again complimented him on his work with the children and thanked him for his time.   In desperate need of a shower, Larry stayed in the left lane with his foot on the gas all the way home.

Ten

As Larry pulled to the front of his house, any excitement from the morning turned to dread. Samantha's car was parked in the driveway in the spot that was typically his next to Maureen's SUV. Sam was supposed to be in school at Cornell, prepping for the end-of-semester exams. Putting his truck in park at the curb, he quietly said, "What fresh hell is this?"

A couple of weeks earlier, at Thanksgiving break, Sam had an issue with Larry's participation in the holiday. Like always, after the meal had been consumed, he sat down with a beer to watch football without a second thought about who would do the cleanup.

Larry's involvement had always been limited to running to the store for the odd stick of butter, making sure guests, such as his mother that day, were comfortable, and, of course, carving the turkey. But this year, when he came into the kitchen to get his mother a cup of tea, Sam told him he had dish duty. Flanked by Maureen and Ashley while he turned on the stove, Sam said, "I'll get Grandma's tea. You're on dishes."

"Excuse me?" Larry said, raising an eyebrow.

"Yeah, we decided that you should clear the table and do the dishes. We cook and clean every year while you drink beer and watch football. It's a ton of work, and we want you to pitch in this year."

Larry turned to Maureen, who would not meet his eye.

"Okay," Larry replied, trying to conceal his fury. "I'll get Ben out here. He can help, too."

"Ben's going for dessert at that girl he's been seeing, Leela's house," Sam said flatly, looking Larry in the eye. "You got this Dad."

"Ah," Larry responded, figuring it out. "I see what this is. I'm being punished because I'm the old knuckle-dragging man—patriarchal penance—Right Moe?

"Larry, please don't."

"No, Dad, it's only fair that you help."

"Excuse me, Sam, I was talking to your mother. Right Moe?" When she wouldn't respond or meet his eye, Larry accepted his punishment and said, "Okay. I got this. Please leave."

"Grandma's tea?" Sam petitioned.

"I'll take care of your grandmother's goddamn tea. Please leave."

"Larry," Maureen pleaded.

"Leave," Larry said, moderating his voice with a controlled calmness.

When his mother's tea was done, he brought it out to her. They had changed the football game to one of those Hallmark Channel Christmas specials. Setting the tea down, he asked if anybody needed anything. Maureen and Ashley shook their heads, and Sam said, "Thank you, no," without turning away from the TV. Larry returned to the task of cleaning up and doing the dishes.

When he was done, he made coffee and set up the pies, plates, and silverware. He called Maureen, the girls, and his mother to tell them that pie was on, but he didn't have any. Instead, he grabbed a beer and returned to the man cave to watch the game until it was time to take his mother home.

***

Now, for some reason, Sam was here again. Larry came into the kitchen from the back door and found her fixing a cup of coffee for herself. "Sam, you're here. Is everything okay?"

"Well, hello to you too," she said. Then she called upstairs to Ashley and knocked on Ben's door, which was next to the man cave, and said, "Dad's home, c'mon."

"Sam, what's going on?"

"Come into the dining room. We have to talk."

Larry entered the dining room and found Maureen sitting at the end of the table, staring through the lacy drapes into the side yard. Larry noticed the blank look covering her face as he assumed his spot at the other end of the table. Ben was to his left, and Ashley was between her brother and Maureen. Sam sat at Maureen's right in front of the window. After a moment, growing impatient, Larry asked, "Moe, what's going on? Is everything okay?"

She gazed at him for a moment, took a deep breath, and a single tear fell from her eye. Sam gently took her hand and nodded at her. After exhaling she said, "There's probably no good way to say this, so I'm just going to say it. A little over a month ago, I had a mammogram, and they found a small mass. A biopsy was done, and it turned out to be cancerous. I have breast cancer."

Ashley was up first. She put her arms around Maureen's shoulders and said, "Oh Mom."

Sam continued to hold her hand while Ben got down on his knees next to her and buried his head into her side. Larry went to the end of the table and stood above them, fighting back tears. After kissing Ben on the head, Maureen looked up at Larry with misty eyes and smiled. Larry returned the smile as a tear ran down his face.

He felt an instant pang of guilt about his Dr. Johnson crush and his contemplation of moving on from Maureen over the last few weeks. Those thoughts were replaced by premonitions of white-coated doctors, hospital rooms, and her being taken from them. In his mind's eye, he could see himself, Sam, Ash, and Ben dressed in black around a casket—crushed by the loss.

Of course, seeing his family huddled so close together, Larry gathered himself and set aside his self-indulgent feelings. There would be a time to process all that, but right now, his brain went to its default setting—work.

Thoughts of willing Maureen through this illness with the application of his unrelenting work ethic raced through his head. He would find the best doctors, get the best treatments, and support her with every fiber of his being. He knew it sounded silly, but he was Larry Plumb and could outwork anything—even cancer. Going forward, all of his energy was going to be extended to beating this illness that threatened to take his wife from him and their kids.

He was adrift in his own head, and it took him a moment to hear Sam gently tell him and her siblings to have a seat, "We have to talk about what this means and the next steps."

Ashley and Ben released their mom and went back to their chairs. Before sitting at the end of the table, Larry also got down on one knee and embraced his wife. She kissed him on the head several times and whispered, "It'll be all right. We'll get through this."

After they were seated again, Sam went into action. The first thing she explained was the prognosis. "I don't mean to be morbid, but there are some hard facts to deal with here. Survival rates for localized breast cancer are ninety-nine percent, eighty-six percent if it metastasizes to other areas of the body. Mom is scheduled for a PET-CT scan first thing Monday morning to determine if the cancer has metastasized. Then, because of a cancellation, she is scheduled to have surgery at the end of the week provided that no problems are found with her EKG or chest X-ray."

Ashley asked what these scans looked for exactly. Sam explained that PET stands for *positron emission tomography*, a body scan that produces images of your organs. To do this, a chemical is injected into the body, and the scanner searches for cells that absorb large amounts of the chemical, which indicates a problem. The CT in the equation stands for *computerized tomography*. This localized X-ray scan used an injectable dye and investigated the tumor from various angles to determine shape and size. Working together, the PET-CT produced highly accurate 3D images.

After answering Ashley's question, Sam continued, "If there aren't any issues with these tests, she'll have surgery to remove the tumor at the end of the week. That will be followed by chemo and then a full round of radiation treatment. Dr. Ying at Buffalo Cancer Institute didn't want to assign a stage without the PET-CT results but seems to think the tumor is tiny, maybe three or four centimeters."

"The stages are one through five, one being the least severe and five, most severe—right?" Ben asked.

"Right. A three-or four-centimeter tumor is stage one, which means detection was very early, so the prognosis is excellent. But, again, we'll get a clearer picture after the scan."

Sam went on to explain that through her clinical work at BCI last summer, she had developed various connections that would be valuable going forward. Hopefully, these relationships would allow her to talk or text with providers directly rather than going through secretaries, nurses, and the other layers of the healthcare bureaucracy. Given Sam's numerous contacts, it was determined that she and Larry would be Maureen's healthcare proxies.

Larry remained passive as he took in this information. He was not phased by Sam being a co-healthcare proxy—she seemed determined to outwork the cancer, too. But he couldn't help being hurt that his partner of nearly three decades had informed their daughter of her diagnosis before him. He again felt a pang of guilt for focusing on himself and returned to thinking about Maureen, but it rang hollow as it circled through his head.

Continuing in team leader fashion, Sam stressed the importance of communication and shared responsibility. They were all part of the support team, which meant that over the next three to six months or however long it took to beat this, everyone would have to be more self-reliant with their own cooking, cleaning, and laundry. She acknowledged that everyone, with their busy schedules, already took good care of themselves, but now they would have to step up and take care of their mother as well.

At that point, Sam stopped and looked at Larry, "You got that Dad?"

Still processing all that was coming at him, Larry hesitated, not realizing he was being called out. When it connected, he saw all of them staring at him, "Yeah," he said. "Got it."

They ironed out the schedule for the upcoming week. Sam had arranged with her professors to stay through the surgery and the following weekend but would have to go back to Cornell for her final two weeks before Christmas break. The rest of the family would have to figure out how to cover these first rounds of chemo and everything else while Sam was at school. Both Ashley and Ben had their phones out and were checking their calendars.

Separated by several feet at the far end of the table, Larry felt as though he was on the outside looking in and not part of his family or the planning process. Ashley cited shifts she could move at Holiday's, where she waitressed, and Ben said he wouldn't have any trouble scaling back his reffing schedule.

When the conversation paused, Sam turned toward Larry again and, in a tone he interpreted as dripping with condescension, asked, "Are you with us, Dad?"

"Yes. I'm with you," he said. And then he looked Maureen in the eye and thoughtfully addressed them. "You guys are really great. I don't want to speak for your mother, but I'm sure, like me, she is really proud and thankful for the way you're all rising to the moment. Obviously, we all want to be there for your mom, but let me say this, I have months and months of vacation time banked, and I can be here the whole time. Do what you think is appropriate, but there's no need to stress yourself out these last few weeks before the end of the semester. I can take care of the cleaning and upkeep of the house, do all the prep for Christmas, and get your mom back and forth to chemo without any issues."

Maureen broke his gaze and turned toward the dining room window while Ben gave him a half-smile.

Sam said, "That's good, but we want to be here for Mom."

"Yeah," Ashley followed up. "We want to be here for Mom. This isn't about you."

Stunned, he silently swallowed this rebuke but could feel his eyes grow big with disbelief at Ashley's comment. Only Maureen caught his response but looked away and said nothing as they continued making plans.

After everything was mapped out, they all gave each other another reassuring hug. Larry took a shower, and the rest of the family went to the living room to watch the Jennifer Lopez movie *Second Act*. When Larry came down from the shower, the girls were cozied up next to each other, and their mother was on the couch. Ben sat on the floor at the same end as Maureen. Larry took a seat a dozen feet away in a love seat with his feet up on an ottoman. The dogs quickly surrounded him. Donald sat next to him with his head on his lap, and Lydia was on the ottoman by his feet.

Though he was late to the party, it took all of thirty seconds for Larry to untangle the plot and see how this clichéd movie would no doubt go—in a blaze of glory, J.Lo would be redeemed after overcoming the stupidity of some privileged white guy who dismissed her out of hand. Sitting there as he worked Donald's ears, he was perplexed that a movie such as this could hold the interest of these intelligent people. Waiting for this torture to play out, he recalled a funny meme about J.Lo and the Dallas Cowboys but couldn't quite place it. Without anyone noticing, he pulled out his phone, did a search, and snickered at the result: "Rings since 1997: J.Lo- 5, Cowboys- 0."

Larry's little laugh came at a moment of high tension in the film—J. Lo was hurt at not being taken seriously—and his family looked at him with furrowed brows. "Sorry," he said. " I just saw something funny on the internet."

By the time the movie ended, Larry needed an escape and offered to buy and pick up some takeout for the family. They got subs, salads, and onion rings from Jimmy's Steakout. Despite Maureen's news today, the mood was light during dinner, with Ben telling another story of some parents coming to blows at the rink earlier that morning. When they were done, Larry wrapped up the leftovers and loaded the dishwasher. After the debacle at Thanksgiving, he had become quite proactive about the dishes.

Instead of watching *The Great British Baking Show* with the family, Larry announced he was headed out to the garage to finish listening to Madeline Miller's Audible book, *Circe*, which no one very much noticed. But as much as he enjoyed the book's first half about the Greek enchantress, he called an audible, opting instead for the sweet melancholy of *Kind of Blue*. It was one of a handful of albums he used to meditate on life. After lighting some candles in his sanctuary, he also eschewed the idea of his controlled forty-two dive and poured himself a big-ass Jim Beam and chased it with a Rolling Rock.

As much as he tried to see the big picture and focus on his wife's health, he could not get past Ashley's rebuke—This isn't about you—WTF, who was she to say that shit to him? She wouldn't know what time it was if she was an arm on a clock, he thought bitterly.

But as the album transitioned to "Freddie Freeloader," Larry struggled to visualize the way forward. He didn't know how he had become so contemptible to his family, but he would have to set that aside for the moment. Right now, his priorities were supporting Maureen and doing the work of defeating cancer.

Just as this was all happening in his head, he heard the mandoor open, and in walked Maureen. He adjusted the volume of the music on his phone, and when he looked up at her in the flickering candlelight, he could see she was apprehensive. Doing her best to hide it, she smiled and said, "I thought you were going to listen to that Greek book?"

"Yeah, changed my mind."

"Mi—Miles Davis?"

"Yes, Kind of *Blue*."

"Ah—Can you turn it down so we can talk?"

Larry obeyed, and she moved the cushioned Adirondack chair that looked out the garage window to the side and sat down. "Can you turn your chair and face me, please?" Again, Larry obeyed and repositioned his chair to face her. She hesitated a moment and then, in a soft voice, stated, "Let me just say I'm sorry for telling Sam about the mammogram results before you."

"It's okay," he said passively. "Sam knows her stuff.

"No, it's not okay," she pushed back. "You're my husband. I should have told you, but I just couldn't do it. You're always so—so Larry."

"Meaning?" he asked, remaining neutral.

"It means you would have just taken over, mapped out a plan, and done all the right things. And, of course, it would have been all buttoned up and on time like everything else."

"So you think I'd manage it like a work project?"

"I'm scared Larry. I see storms, and Sam, Ashley, and Ben will ride the waves with me. You'd just stand there in control, steering the ship in a straight line. I need more than that."

As much as he tried to fight it, Larry was hurt by her characterization of him and thought about his never-ending efforts to get close to her that were consistently rebuffed. Given present circumstances, though, he remained quiet. Even if he did challenge her, in all likelihood, she'd probably write off his desire for closeness as just a play for sex instead of real intimacy. He also didn't like the implication that he was cold and unfeeling. Had she forgotten about the night from just a few weeks ago when she found him tearing up to Springsteen's "Thunder Road" in the garage, and she and the kids had a grand time making fun of his sensitivities? He continued to remain quiet despite his urge to push back. After a short pause, trying not to sound fake, he said, "I get that. I'll try to temper myself and be warmer."

"Thank you."

He then leaned forward, put his arms around her in his sensible way, and said, "Everything's going to be okay. Let's just get you healthy. I love you."

After a moment, she broke free from his embrace and, with tears welling, said, "There's something else I need to tell you."

Larry brought his index finger to her face, gently dabbed a tear running down her cheek, and said, "Hey, it's all right. We'll get through this."

But Maureen turned from his gaze and stared out the window into the evening blackness and then said, "I don't quite know how to say this either, so I'm just going to say it—A few years back in a moment of confusion, I—I made a mistake with a man."

"What?"

"I made a mistake with a man. It was a one-time thing that lasted a few minutes."

"A mistake—" he said, stunned. He paused a moment and then got up from his chair, put his hands behind his head, and peered up at the ceiling. Then, he turned to Maureen and asked, "Who?"

"It doesn't matter."

"Whaddya mean, it doesn't matter?" he said, growing angry.

"I'm so sorry, Larry," she whispered, hanging her head as her silvery hair fell forward, obscuring her face. "I've been trying to tell you since it happened but couldn't. But I can't carry it anymore. I needed to tell you in case something—in case something bad happens. I can't carry this with me into whatever comes next."

Though he wanted to rage at her, she looked so pathetic, hunched over, staring down at the little platform that was absorbing her tears. In all their years together, Larry had never seen proud Maureen O'Donnell so humbled and powerless. Given her defeated condition, the need for her to answer for her betrayal evaporated. He went over to the workbench and tore off a rough paper towel. He handed it to her, then sat down, took her hand, and said nothing while she cried and cried.

When she was done, she blew her nose and wiped her puffy eyes dry, and goddamn, even in this sad, pathetic moment, wasn't she just as beautiful as always. She again apologized to Larry and reiterated it was a onetime momentary mistake.

Slowly she got up and started toward the mandoor. With her hand on the knob, she paused and then turned around and quietly asked, "Can we keep this between us for the time being? The kids don't—"

Larry was already nodding before she finished her sentence. She said, "Thank you," and then left.

Larry sat frozen in his seat, his head overloaded with the day's events. At that moment, time became an abstraction until suddenly he heard the melodic desolation, the measured emptiness of "So What" on the Miles Davis record, which had cycled through for a second time.

With those notes softly filling the air, Larry set his glasses on the workbench, drew his hands to his face, and began to weep.

Eleven

Larry might have stayed in his sanctuary all night staring blankly at the flickering candles, but just as *Kind of Blue* was cycling through again, he could hear Donald and Lydia barking for his attention outside the garage's man door. Though one of the kids or Maureen had let the dogs out, like the chickens, they were primarily his responsibility, and he couldn't have them disturbing the neighbors with their yapping while he sat in a daze, waiting for his brain to reset.

He got up and opened the door, and they rushed in with great excitement. By that point, Larry's tears had subsided. Despite his personal darkness, he could count on the dogs' optimistic bounce to give him a boost. Running his hands around their heads and along their bodies, Larry smiled and spoke to them with affection, asking them in a silly dog-owner voice, *"Who's a good girl?" "Who's a good boy?"*

When that ran its course, he sat back down, picked up his phone from the wide armrest of the Adirondack chair, and turned off the Miles record, which was becoming tedious on spin number three. The dogs cozied up next to him on the platform, and out of nowhere, the word—*absurd*—found its way into his head.

But the word didn't just materialize randomly. Larry had recently read an essay by the absurdist philosopher Albert Camus called *The Myth of Sisyphus*. Sisyphus was a clever Greek king who had cheated death twice and, in the eyes of the gods, comported himself in a way above his human condition. For these disrespectful acts, the gods sentenced Sisyphus to spend eternity in the underworld, rolling a massive boulder up a hill. When he reached the top of the hill, the boulder would roll back down to the bottom, and he would have to start all over again.

Camus proffered that human existence was also an endless exercise of pushing a boulder up a hill only to have it roll back down again. We clean our bodies only to become dirty once more; we consume food only to get hungry again; we wash dishes that will again become messy—and on and on and on. Ultimately, we are no different from Sisyphus—our lives are consigned to a continuous cycle of pushing boulders up hills, which Camus deemed absurd. But rather than despair at the absurdity of these tasks and view life as an interminable act of desperation, Camus thought we should embrace these monotonous tasks with joy and be happy we have something to keep us busy and purposeful.

For the most part, Larry was in the camp where life was a quiet act of desperation separated by moments of grace—but he took Camus's point. However, the avalanche of information he received that day regarding his wife's health and infidelity left him disoriented and somewhat paralyzed, giving rise to the word absurd. "Yes," he thought to himself with a weary smile. "All of this is fucking absurd."

He meditated on the absurdity of it all, and then his mind cycled toward the five stages of grief:

1. For a moment, he denied that Maureen was sick or unfaithful.

2. That led to a surge of anger: How could this be happening to him/them?

3. Another question followed: Self-pityingly, he asked the void—after sacrificing so much for others, how could this be his fate?

4. The futility of all these thoughts was followed by an all-consuming wave of sadness.

5. He never made it to number five: acceptance.

Instead, he came back to the word *absurd*. Again, he thought: "Yes, life is nothing but an absurd fucking joke of unending toil and sadness."

Even with these thoughts twisting in his head, he knew he had to rise to this moment, but how could he turn all of this around and remain positive for Maureen in the coming days? Sitting there trying to tamp down the sting of her betrayal and everything else, he removed his glasses and rubbed his eyes with the tips of his fingers. He needed to find something to steel himself, something he could lean on to strengthen his resolve before going into the house to face his family.

Once more, he turned to Camus. The screen filled with "greatest quotes" pages when he googled his name on his phone. Larry wasn't much of a quote guy—like everything else, they ceased to be effective after seeing them too much, but he needed something to hold him together, especially in front of his unsympathetic kids. Right at the top of the list, he found one that might provide the short-term help he was looking for:

In the depths of winter,

I learned within myself there lay an invincible summer.

Larry didn't like the memey quality of the quote. It seemed as if it should be printed on a coffee mug or worse, on someone's body as a tattoo. But there was something satisfying about Camus's words since he had endured his share of winters and come out the other side. He hoped it would be enough to get him past the kids tonight and hold him till he had more clarity about his present situation.

When he entered the house with the dogs, Larry was tested immediately. Sam was at the kitchen table doing some schoolwork. After saying hello to her and giving the dogs a little bacon treat, she followed him back to the man cave. In a thinly veiled accusatory tone, she asked, "What happened with Mom in the garage? Her eyes were puffy when she came in like she'd been crying."

Larry sat down in his desk chair and looked up at his daughter beneath the doorframe with the man cave placard. She was all sharp angles at her shoulders and chin with intense blue eyes and sandy-brown hair twisted into a ponytail. When you caught her in this posture, her strength was imposing and a bit over the top, like that of a younger version of Maureen. Larry paused for a second, took a deep breath, and in a calm voice said, "She's been diagnosed with cancer. She's upset and scared."

"Of course. Was there anything in particular that upset her?"

Despite Maureen asking him not to say anything about her infidelity to the kids, this question made Larry wonder, like with the cancer diagnosis, if Sam had been clued in about her transgression as well. He paused for a long moment, taking his daughter in, and said, "Yes, there was something. She apologized for telling me second about her diagnosis. She was a little torn up by it."

"Yeah. I get that. Can I say something, Dad?"

"Sure."

"I know you have these mad executive functioning skills, but please remember we're in this together. Mom needs all of us right now. Give us the room to be there for her."

"Whaddya mean?"

"Just, this is our fight too, and we're stronger together. For better or worse, you tend to take these things over."

"Okay. But what I said about taking time off so you guys could finish up the semester made sense."

"I know. But it came off like you were trying to push us out of the way. Please try to be sensitive to what we're going through as well."

Sam's voice was tinged with superiority, and Larry found immediate utility in the invincible summer quote. He removed his glasses again, but this time, he rubbed his eyes with the meaty part of his palms and said, "Okay. Fair enough. I'll do my best to keep that in mind."

"Thank you," she said, like a teacher who had just corrected a student.

***

Larry's general depreciation over the last few years with Maureen and the kids was most acute with Samantha. As best Larry could put together, it started in her second year of college, when she took some history and feminist studies classes to satisfy her humanities requirements before deciding on healthcare. The "MeToo" movement further fueled her diminishing respect for him. Since that time, when it came to Larry, she maintained an air of superiority, questioned his decision-making, and made comments about his male privilege. She even was passive-aggressive about his drinking, referring to him as a—*functional alcoholic* on several different occasions.

This downgrade with Sam broke Larry's heart. Her birth twenty-four years ago had been a revelation. He loved his parents, siblings, and Maureen, but when Sam was born, a thoroughly unexpected wellspring of love flowed from him that was beyond measure.

At work, he thought about her all day, and at home, he tended to her every need. He also wanted to take her everywhere—Home Depot, Wegmans, the gym, even town meetings. Larry remembered long involved conversations with Maureen about the color of her poop, her growth rate, and all her development milestones. He read her countless books about the moon, dogs, bears, and caterpillars. He was so taken with her.

For her part, Sam responded in every way. She was a great, high-achieving, fun kid. Larry recalled fondly when they discovered the Mountain Goats together and when she fell in love with one of his all-time favorite bands—the Clash. Side by side, they read all the *Harry Potter* books as well, but Larry was never any match for Sam's retention of the storylines or the wizarding world facts.

Like her mother, Sam had a real sense of herself and never went along with the crowd. She was the last of her friends to want or get a cell phone—she didn't get the point of being accessible to everyone all the time. She also eschewed all forms of social media and the drama that always seemed to arise from it. She now had a smartphone and limited social media for professional and practical reasons, but she had strong opinions about its adverse effects.

Also, like Maureen in her younger years, Sam wasn't particularly interested in being tied to anyone, male or female. Boys would come and go in quick succession, along with a girl or two. Once, in Sam's last year as an undergrad, when Larry came in from the garage, he found her on the couch, all cozy with a female friend, watching a movie. Later, he made the mistake of asking if she was her girlfriend.

"She's a friend, yes."

"That's not what I asked. You know, is she your girlfriend?"

"Maybe. Why is that any of your business?"

"Just trying to keep up with what's happening around here."

"Don't worry, Dad, I got this. Maybe when you're in the garage drinking beer, you could take in a podcast about female empowerment instead of broing out with Joe Rogan."

"Joe Rogan? Why would I be listening to Joe Rogan."

"Oh, don't all you white guys with pickup trucks do the Joe Rogan thing."

When Larry tried to engage Maureen about her attitude toward him, she took Sam's side, pointing out that he spent a lot of time in the garage drinking beer and whiskey. He pushed back, asking if he was supposed to sit in the house and watch baking shows or listen to murder mystery podcasts with them. She responded, "Yes, that's exactly what you should do."

Larry was shocked at her response and wondered if she knew him at all. He wasn't looking to be congratulated, but it was amazing that they would attack him for his time in the garage in light of years of steadfast devotion to the entire family. With Maureen's help, he provided a nice home where they had few unmet wants or needs. Yet, all of them, especially Sam, seemed to despise him. This too broke his heart.

He hypothesized that, like many young people, Sam was going through an idealistic, self-righteous phase and hoped that, with time, she would soften her stance toward him. He also thought that once Sam, the ringleader of the anti-Larry movement, came around, Ashley, Ben, and even Maureen might see him more positively. But for now, especially with Maureen ill, he would keep his head down, say as little as possible, and work through all of this to the best of his abilities.

***

With Sam gone from his room, Larry took a few breaths, thought about the word absurd and the *invincible summer* quote, and felt a little better. Though devastated by Maureen's infidelity, he was going to have to compartmentalize it for the time being and focus on her health.

Though his family had shot down the idea of him taking on the majority of her care while they finished the semester, he still had all that vacation time and saw no reason not to use it. The kids could be as involved as they wanted while he worked quietly in the background and ensured everything was buttoned up good and tight.

The first step was to call Mac and Burbs and tell them what was happening and that he wouldn't be at work that week. Mac didn't pick up, but Burbs did. Larry was scheduled to work with him for a few days on a project to restore the shelving in one of the elementary schools' libraries. When Larry told him what was going on, Burbs, as always, was thoughtful and supportive. Maureen liked him almost as much as Larry did, which was saying something when it came to his friends. Larry was sure that in the morning, there would be a box of fresh-brewed coffee and a bag of breakfast sandwiches from Burbs on his porch.

Larry called Mac back, and this time, he picked up. Conversely, Mac wasn't Maureen's favorite. Even though they had dated briefly, she didn't like how much he talked or how his volume knob was always pushing toward ten. But his vociferous bullshitting was one of the things Larry loved about him—he was the yin to Larry's yang. And above all, Larry could trust him implicitly, like Burbs.

The three of them had been friends since high school and not once in forty-plus years of friendship did they have a cross word with each other. They had disagreements and different points of view, but never a cross word. And they could talk about anything and everything. Larry was sure he would tell them about Maureen's transgression at some point, and they would listen and offer good counsel on how to find the way forward, but that was down the line.

As he finished his conversation with Mac, Larry mentioned that he had sold a bunch of tickets for his upcoming election fundraiser at the Ironworkers Hall and would drop the cash off at the office sometime this week.

Whether there was an upcoming election or not, Mac held these functions twice a year at the Ironworkers Hall. The fundraisers were more like community get-togethers with pizza, beer, and a shitty band playing classic rock covers. Still, they were fun events that never raised much money—money wasn't an issue anyway, since Mac ran unopposed the last three cycles. It was more for Mac and other local politicians to say hello and have a beer with the people of West Seneca.

As he ended the call with Mac, his mind clicked back to a scene from one of these events a few years ago. Larry was outside the main hall, where the band was playing, in a corridor leading to the men's and women's restrooms. People were shuffling in and out of both restrooms, and just before going in, he saw Maureen three-quarters of the way down the hallway, looking a little disheveled and adjusting her jeans. He paused and then walked toward her.

They had a minor disagreement before going out that night. Maureen was sick of having to attend these things twice a year. Larry told her to stay home if she didn't want to go, but she thought it would look bad if she wasn't there. As an alternative, she suggested they both skip it and go to dinner instead, but Larry liked these events and wanted to attend. Reluctantly, Maureen gave in and proceeded to drink quite a few beers that night.

"You all right?"

"Fine," she slurred. "I just stepped out for a bit of air."

"What happened to your hair?"

"Nothing. It's windy out."

"It's not that windy. Are you sure you're all right? You were doing quite a number on those beers. You didn't throw up, did you?"

"No, I'm fine. I just need to go to the restroom."

She pushed past Larry and headed to the ladies' room. Standing there, unsure of what happened, Larry saw JD come in from outside. He was disheveled too, with part of his shirt untucked. JD was always stepping outside to smoke, and Larry approached him and asked if he had seen Maureen outside—maybe throwing up? He became very defensive.

"I didn't see her. I was just having a smoke."

"She came in right ahead of you."

"I told you—I didn't see her."

"But—"

"Larry, I didn't see her."

Almost as soon as Maureen came out of the restroom she wanted to go home. When Larry pushed back about staying, she became angry and insisted he hand over the keys to the truck, making a minor scene. Larry gave in, and on the way home, he explained the weird encounter with JD and asked if she had seen him outside, but Maureen said she didn't feel well and didn't want to talk about JD or anything else.

It was there, staring down at his phone and the just-ended call to Mac, that Larry had the shocking realization—Maureen had cheated with his old apprentice, JD.

In addition to JD being Larry's apprentice, Maureen had always adored him. He had been like a son to both of them. They had shown him great empathy during his divorce, having him and his daughters over for dinner on a regular basis. Maureen was incredibly supportive through this time, always wanting to talk to Larry about JD's situation.

But now that he thought about it, ever since that night, contact and conversation about JD with Maureen had all but ceased. He and his daughters also had stopped coming to dinner, and she and JD quickly changed the subject when either of their names came up. Ironically enough, after a few turns with her on the dance floor that night, one of the guys said to Larry— "You better watch JD. You know how he likes married ladies." The idea that JD would set his sights on Maureen was laughable at the time, but now he was sure it was him.

"Fuckin JD," he thought angrily.

He got up from his chair, passed Sam in the kitchen and Ashley on the couch in the living room, and started toward his and Maureen's bedroom, taking the stairs two at a time. With each upward step, he grew angrier. When he entered their bedroom, fully intending to call Maureen out, he found her lying on her side sobbing uncontrollably, which stopped him in his tracks.

A little winded, he paused and studied this dismal scene. Another moment passed before his better angels took charge. He went to the nightstand by the bed and pulled a couple of tissues from the box. Then he knelt, handed them to her, and began stroking her hair without saying anything.

Sam and Ashley were not far behind Larry. Seeing how upset their mother was from the door, Ashley asked, "Is everything all right?"

"Yes. Could you give us some privacy," Maureen sobbed."

"Mom, are you—"

"Samantha, give us some privacy," Maureen said, cutting her off.

"Are you sure?" Ashley asked meekly.

"Yes. Please, girls, let us have a minute here."

Larry was still on his knees as the girls skulked away. Maureen started to cry again. Between sobs, she said, "Oh, Larry, I'm so sorry. You've been a rock to all of us. I'm sorry. Please forgive me."

Overwhelmed and a little stunned at the apology, Larry didn't quite know how to respond.

"Please, Larry, lie down next to me and hold me. Tell me everything's going to be okay."

Still unsure of the right course of action, he stoically obeyed, flipping off his shoes and setting his glasses on the nightstand. Without a word, he lay beside her, wrapped his strong arms around her, and held her.

Twelve

Larry went through his usual morning routine on Monday, PET-CT scan day. At the chicken coop, he was heartened to see Littleballs (aka Wynn or whatever the girls called her) hold her ground for a short time against Lazyass. She didn't fight her off as much as she boxed her out like a basketball player setting up for a rebound. Lazyass eventually pushed her out of the way, but it was good to see Littleballs put up some resistance. Watching Littleballs, he thought not only about Maureen's cancer fight but about the rest of the family fighting for her.

Though the power of his *invincible summer* mantra began to wear thin, he again leaned into it when Sam and Ashley questioned him about taking the week off from work. He was proud of how they supported their mom and expected this pushback from them, but what did they expect him to do?

Ben and Ashley went to school that morning while Larry and Sam accompanied Maureen to Clear Image Radiology, where the scan would be conducted. The Clear Image staff was friendly, and the facility was optimistic, with colorful abstract prints on the walls. Larry was quiet while the tech explained the procedure, which would be painless except for a couple of pinches from injecting the radiotracer chemical and the iodine contrast material. Maureen's primary responsibility during the thirty-minute scan was to be as still as possible.

Sam asked about the turnaround for the results, given that surgery was scheduled for the end of the week. The tech saw no issue getting the results to Dr. Ying on time.

Sitting and waiting with Sam, Larry tried to keep himself occupied by mapping out the coming weeks. Accompanied by the light seasonal *Muzak* filling the air, his mind turned to Christmas. One of the things that drew Larry to Maureen and set her apart from other women was her aversion to shopping. She didn't want any part of it—from hunting for items to probing for value, whether at the grocery store, in the mall, or online. She also abhorred listening to friends describe their journey to getting a good deal— *"The sweater was seventy-nine dollars, and then was marked down to fifty-nine, and with my online coupon, I got it for thirty-nine dollars."* At most, she would buy little personalized trinkets for coworkers or close friends and her own clothes. Everything else—the groceries, the back-to-school supplies, the Christmas presents was Larry's job. Maureen would chip in with ideas and suggestions, but the execution was up to Larry. Given his skilled management of money and overall competence, it was another thing he was well suited for and did with great efficiency.

To that end, he tried to make small talk with Sam in the waiting room, asking if she needed him to pick up any last-minute Christmas things for her while he was off that week. But, rather than answer, she leaned over and put her head on his shoulder. Surprised, Larry looked down and saw an uneasy, maybe fearful, crack in the strong angles that made up her face. He started to say something but stopped, reached down, and put his hand over hers, which she accepted without opposition.

***

By the end of the day, as the news of her illness spread through town, dozens and dozens of people reached out to both Larry and Maureen via text message and through her social media accounts. A bounty of casseroles, bagels, and muffins and a full pot-roast dinner with all the trimmings in a big tin pan showed up on the Plumb porch. Mac stopped by with an envelope containing over five hundred dollars in cash he collected from the guys at the shop and during his travels through town that day. The whole family was touched by the outpouring of love and support.

With these good feelings bolstering them, the week went as well as could have been expected. Maureen was cleared for surgery, and the cancer turned out, as predicted by Dr. Ying, to be a stage one, four-centimeter tumor. The scans did, however, reveal that it had metastasized to the lymph nodes in her left armpit. This minor complication was not unexpected and ameliorated during the surgical procedure.

All week long, the kids were super sweet not only to Maureen but also to Larry. Rather than go to his garage sanctuary for his forty-two dive at the end of the day, he found himself sitting with the family at night watching rom-coms and baking shows.

Ashley broke up the routine by suggesting a documentary about Mr. Rogers called *Won't You Be My Neighbor?*. Larry and Maureen were up for it, and Sam agreed with the stipulation that they also watch a documentary about British physician Oliver Sacks. Ben was happy for the break from Julia Roberts' smile—*and how love was there all along*. Ben added that he liked Mr. Rogers as a kid but was freaked out by all the "puppet shit." "I mean, what was up with Lady Elaine's red nose? Was she throwing back vodkas in her puppet dressing room?"

Though Larry was somewhat confused when the real Fred Rogers explained his philosophy, he remembered the PBS show's gentleness and how much he enjoyed watching it with the kids when they were small—though he also found the puppeteering a little disturbing.

Ashley mentioned an article she read in one of her child development classes about the care Rogers used in crafting scripts for the show. He had to make them all as literal as possible. In a segment about a hospital, instead of the nurse blowing up a blood pressure cuff, Rogers edited the line to say puffing up so as not to give the children the expectation of an explosion. The producers of the show called this literal language: "Freddish."

✳✳✳

As well as things were going at home, Larry was left on his own that week to run errands and finish the Christmas shopping at Target and the McKinley Mall. Though busy, he still had difficulty compartmentalizing Maureen's indiscretion. She brought it up briefly when they lay in bed together the afternoon after the PET-CT scan, but Larry hedged, insisting they put it aside for the time being and concentrate on her getting well. At this point, he could not discuss the topic without getting angry, which would cause

Maureen to become defensive and somehow blame him for her actions, which would get them nowhere. Still, following her revelation, he was angrier with JD than his wife.

Marriage was tough business, and Larry was self-aware enough to know besides his many good qualities, he was also distant, and the know-it-all allegation was not without merit. In the name of getting shit done, he bulldozed through things removing any time for natural growth or percolation. His practice in recent years of going out to the garage for his forty-two dive was an attempt to slow things down, but even that was done with a certain fastidiousness. Larry appreciated how his relentless execution of the *to do* list could be taxing for a partner, especially for Maureen, who had now settled into a life of cop shows and rom-coms.

But there was no reprieve or rationalization for JD—Larry was furious with him. He had treated that kid like a son. He saw his untapped potential when JD was a little shithead emptying garbage bins and sweeping classrooms and took him under his wing. He rounded off his rough edges and taught him town politics. When JD messed up, and he did mess up—a lot, Larry defended him. As a result, he was in line for a cush job as Superintendent of Buildings & Grounds that would set him up for life. He wouldn't get rich, but there'd be plenty for his two daughter's college educations, a pension, and good healthcare for life.

The afternoon before Maureen's surgery, Larry could feel his head cycling with rage at JD as he sat at a table with his shopping bags in the depressing food court at the McKinley Mall, sipping a Tim Hortons coffee. Of all the women available to him—*that fuck had to go after Maureen.*

In a weird, outdated, macho way, Larry had always smirked and looked the other way at JD's exploits with women. He felt it was out of his purview, but now, with that chicken roosting in his henhouse, he knew he should have said something. He felt like a dumb politician who is indignant about same-sex marriage until they find out their kid is gay. Still, Larry was apoplectic and feared what he might do if he came across JD in this state.

Sitting there, he took a few deep breaths and considered texting Mac and Burbs. Over a couple of beers, they could talk Larry out of acting on his worst instincts. But it was too soon. Larry needed to make sure things were buttoned up with Maureen's surgery and treatment before he could move forward in processing this mess. He leaned again on Camus to little effect:

In the depths of winter,

I learned within myself there lay an invincible summer.

"Not fucking today Camus," he told himself. What was comforting and helped to calm him down was sitting and thinking about his long friendship with Mac and Burbs. When the time was right, they would help him sort all this shit out.

With a fraction of control returning to his head, Larry began to track a sharp, tall woman in a blue coat and knee-high black boots exiting the 716 Store just outside the perimeter of the barely populated food court. In all the dying malls of Western New York each still had a 716 Store that sold Buffalo-centric items and apparel—from shot glasses to books to Bills jackets.

The woman's blue coat was tied tight at her waist, and a heavy black purse and shopping bag were slung across her forearm. She walked in Larry's direction with a certain purposefulness. A pair of sunglasses sat atop a thick bed of glossy black hair that extended down her neck.

As she got closer, Larry found himself staring her down, not so much because she was pleasing to look at but more because there was something familiar about the confident way she carried herself. The old Tom Petty line, Watch her walk— popped into his head.

As she strolled past him, their eyes met just as a kid struggled to roll up the security gate, opening Panda King. Larry quickly averted his gaze, not wanting to seem creepy, while she went toward the restrooms off the food court.

A few minutes later, she exited the restroom and got in line at Tim Hortons behind several mall walkers. Larry repositioned himself to continue looking at her on the sly while she waited on her order. Once she got what appeared to be a coffee, she turned in his direction. Larry picked up his phone from the table and pretended to look at it as she strolled by him again. 'Who is she?' he asked himself.

When the woman was a few steps past him, she stopped, turned around, and said, "Excuse me, are you Larry Plumb?"

"I am," Larry said in a cautious voice.

A big smile grew on her face, "Oh my god, Larry—Larry Plumb. Kimberly Karney." She extended her hand to shake.

Larry paused for a moment, searching his memory banks, and then stood up. He looked at the woman who was almost eye to eye with him and accepted her hand, saying, "Kimmy from Chamberlain?"

"Yes. Ha, it's been since high school. How've you been?"

Kimberly "Kimmy" Karney grew up on Chamberlain Place, around the corner from Larry's house on Kirkwood Avenue, where his mom still lived. Kimmy's dad worked in the grain elevators on the Buffalo River doing the obsolete and backbreaking job of a scooper. She was the second youngest of six or seven kids. Larry remembered Kimmy as a tawny brunette who wore glasses with rounded brown frames. Her feathered hair and bangs curled around her face, and the glasses gave her a nerdish college professor look. Throughout elementary school, she was taller than all the girls and most boys, including Larry. But in high school, she leveled off at a shade or two below six feet. She was long, lean, and totally unique among other schoolgirls.

She remained lean beneath her blue coat, but she didn't seem so long anymore and was still quite unique from her resolute gait to her shiny black hair. She also had lost the glasses. A tinge of weariness grew outward from her green eyes and mouth.

Larry remembered being taken with Kimmy in middle school, but something was off with her family, which made him hesitate. Throughout their school days, her brothers were constantly being called to the office over the PA system, and when he had a *Courier Express* route, her father gave him a hard time whenever he collected the charge for the paper. He disputed the price and where and when it was delivered—none of which ever changed. Her dad wasn't just giving Larry the business as some other customers might have—the guy was a real prick.

But one spring night during his freshman year of high school, when Larry was past having a paper route and was working with his dad, they were at the same house party, and she was wearing a loose necktie and a vest, working the Annie Hall angle. As much as he liked this cosmopolitan look that Diane Keaton created in the Woody Allen movie, Kimmy wore it much better with her feathered hair falling about her face and brown frames. Larry couldn't take his eyes off her.

At some point, the Edgar Winter album *They Only Come Out at Night* made its way into the musical rotation. It was the side of the record with the instrumental "Frankenstein." But to get to the giant freak-out of "Frankenstein," you had to go through other tunes—one being a velvety song named "Autumn."

While all the other kids were milling about, not paying attention, Larry's gaze followed Kimmy to a plush blue chair in the living room corner next to the picture window that sported heavy gold curtains. She sat Indian-style with her eyes closed and proceeded to gently rock back and forth to the moony, "Autumn."

Larry was drinking a beer and leaning against some decorative molding where the living room transitioned into the dining room. In front of him was a short blonde named Debbie Kidder, who laughed at everything he said and was full of compliments about the way he solved equations in Algebra. But Larry was looking past her, focused on Kimmy pulsing to the silky song about summer love fading into the cold vagaries of autumn.

Throughout elementary school, Larry thought of Kimmy as awkward and hard, like her scooper old man. Yet, that night she was so beautiful and delicate, rocking gently in that chair.

Larry remained locked in on her for the rest of the party. When he saw her getting ready to leave, he headed straight for the door and said, "I'm going too. You wanna walk together?"

"I'm with my friends," she said, looking at two girls flanking her.

"It's okay," Larry said with a smile, "I don't mind."

Understanding his lame attempt at humor, she deadpanned, "Suit yourself."

With Larry a step behind, they strolled down Center Road, which split off to Seneca. They talked nonstop among themselves and totally ignored Larry. But the friends eventually turned down a side street named Delray. Even though they paid him no mind, he got the feeling Kimmy would have gone down the side street too, had he not been there.

With her friends gone, Larry made small talk about school and the upcoming summer to no effect.

With a bit of salt in her voice, Kimmy looked at him and asked, "So, what's up, Plumb?"

"Whaddya mean?"

"Why all of a sudden do you want to walk me home? You hardly said a word to me through ten years of grade school."

"Ten years?"

"Whatever. C'mon man, what's up?

Put on the spot like that, Larry couldn't think of anything to say except the truth, "I saw you sitting in the living room listening to that Edgar Winter song, and you looked really beautiful."

"So that's your thing? You stand around checking out girls when they're at their most vulnerable and then ask to walk them home?"

"Thing? I don't think I have a *thing*. I was fascinated watching you rock out to the song.

"You find me fascinating, do you?"

"That's not what I said. I said I was fascinated watching you rocking to the song. I'm guessing you are fascinating, but you know, that's to be determined."

"Oh, is it? Well, Larry Plumb, did you ever have your heart broken?" she asked rhetorically. "I did. It was on October 4th, 1973, when I was twelve. I had a lovely summer making out with and getting felt up by Donny McAndrews, even though I barely had anything to feel up. And then, out of the blue, he dumped me for no good reason. It was hell; "Autumn" was the perfect song to soothe my broken twelve-year-old heart and it still moves me. Are you going to feel me up and then break my heart, Plumb?"

Larry stood there stunned, not sure what to say.

"Well, Plumb?" she said, looking him in the eye.

"I —I—"

Larry's hands were in his jacket pockets, and before he could respond, she put her hands on his elbows, moved in, and kissed him. It was a short kiss that burned up fast, and stepping back smiling, Kimmy said, "You should see your face."

"Kimmy, what the hell is this?"

"You wanted fascinating—I gave you fascinating."

Larry smiled and said, "Wow, that's something. I'm not sure it's fascinating, but it is something."

"C'mon Plumb, I'm blowing your fucking mind. But you ain't going to feel me up. I don't give that shit away anymore, only to have my heart broken. I learned that the hard way."

Larry laughed and then grabbed her by the elbows and kissed her—really kissed her.

Over the last quarter of the school year, they had a little thing where they talked, laughed, and made out. For all her big talk about not giving it away, Kimmy occasionally allowed Larry's hands to wander all over her body. As much as they liked each other, their little romance, which they both delighted in, was doomed to failure.

Neither of them were old enough to drive, so they were relegated to hanging out at Abbott Pizza, Caz Park and on the way home from school. They tried to go to each other's houses, but Kimmy's asshole dad and her asshole brothers were always around. At Larry's house, it was the same, with his mom and siblings forever present. At that time of year, you could also count on Larry's dad sitting on the porch reading racing forms and drinking beer. On top of that, Larry had to help his dad with side jobs and blew her off for three consecutive weekends.

By then, Kimmy had enough. On the last day of school, Larry was cleaning out his locker when he saw her talking to some friends in the hall. He got her attention and waved her over, and with that Kimmy purposefulness, she marched in his direction and said four words to him: "I don't think so!"

Standing there now, still shaking hands, Larry realized her movements were similar to when she marched up and dumped him all those years ago. There were a handful of girls from Larry's past he regretted not seeing things through in a proper way. Even though they'd been only fifteen, Kimmy was one of those girls.

"Has it been since high school?"

"Probably," she responded, still holding his hand. "Funny, every time I would come for a visit, my dad would say—*That Plumb kid does a good job with the streets.*"

"No kidding. I was sure your dad hated me."

"Oh, he did. Nothing personal," she said with a laugh. "He hated every-one."

"So, he terrorized all the paperboys?"

"He softened a bit in his old age but generally—yes."

Larry laughed and asked, "How's he doing?"

"He's been gone for a long time."

"Sorry to hear that."

"Thank you. My mom is starting down that road now. That's why I'm back. She needs help with the day-to-day, and I'm in a place where it made sense for me to do it."

Seeing how they seemed to be falling into something more than a quick hello, Larry said, "You have a minute to talk?" He gestured for her to sit.

Kimmy looked at her watch, hesitated momentarily, and said, "Sure, I have a few minutes."

Larry shared a brief thumbnail of his life—wife, kids, job. Kimmy followed in the same manner.

Right out of high school, she joined the Army Reserves and met a drill sergeant, a few years her senior, at Fort Drum in Watertown, NY. They married, and she had two sons by the age of twenty-two. The marriage didn't last long, but she stayed in Watertown so the boys would be near their dad, who was phasing out of the army and into consulting work. While managing her family, she took classes at Syracuse University through her twenties. As the boys got older, she worked part-time as a paralegal at a family law firm, Conrad & Conrad. Eventually, she grew tired of the mansplaining from three generations of Conrads and went to law school herself when her boys finished high school.

"The Conrads did contract law. I wanted a more visceral experience, so I went into family law. It doesn't pay, but it's always exciting, and occasionally, you make a difference. Are you still the Highway Commissioner?"

"Not for years. Town politics wasn't my thing," Larry said with a laugh.

"What's so funny?"

"Well, that first night we walked home together, you asked me if I had a thing about watching vulnerable girls. You were so funny."

"That's foggy, but I'm pretty sure I kissed you first."

"Yes, you did."

"Oh, Plumb, what might have been," she said smiling. "Still doing those side jobs?"

"Yeah, I take on some things here and there."

"My mom insists on keeping the Chamberlain house, but it needs a few things done."

Without getting into all the Maureen cancer stuff, Larry said, "I'm booked up at the moment, but I could help you out after the holidays."

"That would be great." Kimmy reached into her purse and pulled out a business card. "Call me when your schedule opens up."

"I will. Great seeing you."

"You too, Larry. Merry Christmas."

"Merry Christmas," he said as they both stood up.

She took a few steps to leave. Larry called to her, "Hey Kimmy, wait a minute." He walked over to her, paused a second, and then began, "At the risk of sounding really silly and embarrassing myself, lemme say something—God, I can't believe I'm going to do this—So, there are some people in my past where things didn't end the right way, and I've had these nagging regrets that I vowed to make right if I got the chance. You were one of those people, and this seems like one of those chances—so I just want to say, though we were really young, I'm sorry I didn't treat you better. I know it was forever ago, but I wish it would have ended differently."

She measured him for a moment with her green eyes, then put her hand on his arm and said, "Larry Plumb, that is so sweet. Unnecessary, but sweet," and then pulled him in for a little hug. "Merry Christmas, Larry."

She gave him one last smile, turned, and walked away.

Thirteen

With the entire family gathered around her in love and support, Maureen's surgery went as well as could be expected at the Buffalo Institute of Cancer, where the staff was gentle and efficient. The tumor and some tissue in the lymph nodes were removed without complication. She also did really well through the chemotherapy and radiation process while enduring the typical fatigue, nausea, hair loss, and a slight case of lymphedema, but Dr. Ying expected a full recovery.

However, with the newness of the diagnosis and the surgery, Christmas was a little off for the Plumb family. There wasn't a sense of doom, but for the first time, a recognition of mortality permeated and maybe spooked all of them. They had, of course, buried both of Maureen's parents, but that was in the abstract before the kids were even in middle school. This seemed more urgent, more real. So, despite the positive surgery results, there was still a sense that nothing was guaranteed, prompting them to acknowledge their time together with a certain tenderness and solemnity.

After the early bumps, where the kids worried Larry would box them out of being part of the support team with his exceptional executive functioning skills, they came to a mutual accommodation and passively tolerated him. He was appreciative of the effort but could feel it wearing thin as the routine of chemo and then radiation became established. Before she returned to school at the end of January, Sam had been Maureen's go-to proxy and advocate, asking well-pointed questions of Dr. Ying and the support staff. Watching the impressive way she communicated, Larry hoped he would be a capable stand-in once she returned to school. Still, it was comforting to know she was just a phone call away.

Though Larry deferred to Sam regarding medical issues, he otherwise was on everything else—really taking over as he had surmised was going to be necessary. As Ashley and Ben returned to school, he took more vacation time to care for Maureen, transporting her for testing, chemo, and radiation therapy. He saw to the day-to-day operations of the house: shopping, cleaning, laundry, snow removal. In quiet moments, Maureen's transgression nagged at him a bit, but he was mostly able to set it aside and live up to his pledge to outwork the cancer in classic Larry Plumb fashion.

In addition to his responsibilities at home, he kept things moving at St. Ignatius while also finding the time to help Kimmy's mom with a few things once the rush of Christmas had passed and Maureen's treatment pattern was established. He was invigorated by going from commitment to commitment, like in the old days when he cleaned up all of his Dad's red ink after his passing.

Beyond the day-to-day operations of the household and everything else, he took it upon himself to keep everyone fed. Larry wasn't a great cook, but he always had a supply of grilled chicken breasts, salmon, turkey chili, mac and cheese, and baked potatoes ready to be warmed up and combined with other staples for easy dinners—never was their fridge so full. The one meal he was pretty good at and did with gusto on Sunday mornings was a big breakfast with all the trimmings—eggs, sausage, bacon, potatoes, pancakes, toast, coffee, juice, and a few store-bought pastries.

For Maureen, eating became a chore. She was sustained by bland foods like oatmeal with some fruit and syrup. Avocado on lightly toasted bread, along with eggs, almonds, and other nuts, became a mainstay. She also developed a taste for warm, flat Coca-Cola. She enjoyed an icy fruit smoothie containing a rotating assortment of items combined with yogurt, and pineapple juice all mixed in a blender.

As she lost her hair, Ben and Larry—though Larry's was already pretty cropped and thin in spots—shaved their heads in solidarity with Maureen. Ashley was student teaching, and there was no way she would face thirty-two eighth graders with a shaved head. Similarly, Sam's semester was primarily clinical work at an Ithaca hospital, and she thought it would be a little unnerving for patients if she looked like one of the female warriors from the Black Panther movie.

Maureen's follow-up treatments consisted of three rounds of chemo and four weeks of radiation. Each course of chemo was five consecutive days of hell, followed by three weeks of rest and healing. From the start, her blood tests and scans trended in a positive direction, and by the end of the third round of treatments, she was also less fatigued and nauseous. She experienced some fogginess, but that subsided, and her appetite slowly returned. By the end of four weeks of radiation therapy aided by further testing, Dr Ying determined there was no evidence of cancer—Maureen O'Donnell Plumb was in remission!

She would still have to do follow-ups every three to six months for two to three years and then every six months until year five. Thereafter, provided she remained cancer-free, it would be annual checkups. But for the time being, she was cancer-free.

The weekend Maureen was declared in remission, Sam came home to celebrate, and Larry took a week off from his Saturday morning St. Ignatius thing. After he had prepared a big breakfast, the family suggested that, in light of service above and beyond, he take the rest of the weekend to himself.

Raising a mimosa, Maureen said, "Let's lift our glasses to your Dad for his dedication to me and this family—and for a *helluva* good job with the laundry. I got to wear my favorite socks every day of the week with him in charge."

They all laughed, agreeing about his mad laundry skills and dedication. Though many things were yet to be addressed with Maureen, Larry appreciated his family's love and felt a sense of accomplishment. Still, he was just living up to his commitments as a husband and father.

But he was all for a small victory lap, and being Larry Plumb, he was full steam ahead with this unexpected reprieve. He texted Mac and Burbs: "Meet me for a beer at Bang Bang."

"When?" came instant replies from both of them.

"Forty-five."

Burbs sent back a thumbs-up emoji, and Mac responded, "Don't be late fucker," which made Larry laugh.

***

It was an unseasonably warm but gray February day when Ben dropped Larry off at Bang Bang. Pulling up to the curb on the opposite side of the street, Ben looked at the saggy old bar and, in a non-ironic way said, "That place is like a broken-down old man. How is it not condemned?"

Larry laughed and said, "Building inspector gets free drinks," and exited the vehicle. With a little jump in his step, he crossed Abbott Road and negotiated the narrow phone booth-like entranceway. Pushing the door open, he was greeted by the fresh day-bar scent of broken dreams. He immediately found Mac and Burbs sitting a few stools down from the regulars, who had their heads craned toward the soundless flat screen set to SportsCenter.

Except for the slow implosion of the building and the upgrades in the TVs, not much had changed at Bang Bang since his Dad drank here in the '70s. It was still the same dark, seedy dive with neon lights advertising Genesee Beer, a smattering of tables, and a six-foot pool table in an even darker back room. Stuck in time too, was the mostly male clientele who busted chops, placed bets, and lived out their lives of quiet desperation, one shot and beer at a time.

Another not-so-big change was Jimmy O'Flarity. Once a young day bartender back when Larry Sr. was a regular here, he wasn't young anymore, and he wasn't just a day bartender—he was the owner of this shithole.

Mac and Burbs had half-finished beers before them when Larry sidled up to the bar, "Hey Jimmy, how you've been? Can you get these bastards another beer and me a Blue Light? And three shots of Beam. Get yourself one too."

"Oh, it's going to be one of those days," Mac said. He then picked up his phone from the bar and, with a few definitive swipes, turned off the ringer.

Larry had been doing some side jobs for Kimmy Karney's mom, for which she insisted on paying top dollar. He pulled a wad of cash from his pocket and flashed it in front of them, saying, "Don't worry boys, I got bail money."

As Jimmy set up their shots, Burbs asked, "What's the occasion, big spender?"

"Maureen's in remission."

His friends, including Jimmy, raised their shot glasses in celebration and congratulated Larry. While acknowledging the ongoing uncertainties, he explained the follow-up process over the next months and years and confidently said the worst was behind them—knock on wood.

Once Jimmy had gone down to the other end of the bar to refill the regulars' glasses, Larry's tone changed. "There's another part to this."

Both friends were well aware of Larry's struggles to connect with Maureen and the issues with the kids in recent years. Knowing that voice, Mac shook his head, "What'd you do now, Plumb? Tuck them in too tightly—set the dinger on their alarm clocks too loudly?"

Despite the warm politician's smile and the gregarious, easy way with people, there was a bite to Mac. He loathed many of life's tiny details and sometimes was impatient. If he couldn't smooth over a problem with his natural charisma and a little bullshit, you were out of luck. This translated into a string of mostly bad relationships and one short-lived marriage that produced a son. And though he showered his son with love, affection, and opportunity, like Larry, he was often rebuffed. This rejection annoyed Mac to no end. His constant refrain was, "We did too much for these little bastards."

Burbs also had one short-lived marriage but didn't have any children. He dated and vacationed with a couple different ladies but was a bit introverted and committed to his independence. Besides being a damn good carpenter, he was a reader too. He and Larry often traded books and fell into long abstract conversations that bored Mac to no end.

Burbs was also at the opposite end of the spectrum from Mac in this idea that parents today do too much for kids. In his job with the town, he mentored a constant stream of interns and BOCES students. He was sympathetic to the pressure today's kids faced, from living with the threat of being mowed down by an AR-15 in school to the endless "connectedness" of the internet, phones, and social media.

Larry was somewhere in the middle between these opposing views. However, he would laugh when Mac would come at Burbs saying: "He doesn't pay for shit, sends them home at 3 p.m. but has all the answers."

"No, I didn't tuck them in too tight," Larry said. "The kids have been pretty good through all of this—and dare I say, even impressed with their old man. It's Maureen."

After saying her name, he paused for a moment, shook his head, and took a pull on his beer before continuing, "On the day she told the family about her diagnosis, she also informed me that she stepped out on me."

"Jesus Christ," Mac said.

"Sorry Lar."

Larry held up his hand and shook his head again. "Yeah, thanks, but that's not the worst part. The worst part—the part I'm about to lose my fucking mind over—is who she cheated with."

"Fuck," Burbs said, now shaking his head.

"Who?" Mac asked.

"Who do you think? Fuckin JD," Larry answered bitterly.

Larry got zero pushback from either of his friends while recounting why he was sure it was JD. He also related that as upset as he was about Maureen's betrayal, he understood it. Marriage was not for the faint of heart. Being with someone for decades required endless diligence and commitment, which was goddamn hard. And, though he was still physically attracted to his wife, he was not thrilled with her mood swings, lack of curiosity, and her indifference at his attempts at intimacy. Given his own questions, it was plausible that things might have fizzled for Maureen too.

Of course, part of him wanted to go all Larry Plumb on their issues—gather facts, examine cause and effect, and then develop practical solutions. But there was another part of him that said fuck it—it wasn't his place to decide what she did or didn't want. She could make her own choices. They had been through a lot together, but if there was one thing Larry understood acutely since his dad had passed, it was that nothing in life was permanent—and that extended, perhaps, even to his marriage.

But the JD thing was altogether different. He could rationalize his and Maureen's problems, but not the JD thing—he had loved that kid like a son, and that son had stabbed Larry in the back like some Shakespearean fuckhead. Larry had hoped his intense anger would have abated as he cared for Maureen, but he still saw nothing but red.

"What should I do? I wanna kill the fucker."

"You can't touch him. You'll lose everything, including the remaining respect of your kids," Mac said reasonably.

"I know, or at least I repeat something like that in my head, but I still want to kill the fucker."

"Has he reached out during the illness?' Burbs asked.

"He sent a card and some food."

"What's Maureen say about it? Mac queried with a severe face.

"She doesn't know that I know. But we're going to have a conversation soon."

Burbs ordered three more beers and three more shots. After Jimmy poured them, Burbs looked at Larry and said, "What I'm about to say is going to suck, but if our roles were reversed, I'm pretty sure you'd be telling me the same thing. What you have to do is get over this JD shit. You have to find a way to get past it. I'm not saying you don't have an honest conversation with your wife about where you stand and what led to this, but you have to keep JD out of it. Pulling him in will only distract from the real issue, which is why she was unfaithful. JD is a fucking asshole, to be sure, but the momentary satisfaction you'll get from throwing him in her face or beating the shit out of him will just come back at you in a negative way a hundred times over."

After taking a small pull on his Beam, Larry turned to Mac and asked, "Whaddya think?"

"I think this big dumb carpenter just hit another nail right on the head."

"You guys suck," Larry said, smirking. "I should've called fucking Rocky. Even though he hates me, he would've been all for beating the shit out of JD. Instead, I get all this high-minded pacifist bullshit from you fuckers."

They had one more round before Larry said he wanted to leave. When Ben had driven him to Bang Bang along Potter Road earlier that day, he'd seen some guys playing winter golf at Caz. Now, Larry suggested they get a twelve-pack and do the same thing.

Burbs went to the convenience store for beer, and Larry rode with Mac to the course. Though Mac hadn't shot a round since the previous summer, his clubs were still in the back of his Jeep. Waiting on Burbs, they loosened up in the sparsely populated parking lot, and Larry, with a wry smile, had a suggestion for Mac, "With it being so warm, you should think about breaking out the Mustang—make you feel young and powerful."

"I see what you're doing. You can come at me all you want with the midlife crisis bullshit Plumb, but you know, and I know, how smooth I look in my pony. And I would, but we know this warm weather ain't going to last."

Burbs pulled up next to them in his Silverado a moment later. A big ear-to-ear grin spread across his long face as he handed Larry his change for the beer and ice and said, "Sorry, man. They didn't have any twelve-packs, so I got three sixes."

This "they didn't have any twelve-packs, so I got three sixes" joke, as stupid as it was, had existed since they were teenagers drinking in the park and never failed to crack them up, and today was no exception.

Breaking up as he put the change in his pocket, Larry said, "It's been a long time since that was in play. Well done, you asshole."

"Maybe after this, we'll go to the liquor store, and they'll be out of liters, so Plumb will have to get three pints," Mac said, laughing.

And the laughter continued all afternoon. The ever-resourceful Burbs got a couple of extra plastic bags with the beer, which they filled with ice and tied to Mac's pull cart. Since they only had one set of clubs to share, they each chose a single weapon to hit every shot—even putts. Mac chose a 7 Wood, Burbs, a 9 Iron, and Larry, a 7 Iron. Although each of them claimed this was the club they hit best—Mac was spraying balls all over the course, which was wet and soggy, and Burbs couldn't adjust to the loft on the 9 Iron when putting. Straight and steady Larry, however, made par on the first two holes and was quite verbose about his superiority and their inferiority. Then Mac came up inches short from a hole-in-one on the par three, third hole.

"That's what the ladies say about you too, Mac—you're always short two inches," Larry laughed.

"Do they say he's short two inches or has two inches?" Burbs chimed in.

"One thing the ladies all agree about is that whatever I lack in manhood, I more than make up for it with my winning personality," Mac said, striking a heroic pose after knocking in his putt.

Despite the soggy ground, bare trees, and brown grass, it felt really good to be out there. As a kid, Larry loved these brief reprieves from the punish-ing Western New York winters and would race off to the basketball courts or come here and shoot a round. Sharing this with Mac and Burbs, he felt both nostalgic and renewed. And, as they slopped around the course, Larry didn't think about Maureen, the kids, or JD for a second. He just laughed and laughed with his two oldest buddies as if they were seventeen again.

But in a quiet moment on the eighth hole, as they scattered in different directions after errant tee shots, Larry looked at Mac and Burbs and was filled with what could only be described as a wave of gratitude. It was one of those transcendent moments he always talked about, dripping with profound feeling, emotion, and, most of all, love.

A warm smile gathered on his lips as he wondered why everything was so easy with them and so contentious with the rest of the goddamn world. It didn't matter where—work or home, especially at home—the world had its middle finger perpetually raised in his face and was waiting to extract a pound of his flesh for even the most minor misstatement or transgression. He used to be afforded the benefit of the doubt, but these days, forces in the universe converged to correct and punish him for his white male privilege at every turn. But there was none of that with Mac and Burbs. It was just easy.

As the day's buzz started to wane during dinner at Mitchell's, Larry, still feeling tender toward his two old friends, asked, "How did this shit happen with us? Why is it that we never get pissed off at each other? Granted, I make allowances for a lot of the half-baked bullshit you guys come up with, but seriously how did this happen?"

"Half-baked? That's some real bullshit from a guy who won't eat a slice of bread or have a French fry but drinks fifty beers a day?" Burbs chuckled.

"It's four beers, two shots, purely for medicinal purposes—sandpaper face."

When the back-and-forth subsided, Mac struck a solemn note, "I'll tell you how it happened. Remember in ninth grade when Katie Auerbach dumped me, and I was—a little emotional?"

"A little emotional? You were fucking pathetic. You cried like a baby for weeks," Burbs boomed.

"To be fair, that girl was smoking hot. She was way too good for any of us, but especially too good for you Mac," Larry jabbed.

"Right, but I was so in love with her, and when she dumped me, you guys supported me."

"As I recall, Plumb and I didn't say much of anything as you went through—your histrionics."

"Exactly," Mac said. "You didn't say much of anything. What you also didn't do was kick me at that moment when I was so fucking weak and pathetic. You let me go through my shit without judgment. Forty years later, It might seem stupid, but you guys were huge, not for what you said but for what you didn't say. It was everything to me. That's why there's never any shit between us."

And just then, as the three friends were having this tender moment, JD ambled up to their table out of nowhere.

Fourteen

With Carrie, the pretty girl from the Golf Club Inn, close behind, JD stood tall in a black leather jacket at the edge of their table cluttered with half-finished beers, chicken wing bones, and remnants of roast beef specials. When JD laid down a little rap about *"three of West Seneca's finest,"* Larry and Burbs didn't quite know how to respond. Mac, sitting to JD's left, did know how to respond.

He slowly got to his feet and, like a gathering storm in an old black-and-white movie, cocked his right arm and torso to maximum tautness, then, in one fluid movement, unleashed a ferocious sucker punch that landed squarely in the middle of JD's jaw. The shot sent JD headfirst into a nearby unoccupied table and then to the barroom floor.

Chaos ensued. Carrie screamed, and with Burbs holding him back, Mac went deep on JD, calling him "a fucking parasite" and "a piece of garbage."

Larry watched as JD slowly got to his feet and put his fingers to his brow. Blood trickled between his finger and down his face. He stepped toward Mac, "What the fuck?"

But standing between him and Mac was the monolith that was Larry, who grabbed two handfuls of JD's leather jacket and stopped his forward momentum cold. Forcefully, as JD, Carrie, and Mac continued to yell, Larry tightened his grip on JD's jacket and repeatedly instructed him, "Look at me—Look at me—Look at me."

When their eyes finally met, with blood oozing from JD's brow, in a calm, serene voice, Larry said, "It's over. Time to go JD."

"What the fuck, Larry? I'm bleeding,"

Still holding his gaze with the same resoluteness, Larry repeated, "It's over. Go JD."

"The fuck it's over." JD pushed without success against the rock that was Larry.

A controlled fury rose in Larry, and a scowl came to his lips. He stoically repeated himself again: "It's over, JD. Time to go," as if he were some barely-holding-it-together Clint Eastwood character.

JD looked into Larry's fierce eyes, and something clicked for him. He seemed to know with unequivocal certainty why Mac had unloaded on him. His body went limp, and he turned away from Larry and looked at the floor. After a moment, he raised his head to say something, but whatever it was, it never quite got to his lips. Larry grabbed a few napkins from his table and handed them to JD.

JD placed the napkins on his brow, took Carrie by the sleeve with his free hand, and said, "Let's go."

Larry watched JD and Carrie walk away as Paddy Mitchell— the joint's owner, gave Mac an earful. Larry followed them, stopping to ask the bartender for a rag. The bartender quickly complied, giving him a clean, dry bar towel. "Could you wet it and throw a few ice cubes in there?"

He jogged out the side door to the parking lot and found them almost to JD's F-150. Larry called his name, but they just kept walking. When Larry caught up to them, they were opening the doors to the truck, and JD was still pressing the napkins to his brow. As he stepped into the passenger seat and prepared to close the door, Larry blocked him and said, "Take this. For your eye."

He turned toward Larry and accepted the rag but didn't meet his eye.

In the transition, a furious Carrie yelled, "What the fuck, Larry?"

as JD put the rag to his brow.

Ignoring Carrie, he looked at JD and said, "You probably should go to the emergency room and have that checked out. Might need a stitch or two."

Larry pushed the door shut and watched Carrie angrily put the truck in reverse and spin the wheels as she pulled out of the parking lot. While they exited, he continued watching JD, who exchanged the napkins for the iced bar rag but would not look in Larry's direction. He tracked them down the street and soon felt conflicted as the truck's red brake lights popped on at the stop sign at Seneca.

Though it all happened so fast, Larry's initial response was relief. Had it been left up to him to deliver this crude but necessary justice, he feared what he might have done in his anger. So, he was exceedingly grateful that Mac had stepped up and handled it for him. But as the truck turned and disappeared down the street, he didn't feel even with JD or that a score was settled. At that moment, Larry was consumed with a bleak kind of desolation as if he had just lost one of his own children or, more precisely, lost another one of his children, but this one had an irreversible Old Testament finality to it.

***

Back in the bar, Mac had calmed down and continued to apologize to a still pissed-off Paddy Mitchell.

Larry pulled out his wad of bail money and took control of the situation. "Paddy, we're really sorry. Would a drink for the bar help right this?

Paddy hesitated momentarily and then turned to Mac, "That's how you apologize."

Larry then addressed the bar, "I'm sorry if we interrupted your dinners. Please have a drink on us in light of the disruption we caused to your evening. Thank you." He raised his half-finished beer, which somehow was still upright on their table, "Cheers."

He settled up with their waitress, giving her a fifty percent tip, and the three of them started toward the door. With Mac and Burbs at his side again, Larry could let go of those feelings of loss. In fact, he quickly recalled what had happened only minutes earlier and could hardly contain his laughter. Once in the parking lot, the three of them let loose as if they had just vanquished a neighborhood bully.

"Oh my fucking god, that was the greatest motherfucking brick in the history of bricks," Burbs roared.

"Remember when Sherry Zipp beat your ass at the ice rink when we were like thirteen? Let's go find her and kick her ass too, Mac," Larry laughed.

Mac did a little two-step dance and then mimicked Muhammed Ali, "I am the greatest—I am the greatest."

Not wanting the day to end and needing to sober up a little, they walked across the street to Tim Hortons. Larry still had considerable bail money left and ordered three decaf coffees, three waters, and a dozen assorted donuts while Mac and Burbs sat at a table in the almost empty shop. Larry was still dizzy with the day's events and forgot himself, saying, "Thank you, sweetheart," to the young girl with aquamarine hair and nose ring who had taken his order.

"I'm not your sweetheart mister," she replied with a certain brusqueness.

Larry had been coached about this by Maureen and the girls and normally would have apologized for the prehistoric *sweetheart* reference, but not today, "Oh, sorry, sweetheart."

After assembling his order, the counter girl stared out the front window of the café and gave Larry no quarter—not even a "Thank you," despite his five-dollar tip.

Larry made multiple trips from the pick-up station, and when he set down the donuts, as Mac and Burbs stirred their coffees, he said, "Thanks for the help, shitheads."

"I just took out your rival. A little respect."

"Rival, my ass. He's lucky you hit him instead of me. But thank you, *really*. I'd be up on charges." With affection, Larry reached across the table and tapped Mac a few times on the arm that wasn't holding a coffee.

"Shoe on the other foot, you would've done it for me."

"For sure."

"Wow, that's beautiful. But before you fellas slip away to the Econo Lodge for a night of scrapbooking and spooning, answer me this—who's going to eat all these fucking donuts?" Burbs asked.

Larry reached into the box, extracted a jelly with vanilla icing, and took a giant bite. "I am," he said as he chewed, the sugary red filling massing at the edges of his mouth.

"Look at Barbie here, stuffing her face. Let's see if she melts?" Burbs barbed.

Mac craned his head across the small table, "Maybe she won't melt, but I can already see the divots in her ass."

"I just want to be loved," Larry said, starting on a peanut stick, but when he was half done with it threw it back and asked, "How do people eat this shit?"

Over the next hour or so, they drank the coffee, hydrated, laughed some more, and made several trips to the restroom as ten-and-a-half donuts sat uneaten in a flimsy cardboard container on the table. Four teenagers came into the cafe shortly before they were ready to leave. One was a kid named Sully, a BOCES student Burbs was mentoring. On the way out of the café, he gave them the uneaten donuts, saying, "Our eyes were bigger than our stomachs."

Larry added, "Plus, we're *magnetic*, I mean *ascetics*. I mean, *diabetics*."

"Dad jokes—am I right?" Burbs asked rhetorically with a shake of his head. "See you Tuesday, Sully."

As they made their way to their vehicles in the lot, Mac said, "C'mon, Plumb. It's time to deposit you back into reality."

Larry went over to Burbs and bear-hugged him. "Love you, brother. Thanks for this."

"Same back at you and you too, Mac—love you." Then Mac came over and gave both Larry and Burbs a big hug.

Noting the size difference between Burbs and Mac as they embraced, with the carpenter being all of six feet five inches and the commish clocking in at six feet even, Larry said, "You guys are cute together—a couple of prom kings or maybe really ugly prom queens."

When the hug ended, Burbs swung around Mac, grabbed him at the waist, and got into a prom-picture pose. Burbs assumed the traditional male position at the back, with Mac in the female position at the front. They sported these hideous, exaggerated smiles—that cracked Larry up. "Wait, let's get a picture of this."

"Goddammit, Burbs, get that thing off of my ass."

"I can't help myself. Your ass is divine."

Larry snapped a few pics, and they laughed at the ridiculousness of their stupid antics one last time. On the ride home, Larry and Mac discussed the fallout when word got around that he bricked JD. They decided that people would not be that inquisitive and just write it off as more of JD's bullshit stepping over the line with women, which was not untrue. At any rate, Mac was pretty sure he could knock back any question with a derisive eye roll or the apparent rhetorical question— "Why do you think?"

***

When Larry got home, he found Maureen and the kids at the dining room table playing the board game Cards Against Humanity. Ashley had just won the most recent round, and they were all laughing at her response to the question: *A recent study shows undergraduates have 50% less sex after being exposed to* ____________ *?* Answer: *Big Bird's brown asshole.*

As the laughter dissipated, Larry said hello and thanked them for his wonderful day of largesse. Then, in a lame attempt at humor, he told them that after he changed into his yard clothes, he was headed out to the garage for a nightcap and to engage in the erudite act of listening to his best John Coltrane mix. They were welcome to join him if they cared to climb out of the gutter of this misanthropic game. Except for Ben, who faintly said, "Have fun," they barely acknowledged his presence as they prepared to answer the next question: *Doctor, you've gone too far. The body wasn't meant to withstand that amount of* ____________ *?*

Rebuffed, Larry smiled and recalled Mac's statement about returning to reality. Then he turned and went into his man cave to change his clothes.

Like Miles Davis's *Kind of Blue*, which had been a companion to contemplating deep thoughts over the years, Larry had also curated a Coltrane mix for the same purpose. With candles flickering, a tumbler of frozen Jim Beam in hand, and "Nancy (With the Laughing Face)" spinning blissfully through the air, he settled into his chair and thought about JD, Maureen, and the day's events.

His earlier feelings of loss when JD pulled away had waned. Now he was thinking about more practical implications, like what would happen when they crossed paths on some work project—how would that go? Though it would undoubtedly be uncomfortable, Larry was confident he could comport himself professionally and get done what needed to get done without any histrionics. Throughout his career, Larry stressed to coworkers and people he mentored that in public sector jobs, the worker pool was narrow and turnover was low, so finding a way to get along even when personalities conflicted was essential. He thought, like him, that JD could be professional and would be able to muddle through as long as there wasn't some big drawn-out months-long project.

Larry also noted the vast change in his disposition from earlier in the day when he could only see red regarding JD. He supposed Mac's sucker punch had done enough to settle the score, which also was a change from how he was feeling earlier. The quick evolution of his mindset surprised him, but so far, the relief was real, and he hoped it would last.

Sitting back in his Adirondack chair with his glasses off and eyes closed, he didn't hear Maureen come through the man door as the mix landed on the mellow beauty of "Naima."

"Larry, you awake?" she asked, touching his knee.

Slightly startled, he picked up his glasses from the armrest, put them on, and said, "I'm awake."

"Can we talk?"

Larry paused momentarily before answering as the flickering candlelight cast shadows across her face. She wore a gray hoodie, sweatpants, and bright yellow yard boots. The soft, silvery fibers between the edges of her forehead and the pulled-up hoodie provided momentary confusion as if she were some unknown entity. He still hadn't gotten used to her thinner, less full body and missing hair, which was slowly returning.

The deficit of hair and her leaner face served to amplify her brilliant blue eyes. Despite the Coltrane, a line from the Who song "Getting in Tune" popped into his head, and he thought about seeing the harmony in her blue eyes, and he felt his heartache soften. He admonished himself for all the years he overlooked those eyes and thought *God, her face was an embarrassment of riches.* Despite her betrayal, he was still so taken with her that he suddenly had the urge to stand up, pull her close, and kiss her fully on the mouth.

His desire to hold her and kiss her prompted yet another song to his mind—"Save it For Later," by the English Beat, which pleaded for intimacy. His amorous revelry didn't break even when she repeated herself, "Larry, can we talk?"

But he desired more than the English Beat song suggested. Instead of just making out, he wanted them to remove their hoodies and run their hands all over each other's bodies. He wanted her to bury her head in his chest and hold him. Then, as they touched, he wanted to kiss her and kiss her some more—kiss till they were breathless. Gasping for oxygen, he would pick her up, set her on the table, and make sweet, gentle love to her in the fog of candlelight and Coltrane.

"Larry, are you all right? I want to talk to you."

"I'm fine. I was just thinking about something."

"About what?"

"I don't know. The day."

"How was it?"

"Great. We had a lot of fun," he said, sitting up straighter in his chair. Shaking his head, he continued, "This might be a weird non sequitur, but even though we've had all this time with the treatments and changes, sometimes there's a second where I don't recognize you. There's a little time lag. Just now, when I opened my eyes, I was like, who is that pretty lady? And, with your face more defined and your hair returning, I notice different things—like how beautiful your eyes are. I'm kicking myself for missing them all these years."

Sitting beside him, she smiled and put her hand on his arm. "Larry, that's so sweet."

He repositioned himself to face her directly. Gazing into her eyes, he moved his hands toward her head but stopped himself, "May I?"

"May you what?"

"Your hoodie."

After a little eye roll, she nodded. He carefully pulled down her hood with both hands and began to caress her fleecy mane, which was like a silver kaleidoscope. Taking it in, he asked, "Ever think of keeping it short? I think it would look good."

She smiled as he tenderly touched her hair, "We'll see. Hey, there's something else I want to talk to you about."

He sighed internally, knowing he had again failed to connect with her. He twisted his body back into place and regretfully moved his hands back to the armrests. "Sure. What's up?"

"I got a text from my Winchester coworker, Ginny Brothers. She wanted to know if you were all right. She said you were involved in a fight at Mitchell's."

Larry laughed and said, "There was no fight. There was a small altercation between Mac and JD, and Burbs and I broke it up very quickly. Paddy Mitchell was pretty pissed, but we apologized, and I bought the bar a drink to make up for the trouble. The whole thing literally went on for less than a minute."

"An altercation?"

"Yeah, Mac punched JD and knocked him to the barroom floor. Like I said, it was over in less than a minute. Burbs held Mac, and I walked JD and his girl Carrie out to his truck."

"At Mac's age, why in the world would he hit anyone?"

Larry paused for a moment and two thoughts pulsed in his head. First, news sure got around fast in this gossipy little town. Second, and more significant, was a question—did he really want to get into this with her? Almost instantly he decided that he didn't. The counsel from Burbs and Mac to not bring JD's name into this was sound, and as far as he was concerned, it was settled for now. But he wouldn't stop her if she needed to liberate a truth. Still, he went to the standard explanation. "It's JD. Why do you think?"

"I didn't know Mac —"

"He doesn't," he said, cutting her off, challenging her to put it together and liberate that truth.

A churning distress came to her face. He would engage but only at her request. He wasn't going to do this for her. He felt a little guilty since she had stared down her own mortality over the last several months. But for the sake of himself, for his own dignity, he couldn't do this for her. Larry again referred to Mac's and Burbs's well-reasoned counsel, that bringing JD up would only distract from their real problems. He was satisfied with the soundness of his decision, and his guilt melted away. He had been as constant as the rising sun for as long as they had been together; she could do this herself.

But the churn and distress evaporated. "Was anybody hurt?"

"Not really. JD had a little cut over his eye. Might've needed a stitch or two."

"That's awful."

"He'll be fine."

She then asked Larry for a little of his whiskey. Given her compromised condition, he wanted to know if that was a good idea. She said she just wanted a sip or two or enough to feel a slight alcohol lightheadedness.

"Oh, that's harsh," she said. "Gimmie one more."

"One more. That's it," he said, handing her the tumbler.

"Ah, that should do it," she said, then winced back a little sip.

Maureen touched Larry's hand as Coltrane's "My Favorite Things" came up in the mix. Initially, she found Coltrane's snappy soprano delightful, but like the whiskey, the discordant improvisation in the middle of the song made her wince. Larry talked to her about Coltrane, his innovations, and his pursuit of a higher understanding of life through the music he made. With a little slur in her voice, she asked questions and seemed interested all the time while holding and caressing his hand.

It was a lovely moment, but Larry was acutely aware that this was probably transitory. There was a chasm between them growing ever wider, and a day of reckoning was not too far off in the distance.

But for now, he would take this, hoping it would end in breathless kisses.

Fifteen

I t was four twenty-five in the morning, and Larry was at his desk with a cup of coffee, working on his Gus Ehrman story in the glow of the famous Ella, Duke, and Tommy Dorsey print at Downbeat Club. Lydia was on the end of the rejiggered sofa bed, which was transformed into a couch, and Donald was directly behind him, curled in a ball in the reading chair. The house was silent and dark except for the dimmed track lights above his head and his laptop screen. It occurred to Larry, with his eyes locked in on the screen and his hand hovering over a wireless mouse that writing was ninety percent sitting there staring at a laptop and maybe ten percent touching the keyboard.

Since Maureen had been declared cancer-free, life at the Plumb house had mostly returned to regular order. Sam was back at Cornell completing her last semester, Ashley was student teaching in the Buffalo Public Schools, and Ben was finishing his associate's program and reffing games. Larry had returned to work full-time, doing the Saturday morning thing at St. Ignatius and the occasional side job.

Maureen, however, still needed some time. Her energy levels were still low, but she was working on it, walking almost eight thousand steps per day, weather permitting, and doing a moderate weight training program she found online. She was close to being able to return to her classroom full-time.

The altercation with JD was a couple of weeks in the rearview and, as expected, produced minimal fallout. The biggest question being asked around town was about the mystery woman JD had allegedly defiled since Mac didn't appear to have a girlfriend. Mac greeted questions with his big politician smile but hedged when pressed, telling people to trust that his actions were justified and to mind their own damn business. JD took a few days off and was expressionless when a couple of cleaning staff newbies who didn't know better asked what was up with his eye, which did need a couple of stitches.

When he took off from work to care for and taxi Maureen to her treatments, Larry had been steadfast about continuing his early morning routine of feeding the chickens, working out, and writing. In fact, the pages of his Gus project, *Shadow Love*, were piling up, and he started to think about the possibility of getting it published.

To that end, he looked over the bestseller lists to see what was trending and if there was a lane for his lo-fi, understated story. He didn't see much hope among the dominant mysteries, thrillers, and romance novels. But there was another thing that really jumped out at him as he scrutinized the lists—most of the top authors were women. A few men were sprinkled among the big sellers, but they were legacy writers like John Grisham, James Patterson, and Nicholas Sparks.

That women were ascendent in publishing seemed right to Larry. In all aspects of life, women were on the rise. Though he was sometimes a step or two behind with these changes, he was all for this new world order. He didn't appreciate the snark that often found its way into how his daughters and Maureen communicated with him about these changes. Still, he understood it was way past the time for a more equitable place in the world, not only for women but for all people regardless of race, gender, religion, sexual orientation, or whatever.

Many of the guys he worked with in town were convinced the elevation of women and others would lead to their disenfranchisement and were filled with grievance. This grievance was cynically exploited by the media and politicians seeking to boost their profiles. Again, Larry understood that though he and his male coworkers had occupied the highest strata of human existence throughout history, the world had quite naturally come to a place where it was over him and his patriarchal white guy counterparts—except when it came to Stephen King and David Baldacci.

Regardless of this reduced standing, Larry knew that as long as he worked hard and was conscientious, he and his family would be fine. And, even with the new order in publishing, he was confident there was enough for everyone, and he would find his place. The Emma Lazarus line he often repeated to himself and made his own popped into his head: *None of us are free until all of us are free.*

So he worked on his Gus story with little expectation, knowing that if the people controlling the levers of the book industry rejected him, he could always self-publish. Larry was drawn to the publishing house model for validation reasons, but he also liked the indie idea where he would be the sole arbiter of his book's fate. Sitting at his desk, still looking at the bestseller list some more, he thought there was a possibility that agents, publishing houses, marketing, and all that other stuff might just be noise anyway. That what mattered and what he needed to focus on was the creative process. That's what was important and what he loved—the process.

In the production of fiction, there were no rules beyond the logic that pushed the story and characters forward. There was no Pythagorean Theorem to apply, and the sum of the hypotenuse didn't need to be added up—most of all, no approval of the goddamn town board was required. With only a few organizing principles to adhere to, he was free to strike out in a million different directions, and he loved that.   And the direction of his story, much to the surprise of both Larry and Gus Ehrman, was towards Rowena.   *When Gus first met Rowena, she managed Socrates Sock Drawer, a nonprofit thrift store. It mainly sold women's clothing but also had a small men's section, some old records, books, and an assortment of unique trinkets. Gus went through the men's racks for lightweight T-shirts to wear under his coveralls. Though he didn't come away with much, he liked the experience the store provided. It didn't have that seedy secondhand store scent, and relaxing Classical music was played over the PA instead of old canned pop songs.   What drew him to Rowena, however, was that she was a puzzle. One day, he was in the checkout line, and a male customer was giving her a bad time because his credit card had been declined on an eleven-dollar purchase. "Try it again, Miss."   Stoically, she responded, "I'm sorry, sir, your card's been declined."*

"Where's the manager? I want to talk to the fucking manager!"

"I'm the manager, and I'm sorry, sir, your card's been declined."

The guy was getting so loud that Gus cut the person ahead of him and put the eleven dollars on the counter, resolving the issue without saying a word. He *got back in line, and the abusive guy left muttering curses. When it was Gus's turn to pay for a Lyle Lovett record, three tees, and a hoodie, all Rowena said to him was, "$16.50, please." She didn't thank him or speak ill of the abusive customer. Just: "$16.50, please."*

Gus found this lack of reaction interesting and started patronizing the shop more than he probably needed to. He liked Rowena's understated look, which consisted of jeans, neutral crewneck tops, and black Chuck Taylors. He tried to strike up a conversation with her about some item he was looking at or was looking for, and she would be earnest in trying to help him but with a certain detachment. After making no headway, he just asked her one day: "Do you want to get a cup of coffee sometime?" And without really looking at him, she said, "Sure."

That was eighteen months ago—

As he read this last part, still with his hand on the mouse, he heard a little stirring upstairs, followed by a toilet being flushed. A minute or two later, Maureen poked her head in the doorway of the man cave and, with a hesitant smile, said, "Do you have a second to talk?"

Larry looked up from his laptop to the doorway as the dog's tails thumped at the sight of her, "Sure."

"Let me get some coffee. Do you need a refill?"

"I'm good."

A few moments later, she was back with coffee. After a brief exchange about her being up uncharacteristically early, she settled in next to Lydia on the sofa bed. She placed her cup on the end table as if to say this would be a real conversation. Both Betty and Friedan, who were named after the author of *The Feminine Mystique*, which Larry had given to the girls in their teens, made their way into the room as well. After purring at Larry's and Maureen's feet, they curled up on a couple of fleecy blankets draped over the top of the sofa bed.

As she settled in Larry sat in his desk chair facing her. With the same uncertain smile, she asked, "How are you?"

"Fine."

"How's the writing coming?"

"Good."

"Still working on that—Gus story?"

"C'mon Moe, what's up?"

"I want to —I want to talk about us. About what happened with that other person. Are you up for that?"

"I guess. The question is, are you up for it?"

"I am. I might get a little weepy, but I think I am. First, I want to apologize again for what I did and thank you for not pressuring me during all the cancer stuff. I'm sorry it took me getting sick to tell you. But I'm glad I finally did."

"Okay, great."

"Are you angry with me?"

"Of course," he said in a voice that was too loud for 5 a.m. He took a calming breath and, in a more subdued voice, said, "I know this will sound bad, but you getting cancer provided a nice little buffer to cool off. It helped me compartmentalize it."

"Ah—" She paused for a moment and then timidly asked, "Before we get into this, do you want to know who it was?"

"I don't need to know. It would unnecessarily complicate things, but that's not my call. That's up to you."

She turned away, and he saw tears welling in her eyes. He got up from his chair and went to the bathroom for some tissues. As betrayed as he felt, he hated seeing her this way, and after handing her the tissues, he sat down, and a small reassuring smile came to his lips.

Maureen moved forward and took his hand. "Thank you. And, again, I'm so sorry," she whispered. "That person never meant a thing to me."

Larry stroked her hand and said, "It's all right."

They sat like that until the tears ran their course. Though the sobbing had stopped Maureen still looked quite sullen and Larry thought she was calculating the repercussions of coming clean about JD. When she was calm again, she leaned back, clutching the tear-stained tissues, and moved on.

"With the cancer, I've had a lot of time to think over the last few months. Besides doing the whole reflecting back thing on my life, on our life, I've come to the conclusion that part of the reason this happened is because something's missing for me, and I'm unhappy."

He sensed she was about to make it his problem. His goodwill toward her evaporated. "Way to narrow it down."

"Larry please, that tone. This is hard, and I'm trying to be honest."

"Sorry. But where's this going? Are you telling me you had sex outside of our marriage because you're unhappy with me? That it's my fault?"

"It's not about you, Larry. Not everything is about you. Yes, I did an impulsive thing that betrayed you greatly. But I think I did it because I've been unhappy for some time. I'm unsatisfied with life."

"All right, it's not about me, but you couldn't tell me you were unhappy or get therapy or sit on the couch and eat ice cream like other depressed people? You had to bone someone?"

"Please don't talk to me like I'm on one of your work crews. And yes, there were better choices than the impulsive one I made. But what would've happened if I told you?"

"I would have helped you."

"No," she said with a certain fierceness, "you would have taken over. You would have put me on some ridiculous middle-of-the-night 3 a.m. exercise plan, given me philosophy books, found yoga teachers, and made organic Kiwi smoothies. You would've applied the bulldozing Larry Plumb method like you did with my cancer."

"So I shouldn't have taken care of you through your cancer?" To lighten things up, he added, "3 a.m. is not the middle of the night—it's first thing in the morning. You 7 a.m. people waste half the day."

"You're not funny, Larry," she said with a small smile. She leaned forward and took his hand again. "You're a wonderful man, and you were so great through all of the cancer stuff and everything else, but the Larry Plumb efficiency method isn't the answer to every problem."

"So what's the answer?"

"I don't know. I've been sitting on the couch watching TV and trying to figure it out, and I don't know. And while we're talking about that—don't think for a minute I missed your judgmental eye rolls about the cop shows because I didn't."

A smirk came to his face, and he said, "Sorry, that's some low-frequency bullshit. Me being judgmental is making you a better person."

Still smiling, she said, "Listen, I think we should go to counseling. Sam asked around and got some recommendations."

Larry paused momentarily. "I thought you said this wasn't about me—that it's about you being unhappy. What am I not getting?"

"Of course, you're part of it. You're my husband—our fortunes are married together. For me to be happy, I need to be happy with you, with us."

"So it is about me."

"You're missing the point."

***

But he wasn't missing the point.

They interviewed several people and settled on an LCSW-R, or more accurately, Maureen settled on this couple's counselor from a local agency. According to Maureen, her name was *Lissa* Smurtz, and she was young and perky with a bright face and had a great vibe. To Larry, she seemed like a slightly older version of their daughters, and he wasn't optimistic about getting a fair shake from her. He also didn't like how she spelled her name— *Lissa*, since she pronounced it in the traditional way—Lisa.

When he voiced his concerns about Lissa, Maureen more or less dismissed them in the same way she had when he complained about the hostility he felt from Sam and Ashley, saying it was in his head or brought on by his own lack of sensitivity and awareness.

Larry's fears about their counselor were momentarily allayed when they entered the waiting room at her office. On one of the walls in big, bold script, ironically enough, was the Camus quote that had given Larry strength when Maureen first acknowledged her diagnosis and infidelity:

In the depths of winter,
I learned within myself there lay an invincible summer.

When Lissa came out and greeted them, Larry pointed to the quote, saying, "Camus, I like it." Lissa responded that she didn't know who Camus was, but it was a great quote. Larry took this as a bad sign; not only did she not know who had written the giant quote on the wall where she worked, but even worse, she asked no follow-up questions about Camus.

Lissa's office was earthy, with an oversized fluffy couch and a couple of chairs. The air was infused with the scent of some undefined essential oil, maybe in the vanilla family.

Maureen told her story first, providing information about the cancer diagnosis and treatments over the last several months. She supplied some background information, including O'Donnell family history, a few facts about Sam, Ashley, and Ben, and several details about her toxic relationship with Andrew Roth. She also went on at some length explaining her unhappiness in recent years, which she believed contributed to her infidelity.

While she was exceedingly complimentary about Larry being a competent, present father, she criticized his odd hours, fastidiousness, and always having the answer and a plan to solve every problem.

She ended by saying she felt as if she was sleepwalking through her life and was tired of having to distill everything through the prism of their marriage. She felt like she didn't have her own identity, that a miniature Larry was sitting on her shoulder, attached to every aspect of her existence.

Of course, in true Larry Plumb fashion, he instantly diagnosed Maureen's problem as a glaring lack of purpose. And, of course, he also had a solution—try some new shit and find a purpose. But trying new shit required effort. It meant getting up early, not turning on the TV, and putting yourself in vulnerable situations. It was a million different things with one requirement—effort. Complaining about his odd hours and fastidiousness was just shade for her lack of effort.

These thoughts were spinning in Larry's head as she spoke, but he made no comment and did his best not to sound defensive as he told Lissa his impressions and gave a bit of background about himself.

A red flag went up for her when he explained his forty-two-dive routine. She asked all kinds of questions regarding his drinking—if he did it in the morning, if he had cravings during the day, if he became angry or violent, etc. And finally, she asked Maureen if it was a problem for her or the kids. When Maureen said it didn't affect them, Lissa proceeded to give a dissertation about the long-term effects of alcohol on the body, mind, work life, relationships, and on and on. She even managed to slip in a term that Sam occasionally laid on him—*functional alcoholic.*

Larry took all this in and thought to himself, *Who is this little shit to lecture me? I do more before 6 a.m. than she does in a week.*

Lissa had great empathy and compassion for Maureen, but the drinking seemed to leave her less enchanted with Larry. She made some practical suggestions to help Maureen keep her mental health sharp as she continued her cancer recovery, including meditating and practicing mindfulness, getting proper sleep, and being physically active. She also mentioned the importance of connecting with others, and—bingo—trying new things.

Before discussing what they could do as a couple, Lissa asked Larry, "Are you angry with Maureen?"

"Yes, of course."

"How do you deal with this anger?"

"So far, I've been able to compartmentalize it. Getting Maureen and our family through this cancer situation has been my focus."

"You said—*so far.* What does that mean, Larry? Do you feel like this anger will surface, and you'll act on it?"

Larry got what Lissa was implying. "Like when I'm drinking?" he asked forcefully.

"Tone, Larry," Maureen interjected, then came to his defense. "Larry's alcohol use is purely recreational. It's an end-of-the-day unwinding thing where he listens to brainy podcasts and music in the garage. If it does anything, it makes him a bit amorous."

"Is that a problem?"

"Not for me," Maureen chuckled. "He gets a little frustrated when I say no but doesn't badger or push. He gets, no means no."

They moved on from that bit of unpleasantness to strategizing about what they could do as a couple to improve their marriage and help Maureen get to a happy place. Larry objected mildly, saying Maureen was complaining that she'd lost herself, that her life was being lived through the prism of their marriage—therefore, wasn't it incumbent on her to find happiness beyond him.

Lissa nominally agreed with him but felt there was an imbalance in their relationship that tilted toward Larry, and he needed to assume some responsibility for both her infidelity and her general unhappiness. Larry couldn't believe what he was hearing but agreed he was there to help Maureen and hopefully salvage their marriage.

Over the next couple of months, Maureen saw Lissa weekly by herself and every other week with Larry. As expected, a large portion of the happiness Maureen was hoping to regain became Larry's responsibility.

He tried to bring her into his world, suggesting they read a book together or listen to a podcast with a drink in the garage, but she refused. He endured excruciating dinners with her and her coworkers, during which they complained about students, parents, and the administration—especially the administration.

They found common ground while taking daily walks with the dogs at a nearby Olmsted Park. But that quickly became contentious. Larry liked to let the dogs off leash to chase the squirrels and rabbits—let the dogs be dogs. But Maureen was nervous they would catch a squirrel or a rabbit and might bother other walkers. Her fears were unfounded—the clumsy dogs couldn't catch a cold, let alone the shifty park squirrels and rabbits, and the other walkers loved the friendly dogs.

As Maureen grew more robust, they took a low-impact ballroom dance class with a forty-something Eastern European teacher named Adriana, who crushed on Larry hard. To Maureen, she would comment, "Ms. Plumb, such a strong, handsome man. You are a fortunate woman."

On top of that, much to his surprise, Larry picked up the steps quickly, moving with a certain adroitness he didn't know he possessed. Adriana always chose him as a demonstration partner for the small class of six couples and seemed to delight in putting her hands on his brawny shoulders and tight waist.

On the way home, Maureen would laugh, "I thought with the way Adriana touched you during the Bachata, she was going to orgasm."

Adriana's apparent infatuation with Larry became a joke in the Plumb house with Maureen and the kids as if it were the height of implausibility that another woman could find him attractive. Larry put up with the good-natured ribbing but thought it portended doom for his marriage since Maureen wasn't exercised in the least by Adriana's overt flirtations.

When one of the guys on Larry's crew needed to get out a little early to drive limo for a Friday night wedding, Larry had an idea that might dispel his tight, fastidious label and be fun and spontaneous.

After arriving home, Larry told Maureen he found a place where they could dance and that she should doll herself up. Part of the problem with taking the ballroom dance classes was that there needed to be a place to dance—but none were available. Larry theorized they could crash this wedding and innocuously get some steps in.

The reception was out in the country at an old barn that had been converted into a banquet hall. Maureen didn't quite realize what was going on until they were out on the floor doing a modified version of the East Coast Swing and saw the bride and groom making the rounds talking to guests.

Larry got drinks after a couple of dances, but Maureen wanted to leave. Larry resisted, saying he was having fun. He also said she was beautiful and loved being there with her. But she insisted they go, making a mini-scene. On the way home, she chastised him for making a mockery of this couple's special day, but what was more upsetting was how he refused to listen to her when she wanted to leave.

"Mockery? It was just dancing. And I heard you, but I thought we were having fun and wanted to stay," he said.

"What if someone did that at our wedding?" she asked.

"I would have thought it was hilarious and had a beer with them."

"Of course, you would have. And you didn't hear me—you just ran me over like always."

Two nights later, after forty-eight hours of near silence, eye rolls, and headshakes, Maureen came out to the garage. With a tear in her eye, she told Larry she thought it would be a good idea to separate on a trial basis.

Sixteen

Though he wasn't surprised by Maureen's request for a trial separation, seeing and hearing the words exit her mouth was like a knife in his side. Tears started to stream down her face, but he resisted the urge to get her some tissues as he would have done in the past.

"Okay," he replied in a low defeated tone. "What's the next step? How do we tell the kids?"

"Sam already knows, but I thought—I thought we'd tell Ash and Ben together once you made arrangements."

"Once I made arrangements?" he asked in a small, questioning voice. "So, it's been decided that I'm the one to go? Who made this decision? You and Sam?"

"Larry, don't make this harder than it has to be," she sobbed.

"Don't make what harder than it has to be? I'm just supposed to go quietly into the night on your word. Do I get a say in anything? Or am I just this plaything to be tossed aside after giving thirty years to you, to this family?"

"I know, I know. This isn't ideal for any of us. But it's just not working," she said as the tears cascaded down her cheeks.

Still with the same tone, he asked, "Moe, what is it? What are you hoping to find? What do you want?"

She took a couple of deep breaths, paused, and then twisted the knife in his side. "I don't know, but I do know I don't want you."

***

After a restless night, Larry got up at his usual time the following morning. He let the dogs out and fed the chickens. Now that they were into the last week of May and the weather was warmer, the ammonia smell in the chicken coop was increasingly prevalent. So, with a lamp attached to his head, he cleaned out the coop and laid down some fresh bedding one last time.

Still, with about an hour until the sun came up, he went into the quiet house, found an old dusty suitcase, and filled it with clean clothes from the laundry and some toiletries. He placed Anne Sexton's *The Complete Poems*, his laptop, cords and chargers in his computer bag. He sent a quick text to Mac and Burbs telling them Maureen asked him to leave. He informed them he was taking the day off and would be in touch sometime this afternoon.

Before leaving, he went into the garage freezer and extracted a just-opened 1.75 liter of Jim Beam and then headed to the no-frills Royal Inn on Transit Road. His idea at that point was to sit in the hotel room and get all sloppy as he tried to figure out his next move. But after pouring himself a drink and watching the local morning wake-up show for about fifteen minutes with a too-chipper host and meteorologist, he set his glass aside, curled up in the fetal position, and cried—all through the morning. Over and over, he cycled through the crushing grief of being turned out so brutally.   Despite the tears, no peace or resolution was achieved and by late morning, when he was all cried out, he drifted off to sleep. When he woke up, he still felt weak and drained, but he was glad he had found the resolve to not drown himself in Jim Beam. He silently told himself he would not be a victim in his story. Though he was far from done processing this blow, his *invincible summer*, for the moment, had returned, and very simply, he was going to put one foot in front of the other and go on.

At noon, he called his mom and explained the situation, and she happily agreed to let him stay with her until he came up with a longer-term plan. He texted Maureen that he was going to be at his mom's and would be by on the weekend to pick up more of his things. He also sent a quick follow-up text explaining what needed to be done with the chickens. She called, but he didn't pick up. She followed the call with a text asking if he was all right, to which he tersely replied: "I'm fine."

Instead of waiting to tell Ashley and Ben, as Maureen had requested, Larry called them. When they didn't pick up, which was not unusual, he sent them a text. Rather than use the word *separate,* he chose to say that he and their mom were working some things out and that, for the immediate future, he would be staying at their grandma's house. He apologized for telling them via text but thought getting out ahead of it was better than having them ask their mother where he was that night. They could talk on the weekend when he planned to pick up more of his things.

Both Sam and Ashley had graduated earlier in the month. Sam was home temporarily studying for her PA licensing test in early July, and Ashley would start in the fall at School #45 on Buffalo's west side as a fifth-grade teacher. They responded to Larry's text with a simple: "K." Ben, who had also graduated from his associate's program and planned on attending Larry's alma mater, Brockport State, in the fall, didn't respond.

He realized he wouldn't be able to get through the week with the clothes he packed, so he picked up a few shirts and a pair of jeans at a local surplus store. Then he had a late afternoon coffee with Mac and Burbs at Tim Hortons near the shop and gave them the play-by-play of what went down. After that, he headed to his mom's house, where Ben was waiting for him. He was sitting at the kitchen table talking to his grandma when Larry entered the room, and in a desperate kind of way, he stood up and gave Larry a giant bear hug.

Larry was stunned by this display of affection and noticed Ben's eyes were wet when he released him from the hug.

"Don't worry. Everything will be fine," Larry said in a low, reassuring voice.

"I know, I know. I'm just really sorry."

"Thank you. That means a lot. Everything will be fine. Whatever happens, you have to look out for yourself. Your mother and I will or won't work this out, but that's on us, not you."

Next, Larry greeted his mom with a hug. She, too, had wet eyes, and he gently reassured her everything would be fine as well.

With that out of the way and it getting near dinnertime, the three of them agreed they were hungry. Larry's sturdy eighty-year-old mom, Helen, said she had pulled some ground beef out of the freezer earlier with the idea of frying up some hamburgers. It was a breezy summer day, and Larry suggested grilling the burgers outside, but when they checked the old Weber in the garage, the propane was out. So, it was decided that Larry and Ben would run out to get a replacement tank along with some store-bought salads, buns, and beer while Helen got the burgers in shape to be grilled.

When they got back, Helen was ready for them. She was spry for her eighty years and exhibited some Plumb-like efficiency, having the old picnic table brushed off and set with a tablecloth, paper plates, plastic utensils, and condiments. She sat like a queen in an old lawn chair, donning a big floppy gardening hat to block the sun, and regaled Ben with stories about Larry Sr., the long-dead grandfather he never got to know, as Larry handled grilling duties.

In a biting voice, between sips of beer, Helen said, "He was a son of a bitch, with all his drinking and carrying on. Remember that Christmas when you were about twelve, Larry, and we had to take all the presents back to the stores because your father always bet on the Bills to beat the Dolphins?

"Ha." Larry laughed. "Of course I do."

Helen continued. "Then, the one time he bets the Dolphins, the Bills win, and that kid plows into him and kills him. A real son of a bitch was that grandfather of yours."

"How'd you know he bet the Dolphins, Grandma?"

"His bookie showed up at the breakfast funeral, and your dad had to pay him."

Larry smiled, "That was ridiculous. But c'mon, Mom, Dad wasn't that bad."

"The hell he wasn't. How you and your brother and sister turned out so good is a miracle."

Helen went on to tell Ben in fuller detail about Larry's exploits, including saving the family from financial ruin after his grandfather passed away. Ben was aware of these stories in a fuzzy way, where Maureen often portrayed Larry as a martyr, but in Helen's account, Larry's actions were nothing short of heroic.

Given the emotional upheaval of the last eighteen hours, Larry appreciated and needed to be pumped up that way, even if it was from his mom. He knew how much he brought to the table, but it had been a while since he had any sense of his accomplishments or goodness.

After Ben had gone home, Larry settled in for the night in his old room, which had been transformed into a neutral space for guests. He was doing sets of push-ups when he received a group text from his siblings, Matt and Nora. Matt was some kind of executive vice president, or a *middle-management asshole*, as Larry liked to kid him, at a medium-sized Midwestern bank based in Indianapolis. Nora was a PhD. Professor of Divinity and Classics at SUNY Albany, where she taught undergraduate classes on the Bible and Greek and Roman literature.

Helen must have reached out to them with the news of his marital issues. Larry had a nice back-and-forth with his siblings where he sketched out the details of his and Maureen's problems in a self-deprecating way— "She's sick of my immense pragmatism." Despite the lack of real information or revealing the depths of their division, Larry was grateful his siblings had checked in with him. After completing summer sections, Nora and her family would visit their mom at the end of the summer. Larry joked that Matt should foreclose on a family farm or something, which would please his heartless corporate overlords and earn him some time off to visit family in Buffalo.

With both siblings out of town and having busy, consequential lives, it was hard to be close, but Larry was proud of them. He and Matt exchanged texts about the never-ending futility of the Buffalo sports teams, and Larry assumed the role of "sounding board" as Matt made his way up the corporate ladder. His relationship with Nora was more intellectual. They would share and talk about articles, essays, and poems via text or email. Some twenty years earlier, he and Matt were boots-on-the-ground present for Nora, helping her physically extricate her abusive first husband from her home. Her second marriage to a Philosophy PhD. named Hanz Pagels stuck, and they had two teenage kids.

As the group chat ran its course, Matt and Nora encouraged Larry to hang in there, which was much appreciated and odd. In the past, Larry had been the steady patriarchal hand steering them forward, and now their words of support signaled a certain parity—the circle between them closed and was now divided into three equal parts.

It occurred to Larry, in the small glow of his cell phone after the texts had ended, that the possible dissolution of his marriage would be the first and most spectacular failure of his life. For a few passing moments, this pending failure created a certain melancholy that gradually morphed into anger—anger at Maureen. It was the first time since her diagnosis and the revelation of her infidelity that he really burned red at her.

He raged in his head at the slights and jokes made at his expense. He seethed about the endless rejection of his amorous advances. And he was incredulous at her petty dissatisfaction with life—*get off the fucking couch and do something about it.* Most of all, the thing that really stoked the flames of his anger was the fucking gall of her saying that she didn't want him after everything they'd been through together.

These angry thoughts subsided before he drifted off to sleep, and grudgingly he acknowledged the courage it took for Maureen to choose to pursue her own happiness. He knew how hard it was to remain committed to the marathon that was marriage, and with tears again pouring from his eyes, he recalled that other immutable truth he had learned in this very house—*nothing lasts forever.*

***

Larry was thankful to return to work the next day and the rest of the week. While the situation with his marriage droned in the pit of his stomach like the thumping hip-hop bass blaring from kids' cars at red lights, the distraction of work was much needed. Helping Mac figure out staffing for upcoming summer projects and running a crew removing a bunch of the town's dead trees gave Larry something tangible to hang on to as his life was being turned upside down.

With his garage sanctuary unavailable for him to workout, he renewed his gym membership at Planet Fitness. Larry had always preferred the solitary-at-home, no-nonsense approach to working out, but with that not being an option, he went to the gym with all the meatheads and tattooed freaks.

He was aware of how out of step he was with the tattoo revolution but couldn't help but be amazed at the permanent chaos people willingly imprinted on their bodies. To him, it was an endless cacophony of distorted shapes and images jumbled together incoherently—none of these people had any design skills. He hated to be judgmental, but he just didn't get it. The last person with any semblance of tattoo cool, swagger, or danger was power forward Dennis Rodman in the nineties. Now, the masses colored their bodies with a sense of style of a first grader. He quietly tried to avert his eyes from these tragedies of the flesh, but like a rubbernecker passing by a car crash, he couldn't help himself.

After the gym, he would round out the day by watching *Wheel of Fortune* with his mom while they ate a quickie dinner. It was nice to spend time with her. Not one to typically imbibe, she would have a beer with Larry while watching the show and say funny things like, "Now I know why your father liked beer and why he ran to the can so much."

For all the discord and tumult Larry Sr. brought to her life, he was still never far from her mind all these years later. As far as Larry knew, she never dated or considered dating after he was gone. She just always kept a vigil for the larger-than-life flawed son of a bitch that was his dad. It was both sad and beautiful.

Larry wondered what his legacy with Maureen would be if there was no course correction—competent and strong, with a tendency to control and suffocate—and always looking to get laid. Though he knew it was pointless to wonder why she couldn't see that his balance sheet, unlike his father's, was all black and no red, it nevertheless made him angry. As the week went on, he grew stronger and started to entertain the notion that Maureen's inability to realize his value revealed deficient reasoning and judgment on her part.

Larry also started questioning himself—why did he want to stay in this marriage? He was physically attracted to her, and there were the kids and the house, but did he love her? Did they connect? Did they have a shared passion, beliefs, and sense of humor? Could it be, he cynically asked himself, that all this time, what he thought was love was merely two people staying together for convenience and comfort? Was love not being loyal to each other, overcoming obstacles, and building a solid structure that would hold against the storms of life? What was love? What were he and Maureen?

***

One place he wasn't plagued by questions about his personal situation was St. Ignatius. Every week throughout the winter and spring, Larry made his Saturday visits to the school, and it was a few hours of pure joy. Dr. Johnson organized a rotating cast of helpers to rehab the school's bathrooms and kitchen plumbing—save for Makayla. Makayla was there every week, ready to work with her gloves, safety glasses, and hard hat. All the kids had some unrealized potential and were willing to learn, but they were—again, save for Makayla— a little inconsistent, which Larry could relate to, having so many of his Saturdays ripped away from him by his dad when he was a kid.

Makayla was a natural. She was good with her hands, asked a million questions, and sopped up everything Larry said, from how to swing a hammer to how much to charge for a side job. Some of the topics Larry discussed with the kids were beyond them, like understanding how projects get funded. But he thought it was good to give them both the macro and micro view and to seed the soil with possibilities. Though these possibilities might not be immediately realized, they remained possibilities nonetheless—a North Star on the rocky road of life.

Of course, Dr. Johnson continued to be a rock star. Larry hadn't quite gotten over his infatuation with her, but like so many things while Maureen was ill, he was able to compartmentalize it. He avoided her Facebook and Instagram pages, and his unscheduled showers were significantly reduced.

A bunch of Ashley's former students from the school, prompted by Dr. Johnson, sent Maureen get-well cards while she was going through chemo. With the cards, Dr. Johnson included a nice little personalized note encouraging her to stay positive. She also suggested that, given the work ethic and tenacity of the Plumb family, cancer didn't stand a chance. Maureen was moved by this bit of thoughtfulness.

Dr. Johnson had words of encouragement for Ashley too. Just before starting her student teaching stint, she sent a card telling her she would do great. She reminded her there was no substitute for good preparation and to call if needed.

Though Larry was able to keep his crush on Dr. Johnson in check, that didn't extinguish the fact that they quite naturally seemed to like each other. Each week, she would welcome him to the school with a cup of Tim Hortons coffee, but by that hour, he'd already had two or three cups and became a little jittery with this extra blast of caffeine.

"You don't have to get me a coffee every week."

"No, no. You're doing an excellent job around here and must be compensated fairly. Right now it's one coffee per week, but if you keep up the good work, there's the possibility of a bagel or a muffin in your future."

"Will that bagel come with cream cheese?"

"We'll start with butter and move to cream cheese, provided your performance remains steady."

Larry laughed and said, "That'll keep me motivated. Okay, but if you insist on getting me a coffee, could you make it decaf?"

"Decaf? Are you a masochist?"

"I'm up early and have already had a few by the time I get here."

"What's early?" she asked.

"Three thirty or four."

"So, what fabulous thing are you doing at that hour?"

Whenever Larry explained his morning routine to anyone, the universal response was disbelief, followed by a question asking if he was crazy, but not Dr. Johnson. Her response when she found out the bulk of his early morning was spent writing was to say: "Is there no end to you, Larry Plumb?" Further, when he explained the style of writing he was trying to emulate, she took it upon herself to read some Raymond Carver. She had a succinct critique: "Very Caucasian and a little dated with all the smoking and drinking, but the everyman quality and the short explosive sentences totally unique and powerful."

About midmorning, Dr. Johnson would often check in with Larry and his crew and pass out bottles of water. One Saturday morning, when it was only Larry and Makayla, she came into the boys' lavatory just as they were about to set a sheet of drywall. Larry couldn't keep the 8x4 sheet in place long enough for Makayla to put a few screws in the studs. Dr. Johnson offered to help.

"Yeah, great," Larry said. Then, he set the drywall down, walked over to his tool bag, and moved a few things around until he found what he was looking for—a flashlight. With a big smile, he handed Dr. Johnson the flashlight and pointed, "Right along this seam. Don't mess up."

A puzzled Makayla looked at them and said, "Wait, I don't get it. We need help holding the drywall in place."

Dr. Johnson grinned and then let out a muffled giggle. She turned her head and took a few breaths, which enabled her to stifle her laughter, but she could not extinguish the grin from her face. "Mr. Larry was being funny," Dr. Johnson told Makayla. "When I was a young person, I would help my daddy with jobs like you're doing here, and he would always have me hold the flashlight and would cuss me something fierce when I messed up."

"Okay—lol, I guess. Let's do this," Makayla responded, not understanding what was funny.

As they held the drywall in place while Makayla sank the screws into the studs, Dr. Johnson looked over at him, still grinning, and Larry could feel a surge of electricity rush through his body at her unmitigated delight with him.

But on this Saturday morning—the Saturday he would face Maureen and the kids and pack up more of his things—he was listless. The plumbing work had been completed weeks earlier. Now Larry, Makayla, and the cast of rotating helpers had moved on to installing a simple security system at the building's various entrances that would feed screens at the security desk and Dr. Johnson's office. The new system would also allow for the doors to be opened remotely.

After Makayla and the other helpers had left, Dr. Johnson, in a peach tracksuit with three rows of vertical turquoise piping, approached Larry as he was putting the last of his tools away and joked that she wasn't sure about the new security cameras and seeing even more of what went on at St. Ignatius. When Larry didn't respond with his typical light-hearted glibness, she was on it. "Is everything okay, Larry?"

A small, fake smile came to his face as he stood there, unsure how to answer. When he couldn't think of anything to say, he became distracted and wondered about her tracksuits for a moment—how many did she have?

Though unsure how to answer, he couldn't stand there thinking about her tracksuits, so he just gave up some basic facts about his current situation and what was waiting for him when he left St. Ignatius: "My wife and I separated this week. After I leave here, I have to go and pick up some of my things and face the kids for the first time."

She looked at him thoughtfully and touched his arm with her long, slender fingers, "I'm so sorry."

"Thank you. "

"Are you all right?"

"I have my moments, but I'm getting by," he said, and with his index finger, he made the up-and-down motion of a wave.

"Where are you staying?"

"With my mom for the time being. That's the one thing that's been nice, spending time with my mom. She's turning me into a *Wheel of Fortune* fan."

She smiled and said, "I hope you can work it out. You're good people."

"Thank you. Yes, me too."

She leaned into Larry with a small hug and said, "God bless."

He smiled at her, picked up his bag, and exited through the heavy wooden entrance door.

Seventeen

When Larry pulled up to the front of the house he had spent decades shaping and molding, Sam's Honda occupied the spot in the driveway next to Maureen's SUV, where he usually parked. He sat in his truck, looking at her car for a moment, and decided he wasn't quite ready to face what was inside yet. So, instead of entering through the front door, he walked up the driveway past the cars, opened the six-foot wrought-iron gate, and tiptoed into the yard with the careful trepidation of an interloper.

Besides being anxious about seeing the family for the first time since being asked to leave a week earlier, he was nervous about the general upkeep of the house and how the chickens were getting on without him. With this in mind, he tried not to be annoyed at numerous dog droppings visible in the overgrown grass as he moved toward the chicken coop at the back of the house, some sixty feet to the right of the garage.

Once he turned the corner, the coop became visible, and he was happy to see Littleballs and Lazyass outside the henhouse luxuriating in the warm June sun. When he entered the pen, they squawked, squealed, and brushed against his khaki work pants as if they had just received a slaughterhouse pardon. He picked up Littleballs, with whom he had a special bond, and she cooed and purred as he ran his fingers through her soft feathers. In a silly pet-owner voice, Larry asked if she missed him. After he set Littleballs down, she and Lazyass continued to squawk, cackle, and get tangled in his feet as he moved toward the henhouse. As happy as he was to see Littleballs and Lazyass enjoying the beautiful summer day when he pushed open the hinged roof, he was irked to find Dumbfuck and Stupidshit sitting in the nesting boxes—brooding.

The birds still had food and water, but no one had removed the eggs in a couple of days, and both Dumbfuck and Stupidshit were trying to hatch them. The birds objected when Larry lifted them out one at a time, set them down in the pen, and then dropped the entrance door to the henhouse so they couldn't get back in. If let back in, both would return and park themselves in the nesting boxes even after Larry had extracted the eggs. In a worst-case scenario, these brooding behaviors might cause the hens to become so agitated they would stop producing eggs. The behavior was extinguished simply by keeping them away from the nesting boxes for a bit of time and removing the eggs daily.

He quickly recognized numerous cracks and fissures in the fragile shells of the eggs the birds had been sitting on, meaning they needed to be thrown out. He hoped Maureen and the kids wouldn't become defensive when he reminded them of the necessity of removing the eggs daily.

On his way to the garage to dispose of the tainted eggs, he heard the dogs barking from the house. The optimism of the yapping dogs eased his anxiety and annoyance. When he exited the man door, they thundered toward him along the forty-foot walkway at the back of the house that led to the garage. Maureen was standing at the opposite end of the walk with a smile on her face, and for a moment, she again looked unfamiliar to him in a Jamie Lee Curtis kind of way with her short, frosty hair. Larry got down on one knee to say hello to the charged-up dogs. Once he stood up, they followed him and continued to jump up as he walked toward Maureen.

She greeted him with a warm embrace and asked how he'd been.

"Fine. But, you know, things are weird."

"Yes, I know. How's your mom?"

"She's hilarious. She drinks a beer with me and we watch Wheel of Fortune. It's been nice to spend time with her.

"Ben said he liked listening to her stories about you and your dad."

"Yes. She told Ben what a son of a bitch the old man was."

"Ben's at work, but listen, when he came home from your mom's, besides telling us stories about you from Helen's perspective, he got into it a little bit with me and the girls about you leaving."

"Whaddya mean—got into it?"

"He was angry."   Larry paused for a moment before responding. "Don't take this the wrong way, but good. We've been waiting for him to say something besides—"I don't know."

"Yes, but you didn't say anything disparaging, you know—about me?"

Larry shook his head, "Of course not. He was there when I came in. He gave me a big hug and was a little emotional. I told him everything would be all right, and you and I would or wouldn't work this out. I stressed his number one priority was to take care of himself. Then we went to the store for a few things and had a little cookout. It was all pleasant boilerplate stuff with my mom telling stories."

"Oh good."

"Yeah, my mom knocked the old man and talked me up. Her usual schtick. Maybe he was responding to that."

"Could be, I don't know," she hedged and started for the back door.

"Moe, before we go inside, can we talk about the chickens for a minute?"

"What about the chickens?"

While taking into account the upheaval of the last week, Larry spoke in a matter-of-fact tone, trying to impress on Maureen the importance of removing the eggs every day so Dumbfuck and Stupidshit didn't fall into the brooding behavior. He could tell she was about to come back at him but held her fire and said she would work something out with the kids.

He followed Maureen and the still-excited dogs into the house and found Sam sitting at the dining room table, staring at her laptop screen. She got up and warmly embraced Larry as well. Hmm, he thought ironically—who knew all he had to do to receive a little affection from his family was to leave?

"How are you?" she asked, stepping back from the hug

"Fine. But, like I was telling your mother, it's been a little weird. How's the studying coming?"

"Okay, it's deciding on a job that's aggravating," she said, sitting back down.

Maureen took her seat at the end of the table. "Sam has a few offers but doesn't know where she wants to work."

"There are plenty of jobs with docs in private practice and hospitals. But primary care seems so boring. I think I'd go crazy writing statin scripts and telling people to lose thirty pounds all day, every day. But if I go for a surgical specialty or ER position at a hospital, it's more school and training, and I'm sick of school and training."

Larry instantly figured out a course of action for her, but he kept it to himself. He suspected Sam knew what to do, but she wanted the perfect no-pain solution that wasn't available to her. There were two possibilities: She would have to get a primary care job and test it out. Or, she might be able to swing some half-measure, like working part-time in primary care while getting some training, but that would require some logistical maneuvering.

Sitting at the table between his wife and daughter, he could feel the pleasant June breeze enter from the open window that looked out on the overgrown grass. He recalled the last time he offered career advice to Sam. She was in the second year of her undergraduate program, taking various classes, but decided that healthcare was what she wanted to do. Larry still had currency with her and the family in those days and advocated strongly for medical school and becoming a doctor, given her skill set and intelligence. He argued she would be at the top of the food chain, which meant more control and options. Scarred by his own experience of having to take a job with the town, Larry was big on having options.

It was then that Sam delivered a massive eye roll, called him a suffocating know-it-all, and accused him of wanting her to go to med school not for her but for himself—to make up for the opportunities he never had because he had to take care of his mom and siblings after his dad's accident. "Again Dad, it's all about you," she sneered.

Larry couldn't believe what he was hearing. Perhaps there was some truth to what Sam charged—that buried within the layers of his own experience, he did want this because of his missed opportunities. But so what? Didn't every parent, since the beginning of time, want more for their kids than they had?

And it was true, he was a know-it-all, but sorry, that was because he fucking did know it all. The record was clear—he had a long history of making smart, rational decisions that advanced the town, himself, and his family.

When he talked to Maureen about it later in their room, she thought that Sam was right—he never went on a decision-making journey with them, and it was very frustrating.

"A decision-making journey? You're joking, right?

"See, right there. You're so dismissive of everyone's process," she clapped back.

"Sorry," he said sarcastically and started to flap his arms and sashay about the room. "Look at me. I'm a butterfly, and I'm on a *decision-making journey.* I was just a humble caterpillar stuck to a tree branch, all hairy and gross, but now I'm a beautiful butterfly on a *decision-making journey.* What riches shall I find?"

Not buying one bit of this cheeky act, Maureen bitterly said, "You can be such an asshole, Larry."

From there, it escalated with all of them, and it finally came full circle last week when Maureen asked him to leave.

And now Ashley drifted into the room and sat in what had been his seat at the head of the table. After a brief greeting, she asked, "What did you say to Ben?"

In an even tone, Larry replied, "Like I told your mother, Ben visited me at Grandma's that first day. We had a cookout, and Grandma told stories about your dead grandfather and what happened after he passed away. That's it."

"He came home and was very angry toward Mom and eventually us."

"I'm sorry to hear that. I'll talk to him. But maybe he was upset that I left."

"Yeah, I guess. He was really mad, called us bitches," Ashley said, looking down at the floor.

"That's not acceptable. Like I said, the possibility of his family disintegrating could have been upsetting to him," Larry offered.

"A little dramatic, Dad," Sam intoned.

Feeling his temperature rise a tick, Larry said, "Dramatic? Given the situation, it's not a plausible explanation for why Ben might have been angry."

"Please don't lecture us," Sam said, exasperated.

"Yeah, Dad, maybe we see it differently," Ashley added.

Larry sort of laughed to himself and then regained his evenness. "Okay, tell me. Why was Ben angry?"

"Sometimes you make us feel shitty and anxious about our decisions. You always have a better way." Ashley said hesitantly.

"Yeah, maybe you vomited up some brilliant dad truth to trigger Ben, and he took it out on us and Mom," Sam followed up.

Larry felt his eyes grow big, not believing what he was hearing, but he chose his words carefully, "Two things—did you ask Ben what he was angry about? And two—even if I made Ben feel bad, why is it on me how he treats you? Doesn't he own that? If I come home from work after a bad day and scream at everyone, is that on me, or do I get a pass because of my shitty day?"

There was a long pause before Maureen responded, "Larry, you need to communicate in a kinder, less aggressive way."

"I don't think he gets it, Mom," Sam said with a shake of her head.

"Yeah, Dad, you want us to listen to your explanation and then get aggressive when we offer an alternative possibility," Ashley added.

"Aggressive? Do you even know what the word means? Let's get a couple of things straight. You can say I'm toxic or privileged, or however the resistance movement likes to characterize guys like me but to say I'm aggressive is just wrong. I've adored all of you, and I've sacrificed a great many things—"

Ashley interrupted and sarcastically said, "Everyone, violins—we've come to the pity party section of the program." She paused and quietly said, "We know Dad, in your twenties, you saved the world, but that was a long time ago, and it's not what's happening now."

At that, Larry stood up, pushed his chair back, and said, "I have to go." He crossed the living room and went up to his and Maureen's room, taking the stairs two at a time like a well-conditioned athlete. He opened the closet, pulled out a suitcase, and packed it with socks, underwear, work tees, khakis, summer shorts, and shirts. The girls were gone when he returned to the dining room, but Maureen was still sitting at the table. She called for him to sit and talk, but he just rolled by her toward his room at the back of the house.

He deposited a few books, his Bose travel speaker, and some charging cords in the suitcase. After zipping up the bag, he looked up and saw that someone had turned the man cave placard on the doorframe ledge upside down. *Is there no end to this fucking indignity?* he thought as he moved from his room toward the front door. Maureen rose from her chair as he passed her with great momentum and said, "Larry, listen," but he kept moving.

He placed the suitcase in the front seat of his truck and then, with that Larry Plumb efficiency, moved past the vehicles, opened the gate, and barreled up the driveway and into the garage to gather some tools and his portable tile cutter for an upcoming job. When Maureen entered through the man door, he was putting his drill, batteries, and charger in his travel tote at his workbench. "Not now, Moe."

"Larry, you need to calm down."

"How would you know what I need to do?"

"This isn't hard just for you," she responded.

"Of course, of course, let's talk about you some more—your unhappiness, how you lost your precious identity. I'll tell you this, someone needs a pity party, and it ain't me." He exited the garage with the tile cutter and tote in opposite hands.

"Larry!" Maureen called.

Halfway down the driveway, he stopped and turned, "WHAT?" he yelled back at her. Her face was a question mark. He waited a second, but she remained speechless, "Now you have nothing to say?" Then he looked at the overgrown grass, "While you're thinking about what to say, maybe you could pick up the dog shit and cut the goddamn grass."

With that, he stormed out of the yard and left.

***

Driving to his mother's, he couldn't remember the last time he had been this angry. Perhaps he was even more angry than when he figured out the JD-Maureen connection. He didn't want to dump this shit on his mom, but he didn't quite know what to do with himself. He sat in front of her house and waited for his breathing to even out and for the urge to take part in some random act of destruction to subside.

On his way over to his mom's, his phone started to buzz. Apparently, speech had returned to Maureen, but he declined the calls. This was followed by a series of texts requesting that dialogue between them continue but in a constructive manner. For that to happen, she said *he* needed to remain calm and not storm off when the conversation didn't go his way.

Larry found this request both infuriating and hilarious. At every turn, he was diminished, disparaged, and disrespected and then was asked to change his behavior—be kinder and less aggressive. He laughed out loud before responding: *How ironic is it that you and the girls beat the shit out of me and then tell me I'm aggressive and need to change my behavior. Ridiculous!*

With that, he turned off his phone and went into the house, where he found his mother preparing to run to Wegmans to pick up some groceries. Though she was fully capable of completing this task independently, Larry decided to accompany her, hoping that walking up and down the aisles with her would provide the distraction he needed.

Though he was still burning hot, he said hello to several people he knew in some capacity from his long service to the town. Then they ran into his old friend from high school, Lucy. She hugged Helen and said, "I hear this guy is staying with you. Is he pulling his weight?"

"So far, so good, but we'll see when we check out if he opens up his wallet," Helen said with a wink.

Larry smiled and looked at the items in the cart. "Thanks, Luc. You just cost me about forty bucks."

"You got loads of cash," she said, prompting a big laugh from all of them. Lucy said she was running late but leaned in and hugged Larry before moving on. In the process, she took his hand and squeezed it. Looking at him with the sympathy of a lifelong friend, she said, "Call me."

Running into Lucy was just the bit of grace Larry needed. Squeezing his hand and looking him in the eye meant so much to him. It was a simple reminder that there were people in this world who loved and appreciated him.

He was fine after that—his equilibrium was restored despite paying a $47.50 grocery tab. When they got to his mother's house, he helped put away the groceries and then gathered his dirty work clothes and his book of Anne Sexton poems. He got a drive-thru coffee at Tim Hortons before heading to the Wash-O-Matic on Ridge Road.

The Wash-O-Matic had become a part of Larry's life when he first made a home with Maureen and was keeping a relentless schedule with the town and his side jobs. Since his work clothes and accessories, like oily rags, filled the basement and washing machine with an odor similar to that of the paint department at Home Depot, it was decided that Larry would take all his work-related garments and add-ons to the laundromat. Usually, he would cram this into his schedule in the late afternoon or early evening on Saturday.

At first, he grumbled about having another task, but he quickly found a Zen-like peace at the laundromat—in the scent of the detergent, the whirring of the spin cycles, the buzzing of the dryers, and the touch of fresh, warm clothes. He also liked the cast of characters he encountered, from the attendants to the patrons, who, unlike him, were there out of necessity rather than choice.

Thirty years down the line, this had become part of his DNA. On this Saturday, he made small talk with the attendant Shirley, a compact lady with a round face, a button nose, and several laundry sacks of grievances. Today she complained about having to go to a bunch of different banks because, for some *goddamn* reason, there was a shortage of quarters. Larry shook his head in solidarity with Shirley as he threw a light load into an old-style top-loading machine. Then he sat in a sturdy but uncomfortable chair in the corner with his coffee and Anne Sexton poems.

He had been introduced to Anne Sexton in a freshman survey class at Brockport. Larry had been somewhat illiterate out of high school, especially when it came to poetry, but he could metabolize a good many of Sexton's poems in real-time, like "45 Mercy Street." He deeply felt the longing, grief, and chaos of her oily life. Although the professor knocked her as a *documentarian* rather than an artist for her confessional style, Larry loved the vulnerability, suffering, and fearlessness. There was blood on the page rather than some wispy fucking metaphor that was impossible to decipher without a PhD. The Sexton poems were real, tangible, and messy.

Just as he was getting through a fat-free tactile poem called "Young," in which you're transported to summer's grassy lawns, ticking crickets, and yellow heat, Maureen entered the laundromat.

When he declined her calls and didn't respond to her texts, besides the one where he said she and the girls were ridiculous, she went to his mom's house looking for him. It annoyed him that after all these years of his going to the laundromat on Saturdays, she still had to go to his mom's instead of figuring it out for herself.

She pulled up a chair next to him and sat down. After explaining how she found him and mini-lecturing about answering her calls, she looked down at the scuffed-up floor, "Ben came home after you left, and it turns out you were right—"

"What? I can't hear you when you're talking to the floor."

She turned and looked him in the eye, "Please, that tone." Then, in a wounded voice, she said, "Ben came home after you left, and it turns out you were right. He is angry you left—he said we don't appreciate or cut you any slack. He called the girls bitches again."

"I'm sorry. I'll talk to him."

"No. It's okay. We—I haven't been great to you."

"Yeah, and you fucking cheated on me too."

She began to weep softly, "I'm so sorry. Come back to counseling with me. We can talk this out."

"*I do*n't think I want to do that." And with an exaggerated voice, he said, "Lissa will have me jumping through all these hoops when we both know what's really going on."

"Don't say her name like that. She's helped me a lot."

"Has she?" he asked rhetorically. "See, I think you want to get in there with Lissa and talk around problems and either blame me or pretend we can fucking solve them with ballroom dancing or some other shit."

"Larry, I've asked you not to talk to me like I'm on one of your work crews. And I asked you not to say her name like that."

"Sorry, I'm allowed to be pissed off and call out stupid people like Lissa. But that's not really the problem, is it?" When she didn't respond, he continued, "Rather than really talking, you want to talk about talking. You want to police my language and make that the issue to avoid going where this has to go. Well, sorry, that ain't going to fly. Say what you don't want to say, but know you should say."

"I talk around the problem and avoid what's happening. So tell me what's really happening—what am I talking around? What am I avoiding?"

"Sorry, you'll have to answer that for yourself."

With a certain deliberateness, he then reached down to the floor, picked up his coffee, closed his book, stood up, walked out the front door, got in his truck, and drove away.

Eighteen

Larry drove around in a flat, meditative state for fifteen aimless minutes, reflexively negotiating traffic before doubling back to the Wash-O-Matic to pick up his clothes. Coming out of his trance in the laundromat parking lot, he wasn't surprised Maureen's SUV wasn't there, and he asked Shirley how long the woman who came in and sat with him stayed once he left. She smiled in a curious way as if asking Larry what was up, "The crying lady? She was outta here right after you."

"Thank you," was all Larry said, demurring.

As he folded his clothes, which had grown cold waiting on his return, he wondered how long it would take Maureen to say what she didn't want to say but knew she should, which barring some miraculous turn of events was—they were done. After the breast cancer scare, it had taken her months to summon the courage to tell him she didn't want him and that he should leave. Larry thought the eulogy and closing hymn for their marriage wasn't far behind, and he half laughed to himself when the perfect song to mark their end popped into his mind—"Closing Time" by Tom Waits. It was a solemn, practical choice that fit perfectly.

However, some impediments needed to be resolved before their relationship could be lowered into the ground and covered with dirt. The first was Maureen's refusal to forgive herself for her infidelity. Throughout their time together it had always been difficult for Maureen to apologize to him for anything. Whenever she committed any kind of transgression or was thoughtless, she sought an angle to absolve herself without taking responsibility. Typically, there was a process where she would avoid the issue while looking for an off-ramp to justify her actions. When it became apparent no escape was available, she would apologize through some act of kindness and declare her love for him. Rarely, however, were the words: *I'm sorry,* ever said.

He theorized that her infidelity was ripping her to shreds. Larry didn't say a word about it all the time she was ill and now only mentioned it in passing. These days, she was the one who brought it up, became all weepy and apologetic, and begged for forgiveness, which indicated to him how heavily it weighed on her. Keeping it from the kids exposed not only her crushing shame but maybe a fear of judgment and repudiation too. She would have to gather the same strength and courage that allowed her to ask him to leave before she could move on, and he thought that meant forgiving herself.

The second reason Larry suspected she couldn't end it was that his ledger contained many durable assets that would provide comfort and stability as they started down the wrong side of life's bell curve. Did she have the resolve in her mid-fifties to jump back into a sea of uncertainty? Was she ready to reconfigure her social life, develop a new financial plan, and find a purpose? Who would do the shopping, look after the animals, maintain the house and cars? And, what about the possibility of a new man—was she ready to accept another dude's bad habits and idiosyncrasies? Was she prepared to accommodate someone else's children into her life? After she'd taken all this into account, perhaps it was easier to keep know-it-all Larry, who took care of himself and almost everything else, too.

In time, Larry thought Maureen, with assistance from *Lissa* and maybe Sam and Ashley, would conclude that her freedom and identity could only be achieved without him. That his strengths—work ethic, competence, and commitment—doubled as weaknesses to stifle and control her and her only way to happiness, her only way to live a life on her terms, rather than through the prism of Larry, was to dump him once and for all.

Larry was strangely calm as he went over this in his mind. In her weepy, apologetic moments regarding the infidelity, Maureen stated how he had been so stand-up for her and the family. But when he tried to use that to defend himself, Ashley threw it back in his face with no objection from Maureen. Though Ashley's words hurt and were unfair, Larry saw the other side too. Wasn't this what he had signed up for when he said I do and fathered her, Sam, and Ben. There was no need to congratulate him for living up to his obligations.

At the same time, the one thing he didn't have an answer for, short of emasculating himself, was what he could change about himself to turn this around. He had come a great distance to extinguish the old boorish codes instilled in him. In his mind, he was kind and sensitive and allowed himself to feel things. Of course, rough spots remained, but he was motivated to learn and grow. Maureen and the girls, however, wouldn't give him credit for anything—they policed his language, questioned his motives, and demoralized him. And when they attacked, he was restrained rather than go back at them, hoping they would come to appreciate his commitment to them and see his decency and efforts to evolve. But all the body blows he absorbed, all the quiet resignation changed nothing. It didn't matter what he said or didn't say; nothing was ever good enough. And now, to save his marriage, his only option was to capitulate fully and totally to Maureen and thus lose himself.

Later, as he lay in bed in his old childhood room, he became emotional. With tears in his eyes, he felt so defeated—how could this be happening to him—to them? Still, he couldn't help but see the crux of their problems with irony. He would lose himself if he stayed, and she couldn't find herself unless he left.

Completely exhausted from the drama-filled day, Larry was still unable to sleep. He recalled scenes from their life—births, vacations, graduations. The triumphs, the failures, the laughter, and the tears. He reflected on how, just before the kid's teen years, he and Maureen would sneak away and stealthily have sex in the family van behind the Rite Aid to save the kids from the possible horror of hearing their parents' little mattress dance. Also, his mind jumped to the absurd beginnings of a phrase that once expressed their physical attraction to each other but was now considered offensive and inappropriate.

They'd been renting a lower flat on Westcliff Drive before they were married. Larry was working around the clock, and Maureen was a second-year teacher at Winchester Elementary. One particular Tuesday night, Larry arrived home at about 9:30 p.m. after meeting with some of the town's politicos vetting him for the Commissioner job. Maureen was sitting in the dim light of their depressing little dining room, correcting essays. She was ready for bed in sweatpants and one of Larry's oversized T-shirts, which conformed neatly to the contours of her buoyant chest. Her sandy brown hair was in a loose ponytail on the right side of her head. Even in the dreary room and mannish nightwear, she was so goddamn cute.

Her jaunty cuteness was made more delightful by the excitement in her voice and her sparkling eyes as she asked a dead-tired Larry a thousand questions about the meeting while he ate a Greek salad. The politicos were well aware of Larry's tireless contributions since coming on as a laborer and quickly rising to crew chief in a handful of years. But they needed to get to know him—see his temperament and his ability to answer tough questions. They also inquired about his personal life—whether he drank and gambled like his old man and his relationship with the fifth-grade teacher at Winchester Elementary.

Larry explained it to Maureen. "They said it would be better if we were married, but living together wasn't a deal-breaker for this job. There was this guy—Joe Littlefield, a Republican committeeman—who said his daughter was in your class. He and his wife like you very much."

"Oh yeah, little Haley. She's a good kid. He's kind of creepy, though."

"Whaddya mean?"

"At parents' night, he gave me one too many compliments."

"He did make a point of telling me what a capable and *attractive* woman you are."

"See, creepy."

Then, very randomly, Larry said, "Yeah, I was getting that too, so I told him you had this *big hairy bush*. It seemed to throw him off a little."

In a questioning voice, she said, "Excuse me, a big hairy what?"

"I told him you had a big hairy bush. I mean, I don't need that fucking guy telling me how capable and attractive you are."

She got up from her chair and walked slowly toward Larry, dragging her index finger across the round tabletop. She pushed his salad bowl aside and then got up on the table in front of him, put her feet on his thighs, and spread her legs wide. As she sat in front of him, he saw that her eyes narrowed with intent, and her breasts had come to life. With a seductive smile, she said, "So you told little Haley Littlefield's dad I had a big hairy bush."

"Yeah, I told him it was like the rainforest down there—pre-global warming rainforest, of course."

She moved her feet from his thighs and started flitting around at his midsection with her toes, "Rainforest, huh. That's the best you could come up with?"

"Listen, I've been in there, and you know—it's glorious. My favorite place in the whole world. I'll do whatever I can to keep it all for myself."

Continuing with her toes and wide-open legs, she leaned back on her elbows and smiled, "All for yourself, huh."

"Do you blame me? You've been there; you know its wonders."

"Yes. Yes, I do, but let me ask you a question. Is that the kind of elected official you'll be—one who lies?" She then moved her hand to the top of her sweatpants, pulled the waistband up, and took a lengthy look inside, "Because that ain't no rainforest. Here, see for yourself." And she sat back up and pulled Larry's head into her lap.

When she removed Larry's head, he stood up and, with a mischievous grin, said, "Mmm, I think you might be right, but I'm going to have to investigate further. Get an inside look."

He pulled down her sweatpants, removed her skimpy underwear, and took her right on the dining room table. Larry's salad bowl hit the hardwood floor and shattered in the heated back-and-forth.

For years afterward, the phrase was a playful precursor to sex— "Is that big hairy bush just for you, or are you going to give someone else a chance?"; "You know Larry, this big hairy bush ain't just for show—it needs attention"; "Hey, landscaper Larry, whaddya say to giving my big hairy bush a trim?;" "It's been a while. How bout I get down there and give that big hairy bush the once-over? I was pre-med for a semester in college."

Larry wasn't upset when Maureen said they should stop using the phrase because it was kind of gross, and they were too old to talk that way. He agreed up to a point but was disturbed that in addition to Maureen gradually not being interested in sex and getting angry about crashing a wedding, there was an absence of playfulness between them—no banter or silliness, nothing provocative or absurd. Part of the rebellious, I-can't-be-tamed

Maureen O'Donnell that he found so attractive was her edge. Now, that seemed to be replaced by obedience to the Resistance and MeToo rules that policed outdated terms, pronouns, and language in general.

Before he finally drifted off that night, he asked himself: *When did she stop being fun?*

***

The weeks dragged on with little communication or resolution. On two occasions, Maureen asked him to come over when she couldn't start the lawnmower. Since Larry had kept the mower well-tuned, he suspected she had over-primed the engine. He explained all that needed to be done was to wait twenty minutes for the gas to evaporate from the flooded carburetor. But she wanted him to come over anyway. He agreed, but only to show her one more time how to prime the engine properly so it wouldn't flood. After that, she was on her own.

He texted her when he arrived, exited his truck, and went up the driveway and into the yard. While he waited for Maureen to come out, he checked the mower and, as expected—flooded. Then he went over to the henhouse and was happy to see it was clean and no brooding chickens were sitting on eggs. There was one problem, though; the entrance to the pen was closed but not secure.

A moment or two later, Maureen came out flanked by Donald and Lydia, who were excited to see Larry. After greeting the dogs, he addressed the entrance to the pen, stressing the importance of securing that door since the golden retrievers were bird dogs, which meant they were programmed to kill birds, and last he checked, egg hens were birds.

But the real problem was Donald. Despite their efforts to integrate the animals, an unpredictability about him made Larry uneasy. She asked him not to be so negative and instead focus on how well they had been removing the eggs and keeping the henhouse clean. Larry almost asked how reminding her to secure the door was negative but thought it would just start a fight and said, "Please latch the door."

Years earlier, Larry had built a side porch off the garage and, in the warmer weather, would sit outside and execute the forty-two-dive looking out into the yard. It was a perfect side-porch type of summer day, and after informing Maureen that the mower engine was indeed flooded, he sat on the patio couch and waited for the gas to clear out of the carburetor. Donald and Lydia lay down at his feet once the excitement of seeing him passed while Maureen eased into an Adirondack across from him. The chickens, however, squawked in the pen, looking at Larry as if imploring him to interact with them. There were a few awkward moments of silence before Maureen asked, "Why don't we have an electric mower?"

"The battery technology isn't that great yet. Next mower. By the way, why are you cutting the grass? Where's Ben?"

"He's on a job with Hank Tomasi."

Ben had a seasonal job with the town doing park maintenance. Additionally, he had been doing side jobs with Larry and guys like Hank Tomasi to stash some cash away for Brockport in the fall. His skill level wasn't great, but he showed up on time, didn't complain, and stayed engaged.

"How's he been? Any more outbursts?"

"No. He's not around much. When he is, he keeps to himself, but no outbursts."

"Good."

"Why is that good?"

"Why is it good that he's not having outbursts? Is that what you're asking me?"

"No. I just told you he's not around much, and when he is, he keeps to himself. Why is that good?"

"I was referring to him not having outbursts. That other stuff, I don't know. He's been fine around me."

"Why did Mac punch JD?" she asked, leaning forward in her chair looking directly at Larry.

"What?"

"Why did Mac punch JD?"

"That's a pretty big non sequitur."

"C'mon Larry, why did Mac punch JD?"

"I told you, there was a beef. Is your next question about the moon? Yes, it is made of cheese.

"Don't be an asshole, Larry. Why did Mac hit JD?"

"If you don't like my answer, you tell me, Moe. Why did Mac hit JD?"

Her body contracted, and she averted her gaze momentarily before meeting his eye again. "Why are you giving up on me and this family?"

In a severe voice, he laughed and then said, "I didn't give up on anything. I've fucking moved heaven and earth for you and this family and would keep doing it. But that's not what you want."

She leaned forward in her chair. "So, tell me what I want—what we want. You have an answer for everything."

"Isn't that part of why you asked me to leave? Because I'm an annoying know-it-all."

She hesitated for a moment, and a single tear fell from her eye, "Is this all there is, Larry? Isn't there supposed to be more? I always thought we were the chosen ones."

Softly he said, "We are the chosen ones. We've sowed, and we have reaped. We have food, shelter, and freedom. Our children are strong, healthy, and educated. We have financial security—we are rich."

When he was done talking, he stood up and went into the garage. He returned a few moments later with a paper towel for Maureen to dry her tears. He also had an earth-friendly poop bag and a plastic glove covering his right hand. He gazed at her for another long moment and then gingerly walked around the yard, picked up the piles, and put them in the bag. After finishing, he threw the bag into the garbage tote and proceeded to the garage. He closed the choke on the mower, pulled the starter string, and cut the grass. Maureen lingered for a minute, watching him cut the straight lines before returning to the house. When he was done, he put the mower away, blew the excess grass from the walkways and driveway, and without saying goodbye, got in his truck and drove to his mother's.

***

A week or so later, as he was pulling into the parking lot at the shop, Maureen texted him asking him to call her—it was an emergency. He quickly dialed her up, and she was crying. "The dogs—the dogs got the chickens—the dogs got the chickens. Please come."

Though he understood what Maureen meant when she said the dogs got the chickens, seeing the birds splayed out and dead in different parts of the yard was way worse than he imagined driving over there. Before dealing with the bird massacre, he went into the house, and Maureen was sitting with the kids at the dining room table. Ben held her hand, and the girls stared out the window.

Grief-stricken and gazing into soaked tissue, she whispered, "I let Donald and Lydia out and then dozed off on the couch, and when I went out to get them—the chickens—Oh Larry."

Larry got down on one knee and reassured her. "It's okay. It's okay."

Though he was trying to be comforting, he couldn't help but feel a certain coldness toward her and toward them. Maybe they picked up on it as he stood up and entered the living room. Lydia looked at him from the floor, and her tail wagged gently. Donald lay on the ottoman and wouldn't meet his eye.

Larry then went into the basement and got four old towels that were stacked and ready to be turned into work rags. He came back up and told everyone he was going to wrap the birds up and bury them. He would get them before filling the collective grave in case anyone wanted a minute or two with them. Ben stood up and offered to help.

They got a couple of shovels from the garage, and Larry set Ben to work digging a ditch in the corner of their lot where they had buried a few family cats and a hamster or two while he gathered and wrapped up the birds.

Stupidshit and Dumbfuck, as expected, were not far from the pen, and Lazyass was in the driveway. Larry was a little heartened to find, though her terror probably lasted longer than for the other birds, that Littleballs had almost made it to the wrought iron fence where she might have escaped through the vertical bars if she were a few steps faster. Tears welled in his eyes as he wrapped his beloved Littleballs in the towel. He wasn't surprised by how much this hurt as he set her next to the other birds on the soft ground and joined Ben in digging the small ditch. When it was ready, Larry sent Ben in to get the girls, and he gently placed the hens in the makeshift grave.

Sam said some flowery stuff about how Kendall and Odin (aka Dumbfuck and Stupidshit) were now in a better place. At the same time, Larry silently apologized to the birds that his family's stupid human shit had caused their gruesome and untimely end. When the Plumb men had finished filling in and patting down the ditch, Maureen asked Larry to make omelets with some of the birds' last eggs. Larry said it was too soon, but she insisted.

He acquiesced, but nobody really said or ate much during this funeral breakfast. Larry was hating all of them and said next to nothing as he turned over his eggs on the plate. Before leaving, he told them he would be there on the weekend to take care of the henhouse.

But when he showed up to disassemble it, he hadn't detached two or three solar lights from the pen webbing before Maureen and Sam were out in the yard telling him to stop.

"Stop, why?" he asked.

"We think we want to get more hens," Sam responded.

"We? Didn't you sign on to work at Strong Memorial in Rochester?" Larry asked.

But it was Maureen, not Sam, who responded. "It's only an hour away, and her schedule is four on and four off. Ben will be away at Brockport, but Ashley will be around, too. Between the three of us, it'll be fine."

"I thought Ash was getting an apartment with a friend?"

"Yeah, but she'll only be about ten minutes away."

"The four of you were here full-time, and there was a chicken fucking holocaust. Whaddya thinking? Nobody picks up the dogshit or cuts the grass, and there were piles of laundry when I was here last week."

"I need this, Larry," Maureen implored. "Caring for hens will give me some purpose and will be healing. We found some at a farm in East Concord."

"You're really doing this?" he said, putting his hands on his head in disbelief. "This is not a good idea. Let me take the dogs then."

"I'm keeping the dogs, Larry."

"It's too much to take care of by yourself."

"I'm keeping the dogs. Don't ask again."

"You have no faith in us and are so negative, Dad?"

Larry pleaded with them, saying it wasn't a matter of faith or negativity; he was being practical. He understood everyone was upset, but it was a terrible idea to make this decision when they were grieving and emotional.

Sam and Maureen just looked at each other and shook their heads.

Nineteen

L arry parked his truck in front of his mom's house after coming home from the gym, and his phone buzzed. It was a text from his old high-school curiosity, Kimmy Karney. She was unhappy with her lawn service and needed a recommendation. He sent her the number of one of his coworkers who had a fledgling no-frills snowplow/lawn service that he did with his college-age son. Larry said he would send the guy a "heads-up" text informing him that she was a friend and would be contacting him. She replied instantly, "Thx Larry. You're the best."

Though their circumstances were worlds apart, ironically enough, Larry and Kimmy found themselves living with their moms in the houses they grew up in a block away from each other. Larry looked at her return text and smiled. She's right; I am the best.

Over the winter, while Maureen was undergoing chemo, Larry tightened up some things at Kimmy's mom's aging house—electrical outlets, railings, and fresh tile and fixtures in an old bathroom. Kimmy had returned to the area to care for her mom and was the new family law attorney at the Ralph Ponsonby Law Firm, which Larry found hilarious.

Ralph Ponsonby was an old-school waspy town elder whose father had been West Seneca Supervisor in the 1960s. The son, now in his 70s, was the head of the Western New York Conservative Party and was noted for his mud-colored dye job, perpetual tan, and blindingly white teeth. He was also known for his disdain of liberals and progressive causes and was constantly popping off in the media about Hillary, Obama, and Erie County's democratic County Executive. And now, with Trump laying waste to civility in public discourse, he was further emboldened.

Through the years, when proposals and policies were being debated and vetted by the town attorney, Ponsonby would sometimes call the town supervisor or a council member, offer his unsolicited two cents, and then boldly invoice the town for the conversation. These invoices were never honored, and he would filibuster and play the martyr at town board meetings about being stiffed for his legal advice while complaining about teachers' and town employees' pensions. He even got after Larry at one meeting—"What exactly is the job description of a Senior Utility Specialist?"

Though he didn't agree with his tactics or ideology he sort of liked Ponsonby. Long ago, when Larry was just starting out, Ponsonby would bring up the old joke about public employees: *How can you tell they're town workers?—One guy is digging a ditch, and three guys are leaning on shovels watching him.* He always dubbed Larry as the guy digging the ditch and asked if he wasn't meant for something bigger than the town. He even gave Larry's name to a local developer with the same ideological bent and big mouth, Carl Worthington. Worthington tried to hire him away from the town for years, but Larry always politely declined.

Ponsonby's addition of a family law component was obviously meant to give the firm a softer image, and Kimmy's taking it on was hilarious. "It's temporary," she said to Larry. And yes, I know nobody else in Western New York wanted this job."

He hadn't talked to Kimmy since the end of winter and was tempted to cut through a neighbor's yard and knock on her mom's front door. He could have been there in less than two minutes. But as soon as he exited his truck, a young guy parked a few houses down on the opposite side of the street got out of a beat-up Ford Fusion and approached Larry. His button-down shirt was rumpled, and he was carrying a legal-sized manilla envelope, "Excuse me, are you Larry Plumb?"

"Yes."

"Mr. Plumb, I'm from the law firm of—" He stopped and nervously looked at the envelope. "The law firm of Ralph Posobenny—"

"The law firm of who—Ralph Ponsonby?"

He looked at the envelope again, smiled, and said, "Yes, Ralph Ponsonby—and I'm here to present you with a Summons and Complaint informing you that you are a defendant in a pending legal matter."

"Legal matter, what?" Larry said, confused.

Extending his arm with the envelope, the kid cautiously said, "A divorce. These are divorce papers."

"Ah, divorce papers. I'll be damned. She's really doing it," Larry said more to himself than the kid without taking the envelope.

"Can you please take the envelope, Mr. Plumb?"

"Sure," Larry said, reaching for the envelope. Once the handoff was complete, the rumple-shirted kid seemed relieved. As he walked away, Larry called to him, "Hey, I've never been served divorce papers. Am I supposed to tip you or something?"

The kid turned around and laughed. "That would be a first. Usually, people want to kill me. But maybe you can do me a favor— instead of a tip, could I use your bathroom? I drank a big bottle of water waiting on you."

Larry let the kid use the john at his mom's house and found out that he was what they called a "process server," and he contracted with various law firms serving all kinds of legal papers to people. He said "divorce papers" were the worst. He thanked Larry for letting him use the bathroom and for not being an asshole.

"Pretty bad, huh?" Larry asked.

"You have no idea," he said as he walked down the driveway toward his car.

***

Later that night, Larry read over the papers, which, in a threatening way, spelled out the grounds for the divorce, the relief sought by the plaintiff—Maureen O'Donnell Plumb—and the deadline for responding. Larry was still a little surprised that she got there. Truth be told, even if it was a way down the road, he was sort of happy this was moving forward. With the dim light of resolution approaching, he could also start planning his next move.

Not liking the angry tone of the summons, the ever-practical Larry texted Maureen to tell her that he had been served and then cautiously asked if it was necessary to waste all this money on a lawyer—especially

Ponsonby. And since their finances were pretty straightforward, couldn't they work this out between themselves?

"That would be great," came the instant reply. "Where and when?"

They volleyed back and forth with suggestions until Larry finally said, "The Wash-O-Matic, Saturday at 5 p.m."

"Really?"

"Yeah. It's a neutral site where we can sit in the corner, talk, and be anonymous—except for Shirley, who might be interested in our conversation.

"Okay. Whatever you say."

He smiled at her agreeableness.

***

Larry arrived at the Wash-O-Matic early on Saturday, not seeking some advantage over Maureen but because he had that week's laundry to do. Inside the sprawling laundromat, numerous overhead fans circulated the warm July air efficiently, yet the room was still hot and stuffy even with the front door open.

As Shirley folded and bagged fresh-from-the-dryer garments, Larry listened to her complaints about the Wash-O-Matic's lack of air conditioning. With a wry little smile, she said on days like this, she was so drained by the end of her shift all she could do when she got home was sit on the porch and sip vodka with lemonade.

Larry smiled as Shirley aired her grievance when Maureen came in with a manilla envelope. She looked all summery and lovely in a peach tank top and a little white skirt. When introducing her to Shirley, he noted that her silvery hair was growing out and that she looked healthy and relaxed.

Maureen complained politely about the hot weather too, saying she wasn't wishing the summer away but wouldn't mind if it was a few degrees cooler.

Once Shirley's conversation had concluded, Larry grabbed Maureen's hand and gently pulled her along to the corner of the building where they had talked a few weeks earlier.

"You look great—relaxed," Larry said. "Can I get you a water or something?"

"No, I'm fine, and thank you," she said, sitting down across from him.

Larry started to pull out his laptop. "I don't have a printer at my mother's, so I couldn't print—"

"Larry, slow down," she interrupted. "I don't need to see any printouts. I know more or less what we have and that we're in good shape. So, if it's okay with you, we don't need to quibble over the money."

Larry took the lead in managing the family's finances, but Maureen was always involved. He was as adept at overseeing that money as he had been with the highway budgets. There was no red ink on the Plumb ledger except for monthly living expenses: groceries, insurance, utilities, school taxes, etc. The girls were moving on to the next phases of their lives and were no longer a financial burden to them. There would be some miscellaneous costs with Ben headed to Brockport in the fall, which they agreed to split. However, the outlay would be minimal since a 529 account established long ago would cover his tuition and living expenses. Additionally, Larry and Maureen had good public sector health insurance, pensions, and robust 401(k)s waiting to be tapped. Neither would suffer any significant financial pain from breaking apart.

For now, they also agreed to punt on the one significant asset they shared—the house. Maureen wanted to see if she could manage it on her own. This was acceptable to Larry, provided she didn't make any major changes that would affect its value without consulting him. Also, in the event that she wanted out of the house he wanted the option to return.

It was their most reasonable, stress-free conversation since Maureen was declared to be in remission months ago, and Larry was a little confused, "What's going on here, Moe? Are you having second thoughts?"

"No, I don't think so. Maybe. We'll see."

"What kind of answer is that?"

"It means I don't know what I want yet. But, and this a big but, when I was in Ponsonby's office drawing up the summons with his divorce attorney, Mary Ellen, it just felt all wrong. She said all these things about my rights, how I was owed stability, and how they had powerful tools to get what was fair and things like that. It felt like they wanted to turn you into this deadbeat and hang you in the public square. And, I just had a moment and was like—I don't want to do this to Larry. In a million years, he'd be the last guy to ever screw me over."

"Thank you. That means a lot to me."

"Don't thank me. You earned that Plumb," she said generously.

"So where does that leave us? Is this divorce going to happen or not?"

She leaned forward and took his hand in hers, "Like I said, I don't know." But I do know I don't want to fight with you."

"Well, I appreciate that, but I want to start moving forward. As nice as it's been to have this time with my mom, it's time I get a place of my own."

"Yes, absolutely do that. Don't wait for me. Move forward however you see fit, but can we postpone making this final?"

"So you want to kick the can down the road?"

"Yes. Listen, Larry, you were right. With the help of Lissa and, to some extent, the girls, I was trying to pin all of this on you. I was trying to make you responsible for my happiness. I would have done it too, if you would've shouted me down and been an asshole to me. But that's not what you did, ya son of a bitch—"

"Hey—none of that teachers' lounge language, and don't say Lissa's name like that," he said, cutting her off.

She smiled, "C'mon, don't make me laugh. I want to finish saying this. By not telling me off or being an asshole, you denied me the permission to blame you. You were just straight and steady Larry, taking care of me and the family—always. And as I sat in that lawyer's office, plotting to take you down, it was just wrong."

"To be fair, you did have cancer. So, there's that."

"I know. But even without the cancer, you would have done the same thing."

"If you thought all this, why'd you have me served?

"Given my transgression, my pettiness, and the way I wanted to blame you, I thought I owed you the opportunity to expedite the process if that's what you wanted—and we still can if you want that."

"Well, what does kicking the can down the road mean? And can I say these are pretty heady revelations?"

"Thanks, " she smiled. Despite what you call heady revelations, the fact remains that I'm still unhappy and dissatisfied with my life."

"I should have quit while I was ahead," he joked.

"Yeah, that might have been a good idea. But seriously, don't take this the wrong way or laugh; I wasn't kidding when I said my whole life felt like it was being lived through you. The house, the kids, the town superstar—you know how many times I've introduced myself as Larry Plumb's wife? Nothing feels like it's mine. It's all Larry, Larry, Larry—

Also, part of how I lost myself was by allowing you to take over everything. You're so efficient in getting things done that, in the last few years, I've become complacent and have been coasting. You know, sitting on the couch with the TV on, more or less paralyzed. So, I think being happy is going to require me to be a bigger participant in my own life if that makes sense?"

"I get it. Yes, that makes sense. I'm really happy for you. Don't undersell yourself—these are heady revelations."

"Thank you."

In light of all Maureen had said, Larry paused momentarily and thought about the implications of kicking the can down the road. Given her epiphany about regaining control of her life, he didn't think she was standing down for the moment because she was afraid of change. It was the exact opposite—she was embracing change.

He also knew that, though it might be easier to just keep him around, it would be out of character for Maureen O'Donnell to stay in this because she was scared to be on her own with Larry as some kind of safe default. Therefore, he trusted she was honestly appraising the situation—that she thought there was a possibility she could be happy with herself and Larry, but she needed some time to test this out.

The question for Larry was, did he want to wait for her to figure it out? He had been preparing as if it was a foregone conclusion that his marriage was over and had made progress in thinking about life on his own. In the two months he had been out of the house, he had grown accustomed to not having his motives and actions challenged or having his language constantly policed. Between his writing project, St. Ignatius, and work, his life was filled with purpose and diversity.

He had also become quite comfortable in his new scaled-down routine of mostly looking out for himself. He laughed, thinking about Maureen wanting to assume more responsibility in her life while he was enjoying less. In this, too, he saw them ironically moving in different directions, but it was a sign of hope instead of signaling doom for the marriage. He decided he could hang on a little longer—he owed that to everyone, including himself.

Until they came up with a final answer, they agreed to split his rent—if and when Larry found a new living situation. It had been a very productive meeting tinged with hope and when it was over, they stood up and embraced meaningfully. With his arms wrapped around her, he felt as if he were holding his warm, soft, triumphant past and his uncertain future. When he looked into her face as the embrace concluded, the hairs on his neck stood at attention. She seemed so close and attainable standing in front of him, and he wished they could melt away their problems just by looking into each other's eyes.

As the moment waned, Maureen said, "We got a new batch of chickens. Do you want to come over and meet them?"

"Um, no thanks.

They're really amazing."

"Don't take this wrong, but I'm out of the chicken business. That was pretty hard on me."

"It was hard on all of us," she said, a touch defensively.

"Of course."

"They've been really good for me, not just the healing part, but for the other stuff we talked about—being more active managing the day-to-day stuff."

"How's Donald been?" Larry asked as they started to walk toward the exit.

"Very standoffish. I've had him on the leash around the pen, and he wants nothing to do with the chickens. He won't even look at them. It's like he knows he did something wrong."

Standing by her SUV in the parking lot, Larry asked, "So what's in the envelope?"

"Just some financial stuff in case this didn't go well. But I think we did pretty good, Plumb."

He loved it when she called him Plumb. "Yes. There might be hope yet."

They both leaned against the quarter panel of her SUV, which was warm, bordering on hot to the touch, and Maureen playfully said, "Guess what else happened at Ponsonby's office that day?"

"Okay, I'll play—they burned Nancy Pelosi in effigy?"

"Ha—that's funny, but no. The old boy hit on me."

"C'mon—really?"

"Yeah, it was so creepy. I was in this big conference room with Mary Ellen going over stuff, and suddenly, her phone rang, and she had to excuse herself to take the call. She left the room for about five seconds before Ponsonby walked in. He sat across from me and went through the whole spiel about getting what was right for me and all their powerful instruments. When he finished with that, he put his hand on my forearm and told me that if I needed anything, I should call him. He wrote his personal cell number on his card and gave it to me while displaying that big creeper smile with those giant white teeth."

"Are you going to call him? He'd probably take you somewhere nice and pick up half the tab."

"Don't even joke about that."

"Why'd you go there anyway?"

"My friend Ginny Brothers used Mary Ellen. Said she was great. She never dealt with Ponsonby at all."

"See how special you are, Maureen? You're getting a twofer—a divorce and a new boyfriend."

"Larry—"

"Think about it—quiet dinners talking about tax breaks, immigrants, government largesse—topped off by not tipping the waitstaff. You better go, Moe, because I don't think I have it in me not to joke about this."

They embraced once more, and coming out of the hug, Maureen reached down, squeezed his hands, and then kissed him on the cheek. They lingered a moment, smiling at each other.

As she pulled away, with the yellow heat of the sun beginning its daily descent into nighttime, a wave of optimism swelled in his gut. But Larry had been in this game too long to be deceived by that feeling. In a twinkling second, his head was filled with the old King of Corinth—Sisyphus.

Given his current situation, Larry wondered if poor, toiling Sisyphus had a momentary wave of optimism in his gut each time the boulder reached its high point? Larry reasoned he must have; there must have been a fleeting sliver of hope. Otherwise, he would have become despondent and given up on having to complete this meaningless, never-ending task. Larry decided, for the time being, he wouldn't think about the absurdity of everything that had happened in the past year. He also wouldn't think about the boulder's soul-crushing descent down the hill. Instead, he would focus on that final hug and kiss and the fleeting hope in the ascent.

Twenty

It had been almost a month since Larry and Maureen had spoken in a meaningful way. Though their last meeting was tinged with hope for their relationship, this possibly was a function of her desire to be a bigger participant in her own life. Instead of verbal communication, she sent many pictures of the new brood of chickens she had acquired. Larry theorized that showing him how well she cared for this new batch of birds was Maureen's attempt at atoning for the mishap that led to the dogs—in all likelihood, Donald—killing their previous brood.

But on the Friday before Labor Day weekend at 3 p.m., just as he was locking up the toolbox in the bed of his town pickup, Larry received a text from Maureen asking to meet at the Wash-O-Matic at 5 p.m. That month, the girls had moved into their own apartments—Sam in Rochester and Ashley off the Elmwood Strip in Buffalo and, on several occasions, needed to borrow Larry's truck. When he asked after their mom, they gushed about how well she was doing.

Though his siblings, Matt and Nora, were in town for a visit, and a barbecue was scheduled for 6 p.m. at their mom's house, Larry needed to see for himself how well Maureen was getting on and agreed to meet with her.

When he arrived at the laundromat, Maureen was in the corner talking to Shirley and waved him over. He had used the time since her text to hit the gym for a quick workout and was mopping his head with a hand towel as he maneuvered through the facility's folding tables, wheeled bins, and banks of washers to the corner where Shirley was standing over Maureen. She was telling Maureen how thrilled she was that her *cheap-ass* boss had hired another attendant to take over the weekend shifts.

As Maureen nodded up at Shirley from her seat, Larry noticed some big changes in her. Her hair was blown out, and she had gone back to her natural sandy color while keeping a few silvery accents. Her eyes were framed with black emo-like eyeliner, and her lips were painted a plush shade of red. She wore a breezy pastel summer dress with a floral print that exposed her arms and shoulders and hewed to the curves of her body. He couldn't get a full measure of her sitting in the chair, but from what he saw, she looked fabulous.

Larry sat down across from her, and after a brief interrogation regarding the whereabouts of his dirty laundry, Shirley took her leave. He turned to Maureen and said, "Well, well, well, aren't you the gorgeous one."

"Thank you. I feel a little silly but thank you."

"Are you headed out on the town, or maybe you have a date with an artificially tanned lawyer?"

"Don't start with that Ponsonby stuff," she smiled.

"Okay, so what's up? How've you been?"

"Actually, I'm doing great. I think I'm really starting to find my stride." Then, pointing at her face and twirling her index finger—"And this is part of it."

"Wearing makeup?"

"Yeah, not so much for what it looks like, but more for my self-worth. Maybe it's how we grew up, but I feel better when I take some time with my appearance. It's like, to be my best, I have to look my best."

"Sure, I get it."

"The girls think it's ridiculous and say I'm surrendering to outdated codes, and I'm opening myself up to not being taken seriously."

"Not to denigrate our daughters, but what the hell do they know? They're smart and everything, but they've barely dipped their toes in the real world. They probably would never admit it, but they've benefited plenty from your good looks. If this helps you feel your best and be happier, you should do it."

"Well, thank you. It's a small thing, and it may be silly, but it helps.

He sensed she was uncomfortable with his assessment of their daughters and moved on. "So besides being good-looking enough not to be taken seriously, what else is going on?"

"Larry—"

"Sorry, just trying to keep it light."

"Okay. Listen, I wanted to meet because we haven't really talked, and there's been some changes with me, and I've made some decisions. Instead of clobbering you at some inconvenient time or having you find out through the kids or some other way, I wanted to sit down and be upfront and transparent."

"Thank you. I appreciate that."

"The first thing is I'm changing jobs. I'm the school district's new Coordinator of Elementary Education."

"Wow. That's great. I didn't know you were looking for something else."

"I wasn't, but on a lark I made an inquiry about this listing I saw, which got me a meeting with the Assistant Superintendent, Janet Kmitch. We hit it off, so I went through the interview process, and she hired me. I was ready to leave the classroom, and this seemed like a good challenge."

"Wow, what a surprise. I'm so happy for you."

"Why is it a surprise?" she asked assertively. "You know I've been trying to shake things up. Or is it surprising that someone would see something in me and hire me?"

"Relax, Maureen, it's just a little out of left field. That's all."

"It didn't sound that way," she said, looking at him sideways

"What's it involve?"

"It's a liaison position between the superintendent's office and the schools. Janet is my boss, and like the job title says, I'll be coordinating and implementing curriculum and instruction models that come down from the state in the district's elementary schools."

"Is there a special degree or training requirement? And why did they wait to hire someone so close to the start of the new school year?"

"My master's in education is enough, and I'll be shadowing the current coordinator, Carol Maston, who is retiring at the first of the year. The timing was perfect since it'll give me four months of on-the-job training. You know Carol and her husband Rick, right?"

"Sure, Ben played hockey with their son, Jason, for a few years. Wow, that's great. I'm so proud of you."

Still looking at him sideways, she said, "It's nice that you're proud Larry, but why? Am I unqualified or undeserving of a different job?"

"So we're going to fight about how I express my excitement for you—is that what we're doing? Next, are you going to come at me with: It's not what you say—it's how you say it. Or maybe you'll find some of my legendary aggressiveness between the lines? In two minutes of conversation, I've been accused of thinking it's unbelievable that someone would hire you and that you didn't deserve a new job when I said nothing of the sort. Instead of projecting, maybe you should look in the mirror."

He stood up, put his left hand over his heart, extended his right arm to the side and then up to his forehead, and saluted. He said, "Congrats, Maureen O'Donnell. All the best in your liaisoning, coordinating, and implementing." He bowed and turned on his heel to leave.

"Larry, wait," she said after he took a few steps.

He turned and looked back at her. "I don't need this, Maureen."

"You're right. I probably am projecting. It's just—everything is happening all at once, and it's a little scary." She tapped his seat. "Please."

Larry stood there wondering if he was self-hating enough to continue this conversation. She tapped the seat again, and he cautiously walked back and eased himself into the chair. "Listen, I get it," he said. "Sometimes, when you take on new things, it feels like your feet are barely touching the ground, and it's scary. But that's how you grow."

"No offense, Larry, but you've been in the same job for decades."

"It's not the same job. I was the commish for sixteen years, and now I have a new job every day of the week," he said defensively, knowing for sure it'd been a mistake to sit back down. "Plus, I have outside interests—like the novel I'm working on."

"Yeah, but you don't think—Nevermind."

"I don't think what?"

"It's just that anybody can write a novel these days. Is there even a market?"

"That's not why you do it—it's about challenging yourself. Look, I have to go."

"No, wait, there's something else." She put her hand on his arm to stop him from leaving.

"WHAT?" he said, not trying to hide his frustration

"Larry—please."

"Again—I don't need this."

"Okay, okay. Listen, I know I already have a lot going on and am a little scared about everything happening all at once, but there's another thing." After hesitating, she made a corkscrew of her face and said, "I think I want to see other people."

He let out a little laugh. "Okay. See other people. Can I go now?"

"Larry, please listen to me. We have to talk about this so we understand each other."

"All right, go ahead."

"I'm not seeing anyone, and I'm not necessarily looking for anyone, but if an opportunity presents itself, I want to feel free to act on it."

"Act away. But you said, *people.* Does that mean women are on the table?"

"You caught that, huh. Yeah, I guess, maybe. I haven't thought this all the way through, and I'm not necessarily attracted to women. Still, after talking to the girls in my golf league, I'm going leave myself open to the possibility of female companionship."

"Wow, that's a long way from the gilded hallways of St. Bridget's. Your parents are probably tilt-a-whirling in their graves."

"Don't say that. And I said companionship, not sex. Again, I'm not seeing or interested in anyone—man or woman. But I'll tell you this, I'm not looking to be courted or chased. Don't take this the wrong way, but I'm tired of being chased. I want to do the chasing if the right opportunity presents itself."

"Chase away Maureen, I wish you better luck than I had. Can I go now?"

"Larry, this is serious. All our time together, and yet, you're so cavalier as if you don't care in the least."

He couldn't believe what he was hearing, and three thoughts jumped into his frustrated head. First, he was right not to make too much of their last meeting, where they parted with a dash of hope.

Second, he was annoyed that she still didn't understand how his mind worked. Given their time together, how could she not know he would have prepared himself for this possibility? That, since his father's untimely death, one of the immutable truths of his life, which he repeated over and over again to her was—*nothing lasts forever.*

Third, was she expecting him to make some desperate plea to save their marriage after she had been unfaithful, regularly rejected him, and was often moody, capricious, and such a pain in the ass regarding his language and everything else?

He was happy and gave credit for the effort she put in to regain the lost meaning and purpose in her life, but he wasn't some dog waiting by the door to be let back in the house.

In her self-discovery, if she had concluded that she could accept him as is and wanted to give their marriage a shot to continue, he would have done that. Larry thought he owed that to what they had built and to not folding in the face of adversity. But he wasn't some kind of mark to be toyed with and strung along, "I'm sorry, but I think you should have known I would have prepared for this."

"Of course, Logical Larry put it all together."

"We're moving from my faulty excitement to name-calling about how I can put simple facts together? I thought you didn't want to fight?"

"It's just your lack of reaction makes it seem like you don't care."

"Would you like me to break a table or throw a bin through the front window?"

"Don't be ridiculous. I was just hoping—I don't know—I guess I was hoping for tender Larry. The Larry who reads poetry and cries to Bruce Springsteen songs, not the cold, rational Larry with all the answers."

"Really? As I recall, whenever you caught me having a *moment*, you and the kids couldn't wait to torture me with it."

"I suppose we did," she said, her voice trailing away. She looked up at the slow-churning ceiling fans above them, and after a short pause, she turned her eyes back to him and gently said, "I guess I'm just conflicted about arriving at this place. Maybe it was irrational, but I thought you might offer some pushback, that you would fight for me."

Larry gazed at her and was again stunned by her lack of self-awareness and, for a moment, thought he might rage at her manipulative, passive-aggressive bullshit. Suddenly, though, he was filled with overwhelming anguish and wanted to take her in his arms and tell her whatever she needed to hear—make everything right. As he had always done. He wanted to turn the clock back to when they were hot for each other. He wanted to return to when they were pushing and striving—building something.

But looking at her beautiful face, he finally accepted that all the pushing, striving, and building hadn't been enough. The foundation had crumbled, and Sisyphus's boulder rolled back down the hill. The task of pushing it back up, which was tinged with hope and promise, would not be repeated. The descending boulder would now crush them. They had failed.

The Wash-O-Matic became eerily silent, and he quietly said, "If I had an answer for everything, we wouldn't be in this mess. You and the kids got everything I had, and I don't want this, but you're on a different path now—a path that doesn't include me. I don't know, sometimes—sometimes things just don't work out."

And it was done.

***

Larry didn't have much time to think about what had just occurred at the Wash-O-Matic with Maureen because the barbecue was ramping up when he arrived at his mom's house. With Ben already at Brockport, Sam stuck working the weekend shift at the hospital, and Maureen otherwise absent, the crowd was unusually thin, but those present—Helen, Matt, Nora, and her kids greeted him enthusiastically. Ashley was also there. Of course, she was a bit standoffish with Larry.

Helen was sitting imperiously in her lawn chair, donning her big floppy gardening hat, and being doted on by Ashley and Nora's teenage kids. Matt handed Larry an icy IPA, and taking a pull, he winced at its bitterness. "Is there some kind of requirement for middle management guys to drink these designer beers?"

"Do you think a man of my stature would put bowling alley beer to my lips like you commoners?" Matt quipped.

They both laughed as Nora exited the back of the house with two trays of nachos. After setting them on the picnic table, she came over and greeted sweaty Larry with a half-hug and told him if he was going to be the grill master, he better hit the shower quickly.

Nora was the most Larry-like of his two siblings in terms of organizational skills and pragmatism. In fact, she typically visited Buffalo after she completed teaching the summer section of "Classics" at SUNY Albany, but this year, she was delayed a week because she had to oversee the installation of a new driveway at her house. When Larry asked why her husband Hanz couldn't do it, she rolled her eyes, "C'mon Larry, Hanz is a brilliant guy, but he's a philosopher. He would've let those concrete guys leave with the job half-done at double the price."

Larry took her point.

On the way to doing what he was told regarding the shower, he handed Nora his IPA, "Here is the stuff Dionysus hands out to the minimum wage demigods like Pan and Demeter to make them feel important."

As the cool water poured from the shower, the crushing reality of what had occurred with Maureen at the Wash-O-Matic hit Larry. He tried to fight it as he stood there with the water running over his head and body, but he couldn't hold back and wept at their failure. He desperately searched his mind for what he could have done better, what he still could do, but every thought, every possibility, every obtuse fancy was a dead end. Seeing no way forward, and a yard full of people waiting on him, he gathered himself and sucked it up for the moment. He exited the shower, toweled off, and dressed in a pair of shorts and his favorite tee sporting the Big Star logo. Noting the new month, he thought of the band's song "September Gurls," and it gave him a small but bittersweet lift.

As he took his place behind the grill, he hoped the evidence of his little breakdown in the shower would go unnoticed. Everyone seemed oblivious except Nora. She approached him, put her hand on his back, and, in a whispery voice, asked if he was okay. His instinct was to nod and say everything was fine, but he knew he couldn't fool her and shook his head. "No, but I'll muddle through."

Nora put her head on his shoulder and ran her hand over his back. In the same whispery voice, she said, "Oh, Larry, what are we going to do?"

This little show of support was a welcome boost. He was further bolstered a few moments later when Mac, Burbs, and Lucy came up the driveway carrying twelve-packs of Rolling Rock and Blue Light.

"Finally, some bowling alley beer," he called out.

From there, the barbecue turned quite festive with grilled burgers and chicken, freshly made salads, baked beans, ice cream, various IPAs, and those bowling alley beers. Matt, Nora and Helen hadn't seen Larry's friends in years and traded friendly updates on family, career, and life. The lighthearted atmosphere helped Larry to keep his emotions in check, but not Helen. With tears in her eyes, after a second glass of beer, she expressed how wonderful it was to have all of them there and how proud that son of a bitch, Larry Sr., would have been to see what fine human beings they all had become. "Except for Mac," she smiled. "He would have been plenty skeptical of Mac."

The joke killed. With that, she took her leave, but not before getting hugs and kisses from the whole group, even Mac. Ashley and her cousins walked their tipsy grandma into the house and helped her get settled.

When Ashley came out, Larry stood by the back door, syncing his phone to his Bluetooth speaker, "How's Grandma?"

"Besides being hilarious, she's fine. I never knew she was so funny."

"Yeah, she has a few sips of beer and becomes a giant cutup. I half expect her to come back out with a lampshade on her head. Where's your cousins?"

"On their phones."

"We're going to have a fire. Feel like staying?"

"Nah. School's starting next week, and I'm still anxious about my classroom. I'm going in early tomorrow to work on some things."

They walked behind the garage, where everyone was getting set up with chairs, coolers, snacks, and small side tables. As Burbs worked to get the fire going, Ashley said good night and gave hugs all around. Everyone offered encouragement and little snippets of advice regarding her new job. Larry then walked her out to her car and, along the way, asked if she needed help with anything. She was good on all fronts. Larry smiled and said to let him know if anything cropped up and thanked her for coming. He then reached in for a hug. When he was about to release her, she held on for a moment. When she let go, she looked at him and said, "I'm sorry."

Larry smiled, "I'm sorry too. I'll try not to be such a know-it-all."

She got in her car, and they exchanged smiles before she pulled away.

Back in the yard, the fire was percolating, and Larry's "Save Me" playlist, which included an eclectic mix of sweet-tempered tunes by Nick Lowe, Philip Glass, St. Vincent, and others, filled the air.

Before long, Matt, of all people, pulled out a vape pen. He explained that sometimes he had trouble relaxing after a long day of *capitalistic domination* and found relief in a couple of nips on the pen. He gave the unschooled group a little in-service on the operation of the device, and what it was they would be taking into their bodies—liquid THC without the smoke or smell. Larry, along with everyone else, took a pull or two and was soon feeling quite fine.

In the course of the conversation, Matt, who had made the quick trip to Buffalo without his wife or kids, giggled about a long-forgotten nickname Larry Sr. gave him while doing a side job.

"Larry was like sixteen, and I was maybe ten. I was pretty useless except for handing off a hammer or taking out some garbage, but the old man was grooming me. Sometimes, I would have to stand around trying not to get yelled at when stuff went wrong."

"You yelled at? That was me," Larry interjected.

"For sure, but I got my share too. Anyway, we're at this dirty rundown house, and our dad is updating some wiring, and there's nothing for me to do. I wander into one of the rooms and there's all these *Playboy* magazines. I start to look at them, and the old man walks in and catches me in a compromised state of growth. From then on, whenever I screwed something up, or he got mad at me, he'd call me *Boner*."

"That's right, I forgot about that," Larry said. "Well deserved—Boner, ya little creeper." He was about to say something else, but Nora cut him off. "

"Him a creeper? What about 1977—the year of a thousand crusty socks? It was the only time our mom was ever worried about Larry."

"That wasn't my fault. That was Ms. Webb, our algebra teacher's fault. She was a year out of college and would prance around in these tight pants and these short little dresses, trying to make algebra fun. And, as my fourteen-year-old self and my crusty socks would tell you—she succeeded. Linear equations were never so fun."

"Yeah," Burbs said. "We all spent the year actively adding up the sum of Ms. Webb's hypotenuse."

"I'll say," Mac added. "Excuse me, I have to use the restroom. Hey Plumb, where do you keep your socks?"

They all laughed as the music spun into a familiar melody nobody could quite place except Larry. That was one of the things he always liked about the THC/pot buzz—music. How crisply it filled his ears.

"What is this?" Lucy asked.

"It's—it's 'You Are the Sunshine of My Life,' but that is not Stevie Wonder," Nora answered. "Who, Larry?"

"Guesses anyone?" When no one responded, Larry gave it up—Jim Nabors."

"Gomer Fucking Pyle?" Mac said incredulously.

"Yes," Larry laughed.

"This is hilarious," Lucy said. Burbs sat beside her, and she stood up and grabbed his hand. They started moving their feet to the zippy flute-inflected song as everyone giggled.

It was a great fun time.

But as the song concluded, it was interrupted by the buzzing of two text messages. Larry looked. "Maureen."

Burbs asked how she was doing. Larry explained that they had met earlier that day, and she looked great and was taking a new job. He gave the rundown on the new coordinator position and, after some consideration, mentioned that he had told them about her desire to see other people.

Unintentionally, he had let all the air out of the buoyant gathering. He apologized and tried to reinflate it by saying he was happy for her—that she had been sleepwalking through life for years and now had a new purpose and was reinvigorated, just without him. He said staying together would only make both of them miserable. Everyone expressed their regrets, but with Larry's toughness, he smiled. "I'll be fine. Lots of life left to live. Now let's play some more Jim Nabors tunes."

On that note, the little party regained some of its buoyancy. When the gathering broke down later, there were hugs and genuine acknowledgments of how great it was to see each other. Lucy hung behind, talking to Nora and Matt for a bit. When Larry walked her to her car, she squeezed him and said, "I should take you home and have my way with you, but you know better than anybody. I only fuck assholes, so there's no chance for that. I love you, Larry Plumb. You're the best."

Larry had the urge to laugh and cry as Lucy pulled away.

Twenty One

L arry had a tumultuous night of sleep. Instead of his old standby dream of hacking on a cigarette, on this night, he was sitting in a splashy office, being assailed by two young men in slim suits with perfectly manicured hair and skinny ties. It was a little murky, but the point of inquiry revolved around his novel, Shadow Love.

The slim-suited dudes were complaining about the lack of dragons and vampires in the story, along with the absence of any gentle boy-on-boy relationships between a white suburban kid with overprotective parents and a Black kid from the inner city with ADHD.

These slight dudes appreciated his efforts but made it clear that no one wanted or needed a story about a blue-collar guy trying to find love and meaning in an angry, unforgiving world, especially a white, blue-collar guy. They said there might be interest if this blue-collar guy went vigilante and started shooting up a bunch of shit, but in its present form, it had no market.

Though he was roundly dismissed in the dream, Larry didn't feel rejected. In fact, he felt smug and superior, knowing unequivocally *Shadow Love* was as valid and vital as any dragon or vampire fantasy. As the meeting concluded, he got up from his chair, stood over his slight inquisitors like a forged-by-time monolith, and said, "Those ties—you can't be serious?"

Then his eyes popped open.

It was the first time in a long time he had woken up with a smile on his face, sort of laughing to himself. Last night's barbecue denied Larry the opportunity to sort through his conversation with Maureen and given the light feeling he woke up with this morning, he decided to ignore that mess a little longer. Instead, he quietly went through his morning core routine in his room, got some coffee, sat at the kitchen table, and opened his laptop.

As his novel unfolded, he found something weird and wonderful about Rowena and decided it was time for Gus to end it with Eileen:

"But she just sits there with those dead, uncomprehending eyes," Eileen said incredulously.

"She comprehends plenty."

"Does she get you as hot as I do?" Eileen asked and then sidled up to him in the small dingy room and kissed him on the neck, attempting to undo his jeans with her hands.

Gus slipped away from her and sat at the little round motel room table. "You don't want me, Eileen. You want danger. Why don't you take a run at Tony Jr.? All kinds of danger there."

"Don't be ridiculous, Tony Jr.'s a joke."

"He's going to have the business soon, and you know there's nothing to his marriage. Maybe you could get a piece of that."

"But I love you."

"You don't love me. You love the excitement and the possibility of scandal."

"So you'll understand when I rat you out to Rowena, won't you, darling."

"That's your prerogative. I did what I did, and I'll live with the consequences."

"I can't believe you really want this. She can't be as fun as me."

"You do make everything hot and sweaty, but Rowena is weird and wonderful—different. She dwells in the shadows outside all the heat and glare. And we both know I'm a shadow guy, too.

It was a productive morning of work interrupted by having to take Matt to the airport for his flight back to Indianapolis. Nora and the kids were driving back to Albany as well. The visit provided a good restorative connection for the Plumb siblings and Helen. At the airport, he hugged Matt and said, "Dad would be really proud." Matt tapped him on the shoulder, nodded, and smiled. Nora, however, having been told those same words back at the house by Larry as they stood with their mom at the end of the driveway, generously responded, "We are as much you as we are him. Thank you for everything, Larry. You hang in there."

"Amen," Helen added.

After they waved goodbye, Larry grabbed his mom's hand and walked her into the house. Like last night and earlier that morning, the opportunity to contemplate the eventful last eighteen hours slipped away as he was due at St. Ignatius at 9 a.m.

Today, he would not be there in the capacity of a plumber or maintenance man but as an ambassador. The summer at St. Ignatius saw reduced programming—reading, math, and health camps on weekday mornings, but the complete after-school program would begin Tuesday, with the start of the new year. There would be an open house in the morning, and Dr. Johnson asked Larry to come in with other staff to greet people and showcase some of the upgrades he had made with Makayla and the rotating cast of St. Ignatius students.

On the ride there, Larry's mind drifted to his meeting with Maureen the previous evening at the Wash-O-Matic. Strangely, rather than feeling the weight of what had occurred, he felt light, airy—unburdened. Their marriage had probably been coming apart a stitch at a time for years, and he had been living with its possible dissolution in an acute way since last Christmas when Maureen revealed to Larry, she had been unfaithful. And now, this Saturday morning, could all these light, uncluttered feelings and the absence of angst and uncertainty suddenly mean it was really over? Could it all have dropped away like a leaf abruptly swept from its branch one fall day?

Larry remembered the last time he found himself in too deep with a girl and was destroyed when she dumped him. It was sophomore year of high school, and Mary Licata was the cute, well-to-do Math League president at North Senior. She was ambitious and energetic and drove Larry and his classmates crazy with the way she poured herself into her Levi's. Navigating school hallways with an adorable pixie haircut and those painted-on jeans, she drew you in like a tractor beam in a sci-fi novel. And it wasn't just Larry and his classmates; it was the upperclassmen as well. A month after being the first girl to tell him she loved him, she got a better offer from the Senior Class President, Tim Miller, and dumped him.

He wasn't as pathetic as Mac when Katie Auerbach put him out with the morning trash—he learned from his friend's mistakes and primarily suffered in silence. The pain was intense for weeks, but suddenly, one day, for no particular reason, it was gone, and she just dropped from his mind. Larry had been preparing for life without Maureen for some time, but could the turnaround happen this swiftly? He didn't have the luxury to sort it out before arriving at St. Ignatius, but he would receive the answer that morning.

***

Instead of his usual work clothes and boots, Larry wore a snug-fitting black golf shirt, khaki pants, and lightweight black mesh summer shoes. With his black-rimmed glasses and close-cropped graying hair, he looked like an advertisement for some super vitamin.

Dr. Johnson greeted him at the school's entrance. The aviators from her Facebook post were sitting atop her shiny, black hair, and with a broad smile, she said, "You clean up nice, Larry."

Like earlier that morning, when he woke from his dream, he smiled and laughed to himself. "Thank you," was all he could say in response, having learned not to comment on a woman's appearance. At a different time, he would have returned the compliment because not only did she exude a benevolent kind of strength, which he found so attractive, but she was tall and lean and goddamn fabulous in a blouseless copper-colored three-piece suit.

The open house was largely a success despite not being well attended. Larry stood with Makayla at his side and showed parents and grandparents some upgrades they had made throughout the building. Safety and security were a top priority with the proliferation of gun violence occurring at schools, so they made sure to also highlight the newly installed security system.

In a quiet moment in The Pit, the open area in the basement where the preschoolers played, Makayla asked Larry, "Did you say something funny to Dr. Johnson again? Because she keeps looking over here and smiling."

Larry hadn't really noticed, but when he gazed across to The Pit, she was throwing a smile in his direction. Larry smiled back reflexively and said, "Yes, I told her the old one about how a screwdriver was great for mental health because, wait for it— because it knew how to turn things around."

"That is so lame, Mr. Larry. I'm not even going to give you a fake lol," she said.

But Larry and Dr. Johnson kept catching each other's eye for the rest of the morning. After hiding out in the boiler room pretending to look at the return stacks he and the kids had replaced months ago, Larry gathered his courage and walked in a deliberate manner from the basement through the school, which was now all but empty, toward Dr. Johnson's office.

He stood outside her open door and took her in momentarily as she sat at her desk looking over some papers. In the growing heat, she had removed her suit jacket, revealing the contours of her long, fit, bronzed arms, which flowed from her summery vest and shoulders like the sinewy filament that held the universe together. She was striking.

He knocked on the door but didn't wait for her permission to enter. Instead, he walked toward her desk and said, "Sorry for the interruption, Juanita, but do you have a second to talk?"

Immersed in the papers on her desk, it took her a moment to detach and say, "Of course, Larry. What is it?"

A bit overwhelmed, Larry felt his face grow warm. He paused, drew in a breath, and then said, "It's been a long time since I did this—since I asked anybody, but when you're done here, would you like to get a cup of coffee with me?"

"Yes," she said instantly, and a slight grin came to her lips. "That would be lovely."

They met at a café Juanita suggested on Hertel Avenue called Mocha Joe's. Larry arrived first, sat near the front door, and looked out a bay window decorated in a flowery summer theme.

Taking in the wonderful smells of the baked goods, he sat like a nervous schoolboy, wondering if this was really happening. The sparse patrons were spread out and plugged in around the room's perimeter. With bent heads, they stared at screens beside walls covered with an eclectic mix of for-sale paintings by local artists as they sipped their cold brews and iced coffees. When the no-nonsense guy in a linen skullcap and baking apron addressed Larry from a boxed-off three-sided counter in the center of the room with a—*Can I help you?*—kind of expression, Larry nodded and said, "I'm waiting for a friend."

Dr. Johnson was a few minutes behind him. When she entered the front door, she was still without her suit jacket, and the aviators were covering her eyes, "Sorry, I had a call. Did you order?"

Taking her in, Larry was a little overwhelmed by her sublime presence, "No, I was—I was waiting on you."

She walked up to the counter, pushing the aviators to the top of her head, and the no-nonsense guy lit up. "Well, if it isn't Dr. J." His bright face turned toward Larry. "And I don't mean Julius Erving."

Juanita laughed. "Larry this is MJ, and I don't mean Michael Jordan. He's the other not-so-tall but just-as-accomplished MJ—Mocha Joe. How've you been, Joe?"

"Getting by. You know summer's a little slow, but pumpkin spice season is just around the corner—cha-ching. Ready for another school year?"

"I'm all over it."

After these pleasantries, Larry and Juanita bucked the bourgeois cold brew, iced coffee trend—he ordered a medium half-caf, and Juanita got a large black coffee. Despite the carbs, Juanita did talk Larry into sharing a couple of MJ's famous scones saying, "They are to die for..."

They went to the farthest corner of the café and sat at a small table facing each other. On the wall next to them was a medium-sized abstract painting called Perplexity— which employed long bending lines and generous knife strokes of red, brown, and green acrylic paint over a cloudy flesh-colored base. Though he didn't quite know why, Larry liked the modestly priced two-hundred-dollar painting. Nodding at it, he asked Juanita, "What do you think?"

She scrunched up her nose and shook her head in the negative. "It's all anarchy and no resolution."

"Do you have something against anarchy?"

"No, but it doesn't go anywhere—it's one-dimensional. I like a little whimsy and tangible shapes in my abstract art. Work off a circle or a cube rather than random lines with no destination or purpose."

"Doesn't go anywhere? I see those random lines as vectors searching for agency." Pointing to a cluster of interlacing lines, he said, "And look, aren't these coalescing into something? Perhaps those lines could be viewed as students gaining strength and knowledge so one day they can transform into highly functional hexagons and trapezoids that contribute to society."

"Now that's some whimsy. You're so cute, Larry Plumb," she said, smiling

"Cute as in smart or are you objectifying me, Juanita?"

"Both. But mostly objectifying you in your little shirt and shoes."

They lingered a moment, examining each other's faces, and then dug into the scones that came with little bowls of frosting and jam. Juanita judiciously broke apart the flaky baked good with a small butter knife and spread a pinch of jam on it. With her fork, she put it in her mouth, then closed her eyes as if tasting something otherworldly. "Oh my, this is heaven."

After devouring half of a scone, Larry passed on both spreads but joked, "You're right; these are to die for. Now take them away before they kill me."

"Interesting. Are you a binge eater?"

"That's a little personal?" he said, smiling

"Perhaps. But I'm not one for a lot of perfunctory conversation, Larry Plumb. I get to the point. Furthermore, how someone negotiates baked goods says a lot about them," she added with a broad grin.

"It's self-knowledge. If you plopped a half-gallon of milk down in front of me, I could destroy every display case in this joint. So, it's easier just not to go there than to stop. So the answer to your question is a qualified—yes. And you?"

"I stop. I'm one of those people who eat small portions every couple of hours."

"My wife eats like that, and having this binge thing, I always finish—" Larry could feel his face flush with embarrassment at his mistake. "Sorry."

"Well, that came up faster than I was expecting, but there's no need to be sorry," she said generously. Then, she set her fork down, casually brought her hands to the table's edge, and locked her fingers together. With a merciful twinkle in her eyes, she said, "Listen Larry, I don't know if you call it intuition, experience, knowing people, or whatever, but if you're the person I think you are, I'm pretty sure you wouldn't have asked me here unless you were ready and I wouldn't have agreed to come unless I thought you were ready. So, relax—I know you've been through a lot these last months. I also know from almost the moment we met there's been something easy, something nice between us. Let's just enjoy each other and see what happens."

Larry's whole body tingled as he stared into her wise face. He reached across the table, covered her hands with his, and said, "Thank you." His touch caused her to let out a little gasp. Worried he had crossed some line, he said, "I'm sorry. Was that too much?"

"No no, you're fine," she said. "Do you want to discuss it, or is this too soon?"

He scanned her face, and whatever had happened when he touched her hands seemed to pass, leaving him confident that anything he said would be met with insight and compassion. "Maureen and I talked yesterday afternoon. She told me she was open to seeing other people. It didn't come as a surprise, but I haven't had much time to think about it with my brother and sister in town and the open house. But I did wake up feeling light and unburdened this morning. It's been a long time since I got dumped, but the last time it happened—Mary Licata, 1978—I remember the pain and hurt just sort of dropped away one day without warning. That's the way this feels."

"Yes, I know that feeling well."

"Really? What fool would dump you?" Larry smiled.

"Not fool—fools, wanting more than I could give."

"Ah, opposite for me. According to my wife, I gave so much it paralyzed her. The general consensus in the family is that I have an insatiable need to control everything. I suppose there's some truth to that, but I never considered it a compulsion. I thought I was just getting stuff done—taking care of business. But she kind of, as it were, got lost in my quality control and now is trying to reestablish herself and regain her identity. Independence was always a big part of that identity, and I respect her effort to evolve, even if it doesn't include me."

"I'm sorry, Larry."

"Thank you, but no need to be sorry. These things happen. Since my dad passed, I've sort of lived by a philosophy of impermanence, nothing lasts forever. Can we talk about something else?"

They decided to continue with an art-themed date by driving together in Juanita's hybrid Honda SUV to the Burchfield Penney Arts Center on the campus of Buffalo State College.

The gallery focused on the twentieth-century watercolor painter Charles Burchfield, with whom Larry had some familiarity. Burchfield was from Ohio but spent his working life in Buffalo and lived in West Seneca until he passed in 1967. The town built a small arts center with an amphitheater and nature trail in his honor. It was funded with taxpayer dollars, and in the last year or so, town engineers discovered that the building was imploding due to faulty construction.

"Of course," Larry said, "when town money is involved, you go with the lowest bid, and this contractor put a load-bearing wall into a concrete channel where water pooled. The exposure caused support beams to rot, and the building is sagging."

"Those must have been fun town meetings."

"Hilarious. Suburbanites get crazy when tax dollars get spent on nonessential things like art and libraries, and if there are cost overruns or the building goes bad—lookout."

However, the Burchfield Penney Arts Center at the college was a proper gallery that housed the most extensive collection of Burchfield paintings, drawings, and notes in the world, along with other exhibits. They both liked Burchfield's style and sentiment but noted that he went from being a pragmatist early on to more of a transcendentalist in later life. Juanita supposed that when a working artist was starting out, they didn't have the luxury of being too out there since they had to keep food on the table. Only later, when they're established, could they test the limits of their imaginations. Larry agreed with this reasonable hypothesis.

After leaving the gallery, they took a leisurely stroll around the campus and ended up outside Ketchum Hall. They discovered they both had been at the 1986 REM concert in the grassy area between Ketchum and Bacon Hall. Juanita was a City Honors High School sophomore, and Larry was already five years in with the town. She went to the show with a group of school friends. One of them was this boy from South Buffalo whom she had made out with a few times.

"His name was Donny Latini. He had this sweet Ralph Macchio kind of face."

"The *Karate Kid*, Ralph Macchio?"

"Yes," she said. "We kissed right here on these steps."

"These steps?" Larry said, sitting down. "Back in the day, I took American Novel 1945-2000 in Ketchum."

She sat down next to him so their knees and shoulders touched. She moved the aviators to the top of her head and turned to face him. "How'd you do in the class?"

"All right. I liked the Philip Roth stuff but was less enthused with Thomas Pynchon. I was working a ton of hours and was exhausted all the time." He stared into her dark eyes for a long moment and then put his hand on her knee and felt a little flutter move through her body. Still looking at her, he moved in, and when she didn't stop him, he whispered, "Did that Ralph Macchio kid kiss you like this?"

When they separated, Juanita smiled and said, "I'm not quite getting the Macchio effect. Why don't you try that again."

A moment later, while they were still kissing, a couple of surprised students walked by, and their faces took on a distinct—*gross, old people kissing*—expression. Larry and Juanita laughed, and she said, "Let's get out of here."

They stood up, and Larry offered her his arm, which she accepted. They walked gingerly to Juanita's SUV, giggling the whole way.

Once seated in the car, they looked at each other and kissed again. Beaming, Juanita said, "Larry, besides your little shirt and shoes making me crazy, I'm feeling really close to you. Normally, I'm not this forward, but we're already pretty well acquainted and I think I want to continue this into the night. Are you good with that?"

"I think I am, but I'm not sure what you're asking."

"I'm wondering if you'd like to have dinner on the rooftop of the Curtiss Hotel and gaze up at the stars with me. I'm told they have a bank of telescopes up there."

***

As the day turned to evening, they ate a beautiful dinner of grilled salmon, sugar snap peas, and roasted potatoes at the Curtiss. Between the long looks and smiles, reality briefly reared its head when Juanita mentioned she recently received a laundry list of violations from a new building inspector, with whom she hadn't been able to make a human connection, which worried her. Larry offered to help, but she quickly pivoted away from the topic, saying she appreciated his offer, but they were "bigger ticket items."

Instead of St. Ignatius's talk, they shared anecdotes about their dearly departed, larger-than-life fathers. Both were uneven—Juanita's dad had an explosive temper—but both had a huge influence on their lives and left behind women who still adored and loathed them many years after they had been gone.

The night remained perfect and clear. The one sour note that stuck in Larry's craw was the music in the bar area. Having a drink after they were done eating, Larry complained, "They have this great upscale dining experience and this beautiful atmosphere, and the best they can do with the tunes is "Legs" by ZZ Top?" A moment later, as if a giant deejay in the sky heard Larry's complaint, Al Green's "Let's Stay Together" began to circulate through the dusky summer night. Juanita grabbed him by the elbow, and they began to move to the tune in time. Soon, they were lost in each other's eyes, and before the song was over, Juanita whispered, "Let's get out of here."

In the half-full elevator, wild with anticipation, Larry stealthily put his hand on Juanita's ass, causing her to let out a small cry as they descended to their sixth-floor room. No one seemed to notice her quivering little shriek, but when Larry looked into her eyes, he could see she was melting with his touch.

Once in the room, she tore off Larry's shirt and kissed him breathlessly. With their mouths locked together, she wrapped her arms and legs around him, and he carried her to the bed. After laying her down, he greedily undid her vest, removed her pants and panties, and kissed her body all over. He felt her thunder beneath his kisses and his probing hands. In that swirling ten-alarm heat, she soon was imploring him.

But standing over her, ready to immerse himself, he quite suddenly had the urge to pause and take in the moment, to burn it into his memory banks forever. He didn't understand why this urge came to him, and he certainly wasn't going to untangle it now, but somehow he knew it was an acknowledgment of how sweet life could be and how blessed he was to be here with this extraordinary woman.

Having been granted this moment of grace, Larry smiled and cheerfully entered her.

Twenty Two

Prior to heading to the Curtiss, Larry had suggested they stop at a dollar store for supplies—bottles of water, toothbrushes, a phone charger, and snacky protein bars. They also bought some Fruit of the Loom tees and undies, and Juanita picked out a summery dress with a floral print for nine dollars, plus a bag to carry it all in. Juanita joked about his forethought, asking him if he wasn't some secret Don Juan?

But sitting at the hotel room table at the end of the bed, watching her sleep at 5:39am, he didn't feel like some Don Juan. Instead, as he pretended to work on his novel, *Shadow Love*, by way of his phone, he was overwhelmed with contrasting emotions—from a giddy infatuation to a serene peacefulness. With Juanita sleeping just feet from him in the dark room, he nevertheless felt the light of the world shining on him.

At the moment the only plausible explanation he could come up with for being in that room with Juanita was divine intervention. Of course, the idea of divine intervention was ridiculous, but what else could it be? —*Thank you, God*, he said to himself as he sat there elated. In this state of euphoria, he had the urge to call Mac and Burbs to tell them where he was and how he had bested the Katie Auerbach and Mary Licata paradigm a hundredfold. His musing, however, was interrupted when Juanita started to stir, moving her hand around the bed searching for him.

"I'm right here."

She leaned up on her elbow and smiled at him, "Good morning," she said in a dreamy voice. "What are you doing?"

"Morning. I'm pretending to work on my novel, but I'm really just sitting here watching you sleep, feeling unbelievably grateful."

She climbed out of bed fully naked and, without a hint of self-consciousness, headed toward the bathroom, stopping along the way to kiss

Larry on the head. After brushing her teeth and completing her morning ablutions, she came out of the bathroom, still in that state of undress. She hit the dimmer switch on the room light and searched the dollar store bag for a bottle of water. After taking a few sips, she went to the end of the bed where Larry was sitting, bent over and kissed him fully on the mouth, "Come lie with me and take off those silly clothes. Did you go somewhere already?"

"Down to the lobby for coffee. Do you want some? It's a bit cold, but there's a microwave.

"Nah, water's fine for now," she said, pulling back the light sheets and lying down. "C'mon Larry Plumb, take those clothes off and get in here."

Larry did as instructed but paused before climbing into bed, "My God, you're beautiful. Can I just stand here for a moment and look at you?"

"Sure. I like the way you look at me, Larry. I have for months.

"Was it that noticeable?"

"Respectfully noticeable."

"What does that mean?" he asked, sitting on the bed's edge.

"Well, not to go off like some preening peacock, but I get a fair amount of attention from men. Some are forward, some are weird, some are offensive, and some, like you, are respectful. I get that men have this involuntary need to look and assess, but committed guys like you are the least threatening."

"Do you feel objectified?"

"All the time, but not by you. You showed up the last half of the year and were serious about the work and kids. It was obvious you were on board with the mission and didn't have ulterior motives. But, on occasion I did notice you glancing over at me—respectfully glancing over at me, which was nice. Ministering to the flock gets a little lonely, and to have the eye of a guy like you was nice."

She was on her side now, up on her elbow, resting her head in her hand, and Larry responded, "Well, the larger world and some people in my life might push back against that assessment."

"Yes, women are finally receiving some long overdue respect and maybe there's a bit of a power shift with the male power brokers—especially the Caucasian power brokers. No offense."

"No offense taken."

"But you're hardly the guy women are pushing back against. If anything, you have what I would call heroic masculinity: emotionally mature, non-threatening, helpful. Do you think any of what happened between us yesterday and last night would have occurred if I didn't feel safe with you as a man? Review how it all played out. After you asked me to coffee, I picked the place, we drove in my car, and then I propositioned and pretty much seduced you. I was in charge all day. On top of that, you were sweet, and we had deep, stimulating conversation. You're not the problem, Larry."

"Thank you, that means a lot. And, for the record, I'm ready for you to seduce me again."

"In time, sir. In time."

"Smiling, he said, "Yeah, my daughters, since their middle college years and more acutely with the "Resistance" and "MeToo" movements, seem to want to police and correct every utterance I make. It's very frustrating."

"C'mon, you get in here next to me." Larry did as he was told. While facing each other, she kissed him and gently caressed his head. "Obviously, I can't and won't speak to your family relationships, but do you remember that morning with Hank Tomasi?"

"When I was a racist asshole to you?"

"Yes, that morning."

"Not my finest hour. But sure, I remember."

"On the contrary. You made a mistake and owned it. That was very impressive, given the power dynamics of gender and race between us. Most people would have become defensive or doubled down, but you owned it and apologized. Often, it's not the mistake; it's the response to the mistake that's important. In my book, the way you responded revealed a highly evolved man. And I'm not saying that because you're cute," she said, grinning.

"Again, thank you. But you must stop before Larry gets a swollen sense of himself and starts referring to himself in the third person."

"Okay, but while we're here, let me just say, you know what I find most sexy about you, besides how you looked yesterday in your little shirt and shoes—your competence. When I read your profile in the Buffalo News, I could hardly believe a person like you existed. The way you navigated your loss, your sacrifice, and your rise to Commissioner. To someone like me, trying against the odds to keep St. Ignatius going, you're an inspiration. And then you showed up that day to help Ashley, and you read that story to the kids so beautifully—I was totally smitten."

"Stop. Call Ashley. I need her to hear this."

"Ha. I won't be calling Ashley. But when I was brushing my teeth, I was laughing to myself and wanted to call some of my boos and tell them I was with Professor Strong Hands."

"What?"

"That's what I call you, Professor Strong Hands. Not only do those big mitts seem to have a sixth sense about touching a lady, but they are sexy as hell—almost as sexy as your competence. I don't quite understand why, but how you carry a toolbox, take your glasses off, and cut that scone with your fork—Lord have mercy! Every time you touched me: at Mocha Joe's, on the Ketchum steps, in the elevator, especially the elevator, I nearly lost it."

"Well, that's a first," he said, reaching across her body and placing his hand on her ass.

"I thought maybe they'd be more grizzled, but they're the right mix of tender and tough. And even now, Larry Plumb, that hand on my butt has me churning."

He moved in and kissed her. Her hand drifted downward as they kissed, and she started manipulating him. When they stopped to take a breath, smiling, Larry said, "You're pretty good with your hands too. But before you have your way with me, I want to complain about something and a couple of things I want to come clean about in the spirit of full disclosure."

"Okay," she whispered.

"First, you lied about the telescopes on the rooftop."

"Guilty as charged, but I think we saw stars anyway."

He laughed and said, "Second, when I was watching you sleep, I had the urge to call my buddies—Mac and Burbs. I was going to brag about destroying the Katie Auerbach, Mary Licata paradigm a hundredfold. Like you, those were high school girls who were too good for us."

"It's sweet you don't know what a babe you are, Larry Plumb."

"Maybe you won't think I'm such a babe after this next thing."

"Oh no, what did you do—not help an old lady cross the street, leave a cat stranded in a tree?"

"You're funny. No, after that first Saturday when I was a racist asshole, I stalked your social media."

"And what, it's making you feel like some kind of deceitful ne'er do-well?"

"Deceitful ne'er do-well? Given the current state of our churning, it's very impressive you're still turning out those snappy phrases."

"Higher education will do that, but whatever you're going to tell me, you better do it fast because, if I'm not mistaken, our churn is accelerating."

"Okay. After looking at your social media, I had to take many unplanned showers. You talk about my hands, but those pictures of you and your boos on the four-wheelers in bikinis and those aviators—you were like some rebel strike force about to do a raid. If I still believed in all that afterlife stuff, most of my sentence in purgatory would come from the way I defiled myself after looking at you in those aviators."

Juanita abruptly stopped what she was doing, threw off the sheets, and jumped out of bed. With her back to him, she bounced over to the room's desk and searched her purse. A moment later, she turned around, and with the glasses covering her eyes, she said, "You mean these aviators?"

"Oh my lord—"

She strutted to the end of the bed and stood at attention, all soldier-like, surveying Larry. Then, she got up on the bed and crawled on all fours and, like a predator closing in on its prey until she was hovering above him and in a fake Rastafarian voice, she said, "You are my prisoner mon, and now I must break you."

With her eyes shaded by the aviators, she climbed up on Larry, her bronzed arms and shoulders rippling. He gently latched his hands onto her hips, causing her to shriek. She now had him right where she wanted him and began to twitch and writhe back and forth, back and forth, and in no time, the prisoner was gloriously broken.

***

Juanita stayed in the shower a few minutes longer than Larry, and when she came into the room, still drying herself off, she found him in a pair of her new Fruit of the Looms. The garment was incapable of holding all of him in and was climbing up his ass, "A little tight, and I'll have to get used to this butt thing, but I think they work. Whaddya think?"

She doubled over with laughter and then went over to him and slipped her bra straps over his arms and shoulders. His meaty chest prevented the clasps in the back from being secured, but he still pranced around the room, striking poses like a runway model before Juanita grabbed him by the hand and giggled while she kissed him, "You'd be such a pretty girl, Larry Plumb." She paused momentarily, her face beaming, and said, "This was wonderful. All of it. Thank you."

"You know how people say *my pleasure* after being thanked, and it's just a thing they say? Well, this time, it's really true. *My pleasure—entirely my pleasure*. And thank you."

After they dressed properly—Larry in a fresh white tee and Juanita in her dollar-store dress—they decided to get breakfast in the first-floor dining room. It was a given they wanted to see each other beyond today, so over eggs and coffee, they were going to discuss how to proceed.

"We're one day into this and already having a conversation about the state of our relationship. I'm willing to put myself out there—I really, *really* like you," Larry joked.

"I really like you too, but we probably need to set some ground rules and expectations for this to work."

"Wait a minute, teach; you said you really like me, and I said I really, really like you—that's two to one. Already, there's an imbalance between us."

She smiled, and then a serious expression came to her face. "How about we talk here for a minute before we eat?" She took his hand and walked him to the little hotel room table. After sitting down, she pushed the information binder on the table to the side in an orderly fashion. She took a deep breath and, with a concerned expression, said, "Listen, Larry, what happened with us yesterday and last night was pretty weird for me. I was very forward with you, but I'm normally the boring workaholic type. I go to the gym, take an occasional vacation, and care for my mom, but mostly, I work. This thing with you last night was cosmic."

"If I could interject for a moment—it was cosmic this morning too."

"Larry Plumb," she giggled, "you're so funny." With the lightness returning to her face, and she continued, "Yes, it was cosmic this morning, too. In fact, it was so cosmic, morning and night and we seem to be such an easy fit that I'm already a little scared. This is weird, but I think we need to slow down a bit. My obligations to my mom, friends, and the gym are manageable and not an issue. What is a big issue is the school and those kids. They are the driving force in my life, consuming most of my bandwidth. I have to be on my game for them, and maybe I'm being a little alarmist, but this cosmic connection we already seem to have scares me."

"Ah, message received. But do you mean slow down or stop?"

"I don't want to stop. I'm just worried this will go too fast, it'll get too hot, and all of a sudden, we'll be in love and have all the complications that come with that.

"Okay, so keep it cosmic, but a slow, simple cosmic, with some space."

"Perfect." She smiled, and reached across the table, taking Larry's hand in hers. "I can't be some moony-eyed schoolgirl dreaming about you in your little black shirt and shoes and how you look at me—I have minds to mold and a building to keep up."

"I promise, despite really *really* liking you, I will do my best not to fall in love with you. But Juanita, if I'm reading how you're looking at me and holding my hand, it's already a little late for you."

She smiled and leaned in for a kiss, "Larry Plumb, you are a delight—and you might just be right."

***

The brightly lit Curtiss dining room was buzzing with activity. The hostess walked them to a small table with dual settings, a summery vase with fresh-cut flowers, and a crisp white linen tablecloth. Before even receiving their coffee, they discussed texting protocols. Both of them said they typically replied quickly and efficiently. Still, Jaunita cautioned that sometimes she was delayed due to circumstances beyond her control, and he shouldn't read anything into it.

"I take it there've been problems."

"You have no idea how insecure some people can be, and by people—I mean men."

"Hey—easy. In defense of my gender, let me say I'm here with you now, which I still can't believe, but I know the second I'm not, I'm going to be dying to hear from you."

"You better toughen up," she said, smiling.

While sipping coffee, they decided to define the agreed-upon *simple cosmic pace with some distance* to mean seeing each other twice a week—Wednesdays and Saturdays as long as work didn't get in the way. The Wednesday night thing could be dinner out or at her place since Larry was still at his mom's—but not a sleepover. Saturdays could be extended destination dates to specific places. Since Juanita had more or less been in charge of what they had done the previous day, she asked Larry if he wanted to choose something for next week. On the spot, Larry came up with the idea of Niagara Falls, saying the last time he was there was when his kids were small, but he knew there were plenty of adult things to do—music, Shakespeare, dining, and shopping.

"I must warn you that if you're a shopper, I'll soft abandon you," he said with a playful shake of his head.

"What does that mean?"

"It means I'll head to the nearest bar and have a beer if you insist on thumbing through a thousand sweaters. My wife, sorry to bring her up, was never much of a shopper, but on occasion, I have been caught in that vortex of indecision."

"Interesting. What if I want your opinion about the way something looks?"

"That's different. I'd watch you model things all day long. But holding your purse while you go through racks—not happening. Judging from how fast you picked out that dress at the dollar store—a nine-dollar dress has no right to look that good on anyone, by the way—I'd bet you're an efficient shopper."

Nodding, she said, "You don't miss much."

"Since we've stumbled onto this, what's with the tracksuits? How many and why?"

"Maybe twenty and Einstein. Same for the suits I wear on school days, but only about ten."

"The Einstein thing where he had three or four of the same suits that he wore all the time, so he didn't have to think about clothes at all?"

"Yes."

"So twenty and ten are the same as Einstein's three or four?"

"Exactly."

"I'm not a math expert, but those numbers don't add up.

"It's the same thing."

"Twenty and ten aren't the same as three or four."

"Yes, they are—they're the same clothing with the added variable of color."

"Oh, that's the catch."

"You can't expect me to just go around in the same color every day. That would be so monotonous and boring. Sometimes, a woman such as myself needs to wear the imposing black power suit to work, and other times, when she wants to catch the eye of a strong-handed man, she wears the peach tracksuit."

When they were done eating, Larry asked about the Rastafarian voice after she had put on the aviators.

"First, you know I'm going to up my aviator game, and second, I thought about doing a Russian voice but didn't think I could pull it off, so I went with the Rasta. Was it good?"

"Yes, on both upping the aviator game and the Rasta voice. I'd hand over every state secret to be interrogated like that. You can take me as your prisoner right now," he said, reaching out his hands to be cuffed.

"In time, mon. In time."

"Can I ask you another sunglasses-related question?"

"If you want me to do some freaky Audrey Hepburn Breakfast at Tiffany's deal, *I could do that too, darling.*"

"Not what I was going to ask, but I will file that away. Nice Audrey Hepburn, by the way."

"*Thank you, darling.*"

"I was going to ask, and you can tell me it's none of my business, but I was pretty surprised by your social media. I wasn't expecting it to be so—so provocative."

"I'm fine talking about it. And yes, I hear some variation of it's provocative a lot—especially from my mom. What it really is, though, is complicated," she said, growing serious. "As a Black woman, I have to fight all these derogatory stereotypes, and since I'm a Black-educated woman with some power, it's even more acute. First, it's the matriarch thing, where I'm just supposed to be this caretaker type of person living my life to look after others. There's some truth to that since I am an educator. But I'm more than that. I want to inspire girls, Black women, and others to tune out all the noisy judgments and be themselves without limitation. I want to show people you don't have to conform to expectations and that you can express yourself any way you want, even as a PhD. who runs a school.

"But that's only part of it. Next, and these are the ones that totally piss me off, is the angry Black woman and Jezebel stereotypes. I know, ironic that I would be pissed off about the angry label. But, if I dare talk about gender or racial injustice, I get tagged as angry. White people tell me to be grateful for how far I've come, and I'm a prime example of how the system works. But it doesn't work for most people of color, and I should not be tagged with that label or dismissed for making that argument—it's nonsense. Then there's the Jezebel thing because I post some pictures that could be considered provocative. The truth, as I said, is I'm a workaholic. I will go on dates on rare occasions, but those are pretty transactional. Before yesterday, it had been a long time since I went on a date that meant anything to me."

"Really?" Larry asked.

"I wasn't kidding about the workaholic thing."

"I get that. My surprise is that—I—we—the first time in a long time, it meant something."

"Of course, silly. I don't put out like that for anybody, or do you see me as some kind of Jezebel?"

"Boy, I walked right into that, didn't I. No, I see you as a beautiful, strong, accomplished woman, and I'm fortunate to be here with you. But, if you wanted to be a Jezebel, that's your choice."

She smiled and, in a soft voice, said, "I mentioned it earlier, but sometimes it gets lonely tending to the flock, and it might be shallow, but the compliments and likes I get from those pictures give me a boost and remind me that I'm a strong, desirable woman. I go back and forth on whether the pics are worth all the aggravation."

Larry looked at her thoughtfully and said, "I can't speak to your situation, but my least favorite part of being Commissioner was dealing with people who felt entitled to comment on my life because they were paying my salary. It was always a balancing act. And the only good answer I ever came up with—which was little more than a Band-Aid for myself—was to tell whoever was passing judgment to 'go F themselves,' under my breath."

"Even the grandmas?" Juanita said with a laugh.

"Especially the grandmas—they were the worst."

***

The drive back to Mocha Joe's to pick up Larry's truck after checking out of the hotel was filled with heady compliments and superlatives about the last twenty-four hours and how they would manage their giddy feelings until they saw each other again on Wednesday. But when they pulled up behind Larry's truck, Juanita presented Larry with another issue he had yet to consider.

"You know I hear from Ashley occasionally via text, and I told her to call me at the beginning of the year to discuss how she was settling into her new job. Have you given any thought to how you're going to handle this with her?"

"No, not really. How about you tell her? She loves you."

"*Larry—*"

"Okay, let's give this a few weeks to make sure we're solid. Then I'll tell her and the rest of the family. Does that sound good?"

"Yes. That seems reasonable."

"Sooner rather than later," he said, nodding.

Larry leaned over from the passenger seat and gave her one last kiss.

Filled with lightheaded infatuation, he exited her SUV and floated to his truck. Once he opened the driver's side door, he turned back to wave and get one last look at her beaming face.

Then, he started counting the minutes until he saw her again on Wednesday.

Twenty Three

Larry quickly found out that Juanita wasn't kidding when she said she was a workaholic. Given the high level of student engagement in his Saturday morning program at St. Ignatius, she saw a full-blown opportunity for a mentorship program in the making. Larry was surprised with this assessment since Makayla seemed to be the only student who was all in week after week through the whole year. However, Juanita had gotten great feedback from students and parents and thought that with some structure and money, they could turn this into something very tangible and not limited to St. Ignatius.

So, after a modest dinner at Juanita's house off Hertel Avenue, they spent their Wednesday date night researching and crafting grant proposals. Of course, Larry was thrilled to spend time with Juanita in any capacity, but combining their different skill sets to create an educational program wasn't what he had in mind when they decided to continue seeing each other. Yet here they were estimating staffing needs and developing a curriculum.

She would always defer to Larry, saying they could watch a movie or go out for a drink, but building an education program from scratch was different from anything he had ever done, and he found the process fascinating. And, just as there was this nice, easy feeling between them when they met, they found working together effortless as well. Larry also began to toss around the idea that when his time with the town was up, something like this might be a viable retirement option since he didn't ever see himself wasting half the day by sleeping until 7 a.m. or playing endless rounds of golf.

Their decision to have the Wednesday night dates not conclude with a sleepover lasted precisely one week. Near the end of the night, Larry would whisper, "The action verbs in this paragraph are really *hot*." She would laugh, and they would kiss, and that kiss would lead to touching, and the touching would lead to more kissing, and the kissing would lead to her bed, where they gloried in each other's company and bodies.

After a month of being together, they determined that, save for the continuing Wednesday-night failure-nonfailure sleepovers, they had achieved their goal *to keep it cosmic, but a slow, simple, cosmic with some space*. There were no communication or texting mishaps, and they had a great time on destination dates at Niagara Falls, Angola on the Lake, and Letchworth State Park.

Besides keeping it cosmic, Larry decided at Letchworth this thing with Juanita wasn't just a fling, that it had all the makings of something more durable. He came to this conclusion, sitting on the porch swing at their rented cottage after a day of hiking. Scrutinizing the wooded expanse before them where the rustling leaves were turning red with the beginnings of autumn, Larry felt so peaceful as Juanita leaned back and rested her head on his shoulder. They cautiously sipped chilled Jack Fire from whiskey glasses when Larry had a musical epiphany—*The Seriously Get Laid Playlist*.

This playlist was made for Maureen back in the day in the hope of sparking some romance, but they only made it through about half of it once, and it didn't lead to anyone getting seriously laid. Larry loved the mix, explaining that he listened to it occasionally, and it always brought tears to his eyes. Given its origins he understood if Juanita wanted to pass on it. But she was intrigued not only by his enthusiasm but also his admission of vulnerability. However, prompted by Ellis & Branford Marsalis' ethereal instrumental of "Maria" from *West Side Story*, Juanita was emotional almost from the start.

In this quiet, beatified peace, tears slipped from her eyes during Chet Baker's "Almost Blue," Charles Mingus's, "Self Portrait in Three Colors," and Joni Mitchell's "Blue Motel Room." In fact, the beauty of the mix made her cry more than Larry, which was saying something. Holding her, he became aware of how happy he was and how Juanita checked all the missing boxes in his life. She was smart, engaging, and fun. She saw him for who he was without judgment, and he didn't have to tiptoe around every word he said with her. She never tried to compete or felt intimidated by Maureen, even when it came to the playlist, which revealed her maturity and sense of self. It was also liberating for Larry that he could be vulnerable with her and not fear petty taunts.

Yet, holding her, knowing how right she was for him, he was quite aware of the fragility of this relationship—that it was hanging together by a tiny thread. There were commitments made that were bigger than both of them, bigger than their easy compatibility, bigger than their connection and infatuation. It was sad but necessary to interrupt this lovely moment and remember the marker put down a month earlier when they started seeing each other—not to fall in love. So, as an act of self-preservation while holding her, he leaned into his old standby, laughing ironically to himself—*nothing lasts forever.*

In the short term, they were solid, but to keep the fragile thread that held them together intact, he knew he would have to minimize any family drama that would unnecessarily strain the relationship. So, as unpleasant as it was likely to be, he informed Juanita, and she agreed it was time to tell Ashley and the rest of the family they were seeing each other.

***

Larry called Maureen and said they needed to talk, and she could meet him at the Wash-O-Matic on Sunday night at 5 p.m. As a result of his and Juanita's Saturday dates, Larry had adjusted his laundry day to Sunday. Maureen requested that he come to the house instead. In addition to talking about what was on his mind, they could also discuss money issues and some changes she was making to the house.

When he arrived, next to Maureen's SUV in the driveway was a beat-up red F-150 that he recognized but couldn't place. Before he knocked on the front door, he walked across the porch and checked on the side yard, where spotty caches of wind-blown leaves from their neighbor's maple tree rested on neatly cut grass. He also took a quick look in the back of the F-150 and saw a contractor's toolbox, some collapsible horses, a five-gallon bucket of joint compound, and a set of women's golf clubs with pink head covers. *Amber Jolly*, he thought to himself.

When Larry knocked on the front door, it set off an explosion of barking from Donald and Lydia. Amber answered a moment later with the dogs at her side, looking very comfy in a Bills hoodie and stocking feet.

"Hey Larry. How are you?"

Larry entered and immediately got down on one knee to greet the dogs. As he petted them, he looked up at her, "I'm good, Amber. How are you?"

"I'm a little pissed at the moment at the Packers shutting out the Bills, but okay."

"I was building a closet for someone this afternoon and listened on the radio. Terrible."

"Especially after the way Allen dominated the Vikings last week."

"Yeah, that leap over Anthony Barr was something. It might take a bit, but that kid is going to be special. Did Maureen watch the game?"

"Yeah. Some of the girls from golf came over. We had fun except for the loss."

Amber was an athletic woman, with short, dirty blonde hair and close-set eyes. She knew Maureen through the women's Tuesday afternoon golf league at South Park Lake, which she won year after year, along with the women's leagues at Caz and Elma Meadows. She was a small-time off-the-books contractor, garnering most of her work from the women in these golf leagues. On several occasions, she took on work that needed a second set of hands, and Larry helped her out at Maureen's request. He was happy to do it, but she never offered to pay or feed him. If you weren't going to pay a guy for his help, it was expected that you would at least feed him.

"Did Maureen watch the whole game?"

"Yes," Maureen said, coming into the room sporting a Bills T-shirt, looking quite fit. "The girls were very patient explaining various aspects of the game to me."

This was a subtle swipe at Larry because it was only in recent years that she became interested in football, and he would get frustrated trying to explain the game to her while watching it. "Good on them," Larry said.

"Yes, it was good, except for how we lost." Maureen smiled and hugged Larry.

Amber slipped on her turquoise crocs, "Good seeing you, Larry. If some work comes your way that you want to pass on, let me know." Then, somewhat awkwardly, she leaned in and kissed Maureen on the cheek.

"Will do," he said as she exited the front door.

A little stunned by Amber's show of affection, after she left Larry asked, "What was that about?"

"Nothing. I think she's hoping something will happen between us."

"Why would she think that?"

"Oh, she's been around a lot helping me, and we've had some conversations, but I don't think that part is for me."

"Does she know that?"

"Yes, but what do they say—hope springs eternal."

"That is something people say."

"C'mon back here, I want to show you something."

Larry followed her back toward his room, where he found that she had started to pack up his things. His books were in boxes, and his pictures and prints were off the walls, stacked neatly against one of the bookcases.

"I hope you don't mind, but I've never liked the color of this room, and Amber offered to help me pack it up and paint it."

Unexpectedly, at the sight of his stuff being readied to be moved out, reality hit him, and he felt a tremendous sinking feeling. With the news that he was seeing Dr. Johnson, Larry thought he was possibly going to deal some kind of blow to Maureen, but she had beaten him to the punch.

"It's fine," he said in a flat voice. "On the first of the month, I'm moving into a place off Center Road. The mom of one of the guys from Building & Grounds is giving me a break on a flat in exchange for taking care of the grass and snow, plus some minor repairs."

"That sounds good. What's the rent so I can pitch in like we agreed."

"It's eight hundred."

Walking back toward the dining room, she said, "Okay. I have something else for you." She handed Larry a check for thirteen thousand dollars.

"What's this?"

"It's half the money in the checking account. I noticed your paycheck wasn't being deposited anymore, so it's probably best we split this up now. I've also had an appraisal done on the house and should be getting the results any day now."

"Okay. So, are you telling me this is final?" he asked somberly.

"No, not necessarily. I'm not there yet, but I want to have a plan in place, just in case. Is it too much, Larry?"

"No no, it's fine. These changes—it's hard to keep up."

She smiled, and said, "Yes, for me too."

"Since we're talking about changes, I guess this is a good entry point to bring up something big with me. I've started to see someone."

"See someone. A counselor?"

"No, a woman."

"Oh, that is big." She paused and said, "Larry, you don't have to tell me. It's not my business."

"Yes, I do because of who the person is. And I have to tell the kids too."

"How come?"

"Because the person I'm seeing is Dr. Johnson, Ashley's old supervisor from St. Ignatius."

"Really?" Maureen said with emphasis, as if there were some breach in the universe.

A little annoyed with her response, Larry said, "Yes, really. We've had this nice rapport since we met, and given the situation with us, well—I asked her out. I thought it was important to be up front about it, being there's a connection with Ashley."

"Are you saying this is serious?"

"No. I don't know what it is other than new. It's just the Ashley thing was important. Otherwise, I wouldn't have brought it up."

"She's Black and very young, right?"

"Yes, she's Black. And if forty-eight is very young—then yes, she's very young."

"I'm sorry, Larry. In a million years I would've never placed you with someone like that."

"I would ask why, but I think that's just asking for a kick in the teeth, so I'll just say she's no Amber Jolly. Also, please don't tell Ashley or Sam. I think they should hear it from me. After that, you can get together and make your catty judgments. Once I'm settled in my new place, I'll come by to get this and the rest of my stuff. Is there anything else?"

"Wow—talk about passive-aggressive."

"I'm sorry, but were you about to say something nice? Were you going to congratulate me and say you hope she makes me happy?"

Maureen recoiled with this rebuke, "It's just surprising."

"If you knew me the way you *should* know me, it wouldn't be surprising. Is there anything else?"

"No."

"Thanks," he said looking at the check in his hand, and moved toward the front door.

He was just about to exit when Maureen called out to him, "Larry—does she make you happy?"

With his hand on the doorknob, he exhaled. He turned around and said, "Yes, it's going well. We're kind of the same person, but it's a bit complicated."

"How so?" she asked with what seemed like genuine curiosity.

From the door, Larry explained the workaholic thing and how the kids and school came first. He went into a more complete breakdown, without giving up any of the intimate details of the relationship. Before long, he was sitting at the dining room table with a beer, spelling out the mentorship program they were developing.

When the news of Dr. Johnson concluded, Maureen gave him a rundown of what was happening with her. The first of her three yearly cancer screenings was in, and it came back clear—no cancer. She talked about her new job and how terrific it was to be challenged again. She missed the day-to-day energy of the classroom and the kids, but it had been invigorating, not dealing with the parents—who cascaded between being too involved or not involved enough. Besides Amber's interest, there was no movement on the dating front, although she had been asked out a couple of times. And finally, she had informed Sam and Ashley of her infidelity.

"Let me guess, they blamed me?"

"Well, not like you think. It was more supporting me and the imbalance women face in relationships."

"I don't want to hear about it, but I'm glad you told them. How about Ben?"

"No."

"That's probably a good idea. Okay, I should be going. My clothes are at Wash-O-Matic waiting to be folded."

She walked him to the front door, where they embraced, and as he went down the walkway, she stepped onto the porch and called to him, smiling, "Larry, I am happy for you."

***

In a text message the following day, Larry arranged to meet Ashley for an early dinner, saying—* it's important.* She suggested a place called Burrito Bliss near her apartment on Elmwood Avenue but said it would have to be quick because she had to write some lesson plans and had a mountain of essays to correct, which was fine with Larry—the quicker, the better.

He instantly liked the trendy little Tex-Mex place and the mariachi music playing at a low volume. After being seated and getting menus, the music transitioned and "Waitin' for the Bus," came into the mix and Larry smiled at Ashley, "Now, this is the type of place where you play ZZ Top."

"Whaddya mean?"

"I was at that upscale Curtiss Hotel, and they were playing "Legs," on the swanky rooftop bar, and it was totally out of place."

"Ahh, I've been up there. I know what you mean, but some people might have liked it."

"I suppose," he agreed.

After finding the Blissed Taco Salad, Larry set the menu aside and looked at his daughter. Ashley hadn't picked up any of his calls recently, so it was with great interest he started to pepper her with questions about her new job—how was it different from St. Ignatius or student teaching; did she like her coworkers and had they been supportive; was the volume of work as expected; what was the demographic makeup of her class? It was that last question about demographics where she became a little impatient with him—as if he was going to make some insensitive remark about the racial makeup of inner-city schools. In reality, he was just interested in the diversity of the classroom and how race, ethnicity, and gender dynamics played out, but, of course, when *he* asked the question, it was somehow offensive or racist.

It was nice to hear the excitement in her voice, nevertheless, and he had achieved his goal of ordering before dropping his big Dr. Johnson news. He thought it less likely that Ashley would walk out on him with a plate of food in front of her than she would have had they not ordered. He gained further advantage when he correctly used the pronoun *'they'* to refer to a nonbinary person she knew from college who was in the restaurant and stopped at their table to say hello.

"Very good, Dad."

A little surprised, Larry said, "I'm glad I got that right. I don't have to tell you, interaction with the nonbinary population isn't all that prevalent in the suburbs."

"So, what was so important that we had to meet?" she asked, as the server set down Larry's salad and her Huevos Rancheros.

"Well," he said hesitating, "I've started to see someone, and we need to discuss it."

"Like a counselor?"

"That's what your mother asked. No, I've started to see a woman."

Her face grew static and closed. "I'm sure I don't want to know about it."

"That's fine, but you should at least know who it is because I met her through you."

Her face went from closed to incredulous, "Who?"

"Dr. Johnson from St. Ignatius."

"No way," she said, stunned, her mouth slightly ajar.

"For about a month now."

"No."

"Over the last year of doing the Saturday thing, we developed a nice friendship, and when your mom decided to move on, I asked her out."

With that, the disbelief turned to amazement, "I can't believe this. I can't believe—you and her."

"Instead of you hearing it secondhand, I wanted to tell you myself," Larry said. And though it was a little perverse, he was sort of enjoying her disbelief.

"I just can't—you and her—she's such a rock star."

"You'd be surprised how similar we are."

"Is it serious?"

"It's very new. You know, she's committed to the school and the kids, and I'm going through a bit of a transition myself, but we like each other."

"Dad, I can't deal with this, I have to go," she said, shaking her head.

"Okay, let me get a box for your dinner. I just wanted to let you know," Larry said, and he scanned the room for their server.

When he turned back to Ashley she had a dubious expression on her face. "I can't believe you would do this. She was my mentor, and now—now you're sleeping with her. This is too much."

"All right. But let me say I'm in a relationship with a woman for whom I have immense respect. That relationship doesn't change one thing between you and her."

"Yeah, I don't know, Dad. I have to think about this. Right now, it would seem to change everything."

Larry caught the eye of the server, pointed to their plates, and mouthed, *Can we get a box*? Then, he turned to Ashley and asked, "How does it change everything?"

"It just feels—it just feels like you're running over me."

"Running over you?"

"You run over everyone and just take what you want."

"Are you saying that I've crossed some line?"

"Obviously, she said, getting angry. "You're dating Dr. Johnson, my mentor."

"Okay. But it's not like you're still working with her."

"Yeah, Dad, I don't know. What about Mom?"

"Your mom has moved on. She's playing footsie with that woman from golf, Amber Jolly."

"This is too much."

"Can't you be happy for me? I know it doesn't seem to come up much, but I've been through a lot too, these last months. Can't you be happy for me?"

"Dad, I have to go. This is too much for me.

"Sure. I'm sorry if you find this disturbing. It just sort of happened. It wasn't my intention to upset you."

The server set the box down just as Larry was done speaking. He said thank you, reached across the table for Ashley's plate, and carefully slid her Huevos Rancheros into the box. He put the box back on her side of the table and looked at her, waiting for a response. She sat there for a few long moments; her face beet red. Finally, without saying anything, she stood up, turned, and pushed toward the exit with a certain fierceness, box in hand.

Larry caught the eye of the server again and ordered a chilled Jim Beam and a Blue Light. Just then, the mariachi horns of Johnny Cash's "Ring of Fire" quietly came into the rotation, and Larry silently agreed that love was indeed *a burning thing*.

***

He finished his salad and drinks and wanting to be done with coming clean to his family about Juanita, he texted Sam saying: *call me asap—very important.* She called as he drove home and talked through his truck's Bluetooth. As expected, she was not happy for him either. She characterized his news about Juanita as a grave betrayal of Ashley's boundaries. She also assailed him for his lack of effort at salvaging things with Maureen. He set aside the trendy Lissa-speak about boundaries and asked her why she never cut him an inch of slack and questioned if she even knew what betrayal meant. When she didn't answer, he said, "It means to be disloyal, deceptive, and unfaithful. Explain how I'm being disloyal, deceptive, and unfaithful to Ashley or your mother?"

Even though he had every right to bring up how Maureen had betrayed him, he didn't go there. He instead asked her not to lecture him about his efforts to save his marriage. He acknowledged his failure and how heartbroken he was for his part in that failure. Becoming a little emotional, he said, "I gave everything I had to your mom and you, Ben, Ashley—it just wasn't enough."

He said a hasty goodbye and wept as he drove home. In the tumult of the evening, he had unconsciously driven to Maureen's house and found Amber's truck again in the driveway next to her SUV. Realizing he was at the wrong house, he turned around and went to his mom's, where they watched *Wheel of Fortune* together. When the show was over, he explained the whole Juanita thing to her. Helen was aware Larry had met someone since he wasn't sleeping there a couple of nights during the week, but he hadn't related any of the particulars. Of course, as always was the case, she was behind Larry, saying: "If you think it's time, then it damn well is time."

A little later, up in his old room, he called Ben, who occasionally did pick up. Though Ben wasn't pleased with what his dating Juanita portended for the family, he was supportive and said Larry had earned the right to proceed any way he saw fit. From there, they had a nice little back-and-forth about how Ben was adapting at school, managing his workload, making new friends, and whether he needed anything. He was good on all fronts.

On a much-needed lighter note, he also confirmed to Larry that the Brockport Rathskeller still smelled like a mixture of piss, Mr. Clean and broken dreams.

Twenty Four

After Larry left that Sunday afternoon, Maureen finished cleaning up from her little Bills gathering, folding serving tables, and putting couch pillows back in place. In the kitchen, rinsing a bowl containing bean dip, she began to weep softly. Though there were still some small plates and silverware to wash, she turned off the water and carefully tore a paper towel from the dispenser adjacent to the sink. She stood there drying her hands and dabbing her tears, and whatever energy she had seemed to trickle from her body like puffs of air slowly being released from a balloon.

Clutching the damp paper towel, she plodded back toward the former man cave and lowered herself into the seat at the end of the sofa bed, where she had engaged Larry in countless conversations. The dogs and, eventually, the cats followed her. Lydia lay next to Maureen with her head on her lap, and Donald hopped up on the chair to her left, still keeping his distance months after the chicken incident. Betty and Friedan curled up on the fleece blanket draped over the back of the thick sofa. With the pets settled, she looked around the room and at Larry's empty chair tucked neatly under the desk, and her weeping intensified. His news regarding Dr. Johnson was another shovel of dirt thrown on their threadbare, almost dead marriage. In her mind's eye, Larry was becoming fuzzy and fading from view, transforming perhaps into a memory. Just as there had been a time before Larry, there would now be a time after Larry.

Despite all the successful steps she had taken to reclaim her life and identity, Maureen was still uncertain about ending their marriage, though Larry seemed poised to move on. Sitting there among his things, she quit pretending that she was going to paint the room because she didn't like the color. In fact, she rather liked the muted slate gray Larry had chosen years ago when he transformed the room into his indoor sanctuary. Like everything with Larry, the smart, practical choices he made were pleasing, and the slate gray walls served as an excellent base to accentuate the prints, pictures, and other artifacts he hung on them.

The real reason for changing the room was because she was tired of the endless reminders of his smart choices, even when choosing a fucking base color for a room. She felt silly for resenting his competence and good taste but couldn't help herself. Her recent growth as a person did, however, allow her to recognize that her pettiness was her problem and not Larry's. Though she wasn't honest with him about why she was changing the room, she was at least honest with herself.

She also understood the tears that trickled down her cheeks were born of grief and fear. She couldn't bear to look at those walls, his books, or that desk any longer without him here. As the years passed, she'd drawn a real sense of stability from knowing he was anchored in that space or in the garage, ready to take on anything life dished out. Now it was sad and scary to think that his steady hand would be gone forever.

But as the tears slowly subsided and despite her lingering doubts, it occurred to her that she had been succeeding quite nicely on her own and had been exceptionally resilient in doing so—beating cancer, reclaiming her identity, taking on new challenges, including a career change. Larry Plumb didn't corner the market on making smart, practical choices. With this in mind, she began to think of how, like her identity, she would reclaim this room as well. In response to Larry's austere earnestness, she would make that space bright and cheerful, with outrageous colors that he would never choose, like watermelon or apricot. In the far corner, she would include a sunshiny mural, prompting her to sing and dance instead of weeping when she came back here.

Emboldened by this positive-self-talk and her new half-baked plan for the man cave she felt a surge of energy return to her body, and grew confident, maybe even a little cocky, and thought—*I can do this*. She took a couple of deep breaths, returned to the kitchen, finished the dishes, and put a few empty beer and soda cans from the party in the recycling bin.

When she was done, she went out into the living room, and rather than put on some cop show, she pulled out her laptop from the coffee table's underneath shelf and began looking at that week's agenda and reviewing a new literacy curriculum called New York Reads, which was a phonics program that was going to be phased in statewide over the next two years. She and her mentor, Carol Maston, would introduce the initiative to the district's elementary school teachers.

Despite the considerable job of explaining and selling the program in the days ahead, she found it hard to stay on task and instead returned to thinking about Larry and Dr. Johnson. Though Maureen asked him to move out and proposed seeing other people, she nevertheless started to think negative, disparaging thoughts about Dr. Johnson and wanted not to like her.

She recalled how Ashley characterized Dr. Johnson as a *rock star* and remembered the thoughtful card she sent amid her chemo treatments. Dr. Johnson had also drafted some of Ashley's former students to send cards. However, now that she was dating her husband, Maureen decided it was all just a ruse to get at Larry and she was a phony. Additionally, she didn't like that Dr. Johnson was eight years younger than him and she thought it ridiculous they were putting together grant proposals and developing a curriculum in the hopes of building a mentorship program. She asked herself—*What the hell does Larry know about education?*

As these negative thoughts swirled in Maureen's head, she was struck by a moment of self-awareness and honesty, recognizing her need to dislike Dr. Johnson was perhaps born of the same petty impulse to change Larry's room. Despite this minor epiphany, the desire to not like her, plus be a victim was still powerful. Larry, perhaps, could have been a little less matter-of-fact and more sensitive in delivering his Dr. Johnson news. He also might have shown some shame or remorse for moving on so quickly. Flashing in her head came the line: How could he do this to me? But almost as the thought popped up, she knew it was false and wanted to escape the pit of recrimination she had fallen into.

With a self-admonishing headshake, Maureen again tried to turn back to reviewing the new reading initiative, but it was no use. Her mind was now cycling to the point where she had elevated Dr. Johnson from someone Larry was seeing to his phony girlfriend. Arguably the best course of action to quash the noise in her head would be a call to Ashley—she might be able to talk her past all this unkind and unproductive Dr. Johnson nonsense—but Larry had asked to be the one to tell the kids. Moreover, Ashley might not have responded positively to her father's dating her former supervisor. But the petty jealousy was now like a carnival Tilt-A-Whirl, chaotically wreaking havoc in her head. Helpless to stop it, Maureen took the next step and searched out Dr. Johnson's social media presence.

With just a few clicks, she found Dr. Johnson's Facebook page, and though she was expecting a rock star, she wasn't quite prepared for just how attractive and put together Dr. Johnson was with her shiny black hair and confident photogenic smile. Long and lean in a crisp power suit, rather than looking like the head of an inner-city school, she had the aura of one of those loud-mouthed Sheryl Sandberg types—a woman who wields her success like a sharp-edged sword not to empower but to cut you—from your failures as a parent to your shitty PowerPoint presentation. Perusing the profile, Maureen was impressed and jealous of Dr. Johnson's educational and professional accomplishments. But shaking her head, she found a way to diminish those accomplishments and the PhD since they were achieved without the pressure of being a wife or a mother.

From there, she moved on to Dr. Johnson's Facebook wall, which was littered with the beginning-of-the-new-school-year happenings at St. Ignatius—the open house, the programs, the new security system. Larry was a bystander in several pictures, but all were in his capacity as a volunteer staff member and none as a boyfriend. The activity of the new school year on her main page precluded Maureen from seeing the provocative skintight dresses and bikinis buried deeper in her profile, that is, until she navigated over to her Instagram page.

After looking at Dr Johnson nightclubbing in sheer dresses, and strolling on exotic beaches in bikinis, Maureen found her mouth slightly ajar. Scrolling through the pics, she didn't look for any secondary meaning. Instead, she reverted to her deeply imprinted Catholicism and decided Dr. Johnson was way too proud of that fit, muscular body and was some kind of exhibitionist slut. It was just what Maureen needed to assuage her petty jealousies and further dismiss this woman as someone who would degrade herself for attention.

She thought about how Ashley and Sam might analyze the provocative pictures. Maureen was sure they would say Dr. Johnson was objectifying herself and looking for approval in an outmoded way. Still, as she continued to scroll, her mouth remaining slightly ajar, she also thought the girls might say Dr. Johnson didn't owe anyone anything and could do whatever the hell she wanted regardless of norms and expectations. Who were they to judge if she wanted to engage the world this way? Despite the obvious contradiction, Maureen abruptly changed course again, now deciding that Dr. Johnson wasn't some starved-for-attention slut, but a brave, fully actualized woman who seemed to be using these pics to tell the world, *Yes, I am all that.*

In a cascading hour of epiphanies, Maureen suddenly had another one. All these changes with her, Larry, and life in general—were hard. In the abstract, she expected he would move on and see other people, but now that it was happening, and happening on such a high level with a smart, driven, beautiful rock star of a woman—it was *really* hard.

She clicked off Dr. Johnson's Instagram page and asked the gauzy void to forgive her trifling pettiness. There was no reason to dislike or disparage Dr. Johnson. And though their spark had fizzled, Larry had always been a good, honorable man who had taken care of her. He had also shown extreme patience in waiting for the decisions she was making that affected his fate. While she was apologizing for her pettiness, she apologized to herself as well—or at the very least, she wasn't going to kick herself for the narrow-minded jealousy that had overtaken her in the last hour, again repeating to herself—*This is really hard.*

***

Further, she wasn't going to kick herself for not being honest with Larry about her dating behavior. Encouraged by her golf friends, she joined the online dating community shortly after she asked him to leave. More curious than active through the spring and early summer, Maureen went on single dates with three different men and then one lunch with her old college flame, Andrew Roth. She met one man for coffee, another on Tinder, and one was the brother of a girl from golf. Her deception was the product of wanting to avoid the possibility of discussing the dates with

Larry, which would only foster more lies because they all had been bad. Or even worse, subjecting herself to his complete indifference.

Though she had been careful and given significant consideration before swiping right, her first underwhelming encounter was over coffee with someone very different from Larry. He was a tech guy at the Tesla plant in Buffalo. Right from the start, he made it very clear to her that his job was to develop and maintain software for futuristic electric vehicles, not to set up the printers for Renee in accounts receivable. A wiffle of a man with narrow shoulders, he gave a new meaning to five feet, ten inches—the stated height in his profile. Though he had a pleasant face with soft eyes, he seemed like a guy who was often overlooked and was desperate to be taken seriously. He was conspiracy minded and went on and on about back-door deals being perpetrated against regular people by elites. Maureen was fascinated by his grievance and insecurity. Still, instead of considering him as a possible companion, she wanted to scoop him up in her arms, stroke his head, and tell him he was a special boy and everything would be okay like a mom.

The second date was with the brother of the golf friend. Tony Vickers was his name, and he was a big, handsome guy with a full head of wild hair and a beard. He was painfully cocky, and when he laid his plucky Popeye-like forearms across the Spot Coffee tabletop, there wasn't much room for Maureen's coffee or blueberry muffin. He owned a canvas covering business that made custom boat and car enclosures. You could tell he was the kind of guy who gave orders and was never wrong. He also finished his pastry in three bites and talked with his mouth full throughout. He was such an asshole that Maureen thought her golf friend had set her up as a kind of joke. It all became too much for Maureen ten minutes into his bragging about his expertise at curing and smoking meat—how everyone at the barbecue ate the brisket he prepared and ignored his son-in-law's. She abruptly got up and left, saying it was time for her dogs—"Um, afternoon surgery."

The last date was with a suave artist, ten years her junior, whom she met on Tinder. This man was purposefully inscrutable, conversing in an ambiguous, sophisticated, open-ended way that she found exciting. His profile was teeming with pictures of him sporting perfectly manicured black hair and sharp-cornered three-piece suits like some sultry Bryan Ferry knockoff. She talked to him for weeks, building what she thought was a playful and pleasant rapport. He complimented her looks and told her that she was fascinating. Maureen soaked it all up, and when they finally decided to meet, since it was Tinder, she talked herself into the idea of a possible hookup, but when he didn't make a move, she was embarrassed at how she misread the situation. Despite this, she hung in with him for a bit longer before finally realizing that was his thing, playing on women's emotions but never consummating. She was pissed at herself for being drawn into his stupid game.

And finally, she had lunch with her old college flame, Andrew Roth. Surreptitiously, she had become friends with him on social media, and they had occasionally exchanged direct messages for the last few years. Andrew did follow through on becoming an attorney and was based in Manhattan but had clients in Western New York.

When Maureen explained she had split with Larry, he suggested they meet for lunch, which she agreed to. He was on his third marriage and was a full partner at Latham Watkins & Roth. Though older and sporting a three-martini porterhouse-potbelly, he still had that sparkle in his blue eyes. He was another one with the bragging, but his were mostly about his billable hours, which did nothing for Maureen. Also, what he lacked in appearance and personality he made up with chutzpah. After complimenting her on how great she looked, he advocated rekindling the magic they once shared, offering to take her down the street to the Henry Hotel as he cut into a giant slice of cherry cheesecake with his fork.

With that, Maureen stood up, reached into her purse, took some money out, threw it on the table, and said, "You're a garbage fucking person. I can't believe I ever saw anything in you. Never message me again."

As she turned and walked away, she could hear him laughing.

When she got home, not only did she curl up in a ball on her bed and cry her eyes out, she called Larry with the intention of begging him to come home. But he didn't pick up, and in the intervening fifteen minutes before he called back, she had steeled herself to continue moving forward on her new path.

The conversation in her head that sustained her was about the distance she had already traveled in taking charge of her own life. She also recognized a happy, fulfilling life wasn't contingent on male *companionship*. Further, she recalled her pledge to Larry and, more importantly, to herself that she would do the chasing instead of being chased. As the tears ran their course, she laughed, thinking, like Walter White in *Breaking Bad*, she wasn't waiting for anyone to knock on her door—she would be the one that knocks. It hadn't worked out thus far, but she was still in the infancy of this new life and decided what was needed was a long-game strategy. She also had to be okay with the possibility of never finding a door on which to knock.

Larry presented another problem to Maureen. Unconsciously, as she sat through her awful dates listening to grievances and braggarts, she couldn't help but compare everyone to him. He would never try to impress anyone with such inane fodder or talk about his accomplishments. He might tell stories in a self-deprecating way and describe what was going on in his life, but he would never engage in frivolous attention seeking conversation. At his core, Larry was like an ancient river, bending and twisting trying to find the truth of the sea. He knew right from wrong and what was and wasn't important. He was curious in both an illuminating and annoying kind of way especially when he would go off on some tangent like why people got down on their knees and prayed to God—"Does an omniscient being need little Joey Dumbass who doesn't have a pot to piss in and never had a chance in life down on his knees before him/her/them? Is that kind of God worthy of belief?" It was unlikely she would ever find a man or anyone who would be equally comfortable deciphering the poems of Anne Sexton and changing out the ball joints on a car.

Given the age of the men on whose door she was likely to knock, Maureen also thought it was unlikely she would find a more well-put-together man. There might be men out there with softer features and better heads of hair than Larry, but there were probably few as fit and firm as him. She was now in the land of short, insecure Tesla software engineers and fat braggarts like Andrew Roth, and for the time being, they would all be measured against Larry.

One reason she had asked him to leave was her life was always being measured through the prism of Larry. In the short term she understood that wouldn't change, and wondered if she would meet anyone who set the bar as high as he had. She liked the idea of this challenge and was optimistic that if she acknowledged the difficulties and effort required to move forward, she would be fine. She also pledged to herself to be patient, and not to give in to petty impulses—too much.

Following his revelation that he was dating Dr. Johnson, she defended Larry and his choices to Sam and Ashley. Though things had fizzled for her and Larry, she pointed out how loyal and hardworking he had been for all of them, and that they should cut him some slack. When both girls pushed back, she acknowledged his flaws but reiterated he had been good to all of them, and they needed to stop being so critical all the time. She reinforced her point with some anecdotes about her disastrous foray into dating. The girls didn't like that she knocked other men to build him up, but they took her point, which was a hopeful sign.

In the same time frame, she also came clean with Ben regarding her infidelity. He went back at her hard, expressing his disappointment, asking how she could look at herself in the mirror. The conversation crushed her, but she was glad to finally unburden herself of this awful truth.

Ben called her back in a few days and was still angry but said he had talked to Larry, who had encouraged him to see this mistake from her perspective, telling him she was lost and unhappy and made an unfortunate choice at a vulnerable time.   Larry didn't ask him to excuse the behavior, as much as he tried to get Ben to understand the nuance of the situation and to extend a bit of grace to his mom. Though he wasn't ready to forgive her, after talking to Larry, he could understand how this could happen, and he was sorry she was unhappy. He told her he loved her and thought it would all be all right with more time. Thrilled, Maureen thanked him for being understanding and told him to take all the time he needed and that she loved him too.

Soon after the second call with Ben, Maureen felt a great weight had been lifted from her. This was the final piece. She forgave herself for the infidelity and petty deceptions of Larry. Now, she was ready to move on.

A few weeks later, after she secured a loan to buy out Larry's equity in the house, they sat down with a mediator, hammered out a few details, and signed or initialed a million papers, and it was done.

The twenty-eight-year marriage of Larry Plumb and Maureen O'Donnell was officially dissolved.

Twenty Five

Despite finalizing his break with Maureen, which knocked him out for a few days, Larry had the wind in his sails and was busier than ever. Fall cleanup and winter prep were in full swing at the shop. The Wednesday night research and curriculum development continued, as did numerous side jobs, Saturday mornings at St. Ignatius, his romance with Juanita, and exploration of publishing options for his recently completed novel. The day-to-day pace of his life was fast and invigorating, which he loved and executed with that dynamic Larry Plumb precision.

The only thing he really didn't have a handle on was his relationship with his daughters. He continued to reach out, asking about their jobs and if they needed anything, but the response was minimal. When he talked with Maureen about it, she encouraged him to be patient and play the long game, as she was doing with dating. She said she had been advocating for him with the girls, pointing out his many excellent qualities, which annoyed the shit out of him. Perhaps if she hadn't hopped on the trendy—white men are toxic train—that had polluted their daughters and instead advocated for him five years ago, they might not have divorced, and their home might not be broken. But she'd been a different, unhappy person then. Still, this failure continued to burn at him.

Though reconsidering the past got him nowhere, Larry thought Maureen was right about needing to play the long game with the girls. He could wait them out and be there without judgment or recrimination when they needed him. More than that, Larry felt this was one of the non-negotiable obligations of fatherhood. He needed to be there for Sam, Ashley, and Ben on both sunny days and stormy ones. With a plate as full as his, he would have little trouble compartmentalizing his issues with his daughters and would wait for them to come around like uptown Lou Reed waited for his man with twenty-six dollars in his hand.

One of the happy things occupying his time was his recently completed novel, *Shadow Love*. He had sent out a flurry of inquiries to agents and publishers to little response, but he didn't find the rejection emails discouraging. Larry knew he still had a long way to go for his true voice to emerge, and unless the world took a weird and incomprehensible turn, it was unlikely he would find himself in the stacks next to Raymond Carver anytime soon.   But the feeling of accomplishment from grinding out his vision with little more than his lunch-bucket imagination and determination was incredibly satisfying. And though he was too close to have an objective opinion, he liked to think he knew the difference between art and artifice and was pleased with his creation: the moody tone, the flawed characters, and the poetic ending.

Eileen followed through on her threat to tell Rowena about her lunchtime affair with Gus. Now they sat at their kitchen table staring at the teapot boiling water for Rowena's afternoon cup of Earl Grey.

"Do you love her?"

"No. It was just sex."

"Just sex? Is it the same with us—just sex?

"Maybe in the beginning, but now I think there's a difference."

"What's different?"

"I guess the difference now is I love you."

The water came to a boil with a soft whistle. Rowena got up from her chair at the table, walked over to the stove, and gazed at the steam rising from the old pot. She turned off the burner and looked at Gus, "Do you want some?"

"No."

She poured the boiling water over the tea bag sitting in the cup, then let the water soak in for a moment. Next, she took the tab attached to the bag between her thumb and forefinger and lifted it up and down a half-dozen times or so until the water was a rich copper color. Having transformed the boiling water, she placed the bag on a spoon and covered it with the tab. With her thumb, she applied pressure until all the excess water trapped in the bag dripped into the cup. She threw the spent bag into the sink. Before walking back over to the table where Gus was sitting, she made several revolutions with the spoon in the cup, looked out the window over the sink, and noted the shifting shadows dancing among the maples.

After sitting down and stirring some more, she said, "Queen Elizabeth drinks Earl Grey. She thinks it's one of the reasons for her long life. She says it boosts your immune system."

"Is that so?" Gus responded.

Rowena looked at him for a long moment before turning her eyes toward the kitchen window again, and a crumb of a smile came to her pink lips.

As Larry waited on responses from the publishing world regarding his novel, another potentially dire challenge arose. His non-elected, non-union position as "Senior Utility Specialist" had become part of a contentious discussion at the recent town board meeting, where they debated the coming year's budget.   Every few cycles when money was tight, fiscally conservative taxpayers, including the old attorney Ralph Ponsonby and his buddy, the developer Carl Worthington, would raise hell at the budget meetings about excessive spending. Larry's six-figure compensation package was among the highest in the town, and guys like Ponsonby and Worthington said the salary was the worst kind of government waste and largesse.

A parade of department heads, successive town supervisors, including the present one, Meghan Wheeler, and Mac, who was armed with a PowerPoint presentation prepared by Larry, would come to the podium to defend him and his position. The PowerPoint demonstrated in real dollars the value of Larry's vast and varied contributions spread across every corner of the town. Most importantly, it showed that the cost of replacing him was more than double his six-figure salary.

That didn't matter this year—bigger than math, bigger than his service, was the anger and sense of grievance throughout town. Rehabilitation of the crumbling Burchfield Arts Center would cost almost a million dollars, and construction of the new town library/community Center was egregiously behind schedule with millions in cost overruns. A group led by Ponsonby and Worthington, joined by other fiscal hawks, was demanding cuts, and Larry and others were in danger of losing their jobs this time.

Larry sat with Mac in his office at the shop. Shaking his head Mac said, "Meghan totally fucked up on the library. She went too big, and now she's trying to cover her ass before the election."

"Even if she caves, what about Judy and Penner?"

"The council is running scared about the election too. The only one backing you is Karen Moby. She's getting destroyed on social media trying to make reasoned arguments about what a great community resource the library will be and how it will cost the town more to get rid of you than to keep you."

"Karen always has my back," Larry said, shaking his head too. "It's stupid for her to take this incoming or lose her seat because of me. I'll text her."

"Then there's this asshole Al Pevco. He's been posting screenshots of employee salaries on that *Fed Up West Seneca Taxpayer* Facebook page. It's a real shit show."

"And my salary is posted?"

"Oh yeah, you're a real lightning rod on that page. Your thirty-seven years make you the longest-tenured town employee. Next to the Police Chief and the School Superintendent, you have the largest compensation package, and the consensus on that page is that your position is some kind of bullshit grift. Terrible stuff about the family being on the payroll—not just Maureen, but your mom and dad too. Even Ben's park job and reffing."

"The old man's been dead almost forty years," Larry said frowning, "I get it, but sheesh."

"Lucy and some people you did side jobs for jumped in and reminded the mob of your community service and Civil Servant of the Year award. Even Kimmy Karney, who works for Ponsonby, defended you."

"Lemme guess, they destroyed them too?"

Mac nodded in the affirmative. "There's even a thread on there with a pic of you holding up that wad of cash you pulled out at Mitchell's the night of the JD incident."

"You're fucking kidding me."

Mac reached in his pocket for his phone and, after a few taps, handed it to Larry.

Larry wasn't prepared for the ugliness. It especially killed him when he saw vicious comments from his long-time coworker, Rocky. Larry was aware that Rocky thought he was full of shit for his work ethic and commitment, but he had always shot straight with him, and it hurt to be so cruelly taken apart this way. "Even Rocky," Larry said, shaking his head.

***

Executing his forty-two-dive later that night in his mom's garage, he thought about how less than a year ago, the entire town had rallied around him and his family with an outpouring of love and generosity when Maureen was diagnosed with cancer. Now, they were out for blood. At the end of the month, just before the election, there was a real chance Larry's job wouldn't be funded in the new fiscal year that began in January.

Larry hadn't considered life after the town besides the mentoring program he was developing with Juanita, but that was in the hazy future. In the short term, if they decided to zero him out, there was plenty of good-paying side work, more than he could probably handle. He also could start drawing on his pension or, ironically enough, get a job with Worthington or some other developer. It was a bad situation, but he wasn't pressed for money and had a couple of months to map out a plan.

Then, all of a sudden, he didn't have time to map out a plan. The taxpayer page posted new pics from the night of the incident with JD. One taken in the wake of Mac laying JD out pictured Larry with two handfuls of JD's leather jacket, staring him down with a pissed-off expression as blood dripped from his eye down his face. The pic captured Larry's anger at the moment but missed the fact that he was defusing the situation. But that hardly mattered in social media, and people responding to the post were outraged, calling Larry an unhinged savage and demanding his immediate dismissal.

Since becoming the Senior Utility Specialist, Larry didn't have anyone he reported to in the town. Thirteen years prior, when he stepped down as Highway Commissioner, Joel Hackenbeck, the Town Supervisor at the time, still had access to a good deal of money the feds handed out after the

9/11 terror attacks. He convinced Larry to stay on of Senior Utility Specialist, which was a great deal for everyone. The town kept Larry, and Larry got to stretch out and do all sorts of projects away from politics without any real oversight for the same compensation he received as Commissioner. But, with the budget outrage and the social media scandal, it was now open season on Larry. However, given the lack of administrative control over his position, nobody knew how or who had the authority to take him out.

Finally, after several meetings with town attorneys the supervisor and council members determined they had oversight power. Meghan Wheeler and the three council members—Judy Palmer, Brian Penner, and Karen Moby would vote on renewing Larry's position at the next town board meeting. It was also decided they would invoke the dubious *conduct clause*. All town employees were subject to the bullshit conduct clause as a condition of employment, but it was seldom used or enforced because of union protection. Larry had no such protection.

As a courtesy, Meghan called him into her office in Town Hall for a meeting. Without looking him in the eye, she explained that she and two of the three council members would vote to eliminate his position and invoke the conduct clause, meaning he was subject to immediate termination. Larry accepted this news without complaint or pushback, but he did offer some advice to the Town Supervisor. It wasn't Larry's style to dress anyone down, but he looked at her and said: "I've been around here since Reagan became president in 1981—I've been through a half-dozen supervisors and countless council members. I've seen 'em come, and I've seen 'em go. You're a talented politician, Meghan, but if you're going to take those next steps, you need ice in your veins. You need to look the person you're fucking over in the eye and not flinch while you're stepping on them. The ones that move up and survive don't blink when they're crushing people. This presentation here? Not meeting my eye—weak. You need to work on that."

With that she looked directly at him as he turned to leave.

Two days later, on Thursday night, Larry sat stoically in the center aisle of the gallery in council chambers surrounded by members of the community, former supervisors and council members, and coworkers past and present. These supporters stepped to the podium, extolled his virtues, and decried this miscarriage of justice. Even JD showed up and sat quietly in the top row off to the side.

But it was not to be. Ponsonby, Worthington, and the Dragon Lady of Dover Drive all spoke with fake outrage about the cost of Larry's compensation package and his moral failings. Facts and context were ignored, and all but Karen Moby voted to eliminate his position in the new fiscal year. They also found him to be in violation of the conduct clause, and he was terminated on the spot in spite of his thirty-seven years of distinguished service.

After the meeting had ended, Larry made the rounds and thanked everyone individually for supporting what was a hopeless cause. Out in the parking lot a huge black Ford Expedition idled in front of his pickup truck. As he passed in front of the giant earth-killing vehicle with its flashers on, he saw the controversial real estate developer Carl Worthington sitting in the front passenger seat.

Earlier that year, when an eight-year-old boy fell from a window and died in the Lovejoy section of Buffalo while his mother was whacked on crystal meth, Worthington popped off in a local weekly newspaper about how some people were not fit to live in society, let alone procreate, and should be sterilized or locked up. "All the queers, illegals and drug addicts," he said. These comments, of course, created a firestorm, but Worthington met the pushback head-on. He would offer no apologies and audaciously claimed he was not exploiting a tragedy. He said such tragedies, no matter where they happened, were the result of failed left-wing education and immigration policies and an overall countrywide erosion of values. This was just the kind of hateful duplicity Meghan Wheeler needed to metabolize if she was going to continue to be a successful politician in the current climate.

Worthington stepped gingerly from the truck and was a little overdressed for the weather in a scarf and overcoat. Like his friend Ponsonby, he had giant capped teeth—teeth bigger and brighter than just polished piano keys. With his blinding smile, he stuck out his hand to shake, "There he is, Larry Plumb. Can I get a word, Larry?"

"Sure," Larry said, grabbing his hand. "That was some show you put on tonight, Carl."

"Thanks. I appreciate how you handled yourself, too. I respect a man that can accept his fate and not carry on like a little bitch."

"You don't have an off button, do you, Carl?" Larry half laughed, leaning sideways, looking for a switch on the side of his scarf-covered neck.

"I do not. Listen, Larry, now that you're done with this bullshit town job, come work for me. We're doing big things in Buffalo and the growth centers down south— Florida and Texas. I could make you happy."

"Florida and Texas? Guns, God, and Waffle Houses—that's your idea of happy?"

"Stay here then. Plenty to do here."

"Thanks all the same Carl, I'll be fine."

"Larry, I did you a big favor tonight. Working for me, you could skate into retirement without a care in the world."

"I appreciate you thinking of me. If I need anything, I know where to find you. Have a good night."

"Think about it, Larry. Opportunities like this don't come around often."

***

Larry sent a group text to the family informing them that he had lost his job and briefly explained the budget crunch, the conduct clause, and the mob-like social media blitz. The girls sent along simple terse regrets. Ben called and was furious, but Larry calmed him down, saying it was just people exercising their grievance and there was no benefit to getting angry about any of it. It was better to move on to the next thing. The good thing was—there were plenty of "next things" available to him.

Maureen called too and offered a generic kind of regret and decried the unfairness of it all, which was big for her. She also expressed relief since she heard whispers at work and was getting her share of strange looks in town. She tried to pump Larry up with some self-help psychobabble, saying how exhilarating and healthy it was to have a new beginning and that maybe he shouldn't be so quick to dismiss Worthington's offer. It was good to hear the kick in her voice, but Larry made a note to himself not to be so familiar when he shared things with Maureen. In the divorce, he felt she had forfeited the right to advise him about his life choices as if she were still his wife. Keep it simple and informative. Establish a boundary that was appropriate for both of them.

When he called Juanita and told her it had gone as expected, she invited him to spend the night with her. As always, Larry was excited about being anywhere near Juanita, but it was getting a bit late, and they both had obligations in the morning. She was meeting with the building inspector, who so far was impervious to the St. Ignatius sales pitch that usually produced time, and a bit of leniency. Larry was moving into his new apartment over the weekend, and now that he didn't have to go to work in the morning, he could get a jump on that. He promised her she would be with him by proxy when he went to bed that night—courtesy of his imagination and devious right hand. She laughed and said she would carry on by proxy as she was in possession of some unruly devices herself, and they would talk tomorrow. ***

After a very productive day, Larry called Juanita, and she was despondent. The meeting with the building inspector hadn't gone well. Previously, he had indicated that for St. Ignatius to continue operating it would need a new roof, costing fifty-one thousand dollars. She had made significant progress in securing those funds, and now he informed her that the structural integrity of St. Ignatius was impaired and was in danger of collapsing.

"That's when I figured out his game."

"Whaddya mean, game?" Larry asked.

"Well, the newest member of the City of Buffalo's Department of Public Works, twenty-something Austin Pennington, told me the building employed a "light framing technique," and had reached the end of its life expectancy."

"That light framing technique was used postwar on some larger buildings but ended in the seventies. Now you find it mostly in suburban houses," Larry said.

"Exactly—light frame was between 1945 and 1970. St. Ignatius was built in 1925."

"What's up with this kid?"

What was up with that kid was—ambition. He wasn't just some wonky engineer type; he was a revolutionary. Lightly read and highly politicized, Austin Pennington had a long face with patches of fuzz that formed a barely legible beard. He was the son of a man who owned multiple car dealerships and he'd grown up in an eight-thousand-square-foot house on ten acres of land in the suburb of Clarence. Before getting an engineering degree, he spent his days riding horses and picking apples at his family's compound.

He was radicalized by his right-wing father and talk radio. Rather than following the standard institutional path to power through electoral politics, the young engineer would make a name for himself by fixing the inner city. Step one of his plan was to raze these just-hanging-on neighborhoods of their aging housing and public buildings. Step two was a murky plan for reinvestment through big hitters like his dad and others from the horse riding-apple picking community. He hadn't quite worked out all the details on that but insisted his portfolio as a junior level Building Inspector be composed of distressed sections of the east side of Buffalo.

"In other words," said Larry, "you're screwed."

"Yes," said Juanita. "St. Ignatius is going to be taken down by fuzzy-chinned Austin Pennington."

***

Juanita's never-ending diligence that September brought new funding to St. Ignatius. Now, the school provided Saturday morning money management, yoga and cooking classes, along with Larry's informal mentoring program. Since the future of the building was in question, they decided to temporarily halt his mentoring program until the issues with Austin Pennington were resolved, much to Makayla's chagrin.

After he'd moved the last of his stuff from his mom's and Maureen's, Juanita met him at his new apartment with the idea of helping him put some things in place, but she was understandably distracted.

"You don't have to stay. I can do this myself. It's not a big deal."

"No, I'm sorry—It's our day together." Still in her gold tracksuit with scarlet piping, she moved toward Larry with a certain deliberation. Standing in front of him, smelling like lotus blossoms, she grabbed his right wrist and then his left wrist and placed his hands firmly on her backside and let out a small gasp. "How about we skip all this mess, pretend we're in college again, and sheet up that bed on the floor. Then you can clear my head with that cosmic Larry Plumb goodness?"

In no time flat, Larry had both of them separated from their clothing and dispensed with the bed, opting for his firmly constructed desk instead.

Afterward, Larry set up the Wi-Fi while Juanita made up the bed. They ordered out Chinese and, from bed, binged two seasons of a decent if a little over the top, Netflix series called *Loudermilk*. Larry's presence and the show's funny one-liners made Juanita laugh and alleviated her anxiety about St. Ignatius's impending doom.

But the relief was temporary. Over the following weeks, she met with countless members of the business community and politicians, including the mayor of Buffalo, seeking financial help and time to get second opinions on the viability of the building. Her petitions were met with disappointing hedges: *We'll see what we can do and get back to you.*

With no time to wait for anybody to get back to her, she and Larry, who now had plenty of open space in his schedule, sought out new locations for the school. But none were suitable. Like St. Ignatius, all the buildings were old and decrepit or had other disqualifying issues that made them unsuitable. Plus, none enjoyed the central location of St. Ignatius, which was on the bus line in the middle of the neighborhood.

The day after Thanksgiving, with the St. Ignatius' situation becoming desperate, Larry saw in the *Buffalo News* that Carl Worthington had popped off again. This time about the Obamas. Worthington said he hoped the former president was using his time out of office to have sex with a Holstein and would hopefully come down with mad cow disease. His wish for the president's wife was that she would return to being a man and go live in the outback with a female gorilla named Bertha. Of course, he claimed his comments were not racially motivated but were simply the result of how much he despised the Obamas and their policies.

But it was bad this time for Worthington. There were incessant calls for him to be removed from corporate boards, and his job bids were dead on arrival. Reading about these stupid statements made Larry laugh, but a moment later, he realized there was an investment opportunity here for Worthington. An opportunity to prop up a crumbling east-side school and rehab his sagging image simultaneously.

Twenty Six

"That fucking racist?" Juanita shouted.

Surprised to hear her curse, Larry smiled and held up his hands, gesturing for her to slow down and listen. "Hear me out."

"Okay, Larry Plumb, but you better come strong—none of this *Wolf of Wall Street* or *Glengarry Glenn Ross*, mess."

Still smiling, he acknowledged that though Worthington was a Waspy old-school racist, there was some good to counter the bad. Over the years, Larry had gone to him several times when a worker with substance issues needed help to pay for rehab or when the son or daughter of a coworker needed a summer job. For years, Worthington had bankrolled the summer reading programs at the nonprofit bookstore Moby Dickens & Company, and he paid for the sandbags and labor to construct a temporary wall to halt the Buffalo Creek from flooding fifty homes along Indian Church Road. Despite him constantly shooting his mouth off in negative ways, there were these instances away from the spotlight where he used his wealth to help people.

"He needs you, and you need him. Otherwise, that little shithead building inspector is going to shut you down."

"Our needs are way bigger than any of your examples."

"Perhaps, but the consequences of his stupid statements this time are way bigger—and so will be his tax break."

Juanita shook her head skeptically at Larry's terrible proposition, "Give me a few days to think and to feel some people out."

Juanita received feedback about what Larry had proposed from staff and community members and cautiously decided the positives outweighed what she hoped would be short-term negatives to her and the school's reputation. Though she remained leery of some unseen consequence, she would take a meeting with Worthington and make her pitch.

On the day Worthington and an assistant showed up in the security camera just behind the school's heavy wooden entrance door for the tour, Larry stood not with Juanita but with the magnificent being that was Dr. Johnson. Dressed in her navy power suit, crisply pressed white blouse, glasses, and shiny black hair pulled tight in a ponytail, she struck a pose of supreme confidence and competence.

Alternating between asking Worthington probing questions about his ongoing projects and pitching the endless possibilities of St. Ignatius, she made quick work of the old guy. Whether it was self-interest or a bit of latent humanity, she got his money—as much as she needed.

His assistant pulled out a notepad and, in a very businesslike manner, started to jot down instructions about reaching out to the building inspector, politicians, and the mayor if needed. Worthington told him to contact all the media outlets except those *pricks* at the *Buffalo News.* He asked if Friday would be suitable for Juanita to do a press conference. And, as he walked out after declining to read a story to the children in The Pit, he told her to wear something nice like she had today and said to Larry, "You're the project manager on this job if you want it."

Larry noted that Juanita's face remained flat in the moments after Worthington made this offer to him. Her less-than-enthusiastic demeanor continued into their weekend date, which took place at a cozy Airbnb in the ski resort town of Ellicottville, south of Buffalo.

Rather than stopping for a late lunch or a drink in one of the numerous establishments decked out with Christmas decorations and filled with people dressed in sweaters and boots despite a lack of snow, Juanita wanted to go straight to their Airbnb. After getting a fire going, they quickly dispensed of each other's clothing, but instead of their typical cosmic interaction, Juanita was clingy and forlorn.

Up on his elbow afterward, with his head in his hand, Larry asked, "Is everything all right?"

Pulling him close, she gently wept, "Larry, I made a huge mistake."

"It's okay. It's okay. Taking that money isn't ideal but think of all the kids it will help."

"No, that's probably another mistake. The mistake is—I fell in love with you."

"Mistake? C'mon Juanita, who are we kidding—I love you too."

Quietly, Juanita went on, "From the moment we met, there was something about you—the humility, the earnestness, the sexy hands. I tried to fight it because I knew we would end up here." She paused, trying to find the right words. "There's been a good deal of pushback from the staff and the community, not only about taking Worthington's money but also about our relationship. I know we've tried to be discreet, but the Saturday staff let me know they are aware of our connection. Others saw your truck outside my house on Thursday mornings. It's coming at me from every direction."

"So that's it?" he asked.

"I'll need to give everything I have to this building project. I also have to do work to re-establish my credibility in the community. Taking Worthington's money and working with him is one thing. Add a white boyfriend from outside the neighborhood; it's too much for some people. I'm accused of abandoning my roots, of wanting to leave my Blackness behind. There's talk of boycotting St. Ignatius. I can't let that happen."

They made love once more before going to sleep that night, but it was despondent—this-is-over lovemaking, unlike the cosmic interactions that had marked their short, fiery time together.

Larry was awake an hour or more ahead of her the following morning and looked with a longing sadness at the beautiful figure sleeping peacefully before him, knowing he would never witness her gentle slumber again. Sitting with a cup of coffee, he assembled the seventeen songs that made up *The Seriously Get Laid Playlist* and linked it to her in a text with a little message: "*I'll listen to this when I'm missing you.*" Checking her messages shortly after dressing, she read the note and then gathered him in her arms as profuse tears streamed from her eyes.

They were mostly quiet on the forty-five-minute ride back to Buffalo. He hated that this was ending and sitting in her SUV in front of his apartment, he was silent for a moment as he gathered the words he was about to say, "When the fog clears from this, I'll remember with great fondness the infatuation and connection that were missing from my life that you gifted to me. Thank you for your cosmic passion and friendship. In a dark, dark time, you made me feel whole again. I'll never forget and will always cherish our time together."

In a whispery voice, fighting back tears, she said, "Larry Plumb, I'll love you forever."

Larry smiled. "I love you too."   He exited the vehicle and started up his driveway with his small bag slung over his shoulder. After a moment she lowered her window and called out to him in a gloomy voice, "Larry, let me know what happens with the book."

***

The previous week, two small publishing houses had offered to put out *Shadow Love* under their imprints. Both offers seemed to be heavily tilted to the advantage of the publisher. Besides some personal validation, he didn't see the benefit of going this route as opposed to putting it out himself through various online retailers.

The book was presently in the hands of an editor he had found online and was going through a second round of edits. Larry had issues with *dangling modifiers*, keeping *tenses* consistent and *echoing* certain words.

So, while he was waiting for the edits to come back, he called Kimmy Karney, knowing she had experience with contract law, and asked if she would look over his publishing deals and give him her opinion about what he was being offered—he thought maybe he was missing something. She agreed and asked that he send along both the contracts and the book, telling him she wanted to get a feel for its marketability before she gave a recommendation.

They were going to talk over coffee, but on the day they were to meet, she texted him and asked if they could get a drink instead, saying— "I know it's only Wednesday, but I've had a long week."

Larry was waiting for her at Mitchell's, sipping a Blue Light at the bar, trying not to think about Juanita. Of course, he had leaned into his old standby: nothing lasts forever, but he needed something more. He thought about the Camus quote he used to get through Maureen's cancer diagnosis and her infidelity, but that wasn't right for this situation. What he needed was a quote about a *hole*—the hole he felt in his life now that she was gone.

He did a Google search on his phone for *hole in life* quotes, and it returned numerous meme-worthy lines from a memoir by Jack Gantos and the lyrics to the Police song "Hole in My Life" from their first record. But those were wrong, too. Suddenly, the John Prine song, "All the Best, " came into his mind." It was about a guy who fell in love and bounced down the street like a little kid wishing only the best for this person he still loved but was gone. That's where Larry was with Juanita, and it was much nicer than thinking about a hole. John Prine could always do that.

But into these musings came a stressed-out Kimmy looking professional but weary in a pair of oval specs, and a dark wool trench coat with a leather document bag slung over her shoulder. Larry said hello, thanked her for meeting him, and helped her off with her coat. She sat on the stool next to his and ordered a Ketel One on the rocks while Larry hung up her coat. When he came back, she was returning her drink to the youngish female bartender, telling her she liked *mango-pineapple* vodka at the beach in the summer, but right now, she preferred a regular Ketel One on the rocks.

Kimmy looked at Larry as he sat down and she complained, "Drinking is too complicated these days. All this flavored booze is nonsense."

"I agree. You need a graduate degree just to order a beer."

She took a deep breath, "I'm sorry, but I need a minute."

"We can do this another day if it's better for you."

"No, this is fine. I gave my notice to Ponsonby, and suddenly, the old man is interested in me. He comes into my workspace with case files and positions himself to put his hand on my shoulder or touch my arm. I'm about to knock him out."

"That guy's such a creep. He made a pass at my wife—my *ex-wife*," Larry said, correcting himself. "Still sounds weird to say."

"Riding out these last days is going to be rough. Sorry about the divorce. How's that going?"

"Fine, an adjustment, but fine. The funny thing is I just got dumped again. I'm with two women in thirty years, and I get kicked to the curb twice within a couple of months," he said with an ironic laugh.

Oh, I'm sorry—"

"Nothing to be sorry about—I'm being silly. What's after Ponsonby?"

"I've made enough contacts to go out on my own. I don't need a big portfolio but want to stay in the mix."

Kimmy ordered a second vodka, and they moved on to discussing the publishing deals Larry was being offered, which she characterized as a step above slavery— "You do all the work, and they get all the profits."

Unless being published by a house was important to him, she thought he'd be better off just putting the book out himself. She read it and liked it, but it was old-school literature. If it were some thriller with gender-ambiguous characters and shape-shifting monsters or a series that could produce a committed following—he might possibly get the publisher to offer better terms or marketing help. But as a one-off standalone, the seventy-thirty split offered by online retailers seemed like a better choice. Plus, he retained total control of his product.

As she finished her second vodka, she apologized, saying she was feeling loopy and needed some water and to eat something. Larry offered to buy her dinner, and they got a table off to the side near the back of the room, but with it being the Christmas season, Mitchell's was unusually busy and loud for a Wednesday night.

After getting a couple of menus, Larry said, "Not much in the way of ambiance here, but the roast beef special is really great."

"I bet, and the fries too. These places always have great fries. But do they have salads? Oh, here we go—Buffalo chicken finger salad. Kind of defeats the purpose."

"I don't watch much TV, but I used to like Anthony Bourdain before the poor bastard went and killed himself. No matter where he was—Greece, Thailand, or wherever—they would just pull something out of the nearest river or lake, fry it up, and splash a little hot sauce and butter on it, and like magic, it was a local delicacy. Same thing in Buffalo, wing sauce on everything."

Kimmy ordered a Cobb salad while Larry did, in fact, get the roast beef special—without gravy or bread, and he substituted a side salad for fries. Kimmy removed her glasses when the waitress was gone and smiled broadly at Larry, her green eyes sparkling, "No bread, gravy, and a salad? Is it bikini season?"

"You ordered a Cobb."

"Yeah, I ordered a Cobb, but if I was getting the roast beef, I'd get the bread, gravy, and fries. You can't order the roast beef and not get the bread gravy and fries," she said with an incredulous smile.

Kimmy raised her hand, calling their waitress to their table, and told her to get this *silly man* bread, gravy, and fries with his roast beef special. The uncomfortable waitress looked at Larry, and with an expansive smile on his face, he nodded his approval. As the waitress turned toward the kitchen, Larry and Kimmy locked eyes for an extra tick or two.

As the moment drifted into the ether, Kimmy mentioned that when the essentials of his book were completed—editing, cover, blurb—it would take less than thirty minutes to upload it to the web and the larger world. If he had some hustle, he could make it available for order and have a signing before Christmas.

This immediately started the wheels spinning in Larry's head. He began thinking about writing the blurb, ordering books and establishing an online presence. He thought about posters, venues and dates. But before going into Larry Plumb overdrive, he stopped and focused on Kimmy and his dinner.   She picked at her Cobb, and he sopped up the decadent gravy with his bread while they talked about Christmas, their moms and kids, and some old high-school friends. He also somberly explained the Juanita thing, which prompted Kimmy to reach across the table and put her hand on Larry's arm, "I'm so sorry."

At her car afterward, Larry thanked her and wished her luck getting through her remaining days with Ponsonby. She searched for her keys in her bag, and when she found them, she smiled and said it was nice to catch up and to let her know what he was going to do with the book. With some hesitation, they leaned in for a quick hug, followed by an awkward moment of getting tangled in each other's eyes again.

***

Returning home, Larry lit some candles in his dark apartment, poured himself a Jim Beam, and cracked open a Rolling Rock. He grabbed a dining room chair, much like the ones he and Maureen had at their first apartment and positioned it near the front window that looked out on the street twinkling with Christmas lights. After he set his drinks on the windowsill, he cued up *The Seriously Get Laid Playlist,* sat down, and let Ella Fitzgerald's "Love is Here to Stay" wash over him.

He wanted to think about Juanita and what the eye contact with Kimmy might have meant. But his revelry never landed as the irony of the song hit him hard. He gazed at his sparsely furnished apartment, and besides the lack of furniture, he suddenly came to the crushing realization he had nothing—no job, no home, no woman, and he was all but estranged from his daughters. He had nothing and was all alone—his life was totally devoid of anything of value. How had he not seen this until now?

Theoretically, many positives and opportunities were available to him, but in this crushing moment, they seemed unsustainable and ephemeral. The soothing melancholy that washed over him minutes earlier had evaporated, and now he was gripped by fear and sadness. Maybe it was the Christmas season or being unmoored from a life that had been rock solid for so long, but his despair quickly became overwhelming. Worse still, the way forward seemed hopeless.

Solutions popped into his head, but what would a job with Worthington, a new home, and another woman get him? In the darkest days of confronting his father's death, and Maureen's infidelity, and cancer, he always had answers, always saw the way forward. But now, sitting there, he felt so alone and empty, like a forsaken man disconnected from everything that ever meant anything to him, an aimless wanderer cut loose from all the ties that anchored him. He looked to the void, and the light that always seemed to find him was nowhere in sight.

Sleep brought Larry no relief. He tossed and turned all night, reliving rebukes from his daughters, he saw dead chickens and Maureen making eyes across some bar at JD. And, just before waking up, he was tangled in a dream where he was hacking on a cigarette.

Most concerning, it was 6:45 a.m.—he hadn't slept that late since his teens, even when he was thick with Jim Beam. He tried to shake it off with coffee and his morning core routine, but he just didn't have it. Halfway through, he rolled up his mat and said screw it—not happening today. Without washing his face or brushing his teeth, he got back in bed and lay there as if paralyzed.

On his way home the previous night, he decided to self-publish, and at 10 a.m.—calling on every bit of strength available to him, he dragged himself from bed. He first pushed back a morning appointment for an estimate on a bathroom makeover till later that afternoon. He also sent a text to Mac and Burbs asking them to meet him at 4 p.m. for a beer at Bang Bang to help him put together an event for the release of his book. They both responded: "Ur buying." That made Larry feel better, but not much.

After dialing up his one-hundred-and-forty song *Power Pop* playlist, which featured the likes of Dwight Twilley, Matthew Sweet, and Bram Tchaikovsky, he spent the rest of the morning on his laptop at the dining room table, coming out from the social media shadows. Clicking away, he sent out upwards of a thousand Facebook friend requests and started following hundreds of people on Twitter.

Even with the upbeat, power pop tunes, he remained listless and depressed. His immersion into social media made things worse. Reading the posts of the people he was contacting saddened him immensely. They didn't really express opinions as much as they regurgitated memes and talking points. Their depth of historical knowledge went back two news cycles, and they had no media literacy or critical thinking skills. This was made more poignant because these were friends, coworkers, and people he respected or was connected to in the community. Yet, post after post, link after link, and meme after meme was mainly the same kind of grievance-filled crap that contributed to him losing his job.

In the early afternoon, he turned away from that task and used free online software to assemble a rudimentary book cover. Once he had something presentable, he shared it with an Indie Writers group on Facebook—one of the positive components of social media.

He instantly received positive feedback and reasonably priced offers to refine his cover and format and upload his book to various retailers. That was a lot of legwork worth passing off, so he hired a woman named Andrea

Edwards, who had a resume that was a mile long and was immediately available due to a cancellation. Besides spiffing up his cover, Andrea gently suggested he might want to take a pen name, or use his initials, or maybe his full name—Lawrence— because the name *Larry Plumb,* didn't exactly inspire excitement. Larry hadn't really thought about it but agreed and decided to go with the initials of his full name, Lawrence Frederick or—L.F. Plumb.

When that was settled, he quickly did his bathroom estimate and arrived at Bang Bang at 4 p.m., not only feeling exhausted but apparently looking exhausted.

"When was the last time you slept?" Burbs asked after a pull on a draft beer.

"I woke up just before seven but didn't get out of bed till ten."   "Well, you look like shit," Mac said. "Better get back to your middle-of-the-night nonsense."

"I don't really know what happened," Larry said in a shaky voice. "I sat down to have a beer last night, and suddenly, I fell into this pit of despair."

"Well, it ain't no secret you've been through a ton of shit this past year," Burbs said.

"Amen to that," Mac added.

Larry took off his glasses and set them on the bar, and rubbed his wet eyes.

"I know, but with every shitty thing that ever happened to me, whether as Commissioner, or with the old man dying, or with Maureen's cancer, there was always something bigger to hold on to that kept me going, kept me focused. Now, I have nothing. I'm just this useless fucking old man with nothing. I don't have a job, I don't have a home, my kids hate me, and women keep kicking me to the curb."

Burbs put his hand on Larry's shoulder, "You got us."

"Let's get out of here," Mac said. "Get a six, drive around and shoot the shit."

"Larry smiled at his friends, picked his glasses up from the bar, and placed them over his ears, "I'll be fine. Sorry for being so self-pitying, but I'm alone and a little broken right now. You fuckers, being here means a lot. I can do this."

"You sure?" Burbs asked.

"Yes."

While Larry tried to assure Mac and Burbs that he would be fine and could power through it, he knew he was full of shit. He had gotten through a lot in life and over this last year, but this kind of desolation was completely unfamiliar to him, and he didn't know how, when, or if it would dissipate.

Twenty Seven

Larry's depression and self-loathing kept his sleep sketchy and his energy levels low. Some quiet moments found him withdrawing, often having to sit or lie down and stare absently into space as he tried to gather the resources to complete daily tasks. Though his body was depleted, his mind willed him forward, and inch by inch, he found a way to execute toned-down workouts and complete setting up his new apartment.

Listlessly, he unpacked books and placed them on the shelves built into the wall. He repurposed some of the artwork from his old man cave, including his beloved Ella Fitzgerald poster at Downbeat Club, which featured an enthralled Duke Ellington and Tommy Dorsey looking on as she sang. The framed poster looked awfully lonely on the eggshell white wall, but like everything in his life at that moment, it wasn't great, but it was a start.

The one thing he found energizing was his novel. He gave it one last thorough review after receiving it from his editor, Nikki. Her comments and suggestions made the book infinitely more coherent, symmetrical, and, thus, easier to read. He also was in constant communication with Andrea, who was putting the finishing touches on his cover and punching up the blurb on the back of the book. Larry found her judicious pruning of the blurb made for a tight, to-the-point pitch to potential readers.

Mac and Burbs were a further bulwark through these dismal days. Burbs took time off to help Larry tie up some loose ends on a couple of side jobs, and Mac secured the Ironworkers Hall for the signing on the Saturday before Christmas from 2–6 p.m. He didn't get the whole hall, which could hold a thousand people, just the lounge area. However, the lounge had folding walls that opened into the larger hall to accommodate a bigger crowd if needed. Though they probably wouldn't need room for a thousand people, they expected a rather sizable crowd. Given the amount of Christmas cheer that was to be consumed, Mac was able to secure the room at no cost.

Mac also got an old high school pal who fronted a local band called Bad Ronald to provide musical entertainment for the signing. Sometimes, Bad Ronald wandered off into Cure-like emo-tunes, but generally, they were a good rocking band with some fun twists and turns.

Finally, as if they were twenty again, Mac, Burbs, and Larry went barhopping every night for two weeks all over West Seneca, South Buffalo, Lackawanna, Cheektowaga, and Orchard Park, hanging up posters announcing the book signing and talking to people. Larry did his best to put a brave face on through all this, but he couldn't break free of the funk gripping him. That's where Mac was so instrumental with all his bullshit. Even though he hadn't read *Shadow Love* or any book in years, he made a convincing pitch—"The book is tremendous; I couldn't put it down. This signing is going to be the literary event of the year."

***

On the Tuesday before the signing, with the book now live online and shipments of product delivered to his apartment, he received a text from Juanita asking if he had a moment to talk.

Larry and Juanita had exchanged several texts since the unceremonious end of their romantic relationship a month earlier. Though he desperately wanted to express how much he missed her, he kept it dignified and straightforward, informing her of his decision to self-publish and giving details about the pre-Christmas signing. She also stuck to a casual informative approach, telling him the building inspector had backed off and prep work for renovations at St. Ignatius was moving forward rapidly. And though she was being pulled in a thousand different directions, she was coping as well as expected.

But once they got on the phone, it was different. They found the time apart hadn't diminished the chemistry between them. Juanita expressed frustration at the challenges of working with Worthington, saying he was a man who was never told he was wrong about anything. He had no filter and was surrounded by people who just nodded and smiled at every misguided and stupid statement he made. When he stopped by St. Ignatius, she did her best to limit his interactions to his people only, keeping him away from the children and school staff—especially staff who would have loved to tell him where he could stuff the garbage that spewed from his mouth.

Larry laughed and complimented her dexterity in managing Worthington and the larger situation. Then he updated her on all the machinations of getting his book live—editing, cover, blurb, and the effort it was taking with Mac and Burbs to get the word out about the signing. He also complained about the evil necessity of social media and how it left him disillusioned with many people he knew, liked, and respected.

He decided not to tell her about the depression he had been experiencing out of fear that she might feel responsible. Juanita, however, picked up on the weariness in his voice and asked if he had been taking care of himself—exercising, eating right, and getting proper rest. Impressed that she knew him so well, he acknowledged he was a little run down without getting into it. Given their present relationship, he felt it was a little out of bounds.   After encouraging him to take care of himself, she got down to the real reason for the call—Makayla. Since the informal mentorship with Larry had ended so abruptly and without a real explanation, Makayla was having some difficulties in school and at St. Ignatius. In both places, there were reports of disruptive and disrespectful behavior, and earlier that day, she was driven home by the police after being involved in a fight on a street corner.

"That seems so out of character for her," he lamented.

"It does. I know it's a big ask, but is there any way you could continue to work with her?"

"Where, how, now that the Saturday thing at St. Ignatius isn't an option?"

"Yes, that doesn't work."

Larry paused for a moment and then came up with a possible answer, "If her parents are agreeable—how about I hire her and pay her to work side jobs with me?"

***

Larry sat at the perfectly set dining room table where Makayla's mom, Janelle, poured him a cup of coffee while her father, James, brought in cream and sugar from the kitchen. Despite the recommendation from Dr. Johnson and Makayla's constant chatter about *Mr. Larry*, the meeting started inauspiciously. It didn't bother them that Larry worked off-the-books cash deals at people's homes. They also liked the idea of Makayla continuing to develop new skills and earning money. What they had a problem with was that Larry wasn't a churchgoing man, and he was expecting Makayla to forgo Sunday services to work with him.

Her education consumed all of her daytime hours during the week, and working after school wasn't practical, since Larry couldn't start his day or break off to get her in the afternoon. Taking this job with him only made sense if they worked both days on the weekend. The expectation of his customer base was typically a full day on Saturday and the first half of Sunday. By noon or 1 p.m. on Sunday, people were prepping for dinner and another workweek.

So Larry came up with what he thought might be an acceptable compromise. He suggested he take her to an afternoon service on Saturday at the end of the day. He did a quick Google search and found masses in areas where he typically worked—West Seneca, Kaisertown, and South Buffalo. They could also attend mass at Saint Louis Church on Main Street, near their home.

"Those are all Catholic churches," Janelle said.

Larry smiled, "It's not ideal, but what's the saying—Don't let the perfect be the enemy of the good or the passable."

Janelle looked at James for a moment, and he nodded, "Okay, Mr. Plumb, that will be acceptable."

"Fabulous," he said, standing up and reaching out his hand to shake with both of them. "Makayla's a great kid—and please call me Larry."

Just then, the front door opened, and Makayla burst into the room and ran toward Larry. She wrapped her arms around his waist and pushed her head against his chest, "Mr. Larry, Mr. Larry, I saw your truck—you're here?"

Larry was a little stunned by this display of affection and smiled at James and Janelle.

"We told you she's always talking about you," James said.

They sat back down, with Makayla occupying the seat to Larry's right. As Janelle freshened up his coffee, he felt a small change in himself. Maybe it was from Makayla bursting through the door, and hugging him, or the excitement in her face as he explained the opportunity he was presenting her. He was also pleased with her serious demeanor when he defined expectations—good grades, no disruptive behavior or fighting, and church on Saturday. Whatever it was, Larry felt a spark, as if his purpose was returning. The foggy depression of the previous weeks began to lift with Makayla's enthusiasm and excitement.

This was further bolstered when Makayla, with her parents looking on, negotiated her wage, "Mr. Larry, at St. Ignatius, you told me the beginning rate for an apprentice laborer was twenty dollars per hour. Since I'm only thirteen, I'll do it for fifteen dollars,"

"Fifteen?" Larry smiled. "Minimum in New York is ten, and since this is off the books, let's say nine per hour."

"How about thirteen, and you buy the coffee?"

"Coffee? I never saw you drink coffee once, girl—eleven," Larry countered with a laugh.

"Twelve, and we buy our own coffee?" She beamed.

"Twelve it is."

The only downside to the meeting was Makayla's disappointment when she learned Larry wouldn't be taking on any new work until after the first of the year due to the holidays, his obligations with the novel, and the signing over the weekend. He shook hands with her parents again, wished them a Merry Christmas, and told Makayla—*Be good*.

In his truck, he texted Juanita: "Mission accomplished with Makayla and family."

She responded instantly, saying, "Great." She followed that with a second text wishing him luck at the signing and a Merry Christmas. She ended by saying: "I miss you."

Larry typed out a message in kind saying, "I miss you too," but before he hit send, he pondered the implications of where this exchange would lead. In another illuminating moment, he asked himself if he wanted it to lead anywhere. Of course, he would do almost anything to lie next to her and experience her cosmic passion, but what would that get them? Temporary gratification followed by the reality that doomed their relationship in the first place.

He sent the text anyway. He saw no harm in acknowledging the simple truth that he was missing her too. What he wasn't going to do, if asked, was see her and possibly give in to the ephemeral pleasure of her heavenly flesh.

He might have jumped at the chance a few days ago, but after meeting with Makayla and her parents, he felt a sense of renewal, and his mind was starting to clear. Staring at the screen of his phone, he knew getting together would only start the pain of their separation all over again. He hated that. It felt like playing not to lose. But, of course, this wasn't just about him—the fates of many kids who deserved the chance offered by Dr. Johnson and St. Ignatius depended on him standing down. It was a bitter but necessary pill to swallow.

As he drove back to West Seneca to meet Mac and Burbs to promote more books, Juanita must have reached the same conclusion since no further texts were forthcoming. Instead of listening to Christmas music, which was so overdone at that point in the season, even on the classical channel, he leaned on John Prine again, dialing up the song "All the Best." He drove along with a smile, thinking about Juanita and feeling grateful for his time with her. And it wasn't lost on him how good it felt to have a smile on his face.

The first snow of the year had begun to fall as he made his way through the dark, wintery West Seneca streets to a somber little place called Morty's Beer Garden. Morty's was in Zone 5, and Larry, still not far removed from his old job, observed the town hadn't vacuumed up the leaves at the residents' curbs yet. The forecast was calling for an extended period of snow over the next few days and into Christmas. If that forecast was correct, the leaves would likely not be picked up till spring.

The last time this happened was in 1990, Larry's second year as Commissioner. The lake effect started coming down in mid-November and didn't stop until mid-March, and the leaves got buried in the snowbanks that accumulated throughout winter. There was no reason the town didn't get to them this far into December, especially with the lack of snow.

When he entered the drab little bar that even Parson Brown couldn't bring a Christmas smile to, one of the residents from Zone 5 was giving Mac shit about the leaves. His name was Ryan Hartling, and he owned a small real estate agency. Hartling was also one of the loudmouths on social media who demanded Larry be fired.

With his biggest fake smile, Mac pointed at Larry as he sidled up to the bar. "Well, Mr. Hartling, remember on Facebook demanding this guy be terminated?"

"Hey." Larry nodded and stuck out his hand to shake. "I think we've met before—Larry Plumb." But Hartling just let his hand hang there.

"Plumb was the guy who coordinated all the crews, made sure all the equipment was in good working order, and buttoned up the whole town before one flake of snow ever touched the pavement."

"Don't you have new people in place?" Hartling asked.

"Of course, but they're a bunch of meatheads that don't know their asses from third base. It'll take years for them to pick up what Plumb could do with one hand tied behind his back while talking up your mom."

Hartling's eyes grew big. "I don't like your tone, and that's not funny, Mr. McNamara."

Still with the fake smile, Mac said, "I don't care what you like, Mr. Hartling, and mom jokes are always funny."

Larry and Burbs tried to muffle a laugh while Hartling paused momentarily. Standing there, Larry thought the small business owner was considering the consequences of escalating. In the end, Hartling retreated back to his table, where a bored woman sat with some drinks. They watched him as he sat down, and when he pulled out his phone, Mac called to him, "Mr. Hartling, would you like a picture to go with whatever poetry you're about to write on social media?"

Mac got between taller Larry and Burbs, and Hartling snapped a picture of the three friends arm in arm, grinning from ear to ear.

Larry and Mac climbed on stools while Burbs leaned sideways against the bar. The chatter in the room made it hard to hear the Sabres pregame on the flat screens above the rows of booze on the back bar. With a sour face, Mac ordered drinks, "Hey Morty, three Jim Beams, and three Blue Lights. Get yourself one too."

"Bringing a constituent's mom into it—nice." Burbs laughed.

"Retail politics at its best," Larry added.

"Fuck that guy and fuck these people. Plumb, do you know how many calls I've taken since you got yourself fired?"

"Since I got *myself* fired?"

"Oh, it's not important. Fuck all these people. I've had it with being yelled at by these whining, entitled suburban jackasses who think the Earth rotates on its axis because they have some shitty little business or they pay taxes," Mac said bitterly.

Burbs looked at Larry. "Out of deference to the shit you've been going through, he's been quiet about it, but his phone has been ringing nonstop since you were let go."

Mac held his phone at arm's length to show Larry and Burbs, "Ten responses saying we're garbage since Hartling posted two minutes ago."

"It's not all negative," Burbs said. "Bravo999 clicked a laughing emoji to what you said about his mom. That's something."

And with his newfound clarity, Larry had an idea, "If you're really sick of this shit, I might have a way out—for the three of us."

Mac and Burbs were aware that Larry had been developing a mentorship program with Juanita. Sitting there listening to Mac complain about all the calls he was taking, Larry thought maybe the three of them, with their unique skill sets, could get a nonprofit program up and running.

"Mac, you could be the administrative part that does outreach and raises money, Burbs has the temperament and experience to mentor, and I could do a little of both—you know, be the guy that fixes all the things you fuck up."

They playfully reminded Larry of some of his fuckups, but both were intrigued. Like Larry, they had pensions to tap and healthy 401(k)s. For an hour or so, they talked it over, weighing the pros and cons, of which there seemed to be many more pros. Mac and Burbs seemed to be up for a change, especially now that Larry had lost his job with the town and was no longer there to lean on or to tie up loose ends.

Before leaving, they hung a couple of posters regarding the signing around the bar, and Larry thanked Morty with a big tip. Heading toward the exit, Mac blew Hartling a kiss.

Out in the parking lot before parting ways, Mac said, "I know there's more to consider, but this nonprofit thing sounds like a good exit strategy."

"We really could make this happen," Burbs added.

It had continued to snow while they were in the bar. "We'll talk more, but right now, it looks like you're going to have to get some streets cleared, Mac," Larry joked.

"Ahhh, fuck me," Mac said with some irritation as the three friends started their vehicles and cleared their windows.

Back at his apartment after he drove home from Morty's, the dining room chair he set up at the front windows weeks back remained in place. Still feeling positive and clear, Larry poured a Jim Beam and set it on the windowsill with a Rolling Rock. Before sitting down to look at the Christmas lights out his window, he synced his phone to his Bose speaker and hit shuffle on his music library. First up was Randy Newman's "Marie," which brought an instant smile to his face, but it was the next tune, "The Girl from Ipanema," by Stan Getz/Astrud Gilberto, that really hit him.

Though the breezy samba standard clashed with the snow falling outside and the Christmas lights on his street, he plugged right into those lines: tall and tan—young and lovely and the *ahh* when she passes on her way to the sea. That imagery of that beautiful girl struck at his core—*ahh*.

He thought for a brief moment how Ashley and Sam would judge him as some kind of sadistic creep for his primal attraction to the sketch of that lovely girl in the song. That somehow the urges coursing through his and every man's body were to solely dominate and control and were without poetry, charity, and love. Larry never wanted to dominate or control—he wanted the alluring verses, the compassion, and the love. He and Juanita had reached those highs—reawakening Larry's long-dormant sense of in-fatuation and connection.

Regardless of the outside forces that brought him and Juanita down and the price they both paid in grief and loss, that infatuation and connection remained the apex of life's sweetness, and he wanted more of it. Awards, money, status—those earthly riches couldn't measure up to the way a woman walked, her laugh, or the wanting look in her eye. He rose from his chair, and started to dance around his apartment, wishing his old instructor, Adriana, were there to accompany him. While he moved about like a moonstruck fool, he told himself he would share that love with someone again regardless of the cost.

Twenty Eight

I t continued to snow throughout the night. Larry was back on schedule, waking at 3:46 a.m. with the lovely image of that tall and tan girl still in his head. He sipped coffee, looking at the lights outside his window that had been left on all night, and for the first time during the holiday season, he felt a tinge of Christmas hope.

He sailed through his core routine, posted reminders about the signing on social media, and even had time to read a short story by John Cheever, which left him thinking Mac was right—*these whiny suburban fucks believe the Earth does rotate on its axis for them.* After shoveling almost a foot of snow in his driveway, he had coffee with his appreciative landlady and headed to Maureen's.

When he decided to self-publish, he sent a group text to Maureen and the kids to inform them of the signing and that he would drop books off for them at the house. The response, as expected, was less than enthusiastic. Sam extended regrets about not being able to attend because of work, and Ashley's rejoinder was a single word: Congrats. Ben gushed, telling Larry he was really proud of him and was looking forward to the signing. Maureen also provided terse congratulations. As a courtesy, she also sent a separate text telling him that she had started seeing someone—one of the town's finance guys, Tim Watts.

Larry had known Watts in a peripheral way in high school. He played alto sax in the school jazz band and was kind of a dashing guy, always sporting porkpie hats, turtlenecks, and tweed jackets, like Thelonius Monk. He had gone to Chicago for college and stayed, making a fine living as an analyst for a myriad of Fortune 500 companies.

After a divorce, he returned to Western New York to semi-retire and take a part-time job with the town. One afternoon, Larry met with him while dropping off employee rosters for Mac at Town Hall. He heard some Paul Desmond leaking out from a corner cube, and when he investigated, there was Watts. Though he was a little thin on top and kind of a slight guy, he had aged well and was still dashing in a tweed jacket. After catching up, they had an extended conversation about Paul Desmond. Maureen had met Watts at a fundraiser, and now they were dating. Not only that but in her text, she said he *adored* her. It was an odd thing to tell her ex-husband, and Larry wasn't sure if she was gleeful about this new relationship, or she was trolling him. Whatever it was, it hardly mattered now.

The snow closed schools for the day, and when Larry arrived at Maureen's, she was in the garage with Watts, trying to figure out how to start the snowblower. After taking a moment to pet the excited dogs Larry greeted them somewhat awkwardly and diagnosed the problem from the gassy odor as a flooded engine, like in the summer with the lawnmower.

Watts was, of course, dashing in a navy peacoat, wool scarf, and plaid trapper hat. However, he seemed very uncomfortable with the cold winter morning—too uncomfortable for a guy who had spent his life in Chicago. Maureen, dressed in her knee-high black boots, fleece beanie, and parka, looked great, as usual. Though they were similar in height and dress she seemed to have a greater, more impactful presence than Watts. At any rate Larry told them they would have to wait about twenty minutes for the gas to clear from the carburetor for the machine to work. He handed Maureen the bag of books and turned to leave.

But before he could go, she asked if he would help dig out Watts's BMW. Maureen had the day off, but he was expected to be at work. Watts protested, and Larry, unsure what the play was, then looked at Maureen and figured it out. "Sure," he said.

In that telling moment, Larry could see that the power dynamic of the relationship was heavily tilted toward Maureen. He also understood why she asked him to help. Like an improvised sax solo that jumped wildly from one note to the next, Watts was all over the place and quite inefficient at moving snow. Plus, he really didn't have much strength or stamina.

Once Watts' car was liberated and he was on his way, Larry said, "That was interesting," as he and Maureen trudged through the snow back toward the garage to check on the snowblower.

"He has ADHD. He's a sweet guy."

"A finance guy with ADHD?"

"Larry, be nice. He's been very successful."

"Okay, okay," he said.

After he showed her how to start and use the snowblower he got in his truck and headed to finish up a hardwood floor install with Burbs. Carefully negotiating the snowy streets, he thought about Watts and Maureen and how—he adored her. Waiting on a red light, Larry reflected on how he had adored her too, but it wasn't enough. As the light changed, he maybe stumbled onto another reason why he and Maureen didn't make it. Ultimately, they were competing alphas who couldn't coexist. Larry liked to think he tried to meet her halfway as a co-alpha, but maybe that wasn't right, and he was fooling himself. Again, it hardly mattered now. One thing was certain with Watts—she was the alpha, and he was the beta. Good for you, Maureen, he mused. *You deserve to be adored on your terms.*

***

On the day of the signing, Larry and Ben pulled into the Ironworkers Hall parking lot, which was already half-full an hour before the event began. His long history in the town, his due diligence on social media, and all the reaching out with Mac and Burbs seemed to have paid dividends. Although over a thousand people clicked that they were interested in the event, and some seven hundred said they were attending, the half-full lot still surprised him.

He consulted with his Facebook Indie Writers group, thinking perhaps the five hundred books he ordered wouldn't be enough, but the consensus was his estimate was probably in the ballpark. From scrutinizing social media, he also cynically reasoned that not many people actually read books or novels, and perhaps the high level of engagement was just a reflection of people wanting to go to a party.

When Larry and Ben entered with the first load of books, people in the already busy lounge started clapping for him. Embarrassed, he smiled and waved as Burbs directed him to a table across from the bar. Bad Ronald was setting up at the opposite end of the room, which was decorated with festive wreaths, lights, and two oversized fake trees. Seeing the turnout already, Mac opened the folding walls that led to the greater hall to create more space and said to Larry, "This is going to be big."

Larry and Ben, with the help of some of his former coworkers, including Rocky, ironically enough, made quick work of getting the remaining cases of books into the venue and to the table where he would be signing.

Larry looked at Rocky and laughed, "The book is still full price."

"I'm not buying your stupid book, Larry, but I will get you and your kid a beer."

Larry could feel the Christmasy buzz in the air, and by the time Rocky returned with the drinks, everything was in place: Sharpies, stacks of books, instructions for digital payment, and two enlarged cutouts of the book cover resting on either side of where he would be standing and signing. Rather than him sitting down at a table, it was decided that Larry would stand and sign at a raised cocktail table. This would give him a chance to say hello to people in a more personal way and snap pictures. Ben would be close by facilitating the whole process. It was a good plan since people would undoubtedly post those pics to social media, thus creating more buzz about the book.

Larry and Ben thanked Rocky for the beers, and they knocked their bottles together and said, "*Cheers.*" Then, something strange happened—for the first time in thirty-plus years of working with Rocky, they had a moment. It wasn't much, but there it was—a human connection. Above his long, full beard and cheeks, Rocky's angry, resentful blue eyes softened as he looked at Larry. "The shop isn't the same without you," he said, staring at Larry in a penetrating way. He paused briefly and then said, "Merry Christmas, Larry."

Larry put his hand on Rocky's shoulder, "Merry Christmas Rock."

Larry was quite moved as he watched his old nemesis walk toward the bar. Inspecting the increasingly frenzied room, he was reminded of the yearly Christmas Bazaar from grade school. But his mind drifted from those care free days to his recent depression and his year of loss—Maureen and Juanita, his job, and his home. Yet, despite those defeats he was still there, having a moment with a longtime rival as a line formed to buy his first novel, which he created through bold persistence and imagination. Yes, he thought—I'm still here. You could kill his dad, steal his youth, take his job, dump him, disrespect him, ignore him; it didn't matter. Larry Plumb was still here. Larry Plumb was built to last. Regardless of the obstacles he confronted and the losses he took, he would pop out of bed and continue to attack each day with good sense, determination, and a desire for love.

As he watched Rocky melt into the crowd at the bar, it also occurred to him that maybe he was wrong to think of life as impermanent, that *nothing lasts forever.* He turned to Ben, who was so proud to be there with him, and he thought of Makayla, who was so eager to work with and learn from him. He gazed out at the lounge filled with friends, former coworkers, and people wanting to share Christmas cheer with him—it was all a testament to how he had touched their lives and how he would live on in them.

Though his relationships with his daughters remained strained, perhaps his most significant impact was on them. Their obnoxious, hurtful rebellion would not have been possible had he not been such a conscientious father, feeding them books like *The Feminine Mystique,* and music like the Clash, or had he not imbued them with the lofty Emma Lazarus ideal that—*None of us are free until all of us are free.*

Going forward, Sam and Ashley would move through this world demanding equity and equality. In their work and life, they would inspire others to do the same, and rippling across the universe, the arc of history would bend ever so slightly toward justice. Larry was there too.

It was an incredibly satisfying moment—a moment in which if he were some paragon of manhood like "Dirty Harry," he might be holstering his .44 Magnum with dead guys all around him. If he were some jacked-up football player, he might have been spiking the ball and flexing obnoxiously like a conqueror of worlds. But he was Larry Plumb, former town employee, reader of poetry, and first-time author, trying to move forward and adapt to a changing world with humility, goodness, and love. He felt a small, gratified smile come to his lips, and then he got to the work of signing books.

***

In the end, Larry sold four hundred and eighty of those books. On top of that, with the help of Mac and Burbs, he hosted a great party. Given the half-full parking lot an hour prior to the start of the event, two auxiliary bars were set up and staffed by a rotating crew of old coworkers from Highway to keep the drinks flowing. Bad Ronald played a lively set of holiday and cover tunes at a volume that still allowed for conversation to occur. The big hit of the first set was the Kink's "Father Christmas." Mac and Burbs worked the line that proceeded at an uneven pace depending on how well or how long it had been since Larry had seen someone.

People from every phase of Larry's life showed up. Not only coworkers but also people from his mom and dad's day, former town supervisors, council people, and support staff. It was like a fifty-year reunion of town workers.

There were also many surprises with old classmates and girlfriends like Mary Licata, the first girl who told Larry she loved him. Also in attendance was the recently divorced Katie Auerbach, who stomped on Mac's heart freshman year. She was still out of Mac's league at fifty-six, but he zeroed in and chatted her up regardless. Another woman who was in line to get a book, still looking pretty great, was their old teacher, Ms. Webb, who taught Larry, Mac, and Burbs algebra her first year out of college. She laughed when Burbs told her how hard it was to solve for x when she wore tight pants or a short skirt. Their friend Lucy was there as well. She had recently dumped her crotchety boyfriend, Gene, and with good humor, told Larry, "So, ya know I'm in the market for some new asshole."

Helen, flanked by Nora and Matt, received almost as much attention as Larry. Sitting at a table just off to the side where he was signing books, she thanked people for coming, asked after their kids and grandkids, and wished everyone a Merry Christmas. The only person she didn't have a kind word for was Ponsonby, who strolled up to her table with his giant white teeth at full force and his mud-colored dye job. But Helen was having none of it, telling him, "You have a lot of nerve showing up here after what you did to Larry." Turning to Nora, she said, "Look, the cheap bastard didn't even buy a book."

With an embarrassed expression, Ponsonby cast his eye toward Matt as if searching for relief from Helen's rebuke, but none was forthcoming. Matt, like his mom, wasn't having it. He did say, "If you're looking for a book, Mr. Ponsonby, I would be happy to walk you to the back of the line where you could wait with everyone else." Ponsonby's giant white smile receded, and he slithered away like a small, wounded garden snake.

Larry was catching up with an old neighbor when he noticed a few people back in line, JD's friends, Carrie and Lynn, from the Golf Club Inn. They looked very cute in festive sweaters and Santa hats and seemed to be talking to Mac in a friendly way. Apparently, something had changed since that night at Mitchell's when Carrie was screaming at them after Mac sucker punched JD.

When it was their turn, both ladies skirted the cocktail table, hugged Larry, and congratulated him on the book and the great party. Like others, they expressed surprise at his literary ambitions. When Ben placed some books on the table to be signed, Lynn asked, "L.F. Plumb? What does the "F" stand for?"

Before Larry could answer, Ben said, "Larry *Fucking* Plumb."

They all laughed, and looking at Ben, Carrie said, "This is your son, right? He's a younger, bigger you?"

"He's funny and cute," Lynn smiled.

"Yes," Larry said, and introduced Ben. "It was mentioned that my name, Larry Plumb, didn't exactly inspire excitement. So we went with my initials. And despite what Ben says, the "F" stands for Frederick."

Ben put an exclamation point on his dad's explanation, "See, Larry *Fucking* Plumb—much better!"

They all laughed, and it was time for the line to move again. Larry quickly signed the books with a play on the title, *Shadow Love*—Heed the Shadows, L.F. Plumb. He thanked them for coming and wished them a Merry Christmas.

When he handed Carrie her book, she grabbed his forearm, leaned in, and whispered, "Hey, just so you know, JD and I are pretty much done. He would never tell me why your friend punched him, but I have a pretty good idea. Look me up if you want to exact a little karma on him." She stepped back, smiled at him seductively, and then turned toward Ben. She said it was nice to meet him and to stop at the bar and have a beer with them when he was done there.

Lynn hugged Larry and said she was looking forward to reading the book. She also encouraged Ben to have a beer with them.

Not sure what just happened, Larry looked at Ben, and Ben looked at Larry, and they both muffled a laugh.

The line continued to move, and a minute later, seemingly out of nowhere, Makayla was standing next to Larry, as he talked to the secretary at Maureen's old school, Alphie Coyne. Alphie needed some rooms freshened up—drywall, paint, light fixtures, outlets. In addition to moving books, the signing proved to be quite valuable in securing new work. He introduced her and told Alphie that Makayla would be his number-one assistant on the job. Showing some customer service chops, Makayla said she was looking forward to working on her project and wished her a Merry Christmas.

When Alphie left them, Makayla asked, "How'd I do?"

"Perfect. Who are you here with?" Larry asked, smiling.

"Dr. Johnson."

Larry scanned the room, and halfway between his table and the bar, Juanita stood tall in a circle with a big smile, talking to Maureen and Ashley. Watts was off to the side, looking as if he was about to take their drink order. When Larry stopped over to pick up the last of his tools earlier in the month, he'd told Maureen about the situation with Juanita, knowing she would pass the information along to Ashley. Maureen asked questions, but he was tight with answers, telling her it was "amicable" and that "sometimes things just don't work out."

He waved, and Juanita responded first, followed by Maureen and Ashley, while Watts looked confused. They were all beaming as they waved back, even Ashley.

While they talked, Larry quickly introduced Makayla to his family and put her to work with Ben. It was evident from the first fist bump she was a bit smitten with Ben, but that didn't keep her from doing a good job. Ben liked her too and told her stories about his time working jobs with Larry as they put books before him.

After a torrent pace, the line eventually whittled down to random people, and Bad Ronald started to pack it in. Juanita broke away from Maureen and Ashley and spent a few minutes yucking it up with Mac,

Burbs, and Lucy before coming over to say hello. Immediately, he sensed the gravitational pull between them was still immense. With this in mind, like with Maureen, he kept their interaction small and tight. This was the best course of action for both their sakes.

Before he introduced her to Ben, who was being closely shadowed by Makayla, he made a joke about surviving his friends and not to believe any of the damn lies they told about him. A moderate smile came to her face, and she congratulated him on the great turnout and party. With the same kind of circumspect demeanor, Larry thanked her for coming and asked about the progress at St. Ignatius. He also mentioned all the work he secured today and how it would keep Makayla busy throughout the winter.

To avoid further awkwardness, he brought her over to Helen, Nora, and Matt, and she did her Dr. Johnson thing, charming and delighting his family with her bright, easy disposition and interest in them. While she talked with Nora about her time as a college professor, Ashley came over to say hello. She assured Helen that she would be by in the morning for Christmas breakfast and then gave Larry a real hug and congratulated him. Larry sensed her discomfort, but still flush with his earlier thoughts about her and Sam being masters of the universe, he took the hug as progress between them.

Maureen sent a text to Larry saying she wasn't ready to engage his family as his ex-wife yet. She congratulated him again and asked him to extend her regrets to Helen, Nora, and Matt.

As 6 p.m. approached and the signing was ending, Juanita gathered up Makayla. Before heading out, she expressed how nice it was to meet everyone and wished them all a Merry Christmas. Makayla did the same and gave everyone a hug except Larry. She fist-bumped him, saying, "Since we're going to be colleagues, we should keep it professional," which drew a huge laugh from the group. Juanita did give him a hug and an awkward kiss on the cheek and congratulated him once more.

As Larry watched them leave, Nora came up from behind him, put her hand on his back, and said, "That is one impressive lady—and so *fucking* hot. Never hearing Nora curse, Larry busted out laughing. "Seriously, I think I'm in love," she said and Larry laughed even harder.

It was just the reset he needed to ease the longing he felt as Juanita walked away. But, as Juanita and Makalya went toward the exit, another tall woman with glossy black hair and a familiar gait headed in Larry's direction. It was Kimmy Karney, looking fabulous in ankle-high boots, jeans, a thick black turtleneck, and a thin winter vest. As she stepped closer, Larry could feel a smile coming to his face. She was smiling too.

Kimmy greeted him with a hug and said, "Quite the blowout. I hopped over three piles of vomit in the parking lot on my way in."

"Only the most high-minded people attend these literary events," Larry joked.

He thanked her for lighting the fire that resulted in a very successful day, and then he pivoted to introduce her to his family. While Nora and Ashley helped Helen, who was a little drained from the event, with her coat, Larry explained it was on Kimmy's advice he fast-tracked putting the book out and doing the signing.

Then, with a certain devilishness, he told Helen that Kimmy was an attorney, and she worked for Ponsonby. Helen perked up instantly, calling Ponsonby a *son of a bitch* and a *sycophant,* producing a huge laugh from all, including Kimmy. She smoothly confirmed it was a job of convenience and was no longer employed there.

After one more hug, Nora, Matt, and Ashley left with Helen. With things winding down Kimmy agreed to have a drink with Larry. Ben said he was going to have that beer with Carrie and Lynn. Larry cautioned him that those girls had a never-ending party going and to be careful. He thanked Ben for his help, and they embraced like two hearty bears. Larry gave him a hundred-dollar bill—to cover an Uber and whatever, but mostly for an Uber.

Despite the event being over, the lounge area was still quite full and festive. The digital jukebox had replaced Bad Ronald with Christmas songs and a not-so-great mix of tired classic rock songs. Carrie and Lynn's crew, which now included Ben, were at one end of the bar, and Burbs, Lucy, Mac, and believe it or not, Katie Auerbach were at the other end with a sizable crowd between them.

Larry set his remaining case of books and cover cutouts on a nearby table and, flush with cash, bought the bar a drink. As the old friends laughed, busted chops, and caught up, especially with Kimmy and Katie Auerbach, Larry had another epiphany.   Throughout his life, he was gifted certain moments of grace, when some supernatural force seemed to tap him on the shoulder and say—mark it down; it doesn't get sweeter than this. Larry paused, as he had before that first time with Juanita, and in that little nothing lounge sharing laughter, joy, and love with Rocky, his family, and these friends—he took it in and marked it down. Erect and triumphant, he felt as if he occupied the very center of the universe. It was as near a perfect moment as he had ever experienced and there was nowhere, he'd rather be. If that wasn't enough, Kimmy kept sparkling him with her eyes, which were the green of Christmas promise.

Larry stepped away from his seat at the bar to talk to an old coworker. When the conversation ended, he went over and pumped a few bucks into the jukebox before returning to his stool. After further laughter, another drink, and more eyes from Kimmy, she excused herself to use the restroom. On her way back, as she moved with that distinctive gait toward Larry, who was facing her on his stool, suddenly, from the ashes of history, the air was filled with those first velvety bars of the Edgar Winter dirge "Autumn." The song Kimmy used to soothe her broken twelve-year-old heart when Donny McAndrews dumped her. It was also the song that prompted Larry to pursue her at that house party all those years ago.

"What are you doing, Larry?"

"What I'm doing is—*blowing your mind.*" And, from his barstool he made a fist on either side of his head. Then he unfurled his fingers simultaneously as if an explosion was occurring. A dreamy smile grew on her face and knowing that he had succeeded in blowing her mind Larry stood up, looked her in the eye and kissed her.

She grabbed his hands and kissed him back. When the kiss dissolved, she said, "I promise not to go all Donny McAndrews on you."

"Yeah, you say that now, but when you do, it'll still be so worth it."

Over the last year, if he had learned anything, it was that without loss and heartbreak, this glorious moment with the beautiful green-eyed Kimmy Karney wouldn't have been possible.

Larry Plumb was still very much here, and he was ready for everything.

Acknowledgements

First and foremost, I need to thank my wife, Donna, who designed and generated the artwork for Larry Plumb Is Still Here. She also served as the book's final proofreader, uncovering numerous errors and inconsistencies in the manuscript. Most of this book was conceived and written during the middle of the night, and her patience with lights being turned on, coffee being made, and pets being fed was endless. Most importantly, thirty-plus years into our partnership, she still shares all her sandwiches with me and makes me laugh.

I would like to express my extreme gratitude to the early readers of this book: Jeanne Moran, Joe Kane, Peter Kane and Jesse and Mary Lou Nolan. All provided invaluable feedback in shaping, molding, and chipping away the rough edges of this book.

Special thanks also go to Tom Schappert for providing key insights about the functioning of town government.

Also, special thanks to Mark Bova, whose work ethic and smarts would rival that of Larry Plumb. Raising and caring for a real brood of urban egg hens Mark provided insight and expertise about all things chickens in this book. He wasn't a bad guy to work with for nearly three decades either Though workshopping wasn't really for me,

I'd like to express gratitude to Kelly Dwyer and my classmates at the Iowa Writers' Summer Festival for the honest feedback, which provided fresh perspective and helped to tame my worst impulses.

I'd like to thank Tom McDonnell and Dog Ears Bookstore and Café, not only for carrying my books but for their dogged pursuit (pun intended) of making reading, writing, and literature an essential part of developing a caring, kind, and well-informed community. Plus, it's the coolest coffee shop in all of Buffalo.

About the author

P.A. Kane lives with his wife and son (who is taking his good ole' time finishing his masters degree), plus their dog, Kaya Francis Bean and their cats, Luna and Olive in West Seneca, New York. Kane worked for nearly three decades in the transportation business and has a English background from Buffalo State College. In addition to *Larry Plumb Is Still Here* (2024), he is the author of *The Last Playlist (A Sonic Epitaph), Leaving Jackson Wolf* (2018) and *Written In The Stars: The Book Of Molly.(*2016) He also writes and publishes the satire website BuffaloMud.com. Official website is: PAKane.net. Kane is on Facebook, Bluesky and YouTube. On YouTube you can find a playlist of the artists and songs mentioned in this book plus many others.